MW01113835

A Trace Of **SMOKE**

A Trace Of **SMOKE**

A Novel By

O. J. Bryson

To
Margo,
I loved all our
little talks on the
cruise!
Your New friend,
Jay
10-12-01

ISBN 1-58721-205-6

This book is printed on acid free paper.

1stBooks – Rev. 7/27/01

"O. J. Bryson's writing (*A Trace of Smoke*) combines an engrossing plot, vivid characterizations and deftly-paced action into a genuinely pleasurable read. But even more importantly, he manages to capture the sights and sounds of the Tennessee/Carolina mountains and their people. His ear for natural dialogue adds a dimension to rival the best of Sharyn McCrumb.

Bryson's soon-to-be released novel *The Box* is a fast read, and I couldn't wait to find out what was in the box."

—William Thompson, Editor Emeritus for John Grisham and Stephen King

---

John Grisham: "To Bill Thompson, who started it all." (Mr. Thompson edited *A Time To Kill* and *The Firm*.)

Stephen King: "Bill Thompson was very important in my life as a writer, and, other than my wife, he was probably the most crucial influence during my earlier years as a novelist."

"What a thriller!" —Fox TV

"Jay Bryson's 'Trace of Smoke' is both a gripping thriller of political intrigue and a tale of personal courage. It's also prescient in predicting the fallout from the machinations of the tobacco lobby—how did he know this stuff before the headlines?

Bryson has created an appealing and credible ingenue—no, let's call her a superhero—because she's smart, attractive and a very strong woman fueled by integrity.

Bryson's ear for dialogue is uncanny. And his descriptions of the places where the action is set in the heart of the Smoky Mountains brings the scent of burning {oak?} firewood to the reader's mind.

The action in this novel is fast-paced and holds suspense to the very last page. I can't wait to see what else Mr. Bryson is writing."

—Rosalie Muller Wright, Consulting Editor, *Sunset Magazine*

About The Book

When the tobacco cartel suddenly learns it is one vote shy on a winner-take-all bill in Congress, it taps Todd Carrington as its tie breaker. But Todd hates the tobacco industry. So the tobacco boys go after his fiancée, Barbara Dare—if *she's* hiding anything, they'll use it to pry loose *his* vote.

Barbara Dare is hiding something all right—hiding it in the mountains. The Dare family secret has been lying dormant all these years, like a powder keg next to a smoldering campfire, waiting for someone to kick a hot coal its way. The tobacco cartel is in the business of kicking hot coals at powder kegs. Everything is all set for the explosion.

It will appear tiny at first, little more than a Fourth of July firecracker, hardly enough to knock a man in a closet out of his wheelchair, and the word count will take up less space than if someone had whispered at an all-day-singing and dinner-on-the-ground that the preacher had run off with the piano player, but the fallout will be massive. The Great Smoky Mountains will be hit worst of all, especially the apple blossoms.

Barbara Dare has known all her life that one day some men—and they won't be nice men—will be coming for her. She just doesn't know it will be today. She has always planned to run when they come, so running is what the beautiful young coed does best. Thirty minutes and counting.

ACKNOWLEDGEMENTS

I am indebted to Scott and Tina and Chris, who were generous to me with their time. I owe a debt to the members of the Dallas/Fort Worth Writers' Workshop for their critique; thanks also to Dr. Roger White, Amy Rushing, and Marlene Mackasey for their careful reading of the manuscript. A special thanks goes to Carlene Thompson (*Black Is For Remembrance*), my teacher in WRITER'S DIGEST SCHOOL's novel-writing workshop and my escort through the minefield of revision. Mostly, I thank Stephanie James who edited the manuscript, her third book with me.

For Buddy and Maggie who lost their way and went running for the skies. And for Ben who is coming this way.

To a fleeing rabbit, every shadow on the wing is a hawk, but eventually, the hawk itself takes flight.

—O.B.

Find the four finest steeds in the land...
Tie one to each foot and one to each hand...

—***The Song of Roland***
Medieval French Epic

PROLOGUE

(The Situation)

Thirty minutes to the explosion.

Barbara Dare wore a freshly-picked apple blossom in her hair as she trotted across campus toward the gym, confident there were no pictures of her in existence. Not one. Not even in the university's yearbook. For four years she'd managed to elude the school's photographer on picture day.

She had known all her life that one day some men—and they wouldn't be nice men—would be coming for her. She just didn't know it would be today.

The campus was unusually quiet, considering all that was about to take place; the heat had chased most people inside. Somewhere in the distance, probably at the stadium, she could hear the band practicing "Rocky Top." Wonder if they know "Here Comes The Bride"?

Intoxicated with thoughts of last night's proposal of marriage, she bent over, peeled off her sandals, and walked the rest of the way to the gym barefooted, her shoes dangling, one from each hand. The freshly-watered grass between her toes made her feel light-headed and frivolous and sent her skipping and dancing and whirling across the lawn. How wonderful, this moment of frivolity, this moment of escape.

Once inside the gym, she hurried through the smell of stale sweat to her locker, removed the calf-length, navy-blue skirt she was wearing, and slipped into her orange racing shorts. She straddled the bench in front of the locker, unbuttoned her white frill blouse, removed her lacy bra, and pulled on her much sturdier sports bra. Then, for good luck, she rubbed the beads on the Cherokee mud-bead necklace around her neck, unaware that though they had no description of *her*, they did of the *necklace*.

Twenty-nine minutes and counting.

Barbara Dare had been old enough to vote for two years and

xv

a bit, occasionally watched CNN, and less occasionally read the headlines in the *Knoxville News-Sentinel*. She had paid only slight attention to the President's impeachment trial, and, in general, had little interest in politics. She had never heard of the "tobacco cartel," and the cartel had never heard of her. But all that was changing by the minute.

She toyed with the engagement ring on her finger, getting used to its feel and promise. Then she reached inside her locker for her orange-banded socks. When she leaned over, the white apple blossom in her hair teeter-tottered, so she tucked it under her orange and white sweatband.

Twenty-eight minutes and counting.

In Washington, D. C., that city where people take their dreams to have them whipped, the tobacco cartel was in trouble. The FDA was hot on the heels of the tobacco industry. The impeachment trial was all over, and the Senate hearing on "regulating nicotine" had become the hot potato. The explosive hearing had just taken a thirty-minute recess, twenty-eight minutes left. None, save one, had ever heard of Barbara Dare. Within the hour her name would limp through the Senate like a singed rabbit running from a Smoky Mountain brushfire.

Down a couple of halls from the Senate Hearing Room, bushy-browed Krandall Kaufman, the tobacco cartel's head watermelon on the vine, hid in a closet and watched it all on closed circuit TV from his wheelchair—arthritis in his knees and hemorrhoids where people have hemorrhoids—a headset propped cockeyed over his thick black hair. For thirty years now he'd been building the bomb. He, too, had never heard of Barbara Dare, but he was minutes from dogging her the rest of her life. Or until she knelt before him.

The Dare family secret had been lying dormant all these years, like a powder keg next to a smoldering campfire, waiting for someone to kick a hot coal its way. The tobacco cartel was in the business of kicking hot coals at powder kegs.

Everything was all set for the explosion.

It would appear tiny at first, little more than a Fourth of July firecracker, hardly enough to knock a man in a closet out of his wheelchair, and the word count would take up less space than if someone had whispered at an all-day-singing and dinner-on-the-ground that the preacher had run off with the piano player, but the fallout would be massive. The Great Smoky Mountains would be hit worst of all, especially the apple blossoms.

Twenty-seven minutes, one second.

1

In Knoxville, Tennessee, Barbara Dare, a pretty, blue-eyed blond—people said she looked like Princess Di, only tanner—sat on the bench in the locker room, lacing up her white Nikes and dreaming of an apple-blossom wedding. An Arby's "buy one, get one free" coupon was stuffed in the tiny pocket of her orange running shorts. A dozen long-stemmed red roses and a telegram lay on the bench beside her. She was about to run her last race for the university.

After graduation next week, Barbara hoped to find a job in the Human Resources department of some small lab near home. She had simple tastes and, other than her career plans, felt she wanted what most mountain girls wanted—maybe not big city girls, but, for sure, girls like her: a marriage to a good man, a small home in the mountains, and a quiet life. But one thing separated her from all other girls in the mountains. When she was little, Grandmother Dare had whispered a terrible secret to her. The secret now threatened the career, the happy marriage, the small home in the mountains, and the quiet life. It was becoming clear, if she was going to realize these dreams, sometime soon she was going to have to fight for them. Sometime soon she was going to have to risk it all.

The first risk she would take would be to call Todd and tell him. She wouldn't tell him everything—she couldn't—but she would tell him enough. She glanced at her Timex. She had just enough time to make the call before the race. She started for the pay phone hanging on the wall, remembered she needed change for the call, and hurried back to her locker.

Tamika, her teammate and best friend, a tall African-American girl with high hips and loose lips—she could make anything funny and usually did—stood next to Barbara loosening up and stretching her long leg muscles, using the bench as a brace. A Dairy Queen cup filled with water sat on the bench between the two of them. Tamika had grown up in the back alleys of Atlanta and could outrun the MARTA—Atlanta's rapid-rail train for commuters—for the first hundred meters. The picture of her doing so had been in the Knoxville paper.

The locker room was quiet as a morgue. It usually was before a big race. Tsu and Brandi, the other two members of the cross-country team, had already gone to the stadium, and the out of town teams were dressing in the visitor's gym.

"If you gonna make the gun," Tamika said good naturedly, and without looking up from her stretching, "you better move it. Finish gittin' yo' self ready." Tamika was always big-sistering her.

Barbara took five quarters and a dime from her purse. While she had the purse open, she retrieved the Arby's coupon from her pocket—a free sandwich was a free sandwich—and dropped it inside the purse. She tossed the purse back inside the locker. "I have to call Todd."

"Give it a rest, hon," Tamika cackled. "He ain't backed out. If he was gonna back out, he sho' wouldn't a put them five carats on yo' finger last night."

Barbara acknowledged the comment with a sincere smile.

Tamika had now broken a sweat and was drying the back of her neck with a white towel. "You the catch, and that tobacco boy knows it."

"Todd wouldn't like you calling him a *tobacco boy*. He doesn't even smoke." She knew Tamika knew this, but her loyalty to Todd made her defend him anyway.

"Not 'cause he smokes, girl," Tamika said without condemnation, "'cause he grows the stuff."

"You know he doesn't grow the tobacco. And he's crossways with his father because *he* does."

"Girl, I don't care if he grows snuff, long as he treats you right," Tamika said laughing. "I ever hear he don't, I'll knock him down the steps and beat him over the head with his shoe."

"I'll give him your kind regards."

"While you're at it, remind him I was the one that introduced y'all."

"Only," Barbara challenged, "because you met him one minute before I did."

"'Cause you wuz hidin' in the toilet, cryin'," Tamika said,

tossing the towel at her. "But he better be good to you. My aunt Maudie, back in Atlanta, says, 'If I likes ya, I lets ya. If I loves ya, I heps ya.'"

Barbara laughed and nudged her locker shut with her knee.

"I loves ya, and I'm gonna hep ya." Tamika took a sip of water from the Dairy Queen cup. "But if you gonna catch me in this race, you better get to loosening up." She reached the cup toward Barbara, offering her a drink.

Barbara thought of the bitter pill she had to swallow—telling Todd—and became deadly serious. She received the D.Q. cup from Tamika's long black hand, like it was the Holy Grail being passed between the Disciples at the Last Supper.

Just as she raised the cup to her lips, Tamika said, "Hey, you way too serious. Did I ever tell you 'bout the man that went blind from drinkin' tea?"

"*Blind from drinking tea?*"

"Yeah," she said, slapping her thigh, "left his spoon in his glass."

Barbara tried to laugh, but it was a mirthless chuckle. An apple-blossom wedding was riding on the phone call she must now make, but she couldn't tell Tamika, her best friend. She couldn't tell anyone.

"Speaking of tea," Tamika said, walking toward the stalls, "I gotta make a pit stop 'fore the race."

Alone now, Barbara raked the fingers of the hand with the new diamond on it through her long blond hair and, half-dressed, walked slowly toward the phone, deliberately pigeon-toeing her Nikes into the concrete floor, like a little girl being pushed toward a whipping that wasn't hers, her orange and white jersey draped across her shoulder. The mud-bead necklace hung down over her running bra. Because of the Dare family secret, she wore the necklace everywhere. She wouldn't be caught dead without it.

The phone call would put it all on the line. She picked up the receiver, deposited the five quarters and the dime—exactly what it cost for a three-minute call to Chapel Hill, North Carolina. Todd had graduated from the University of Tennessee, but was getting his Masters at UNC—and started dialing, still

3

trying to decide, Should I tell him before or after the race? She had practiced the words a thousand times since last night. "Sweetheart, if I told you something...something bad...something real bad about myself, would you still love me? Would you still want to marry me? It's not my fault. Honest, it's not my fault."

"What ain't yo' *fault?*" asked Tamika, back from the bathroom.

Realizing she'd been speaking out loud, Barbara quickly popped the receiver back on the hook. "Nothing. Just talking to myself."

The change trickled down through the phone and clanked in the coin-return, sounding like a skeleton dancing in a can. She picked up the coins and tossed them into the blue plastic bin in the bottom of her locker.

Tamika pointed at the clock on the wall. "We better get on over there, girl."

Barbara knew time had run out. The clock had made the decision for her. She would call Todd *after* the race. She slipped the orange and white jersey over her head, then asked Tamika, "What do I do with the roses?"

"They won't keep without water."

"Could I borrow your D.Q. cup?"

"Sure."

Barbara stuffed the long-stem roses into the Dairy Queen cup and propped them against the wall in the bottom of her locker. She then quick-walked to catch up to Tamika, who was almost to the door. The heat hit them as soon as they came out of the air conditioned gym. They walked without talking across the green grass toward Neyland Stadium, dodging the sprinklers.

The bulk of the crowd had not gathered yet; it was not the *beginning* of this marathon, but the *finish* that would be exciting, the stadium lap in front of the home folks. Ancient marathons were about twenty-five miles, the distance between the Grecian cities of Marathon and Athens. But when Britain's King Edward VII wanted to watch the *beginning* of the 1908 Olympic race from his home, the distance was changed to *26 miles 385 yards,*

4

because that's how far it was from Windsor Castle to the Olympic stadium in London.

Today's 26.2 mile race would take Barbara Dare and the other runners a little over two hours. And so, two hours from now is when most of the fans and the press would show up. Track and field events had been going on for three days. The marathon through the mountains would be the grand finale.

Barbara liked the camaraderie with the other girls and wasn't worried about the race. They all knew she was the fastest and strongest of the pack, but she had never won a race, and they liked that. She could help her team win, but she, personally, must not win. When you're that fast, *not* winning took some planning and kept her coach frustrated. But the Dare family secret required that she must never win.

At the starting line, unconsciously, Barbara started humming, "Hear The Voice of My Beloved," a plaintive and mournful folk song, as if she had a premonition that death would be running in the fast lane.

"Dare, get your mind on the race," yelled Coach Prissy Simmons, slapping her on the rump, "and save something for your final kick."

The gun sounded and the cross-country race got underway. Eight teams—four on each team—from eight universities, dressed in their school colors, jogged off down the hill, appropriately nicknamed Widower-Maker Hill, and headed toward the Great Smoky Mountains.

Barbara took the lead. She always did. Tamika fell in behind her. She always did. First among innocents, Tamika would be the first to fall.

5

2

Twenty minutes, thirty-two seconds.

The storm was coming and it was coming fast, from all directions. It would take seven of them to bring her down, though some were on her side. They weren't the *Magnificent* Seven, but *seven* there were. One would make the bomb, one would light the fuse, one would deliver the death warrant, one would weep, one would warn, one had no idea what was going on, but the one who cared the most would just sit and wait.

Seven tiny scenes, cameos of coming events, were simultaneously unfolding. The cast of characters was as varied as a bucket of potatoes, but they all had one thing in common: Barbara Dare's secret could destroy any of them. Everyone was at his post:

Scene 1: At the nation's Capitol, and down the hall from where Krandall Kaufman was hiding in the closet, sixty-five year-old Senator Charlie Carrington—Tarzan in a three-piece suit—paced his office, staring at the black vibrator-pager on his desk. This consummate Capital Hill powerbroker with an impeccable reputation was about to have his last fight with the Senate. He would trigger the explosion. The blast would launch the death warrant on Barbara Dare.

Scene 2: In Asheville, North Carolina, Tumbler, the mouseman—a small, watery-eyed man with a pencil-thin mustache over a pencil-thin upper lip—nibbled on a piece of yellow cheese, gnawed his fingernails to the quick, and watched the phone. He'd fed the farmer to the hay baler this morning. Barbara Dare would be his afternoon project.

Scene 3: In Cell Block 13 at Sagebrush Prison near Knoxville, Tennessee, Buzzard Mackelroy—a medium-built man in thick, goggle-type glasses strapped on with a ragged elastic band, and doing life without parole for murder—was being courteously escorted, like a king, to solitary confinement. He would hear none of the explosion, but it would rip his heart out. The warden would say he didn't have one anyway.

Someone would have to pay. Buzzard Mackelroy would deny he ever knew Barbara Dare.

Scene 4: In France, Roland—nephew of Charlemagne and hero of children everywhere—innocent, brave, young Roland, slain at Roncesvalles Pass in 788 for his noble political dreams, got on his knees and screamed from the grave, "They won't listen! Go back! Go back!" But Roland's warning went unheeded by his twentieth century counterpart in New Bern, North Carolina.

Scene 5: In New Bern, a naïve young politician by the name of Todd Carrington—a Greek god in a blue tank top and khaki shorts—hurled himself headlong toward the bright lights of Washington, D. C., dreaming Roland's same noble dream: champion the underdog, include the excluded, offer hope for the hopeless, and that help only need be summoned. A lamb to the slaughter.

Scene 6: Last night Todd Carrington asked Barbara Dare to be his bride.

Scene 7: In Cades Cove, Tennessee, an apple blossom clung tenuously to a limb, and Grandmother Dare, her running all done, rocked away the hours and waited for the tragic end to come. But her wobbly old legs had one last run left in them. She would run through the Valley of the Shadow of Death with Barbara Dare, the one she had taught to run, arguably the fastest girl ever to come out of the Smoky Mountains to run for the University of Tennessee.

An apple blossom was about to fall.

3

In Washington, D.C., the Senate had been fighting all morning and now the *lawyers* were at it. They'd finally gotten to the crux of the matter.

"You're spiking cigarettes!" argued Morgan J. Schubert, the FDA's top lawyer.

"Prove it," responded Maxwell "Bones" Talbert, lead attorney for the tobacco industry. Talbert, an African-American, was a beanpole of a man with honey in his voice. He had gotten the nickname "Bones" from all the corpses he'd left strewn in courtrooms around the country.

Morgan Schubert, on the other hand, was a strident sort, more like he had vinegar in *his* voice. The short fat man wore thick glasses, was prematurely bald, and had a bulbous red nose.

The smiling presidents of the nation's largest tobacco companies sat leaned back with their legs crossed, lounging among their twelve attorneys, all watching their man, Bones Talbert.

Morgan Schubert held up a pack of cigarettes and shook it at the tobacco moguls. "You're addicting the nation!"

"Prove it."

Stalemate.

Krandall Kaufman watched with bated breath from his hiding place in the closet as the fight raged on. Kaufman's main worry was about collateral damage to the tobacco industry, not about the eventual outcome; the deck was stacked, and he was the man who'd stacked it.

The stage was set and the lines were drawn.

The battlefield: a Senate Hearing Room.

The opponents: The FDA vs. the tobacco industry.

The audience: national TV.

The prize: billions, enough to balance the national debt.

The risk: annihilation of the tobacco Industry.

The plea: one vote. The votes were split right down the middle—the chairperson would break the tie.

Chairperson: Charlie Carrington, Republican senator from North Carolina.

Still holding the pack of cigarettes, Morgan Schubert strutted around like a man who had just gotten paid. "All right," he announced with a confident smile and with no more arrogance than most lawyers. "For our next witness, we call Maynard 'Tubby' Humphry."

"Tub" Humphry, in his mid fifties, a prosperous tobacco farmer from Winston-Salem, North Carolina, had been in the news of late. The stout, red-faced, rotund man with a farmer-tan and bibbed overalls had been encouraging other tobacco farmers with large holdings, like his, to switch from tobacco to alternative crops, a not too popular argument in Winston-Salem, a town where most residents' livelihoods came from tobacco, in one way or another.

Tub Humphry did not appear when his name was called.

"Maynard Tubby Humphry," called lawyer Schubert, a little louder, impatiently looking around the chamber.

Tub Humphry, supposedly, had proof that the tobacco industry was secretly developing a new and more powerful tobacco plant, one that was far more addictive. The tobacco cartel had been growing the secret plant in some undisclosed foreign country and now had it developed sufficiently enough that they wanted to test-grow it in the States. Tub Humphry had been contacted by an unnamed tobacco mogul and had agreed to use his plantation for the experiment. Soon after his handshake with the tobacco representative—nothing in writing—his twenty-three-year-old son came down with lung cancer. The boy didn't smoke but the daddy did. The doctors blamed it on auxiliary smoke and gave him six months to live. He died in two weeks. At breakfast, the morning after the funeral, Tub Humphry's other son, sixteen-year-old Clarence, threw a piece of grape-jellied toast in his dad's face. "You killed him, Dad! Mom tried to tell you. You and your tobacco crops." Last week, Tub Humphry had contacted the FDA. He wanted out of the tobacco growing business. He would tell all.

If true, such information would be the nail in the tobacco industry's coffin. The word on the street was that the FDA already had them on the ropes. The legal tide was about to turn against the tobacco boys.

Tub Humphry still did not answer the summons to the witness table. A page was sent to see if he was waiting in the hall. He was not in the hall. No one had seen him.

Lawyer Schubert turned to Chairperson Charlie Carrington. "I request an arrest warrant be issued on Maynard Tubby Humphry for failing to answer a Senate subpoena."

"Without objection," Charlie Carrington said. "I'll have it faxed immediately to Sheriff Johnston in Winston-Salem. Meanwhile, let's take a thirty-minute recess."

Earlier in the week, someone had whispered Tub Humphry's story to someone and that someone had whispered it to…Now all D. C. was secretly frothing at the mouth at the thought of getting their hands on all that tobacco settlement money. But until Tub Humphry's name had been spoken in the hearing just now, it had been only rumor. Now it was as good as fact. And in a city where rumor was sometimes better than fact…everyone knew the tobacco industry was on its last leg. All that money was about to be divvied up, and Krandall Kaufman, head of the tobacco cartel, was not a happy camper.

Everybody started grabbing.

The President rushed to the Rose Garden for a hastily called news conference and announced to a national TV audience, "I can save Social Security…."

Senators dashed to the phones and called constituents back home, shouting, "Looky, looky, looky…"

Pin-striped, high-powered New York lawyers ran to the sewers, promising sewer rats, "If you can cough, I can get you millions. If you can spit up blood, I can get you twice that. You did used to smoke, didn't you?"

State attorneys general called one another, congratulating themselves…The Heart Fund became giddy with the prospect of…

Everybody was "eat up" with the grabs, and Krandall Kaufman was in town to see that anybody grabbing too hard drew back a bloody stub. He had a collection of bloody stubs.

11

All this had happened earlier in the morning and now there were nineteen minutes left on the thirty-minute break.

Krandall Kaufman had heard the rumor about Tub Humphry's tall tale, too, but he wasn't worried about it. And he wasn't worried about how the vote in the hearing would go. Chairman Carrington was *his* man in the Senate—had been for thirty years. Kaufman had personally hand-tooled him to do his bidding. Charlie Carrington's reputation was above reproach on the Hill. Of course, everyone knew and accepted that Senator Carrington had a blind spot when it came to tobacco. They assumed it was because he owned several tobacco plantations. No different than a senator from a coal mining state having a *coal* blind spot, they reasoned, or a senator from Texas or Wyoming having a *cattle* blind spot.

But Kaufman knew the real source of Senator Carrington's blind spot: the senator's wife. Lady Carrington was Kaufman's ace in the hole. Quite early, he had unearthed an indiscretion on her part; her indiscretion had been an attempt to cover her *husband's* indiscretion. Ever since, Kaufman had owned the senator. With that experience, Kaufman learned that you can whip a man physically and he'll come back to fight another day. But if you threaten to shame his wife, you can lead him around like a whipped puppy. The blackmail had made a vegetable of Lady Carrington, but the senator had held up pretty well.

Kaufman trusted Charlie Carrington…as long as he could see him, and he was watching him right now…on the TV monitor. A hidden camera, the work of Kaufman's night man, Tumbler, mounted in the ceiling of each of the four corners of the senator's plush office, caught his every move.

From his cramped quarters in the closet, Kaufman peeped in, courtesy of the hidden cameras. Senator Carrington was standing behind his desk, his arms folded, staring out the burgundy-draped window, probably planning his next move in the hearing.

When there's that much money lying on the table, you'd better plan. It was the most money that had ever been laid on a table. Enough to die for. And some would; Kaufman would see to that. He had killed more people than a small war—not

12

personally, but his goons, mostly Tumbler. He didn't count the ones nicotine had killed. He couldn't afford to acknowledge that, even to himself. In spite of all this, Kaufman considered himself a patriot, and wore a red, white, and blue flag-shaped lapel pin laced with diamonds and rubies to prove it. At a ballgame, Kaufman, the jingo, was first to salute the flag.

The massive mahogany desk occupied the eye-catching part of the senator's office. Behind the desk sat a large, padded-leather chair that leaned and turned, and looked like it had never been sat in.

The desk was uncluttered. A gold pen set and a matching gold container, about the size of a Campbell's soup can, sat on opposite ends of the desk. The can was filled with fifteen-cent red, white, and blue senatorial give-away pens, paid for by taxpayers. A thin, leather portfolio that the senator usually carried tucked under his arm, lay on the desk in front of the chair, as if waiting to be opened and its contents reviewed.

Between the pen set and the can of pens stood a gold-framed picture. It was a photo of the senator at the helm of his yacht, somewhere off the North Carolina coast. Beside him stood a dizzy-eyed brunette with a harmless smile, yet, at sixty, quite attractive. That was Lady Carrington. Manning the spinnaker was a handsome young man who looked just like the senator. The young man was their son Todd. All three were decked out in blue and white yachting clothes. The portrait had been taken last year on Todd's birthday. Todd's girlfriend, Barbara somebody, had been on the yacht for the party, but for some reason was not in the picture. Kaufman figured a kid as handsome as the Carrington kid, and with all that money to inherit, probably had a stable of fillies.

A black vibrator-pager lay on the corner of the senator's desk—the corner closest to the door. It looked like the kind of pager they give you at a restaurant to silently signal you when your table is ready. The vibrator-pager was the only thing that looked out of place.

Kaufman studied Charlie Carrington like a prize pig he was taking to market.

The broad-shouldered senator, standing there in his dark-

13

blue suit and club tie, as erect as a light pole, was a *young* old man. His sixty-five years, same as Kaufman, showed mostly in his steel-blue eyes. He had another good twenty years in him, Lord willing. During the last five of those years, Kaufman would start grooming a successor for him. But it would be hard to find another Charlie Carrington. Unlike the cartel's other five senators, bought and paid for, Kaufman had never paid Senator Carrington a dime, and yet Carrington had never said no to him. Not once.

Suddenly the calm was broken by a gentle tap on the senator's door.

Fifteen minutes and counting.

4

Startled from his daydream, Senator Charlie Carrington strolled across the thick, gold carpet. But as he reached for the knob, the door cracked open and a stubby lady, with a blunt haircut and bangs that came almost to her eyebrows, wedged her head through. Senator Carrington shouldered the door to a crack.

"Got a second, Charlie?" the woman asked, leaning in on one foot. She was perspiring profusely.

"Just." He glanced at his Rolex, revealing diamond-studded gold cufflinks.

The middle-aged freshman senator started crawfishing. Kaufman had seen it a hundred times. He smiled, lit up a Marlboro, and settled back in his motorized wheelchair to watch Charlie Carrington work his magic.

"I'm getting cold feet," she said. "The polls are saying—"

"Polls, schmolls. Polls is just another way of talking out of both sides of your mouth. Only you use someone else's mouth."

"The polls don't lie."

"They do if you want them to," Senator Carrington said. "It's all in how you ask the question. It's whether you're pitchin' or catchin'. If the White House can do polls, we can do polls. We'll do our own. It's like that book *Lying With Statistics.* Somebody ought to write a book and call it *Lying With Polls.*"

"But...but," she stuttered, "my constituents back home see this tobacco thing as a simple black or white issue."

"Tell them it's a funny shade of gray," he said with a chuckle.

"Am I supposed to laugh?" she asked brusquely.

"Sorry," he apologized, holding his wristwatch up. "I've got to get back in there to the fight."

"Understood. But I didn't understand your joke." She blew a blast of air, like a tea kettle letting off steam, parting her bangs right in the middle of her browed forehead.

"Tell your constituents, Senator Smith, it's a *gray* matter.

Gray can get you out of anything. Didn't you watch the impeachment?"

So it would be the gray argument, Kaufman thought and widened his smile. "Captain Gray" was about to strike again.

"I was on the *President's* side," she boasted.

"And you won. I'm not begrudging you that," said Senator Carrington. "You snookered us. Shucks, I'm on the President's side on a lot of things. *I'm* leading the fight on his new budget. But I'm not talking about *sides.* I'm talking about getting things done. Here on the Hill, gray is king. It's like stockbrokers. Stockbrokers make money whether the stock goes up or down. Like stocks, gray doesn't care which side it's on. My friend, the longer you stay on the Hill, the more you will come to know that gray is more valuable than gold."

Her wide eyes widened. "You surprise me, talking that way, Senator Carrington. *Gray more valuable than gold?*"

"It's quite simple, Senator Smith. Most senators are honest—we all come here honest; I did too—and wouldn't sell their vote if you offered them a gold mine. But most will *trade* votes. Color your legislation *gray* and they'll trade their *gray* vote on your *gray* bill for a reciprocal *gray* vote on their *gray* bill. See the logic? If you can't buy a senator's vote with *gold,* but you can with *gray,* then gray's more valuable than gold."

"Isn't *gray* just another word for *compromise?*"

"Ah, but here's the difference. Compromise has integrity. Gray is a schoolyard bully."

"I don't see the difference."

"*Compromise* is when you trade your vote on a bill that you may not like, but that won't hurt your constituents back home. *Gray* doesn't care."

"Let me see if I understand. You don't trust the senators, you don't trust the White House, you don't trust the polls. Whom do you trust?"

"Trust the people. Trust the man—or woman—who doesn't whisper his ideas to you behind closed doors. Trust the one who says, 'I don't mind if you record this conversation.' Trust the people, my dear. If the people are wrong, we'll all have to find that land of beginning again."

"That's all well and good," she said, "but we don't grow *tobacco* in my state. I'm not sure—"

"You grow *old folks*, don't you?"

"I don't follow."

"You want my six votes on that Social Security bill of yours, don't you?"

"But you promised," she whispered, then glanced down the hall as if afraid someone might be listening. "And I promised I'd deliver—"

Senator Carrington opened the door enough for her to step on inside. He immediately put his long arm across her round shoulders, and then politely guided her back through the cracked door. "Senator Smith, I trust your judgment. You go on out there and be your regal self. Vote your conscience. Any committee I chair, I tell senators to vote their conscience. I'm telling you, personally, vote your conscience."

"Thank you," she said, looking quite relieved.

"Then when your Social Security bill comes up next week, I'll vote mine."

"Oh." She bit her lip. "I'll study about it."

"Fine. But I want your decision before you close that door. I'm hoping to drag this hearing out for a few days at least. But any second someone might jump up and call for the question. If you're not with me, I only have a couple of minutes to talk Senator You-Know-Who into voting *his* conscience on my tobacco legislation, and he's very much against your Social Security bill. He's not scared of *gray*."

"Gray it is," she said, meekly, and left his office.

Chalk up another one for "Captain Gray," Kaufman thought as he watched the scene come to an end, remembering that gray had reached its zenith during the impeachment. No matter which side you were on, with few exceptions, gray, the schoolyard bully, had provided political cover.

Charlie Carrington's reputation on the Hill as a master negotiator was well-deserved, though it was Krandall Kaufman who sat in the tobacco industry's catbird seat, calling the shots. No one knew where the catbird seat was located, and few, even within the industry, knew that such a person as Kaufman existed.

17

But, like in the Mafia, those who needed to know knew. Even a simpleton, no matter which side of the fight he was on, knew that someone somewhere was brilliantly orchestrating the tobacco industry's death match in Congress.

Kaufman watched Senator Carrington turn and start back across the lush carpet toward his desk.

A sudden violent and rapid knock came from the senator's door.

The senator wheeled around and quickly cracked the door again. Kaufman expected it to be the same lady, having another change of heart.

It was Morgan Schubert, the FDA counsel. Schubert bolted in without waiting to be asked, his red nose glowing. "Tub Humphry's dead."

"*Dead?*"

"Farming accident. Got caught in a hay baler." Schubert was carrying a manila folder which he nervously shifted from one hand to the other.

"*Hay baler?*"

"His boy found him and called the Winston-Salem sheriff."

"When?" Charlie grabbed a notepad as he pulled the Montblanc pen from his lapel pocket.

"Early this morning. Must have happened about milking time."

"*Milking time?*"

"Still had his milk bucket in his hand. And there was milk in it."

Charlie scratched his chin. "Something mighty peculiar here."

"Why?"

"Milking time's at daybreak. Dew'd still be on the hay."

"*Dew?* What's that got to do with milking?"

"Nothing. But it has everything to do with haying."

"I don't understand."

"You make hay when the sun's shining, not while it's wet."

"Oh. I live in New York City. We don't grow much hay."

"I know Tub Humphry," the senator said. "He might milk his pet cow, but he's no fool. He wouldn't be haying at daybreak—" He stopped talking, turned and stared out the window again.

Kaufman watched him. Defeated-like, the senator flopped down in his chair. He leaned back, thinking hard, like he was putting two and two together. Kaufman knew Charlie wouldn't be foolish enough to announce to the FDA his opinion about what might have happened to the dead farmer.

"What do you think we ought to do?" asked Schubert, back to shifting the folder—probably full of questions he had planned to ask Tub Humphry—from hand to hand like it was a hot potato.

"About what?"

"The hearing."

Charlie, ever in control, looked up at him, and said without hesitation, "Call your next witness."

Schubert started for the door.

"I'll be on in there in a minute. You might alert the chaplain that we'll want him to lead us in a moment of silent prayer."

"Yes, sir." Morgan Schubert left and closed the door.

Charlie Carrington sat there slump-shouldered, like he was in shock. Like he knew who had fed Tub Humphry to the hay baler. But only Kaufman and Tumbler knew for sure.

Ten minutes, two seconds to the explosion.

Barbara Dare was halfway down Widower-Maker Hill when she heard Tamika call out from behind her in a high-pitched voice, mimicking the coach's last comment, "Save something for yo' final kick."

Without looking back, Barbara threw a "thumbs up" over her shoulder.

By the time she reached the bottom of the steep hill, she was beginning to feel the humidity in the unmerciful heat. She turned onto a footpath that would lead along the river, the Tennessee River. The stadium quickly vanished behind the thick growth along the banks, but she could still hear the cars on the four lane. The other girls were nowhere in sight. A couple of hours from now she and the teams would re-trace these steps, going in the opposite direction. That's when the Widower-Maker would earn its name.

But the hill wouldn't bother Barbara. Where she was from, the Widower-Maker would be called a *mole hill.* She was from Cades Cove, Tennessee, a land tucked away in the Great Smoky Mountains, as remote and breathtakingly beautiful a place as ever there was, not far from Gatlinburg.

And that's where Barbara went every weekend, sometimes to train for events like today, but mostly to see Grandmother Dare. The Cove's unspoiled beauty had not gone unnoticed by Hollywood. Columbia Pictures brought Ingrid Bergman and Anthony Quinn there to film the movie, *A Walk In The Spring Rain.* And Jane Fonda, before she became Ted Turner's wife, came to the area to film *The Doll Maker.*

Around 1820, the State of Tennessee acquired Cades Cove from the Cherokee Indians, then speculators bought the land from the state and sold it to settlers, about 137 families. But years of wars, diseases, and isolation sent most of the heirs of the original families packing, leaving the blacksmith shop, the cantilever barn, the mill and dam, the smokehouse, and the corn crib, all in different stages of deterioration.

Barbara's grandmother was born in Cades Cove and still

held the original land grant on a hundred-acre farm there, with a small cabin. When the other settlers left, she stayed. She and Barbara liked the isolation, and for good reason. The isolation kept them alive.

The log cabin, embedded in the midst of blue-misted mountains, overlooked a meadow of wildflowers of every color, a cornfield with a scarecrow, appropriately named Mr. Scarecrow, and a mountain stream with a bridge over it. Besides the scarecrow, the farm boasted one horse, named Ned, twelve gray-speckled Dominiquer hens, a few baby chicks, and one very busy rooster.

An eleven-mile loop road encircled Cades Cove. The road followed the old wagon trail, including occasionally having to ford the stream. It was that eleven-mile loop where Barbara first learned long distance running. Until she went off to college, hardly a day had passed since she was old enough to remember that she hadn't run that loop, summer, winter, spring, or fall, in rain, sleet, snow, or hail. Some days she ran it twice, then headed higher into the mountains to run some more with the deer, the bears, and the wolves. Then she jogged home and took a dip in the ice cold stream, in the raw.

From the high ground of the bridge that peaked the loop, she could see when a strange car was coming up the mountain, giving her time to race across the cornfield, past Mr. Scarecrow, hurdle the split-rail fence, sprint through the meadow of wildflowers, past the corn crib, through the yard full of chickens, and up the porch of the cabin, grab Grandmother Dare by the hand and flee into the forest until the danger passed.

She had learned to live on the edge of flight. But not without cost. She wet the bed until she was sixteen. On her sixteenth birthday she got her driver's license, and that was the day she stared the family secret in the face for the first time. She never wet the bed again.

Until high school, most of her formal education had been "home schooling" by Grandmother Dare, and most of her dates had been with TV stars like Andy Taylor and Barney Fife and Don Johnson and Jerry Seinfeld, but only in her dreams. Grandmother Dare had always told her she was pretty, but as for herself, Barbara had no way of judging. But once she reached high school, and the boys started coming around in droves, especially hanging out around the creek when she was swimming, she figured she must be a little pretty. Of course when the boys were around, she wore her bathing suit or her jogging outfit. But dates were out of the question. The secret would tolerate no social outings. So, in high school, she hung out with the girls, and the girls liked that, once they saw she was no threat to them.

Now, as a college senior, she, like her classmates, occasionally watched the popular TV sitcoms, along with Cheers and Mad About You reruns. Because she was a runner, she had never smoked or done drugs. An aspirin made her high. She was widely read in the classics—Grandmother Dare had seen to that—but not widely traveled. Other than a couple of trips to the North Carolina coast to visit Todd—when she visited him at his parents' coastal mansion, he took her *yachting*, when he visited her at Grandmother Dare's cabin, she took him *hickory nut hunting*—Barbara had never been out of the Smoky Mountains. The cruel family secret required she live out the rest of her life near the mountains.

"Stay near the mountains, and when they come for you, run as fast as you can," Grandmother Dare had always warned her. And that's what Barbara was doing today as she continued the marathon through the mountains for her university.

She had no particular political leanings, and politics was the furthest thing from her mind. She never considered that Todd might have enemies too, that his enemies might want to talk to her enemies, nor that politics could be as dangerous as a four-poster bed full of copperheads.

Unconsciously, she widened her stride and thus the distance between her and the other runners.

Three minutes and counting.

6

Still in his office, Senator Charlie Carrington had just received word about the death of Tub Humphry, the Winston-Salem farmer. He started pacing nervously.

From his hidden closet, Kaufman watched him.

The senator stopped and stared with great disgust at the black vibrator lying on his desk, like he wanted to spit on it. After what seemed forever, he picked it up, dropped it into the left front pocket of his pants, and shuffled, droop-shouldered, toward the door that would lead him back down some halls to the Hearing Room. Before he opened the door, he paused, awkwardly. He walked back over to his desk and reached for the phone.

One minute, nine seconds.

Kaufman watched him, curiously, and leaned closer to the TV monitor. The senator was acting funny. What was he up to?

As he started dialing, his home phone number flashed across Kaufman's screen. The stooge was calling New Bern, North Carolina. Why now? With the hearing due to start any minute?

The senator's wife answered on the second ring. "Hello?"

Lady Carrington spoke the word with such charm that the most casual observer would have known Southern aristocracy was on the other end of the line, her voice so soft that Kaufman had to turn up his headset.

"Daddy's coming home, darling," said the senator. "I—" The deep Southern voice, that for years had resonated through the halls of Congress in stentorian tone, striking fear in his opponents, now sounded tired.

"Todd's engaged!" Lady Carrington screamed, interrupting him, her voice all full of happy excitement. "I've been trying to get through to you all morning."

"*Engaged?*"

"To Barbara."

"Why am I surprised?"

"You sound troubled. You like Barbara. You always said you liked to dance with her. She's—"

"I do like to dance with her, but—"

"You think our son can do better, don't you?"

"We don't know anything about her family, or—"

"It's that mud-bead necklace she wore to the Wine Conferee last month, isn't it?"

"Not necessarily. It's—"

"I knew the necklace bothered you."

"I don't think mountain mud beads go with an evening gown." Still standing, the senator removed one of the give-away pens from the gold can and tapped it, nervously, on his desk.

"I think it shows character. She says she wears them because they mean so much to her grandmother."

"A college senior should know better."

"Oh, she *knows*, all right. It was a statement. She's high-minded. You're just not accustomed to being around high-minded people."

The senator gulped. "High-mindedness can be dangerous."

"I love the way she bends over when she talks to children, and the dignity with which she greets Samson. She talks to him like he's one of the family."

"She has no concept of one's station in life," the senator said as he tossed the give-away pen on the desk.

"Samson likes her, and he can spot a fake."

"Samson's a servant, dear. He has nothing to barter with."

"All the more reason her courtesy is genuine."

"It may be simple mountain snobbery. Whatever it is, no lady of breeding would have worn that crude necklace to such a formal event."

"I would."

"You?"

"If *my* grandmother had given it to me."

"Your grandmother gave you plenty."

"I would trade all these tobacco farms to have had a relationship with my grandmother like Barbara has with hers."

Fifty-nine seconds.

"That's because of your disapproval of tobacco, darling." He sat down on the edge of his desk. His right leg immediately began to bounce up and down, nervously.

26

"That's another kettle of fish, dear." Lady Carrington cleared her throat like a fishbone was caught in it, then, in a weepy voice, said, "Todd loves Barbara. Other than the mud beads, you like her, don't—"

"*Like* has nothing to do with it." He lit a Winston. "Engagement's a little sudden, don't you think?"

"*Sudden*, dear?" said Lady Carrington, still in a prim and proper voice. "Four years is hardly sudden. They've dated all through college. Todd is so in love, he can hardly sit. By the bye, this afternoon Barbara is in a cross-country race, or some kind of race, at the university. I sent roses and a 'Good Luck Telegram' from you and me. I didn't know what was appropriate for that style of event."

As Kaufman sat there in his wheelchair eavesdropping on the chitchat between the senator and his wife, he felt a little foolish—the head of the world's largest industry, hiding in a closet, listening in on a man talking to his wife—and thought he might should feel a little guilty. But he didn't. After all, it was no different than looking in on the President in the Oval Office. And videoing it. Rumor was that the tobacco cartel might have a video of several of those Oval Office moments, and Kaufman did nothing to squelch the rumor. Everyone knew that the tobacco industry's surveillance was superior to that of the White House. The White House was constantly complaining to the media that some foreign government had tapped their phones. Most credited the rumor about the cigar video for the White House's sudden shift from *frontal assault* on tobacco legislation to *friendly foe*. The tobacco industry had never lost a case. To Kaufman, the reason was quite simple: keep your ears open—surveillance, and your mouth shut. A fish can't get caught unless he opens his mouth.

Tumbler, Kaufman's night man, a surveillance guru, who claimed he could hotwire a 747 in flight, usually manned the closet. But early this morning he had taken the cartel's jet to Winston-Salem, North Carolina, to visit a tobacco farmer. The farmer had become a little too vocal, to the point of organizing a rally of mega farmers to encourage them to plant crops alternate to tobacco. It would be newsed as a farming accident—the cow wouldn't tell—and the other farmers would get the message: Don't talk out of school.

"That's good," said the senator. "Roses are appropriate. But we don't know that much about Barbara Dare. Her family and--"

"You're so suspicious, dear. You've been in politics too long. She holds currency with me."

"My office will run a background check on her." He took a deep draw on the cigarette and let out nervous little puffs of smoke.

"Todd won't like that," she said, lightly.

"I don't like it either, darling, but a background check has to be done if she's coming into the family."

"But, yes of course, dear," she said, submissively. "And here I've done all the chatting, yet it was you who called. Did you have something to tell me, or were you just being your usual sweet self and inquiring about Todd's party?"

The honey oozed from her mealy-mouthed voice, but Kaufman knew why the verbiage had no spine. Though he had never met Lady Carrington, heiress to the largest tobacco plantations in the Carolinas, it was he who had robbed the hive of her soul, leaving the corpse to flit about like a social butterfly with no compass.

Twenty seconds.

"Daddy's coming home, darling." The senator's voice sounded more tired. "Before I can come home, though, I have to confess something to you."

Kaufman couldn't believe his ears.

"*Confess?*" she asked, softly.

Kaufman adjusted his headset. Was the fool going to tell her?!

"Thirty years ago, something foolish happened," said the senator, almost whispering. "The tobacco cartel found out about it. All these years they've been holding it over my head. I finally—"

"I know all about it, dear," she said. "I knew the day it happened. I knew the day you changed. You did it for me."

"You've known all along?"

"Todd really is *your* son, dear."

28

"Don't, sweetheart. Don't mention that again—"

"Well, he is."

"I know that. Let's just not talk about it any more. You've been hurt enough. And please don't ever say again that you think that I might doubt that Todd is my son. Promise?"

"Indeed. You will always be my hero."

Lady Carrington wasn't as senile as she acted, thought Kaufman. He may have misjudged her. In fact for the first time, he sort of admired her. Not many women could have kept their mouths shut about something like that. And for thirty years.

"Thank you, darling," said the senator. "That makes what I have to tell you easier."

Five seconds!

Uh oh. Kaufman started squirming. He'd been building the bomb for thirty years, but didn't know it was about to blow up in his face.

"I've never said *no* to the tobacco cartel before, but I'm saying it now. I'm through."

All of a sudden the leather seat in the wheelchair was soaked with sweat.

One second!

"This is my last fight. I'm retiring."

Kaboom!!

Kaufman almost fell out of the wheelchair. It couldn't have created a bigger explosion if the senator had dropped the atomic bomb. The tobacco industry, the largest business the world had ever known, was in the fight of its life. Right now. This very moment. And, Charlie Carrington, their point man, their swing vote for thirty years, had thrown this bomb into the mix: He was retiring! He couldn't *retire*! That would leave the tobacco cartel one vote short! But the jig was up. The genie was out of the bottle. He couldn't blackmail Charlie Carrington again. And he thought he had him by the yin-yang for another twenty years.

"I'm delighted you're leaving politics," Lady Carrington said as if he had just told her he was out of cigarettes.

Senator Carrington stood and stared blankly out the window. "I should have left long—"

"Oh," interrupted Lady Carrington, "Todd invited Barbara to

his graduation party. Don't forget, it's here at *this* house, tomorrow night. That's when Todd wants us to announce his engagement."

Kaufman pulled the fine linen kerchief from his silk coat pocket and wiped at his forehead, trying to catch his breath.

"It's too soon for any *engagement* announcement," said the senator, now standing taller, and looking like the world had been lifted from his shoulders. He stared at himself in the mirror, adjusting his tie.

Kaufman glanced at his other TV monitor, the one that showed the Hearing Room—The hearing was open to the public, but he couldn't afford to be seen in there. The senators were wandering in and standing around in little caucus groups, no doubt discussing the Tub Humphry accident. But they couldn't start without their Chairman, Charlie Carrington.

What could he do about Charlie Carrington's retirement? What should he do? The news would leak. He had to move fast...before the media got wind of it. They would announce it as another nail in the tobacco coffin, and Kaufman knew it was. A small hole can sink a big ship, and Charlie Carrington, the louse, had just torpedoed the tobacco industry.

"Speaking of announcements," Lady Carrington was saying, "Todd has something to tell you. He's decided to enter politics."

"*Politics*? Todd!?"

Bingo! Kaufman almost shouted. There was the solution. Trade an old senator for a young senator. Trade a king for a prince.

"You know what an idealist he is," Lady Carrington said.

"That's a very dangerous decision."

"He's all wide-eyed about it. He says he wants to build a better world. You did too, remember?"

"I'm not sure there is a *better world*." The senator sounded tired again, discouraged, and broken.

"I hope you'll talk him out of it...."

But Kaufman wasn't *discouraged*, and he wasn't *broken*. But he was in a *hurry*. He popped the monitor off and grabbed for the phone.

The solution had fallen into his lap. All he had to do was get

Todd Carrington elected to the Senate. No problem. Getting his *vote* might be. Maybe he could pull the same trick on the son that he had pulled on the dad. First he had to find some dirt on Barbara Dare, the bride-to-be. Wonder if she was hiding anything? If she was, Tumbler could squeeze it out of her.

He called Tumbler who was still waiting by the phone in Asheville, North Carolina. "Get to that cross-country track meet at the University of Tennessee. I'll order a computer search on Barbara Dare immediately. An email photo and full description will be on your dashboard computer by the time you arrive in Knoxville."

"I'm taking Mickey...to chauffeur," Tumbler said.

"You need to get rid of that dummy."

"I may have to...cut him a new head." Tumbler, brilliant as he was, could hardly complete a sentence.

"Just don't hurt the girl. Do you hear me? *Don't hurt the girl.* And keep that knife in your pocket."

"What do I...wear?"

Kaufman ignored the question, leaned back in his wheelchair and rubbed his knees through his thousand-dollar suit. The arthritis hurt worse when he was tense.

Who was this Barbara Dare, anyway? he asked himself. All he knew was that she was a UT coed, a senior who liked to run. But before dark he would know what she had for breakfast, the color of her toenails, the balance in her bank account, how many men she had known, and her parents' blood type. By dark, he would know more about her than did her fiancé.

Whoever Barbara Dare was, she was about to have a visitor, the likes of which she had never seen. Tumbler would ride into Knoxville like a brick out of a dark alley. That little hillbilly bride-to-be had better not be hiding anything.

"What do I...wear?"

"Huh? I thought you'd hung up," Kaufman said. "What'd you say?"

"What do I...wear to a foot race?" Tumbler's voice trailed off like an undertaker's.

"It doesn't matter."

"What do I...wear?"

Tumbler, a true person of the night if there ever was one, was seldom out in the daylight and had never been to a sports event. Kaufman, hot and irritable from having to stay so long in the stuffy closet, managed to responded resignedly. "Wear whatever you want."

"What do I...wear?"

"I don't care what you wear!" Kaufman yelled into the phone. "Wear a purple suit if you want to!"

"*A purple suit?* That what they...wear?"

"With a *purple* polka-dot bow tie!" Kaufman shouted in frustration. "Get a *purple* umbrella to go with it. Just keep that knife in your pocket!"

7

An apple-blossom wedding. That's what Barbara Dare was trying to think about as she ran through the woods. How many attendants? What colors? Choosing the colors was easy; the apple blossoms would dictate the colors. The proposal of marriage was as fresh as last night's stars and had already survived the morning; she'd see about the afternoon.

Barbara was happiest when she was running and when she was in the mountains. Today she had the best of both worlds; she was *running* in the *mountains*.

Twenty miles to go. She'd already run six.

Her mud-bead necklace flopped wildly on her orange and white jersey, keeping time with her breathing. She could feel her chest heaving, and not just from being winded—she was truly exhilarated. By habit, she reached up and rubbed the beads between the tips of her tan fingers, calming them and herself. The necklace was her security blanket. She would wear it to her grave.

It was a peaceful afternoon in the Great Smoky Mountains. The calendar said May, but the smell of the pines said Christmas. Every tree had a bird in it, and every bird was singing at the top of his voice, serenading her in a major key—"Here Comes The Bride." That is every bird but one. High overhead, a buzzard floated in the cotton-candy clouds, looking for something dead or dying. The buzzard was not singing.

The lazy sun penetrated the crowns of the pines, the hickories, and the oaks, and played peek-a-boo with her fast-moving white Nikes. Without breaking her long stride, even as she dodged briar patches and kicked over mushy, white toadstools—booby traps to the city girls in the race, but to her as comfortable as a pair of soft gloves—she adjusted the orange and white, cotton sweatband strapped around her forehead—the apple blossom was still there—and got back to planning the wedding.

Seventeen miles to go, according to the posted mile-marker.

The birds had brought up the matter of the music. What

about the *music*? Todd liked Brahms, so Brahms it would be, mostly. She might slip in one bluegrass number, or a Dan Seals song. And her bridesmaid? Tamika. Yes, *Tamika*, her teammate. Tamika was a little salty, but she would be her bridesmaid. But who would give her away? Grandmother Dare. Definitely Grandmother Dare would give her away. And where would they have the wedding? Todd didn't care. His daddy might, but he didn't. She would consult with Todd's mother, but if they left it to Barbara, the wedding would be at the church near Grandmother Dare's cabin in Cades Cove. The church was built in the late 1800s, the work of one man, a blacksmith/carpenter. The man built it in 115 days for $115, then became its first pastor. It was a tiny, one-room chapel with an oak floor and oak benches, and was situated in the middle of an apple orchard. Perfect. If they waited until next April, the apple trees would be in bloom.

As Barbara ran, a happy smile, the only one to visit her in some time, crossed her face and peeped inside her heart. But suddenly the real world slammed the door to her heart shut. Who was she kidding? A wedding. She should live so long. The real world didn't play fair. Girls should be allowed to have weddings. She wanted to cry but to cry she would have to stop and if she stopped she would be caught. Her heart started pounding like a jackhammer on a lullaby.

Fifteen miles to go.

When Grandmother Dare had warned her that some not so nice men would be coming for her some day, she didn't tell her *who*—she didn't know who—but she told her *why*. And she told her to always stay near the mountains where she would be safe, and to make good use of her long legs, to train herself to run.

So right from the very start, Barbara took her advice, staying near the mountains and training to run as fast as she could. At first she could only outrun a chick—a baby chicken—then a pig and then a goat. She not only became very fast, but also very quick; she could catch a rabbit with her bare hands. She became very wise in the ways of the woods. And her touch. She could move a hornet's nest full of angry tenants from one tree to another so gently she never got stung. As she got older and her legs got longer, she could almost keep up with Old Ned, the pony. She had had many a race with Old Ned in Grandmother Dare's front yard. Her front yard was actually the meadow of wildflowers, full of honeybees and monarch butterflies. Grandmother Dare would sit on the porch and cackle and yell encouragements to her from her rocker. And sometimes Grandmother Dare cried.

Barbara was never a tomboy, always preferring lacey, pretty things, mostly mail-ordered from catalogues. Even in the woods, when she wasn't running, she wore a dress. Grandmother Dare saw to it, and constantly encouraged her in the queenly elegance of mountain ways, using Princess Diana as a model, pointing to her on TV, saying, "Now that's how a proper lady holds a teacup, that's how a proper lady carries herself, that's how a proper lady speaks, that's how a proper lady leans over, humbly, and greets a child or a sick person," so much so that when Princess Diana died, Barbara cried. On other occasions when she was little, Barbara would sit in Grandmother Dare's lap in the old Shaker rocker, and they would while away the hours thumbing through the pretty clothes in the Sears catalogue. You do those sorts of things when you're hiding high in the mountains, deep in the forest, cut off from most of the world. Quite early Grandmother Dare bought her a sewing machine and taught her to use it. But she didn't teach her to cook—Barbara didn't like to cook.

She chuckled at Grandmother Dare trying to teach her to cook. She still didn't like to cook, but Todd didn't know that. She let out a slight giggle. Some things you don't tell a man till after the wedding.

Thirteen miles to go.

Barbara had chosen the University of Tennessee because it was in the mountains. And Knoxville, a friendly town where folks still greeted each other with a howdy and a handshake, was less than an hour from Cades Cove where Grandmother Dare lived. When Barbara arrived at the university, she hadn't known they had a girls' track team. But one day after class she was running alongside the Tennessee River, in front of the football stadium, and came upon some girls running; she learned later it was their cross-country team. She jogged a ways with them without speaking, then passed, and sprinted off into the woods. When she got back to the dorm that night, the girls' track coach, Pricilla Simmons, was waiting for her. Barbara recognized the coach, a young, middle-aged woman, as one of those who had been jogging that afternoon down by the river. The next week, the student newspaper quoted Coach Prissy Simmons, "A runner has come to us from the mountains. Her name is Barbara Dare. The University of Tennessee has never seen a runner like Barbara Dare." Barbara was pleased with the comment. But Coach Simmons had no idea how right she was, nor how dangerous her statement. If she only knew. No other girl had ever had such a reason for running. It was simple: A frightened girl runs faster. And Barbara felt she could tolerate that bit of publicity; the student newspaper wouldn't be going off campus.

Ten miles to go.

Now, suddenly the birds stopped singing and the woods became very quiet. The only sounds she could hear were her feet courting the ground and the haunting creak of the hardwoods rubbing each other in the polite breeze. They must be gaining on her, she thought. Planning a wedding had cost her, so she tried to pick up her pace. The birds were accustomed to her comings and goings in their forest, but not those tracking her. The birds' silence seemed to trumpet a harbinger's warning that last night's proposal of marriage was in trouble. Tonight she would try to find out how much trouble.

The sweatband kept the perspiration out of her eyes, but the rest of the salty juice ran down her back and legs and puddled in her shoes; her orange and white jersey, number 20—the same as her age—was soaked as were her orange racing-shorts and her orange-banded socks.

Eight miles to go.

She'd used up eighteen miles of the forest. Soon the clearing would come into view. She would have to leave her place of safety, the woods, and go into the dangerous part of her run, out into the open where she would be exposed.

They would chase her to her death. She knew that. Maybe not today, maybe not tomorrow, but one day soon. All her life she'd been preparing for the day they would come, and running was what she did best.

Today was the culmination of all of her training to become the fastest. Today was her last race for the university. And right now, she was in this cross-country race that she must *finish*, but must *not win*. She could tell no one the reason why she must not win, and the clock was already ticking.

Since she didn't know *who* was coming, much less *when*, she decided that, just for practice, she would play like today's race was when they would deliver their *coup de grace*. And so, in her mind she began to play it all out, pretending that her opponents in this event meant her harm.

Already in front of the other contestants, she began to claim every speed-enhancing emotion in her being. First she thought of graduation, then she thought of the wedding again, and then her twenty-first birthday. But those thoughts only slowed her. If somehow she didn't become faster, there would be no graduation, there would be no wedding, and there would be no birthday.

Finally, she thought of Todd and the danger her secret had placed him in. That did the trick. That was the emotion she was hunting. She pretended she was leading them further and further away from Todd, and that made her run like a woman with her hair on fire.

A senior now, she had met Todd Carrington when she was a freshman. She laughed now at their first meeting, but at the time it wasn't very funny. She had received, as did all freshmen, an invitation to the President's Reception Ball. The invitation stated: Formal, Black Tie. She took that to mean "Sunday go-to-meetin'" best, so, for the occasion, she ordered from the Sears catalogue a baby-blue Angora sweater, enough white wool fabric to make a pleated skirt, and a pair of burgundy penny loafers. She planned to walk over to the dance with Tamika, Tsu, and Brandi, her teammates.

The night of the big event arrived, but when Tamika called and said they were on the way over, Barbara was still sewing the pleated skirt. "I'm not ready," she said. "Y'all go on. I'll catch up." She finished the skirt, slipped on the sweater and loafers, with a penny dated 1959 in each slot, and, proud as a princess, struck out across the manicured lawn toward the President's home. When she opened the door, the men were wearing dinner jackets, and the girls were all in dresses like those Princess Di wore. But the catalogue didn't carry dresses like that! She froze in horror, then dashed to the powder room and wept.

Momentarily, Tamika came to the door. "Are ya decent?"

"I'm not going back out there," Barbara said from the stall, so embarrassed she could die.

"There's someone here who wants to meet you," Tamika said. "Come on out."

"I don't want to meet anybody."

"I think you will," Tamika said with a proud laugh. "It's the President of the senior class."

Holding a piece of toilet paper to her eyes, Barbara cracked the door and peeped out. There stood a tall, broad-shouldered, all tan, Greek god.

"Hello," he said with a deep Carolina drawl.

Lord, all this and he speaks, too.

Without even introducing himself, he gently led her with his large, powerful hand out of the bathroom, straight to the dance floor where he taught her to waltz in her white, pleated skirt, her baby-blue Angora sweater, and her burgundy penny loafers, right there in front of everyone, to the envy of every girl in the room.

All that was a long time ago. She had now become a specialist in what to wear where, and last night the Greek god asked her to be his bride.

Seven miles to go.

Barbara now broke out of the woods, running at breakneck speed, at least it was breakneck speed for a marathon. Hard-pounding footsteps came from the woods behind her, crackling kindling underfoot.

She glanced back. Colors. Every color of the rainbow it seemed was chasing her, darting in and out between green pine trees, making the bright colors flash like strobe lights.

Like a child fleeing a ghost, she lit out across an open sage field, scattering the butterflies. But the rainbow chased her into the field. The rainbow was now spread out, making a swathe like a scythe through the sweet smelling sage.

The sun bore down, the chiggers began to bite, and overhead a hawk cruised the skies. Suddenly a fleeing rabbit, trying to make it to safety, hopped across her path, almost tripping her. But the hawk was already in a death dive. The rabbit would receive no mercy. Fleeing her own kind of hawk, twenty miles lay in her wake.

Six to go.

8

Barbara Dare was out there in the woods somewhere, running. Tumbler could never catch her in the woods—few men could—but he knew where she was headed. She would come storming into the stadium any minute now. All he had to do was pick his spot and let her come to him.

But first he had to get parked. No easy task when you're stalled in traffic inching its way down Stadium Drive past the front of the stadium, everybody hunting a parking place. And his new suit itched. On such short notice, he liked to have never found a purple suit. The purple polka-dot tie had proven to be even more difficult to find.

From his seat in the rear of the big white Mercedes, Tumbler noticed in the rearview mirror one of those pickups with unusually big tires and a suspension lift that makes it sit high off the ground. The black truck was also stalled in the traffic, had red mud splashed all over the cab, and its diesel engine clattered like it would explode in the heat. The front tag read: Go Vols, National Champs. The driver wore a UT ball cap, and a coon dog rode in the front seat beside him. A shotgun rested in the headache rack mounted below the truck's rear window.

Up ahead of Tumbler's Mercedes, a frustrated young man dressed in jeans, tennis shoes, and an orange and white vest over a sweaty T-shirt raced about in the middle of the street—Barney Fife-like—wildly directing the stand-still traffic to nowhere in particular.

Tumbler rolled down his window and signaled the young man to him.

The kid ignored him at first, then evidently saw the white press card propped in the windshield of the big Mercedes. He quickly hurried over, stared into the backseat, and gulped. "Don't that take the rag of the vine. You drive that thang from the backseat?"

"Yeah." Tumbler, sitting in the back seat on the passenger side, gripped the steering wheel and kept his head down.

"Then why's *he* wearin' the chauffeur's hat?" The parking attendant pointed at Mickey, in the front seat.

Tumbler ignored the question and pointed toward a lot next to the stadium. "I'd like to park over there."

"You with the press, ain't you?"

"Yeah."

"Well, that's where the press parks. That's where I'd park if I had me one of them white cards." He leaned in, gawking, as if trying to get a better look at the clever, rear-seat-drive setup.

Tumbler revved the twelve-cylinder engine and began inching the window up.

The boy jerked his head out just before the glass caught it. Meekly, he said, "Just a minute. I'll help ya across." He raised his arm, revealing perspiration stains in his arm-pit, stopped the already stopped traffic, and motioned Tumbler through.

Tumbler pulled across the street and parked under a large oak. He told Mickey to stay with the car and that "the Barbara Dare project" shouldn't take long. "What a stupid girl. A 4.0 GPA and do something this stupid."

"She *must be* stupid," he thought he heard Mickey say.

"Yeah." Tumbler opened the door, slid his wiry frame off the thick, purple cushion, and climbed down to the ground. "Got herself engaged. If she hadn't *gotten engaged*...this trip wouldn't have...been necessary."

Mickey didn't respond.

Tumbler found some shade under a sycamore tree in front of the stadium, hid behind it, and watched the crowd gather. A weak bark caught his attention, causing him to glance over his shoulder. A long-eared hound, his tongue hanging out, was chasing a calico cat down the street and they were both walking. It was that kind of hot in Knoxville. Everybody was hunting shade.

Tumbler peered from behind the tree and studied his escape route. He only had to remember two landmarks: Widower-Maker Hill and the Smoky Mountains. He was standing on top of Widower-Maker Hill, and he could see the Smoky Mountains. That's where he would run to. The pretty blond, whose marriage plans had sent his client into such a stupor, was somewhere between those two points, coming his way. On foot.

From behind the sycamore tree, Tumbler looked at the one-page description Kaufman had just emailed him. The target was not adequately described.   Tumbler had to have a better description. His reputation was on the line. He had never taken out the wrong target before.   On his cell phone, he dialed Krandall Kaufman's closet in Washington, D.C.

Kaufman answered on the first ring. "What's wrong?"

"The description you sent…is not sufficient. It could fit any of the girls she runs with."

"That's all we have on her."

"You ever heard of…hillbilly justice?   You don't mess around with these mountain people, and I'm staring at 30,000 of them…right now.   I don't want to get the…wrong girl.   I…I think we should call it off until you can get me a better…description of her. We need more time."

"We don't have *more time*!" Kaufman shouted.   "That Senate hearing is underway right now!"

"Nothing new. Been going on for a week."

"But Senator Charlie Carrington is retiring! Do I have to spell it out for you? He's our swing vote. We want his boy to take *his* seat in the Senate! His boy got engaged last night. To Barbara Dare! If you don't get to her, how are we going to force his boy's vote?"

"His boy is not even running for office. Much less been elected."

"He will be," Kaufman said with quiet assurance. "He will be. I'm meeting with his dad at 11:00 in the morning. I'll make him stay on until we can get his son groomed."

"How?"

"He confessed everything to his wife, but he still wouldn't want her humiliated in public. If I have to, I'll threaten to leak the news about *her*."

"That should keep him in line…a while."

"Call me at 11:05 in the morning with your report on Barbara Dare. That report will be the trigger mechanism that launches the boy's political career."

"It'll launch something else if I...get the wrong girl. Call it off until you can send me a picture...or a better description of her."

"I don't have a *picture* of—" Kaufman interrupted himself. "Wait a minute—"

"What?"

"There may be something else. Lady Carrington said something about...Mud beads."

"*Mud beads?*"

"Mud beads. Barbara Dare wears a mud-bead necklace everywhere she goes."

"*Everywhere?*"

"To the point of embarrassment, the senator thinks."

"That's good," Tumbler said, relaxing. "That's all I need. I'll call you at 11:05 in the morning." Tumbler hung up, turned, and stared into the Smoky Mountains.

The Smokies, as the locals called them, were silhouetted in their always smoky haze. The whole area was generally referred to as the Smokies, but the actual entrance to the Great Smoky Mountain National Park was about thirty miles away as the crow flies. Forty in a car. Tumbler and Mickey had checked it twice that morning. Thirty-two minutes flat...if you took the back roads and if you let the hammer down and if the stream of tour buses didn't trap you in Pigeon Forge or Gatlinburg. But if Dolly was appearing in person at Dollywood, look out. But she wasn't. He'd checked that too.

A man could get lost in the Smokies. A lot of men had—an accused abortion clinic bomber was said to be hiding there right now. But not Tumbler. He was scared to stay too long in the mountains; a rat was not very high on the food chain in the mountains. And Mickey would spoil without air conditioning. Asheville, North Carolina, lay on the other side of those mountains. *Asheville* was more to Tumbler's liking; his client already had a hideout there.

From behind the tree atop Widower-Maker Hill, Tumbler could see his white Mercedes. It was backed in, the motor running. Mickey hadn't moved an inch; he was still looking straight ahead. Good old, loyal Mickey. This was Mickey's first job. He looked a little pale today and was starting to lose some of his color. Mickey was his best friend. His only friend. If he ever did Mickey in, it would be to steal his name. He had always wished his own name was Mickey and had never forgiven his mother for not naming him that. Just to spite her, MICKEY was the name printed on his North Carolina license tag. Mickey didn't care.

The Mercedes was a four-door, an S600, the biggest they make, and was deceptively fast. Tumbler had chosen it because one just like it had recently been in the news—with the death of Princess Diana, though hers was black—and the French paparazzi had said the car was fast. If it proved not to be fast enough, he'd just get another one. Money was no object with his client. Being a little man, the Mercedes was a little bigger automobile than Tumbler preferred, but his purple cushion helped him see over the front seat and tan leather dashboard.

He was pleased with his decision to leave the motor running. A hasty departure was everything. This was a little job, but he took the same care as if he had been going after the senator himself. Kaufman had instructed him not to kill the girl, but Tumbler had his reputation to think about. He never did a job without killing someone.

He looked off down the steep hill to his left. One glance at the incline verified that Widower-Maker Hill was appropriately named. The street was roped off with orange tape for the foot race. Widower-Maker Hill would be his escape route. God help the poor girl that was lagging too far behind Barbara Dare when the Mercedes tore out.

Everything was all set.

Now for the fake press badge. Tumbler removed the yellow badge from his pocket and nervously fumbled with the pin. This was his first daylight job so he was nervous beyond his usual state of nervousness. He jabbed his finger twice, trying to pin the badge to the lapel of his mouse-belly-purple suit. His finger bled a little, but he sucked the blood off. *Blood* didn't bother him. *Little tasks* bothered him. Things like pinning on a badge. But he finally got it on.

He stepped from behind the sycamore, then moused his way

into the stadium amidst the smell of peanuts and popcorn and hotdogs and beer and sweat. He wasn't comfortable at all at the sporting event and felt as out of place as a potatobug at a radish convention. He took a seat near the finish line with the rest of the paper-rattling, loud-talking, camera-toting press. A creature of the night, he opened his purple polka-dot umbrella that matched his purple polka-dot bow tie, and squinted into the sunlight.

A sea of orange stared back at him.

Thirty-thousand binocular-eyed, skimpily-clad fans, mostly University of Tennessee students, lounged in the hot afternoon sun, drinking and watching—drinking whatever cooled them and watching for the teams to come off the river trail, round a far tree-laden curve, head up Widower-Maker Hill, and then sprint into the stadium.

National sportscasters, herds of them, had descended on Knoxville and they were all predicting that Tennessee's Lady Vols, the out and out favorite, would win the cross-country marathon, making them national champions.

Tumbler adjusted his binoculars and began to watch for the orange team to break into the clearing. He would get his first glimpse of her when she reached the trail that ran alongside the Tennessee River.

The river would escort them to Widower-Maker Hill, and Widower-Maker Hill would escort them into the stadium.

Like a master carpenter, Tumbler found it better to measure twice and cut once, so he removed the brief email note from his pocket and read it again. He didn't have to. He had perfect recall...or so he claimed to himself. No matter, this *second measuring* would make sure he had the right girl.

Besides saying that she was brilliant, and listing her grade-point average, the note described her as a tall blond, and further stated that she was pretty, she was fast, and she was clean. Actually the note said she was beautiful, but Tumbler's stuttered mind didn't make the distinction between pretty and beautiful. How a girl looked was of no interest to him. His delight was in the chase, especially when they tried to get away.

They had definitely sent the right man. When they sent him,

it was for a killing. But this trip was most unusual. This trip was for *gathering information*, not for *killing*. And he'd been warned not to make up one of his lamebrain excuses for hurting the girl. The killing would come later.

Not having a picture of the target still bothered Tumbler, but Kaufman had solved that problem when he revealed the girl's fatal flaw—more of a habit than a flaw—a flaw nonetheless, as identifiable as a birthmark and as predictable as the sunset. That flaw separated this girl from all others in the race. Armed with that speck of information, he could do what he had come to do. What delight: a mud-bead necklace around her throat. Ah, the throat.

Like a thirsty man in the desert staring at a bucket of cool water, Tumbler salivated, tantalizing himself with the thought of taunting her into some action that would justify killing her on the spot.

From his vantage point near the finish line, he could reach out and touch the winner. He didn't know which of the speedsters bore her name, but one of those four University of Tennessee girls was Barbara Dare, and Barbara Dare was the one he'd come for.

He felt inside his pants pocket to make sure the knife was still there.

9

Six miles to go.

Barbara Dare couldn't concentrate on how far she had to go. Her mind raced faster than her feet, making her forget that there were only six miles left.

She soon passed the city limit marker and began clicking off the streets of Knoxville. She raced past a small gray house with a tin roof where two old men in faded overalls were usually playing horseshoes in the all-dirt, front yard. Today the sun had chased them to the shade of the porch. One man was lounging lengthwise in the porch swing, with one foot on the floor, the other foot in the swing, and his ball cap resting on his knee; the other man was leaning against one of the two posts that propped up the dilapidated porch, fanning himself with a tattered straw hat. It was just too hot to play horseshoes.

As Barbara trotted by, the two old friends she had never met waved and she waved back.

She glanced over her shoulder. In the distance, a black girl, a brown girl, and a white girl—the orange part of the rainbow— were racing after her. She didn't worry about them; they could never catch her. And if they couldn't, the others certainly couldn't.

Barbara Dare—she wore her grandmother's last name—was brave as an Indian warrior and skittish as a thoroughbred racehorse. At least she *wanted* to be brave. She *meant* to be brave. When the end finally came, she would *be* brave. And she had reason to be *skittish*. The more she worried, the faster she ran. Lost in what was to come, she ran another five miles and was coming down hard on the last mile of the way.

One mile to go.

She had now reached the Tennessee River—she could hear the cars on Stadium Drive but couldn't see them for the thick foliage—and raced alongside it enjoying the cool shade of the sycamores, smelling the wild fragrances, and splattering the soft mud. She and Todd Carrington had had many a picnic there on the beautiful river's lush green banks. He brought the caviar and she brought the fried chicken. And Moon Pies.

Suddenly a foul odor struck her nostrils. It was a skunk. Like the sound of a rattlesnake, and there were plenty of those around, as well as water moccasins and copperheads, the smell of a skunk would be unmistakable, even to a city dude. The skunk had probably come to the river for a drink, but he might still be lurking nearby.

The odor caused Barbara to jerk her head up. When she raised her head—

She saw the stadium! And heard the crowd, jarring her back to reality. "Oh, Lord!"

She was too far out in front of her competition. She was about to win the race! That she must never do! Trapped! Any way she looked at it, she was trapped. She had run too fast. Thousands of screaming fans and the national media—some, it seemed, had set up camp there since the Vols won the national football championship—waited for the winner to burst into the spotlight.

It was the race of her life; everyone had said so. And in her four years at the university she had never won. The goal was in sight. Her calves ached, her lungs begged, and her mouth tasted of copper. What would it be like to win?

"And this time," Coach Persimmon—that's what the girls called Coach *Prissy Simmons* when she pushed them too hard— had screamed at the starting line, "please save something for your final kick!" Some said Barbara Dare always choked at the finish, but her coach blamed it on burning too much energy early in the marathon, saving too little for the stadium lap in front of the fans.

Barbara longed to tell them all that this was far from being the *race of her life*. Still, the little girl inside her—that part of her that would not acknowledge that Death was coming down hard on her, that part of her that was all full of dreams, that part of her that every bright-eyed mountain girl owned unto herself— wanted to win. Usually only the campus paper covered track events. Now, if she dashed into the stadium in the lead, the national media would swarm her, asking questions and demanding answers.

Then everyone would know.

Then it would all be over.

Then day would turn to night and the night would never go away.

Still at full stride, she fought the temptation to satisfy the hunger in her heart to win, to dine just one time on the sweet roar coming from the stadium, now booming like thunder. Just once. That's all she wanted.

Track meets were usually held at the track field, but this, a national event, was in Neyland Stadium; Neyland would hold three times the number, but this was quite a crowd for a track meet. Oh, how she wanted to win. For Todd. But alas, such was not to be.

No way around it, she was trapped. She couldn't win because of the press and she couldn't lose because of her team. But she had known since she joined the team that her personal goal was to become the fastest, not to win. She must never win. But that didn't keep the rebel inside her from wanting to. Just one time she would like to cut loose on that final lap. She felt like a mother trapped on the median of an eight-lane highway, holding a child by each hand, trying to get across four more lanes of seventy-mile-an-hour traffic. The mother might do it, but she would pay a high price. And so would Barbara.

It would do no good to cry. It would do no good to pray. And so Barbara Dare made the only decision she could. It all happened in a flash. Halfway up Widower-Maker Hill, she feigned a cramp, bent over, and watched between her long, perspiration-drenched legs for the others to catch up.

An eternity of seconds passed. She knew the binoculars in the stadium were trained on her. The stadium became silent as a tomb.

Tamika, Tsu, and Brandi, her Lady Vols teammates, soon came flying around a far, tree-laden curve, North Carolina and Kentucky hot on their heels; it was a team race. The herd started climbing the Widower-Maker.

Closer. Closer. Closer.

A small girl from TCU lagged in the distance, her purple uniform bouncing and shimmering in the hot afternoon sun, bringing closure to the rainbow.

Barbara began jogging in place, shaking out the phantom cramp. Then she started trotting. Like a runner awaiting a baton, she segued in front of the oncoming heavy breathing, heavy footsteps, and big time sweat now blending with the smell of honeysuckles alongside the street. Her teammates, leading the rest of the pack, had now caught up to her. Dressed in orange and white, Tamika was black, Tsu was Chinese, and Brandi was white. For four years they had traveled, laughed, and cried together, and this was their last race as a team.

Barbara gave the signal, the last she would ever give them. They grabbed hands and, four-abreast, sprinted into the stadium, running, laughing, and crying all at the same time, bringing home The Big Orange

Her heart almost burst with pride when the stadium erupted into "Rocky Top." Fans came to their feet, stomping and screaming. Some even climbed into their seats and stomped, tempting her one last time to cut loose and outrun them all. But *living* was more important than *winning*, so, as preordained, she fell slightly behind Tamika, Tsu, and Brandi.

They made the final turn. She bunched right up next to her teammates, hiding from the cameras, making sure she was at least fourth; that way her team wouldn't be penalized. The press would pay little attention to fourth place.

She shot across the finish line and, holding her elbow over her face, and without breaking stride, headed straight for the showers. She couldn't take another lecture from her coach about pacing herself. If Coach Simmons knew what she knew, she would have faked a cramp, too.

10

Tumbler watched it all from the press box near the finish line. But he saw no mud-bead necklace.

The short Chinese girl won, and so all the reporters and camera crews rushed her. All but Tumbler. When the girl whom he suspected was Barbara Dare had crossed the finish line, she threw up her arm, blocking his view. He couldn't tell if she was wearing a necklace of any kind, much less a mud-bead necklace.

So he strolled over to the leggy black girl with the high hips who had come in third. No one was around her. He peeped from under his purple polka-dot umbrella. "That Barbara Dare?" he asked, "who came in fourth?"

"Yeah," said the black girl, bent double and breathing heavily.

Uncomfortable with conversation of any kind, especially in the daylight, Tumbler nervously lit the Marlboro in the ivory cigarette holder he was chewing on. "She didn't stay around for the interview. Why?" he asked in his best undertaker tone.

Still bent over, the black girl looked up, giving him a scowl. "You stupid? *She* didn't win!"

Tumbler bit hard on the cigarette holder. He had never killed anyone just for killing them, but this girl deserved killing and he might oblige her. As soon as he finished his *other* job. He just stood there puffing on the Marlboro and twirling the umbrella, hiding from the sunshine. The white cigarette holder amplified the paleness of his skin and the thinness of his pencil-thin mustache over his pencil-thin upper lip. And he liked that. All the attention to his appearance gave him a chance to size up his quarry while they dwelt on his mouse-man look. He was especially thankful to Kaufman for suggesting the color for his suit and matching accessories. Purple suited him just fine because purple was the color of a mouse's stomach, soon after it had been killed.

The black girl must have realized she had offended him. "I'm sorry," she said apologetically, "but I just ran twenty-six miles. I got my breath back now." She grabbed a bottle of Gatorade and began gurgling it down. "The name's Tamika."

Then, like a rat plotting a cheese burglary, Tumbler locked his watery, mousy eyes on her, and with his practiced undertaker-tone said, "I asked you why Barbara Dare didn't stay for the interview?"

Tamika straightened up, towering over him. She wiped the sweat from her face with the bottom of her jersey, revealing her pale-brown, outtie navel. "You see, Barbara's our—" She grabbed another swig of Gatorade and swallowed fast, "Homecoming Queen-elect and she gets pretty tired of answering questions about—"

"Barbara Dare? *Homecoming Queen?*"

"*Elect.* Homecoming Queen-*elect.*"

"No matter. It appeared she could have won the race."

"You noticed," Tamika said, smiling. "Now, that's a story for you. She *could have* won. She's the fastest on our team."

Tumbler couldn't care less who was the fastest. He needed other information. "Where is she from?"

"Cades Cove, Tennessee. Hey, how come you ain't interviewing Tsu, the winner?"

Tumbler, still wearing his fake press badge, glanced toward the winner's circle where reporters were still hounding the Asian girl. "I don't speak Chinese."

Tamika laughed, but Tumbler didn't. She gestured with her palms open. "Then interview me."

He ignored her comment, turned and walked toward the women's gym. As he did, he heard Tamika call out, "Barbara Dare don't grant no interviews."

As soon as he was out of sight, he tossed the yellow press badge onto the green grass beside his white Mercedes. The women's gym was about a block away, so he decided to drive. He closed his parasol and climbed into the back seat, on the passenger side. He adjusted his purple cushion, shoved the car into gear, and drove, always from the rear seat, right out across the lawn, the sprinkler system going full blast. Mickey sat in the front seat, his head teeter-tottering from side to side each time Tumbler bumped over one of the metal sprinkler-pipes.

Tumbler had good reason for driving the Mercedes from the back seat, an idea he got when he called the factory in Europe to order it. Plant officials asked, "Do you prefer left-side or right-side steering?" He thought about it a minute and replied, "Backseat, right-side." After more than a few moments of doubt and explanation—their doubt and his explanation—they agreed to modify the automobile to his specifications. The brakes, accelerator, and steering mechanism were extended to accommodate his small size and his fancy for driving the car from the rear seat. Since he was paying cash, he didn't feel it necessary to reveal his reasoning, which to him was quite logical. Most of his jobs were at night. Anyone chasing him would naturally shoot out the driver's side window. They would never think of the driver being in the backseat, and certainly not on the *right* side of the backseat. That's how his friend Mickey came into the picture. That and the fear that the highway patrol might become suspicious of a driverless car. Tumbler had mounted a dummy with a chauffeur's uniform in the seat where a driver would normally sit. If his pursuers shot out the window, he wanted them to think they had hit him; he needed a head for the dummy that would splatter. So he gave Mickey a real pumpkin for his head and glued a wig and chauffeur's cap on it.

Tumbler now drove slowly past the girls' gym, studying it. He then turned into the alley and parked by a door that read, "Women's Locker Room." He turned the windshield wipers off and climbed out. Mickey stayed in the front seat with the motor running.

Peeping and stalking, Tumbler stole toward the door. As he walked, he kept his small round shoulders hunched up against his head, making it appear he had no neck, and furthering his mouse persona. Like the voice, the look was practiced. He used a special tear solution to make his eyes leak. As a *man*, he appeared small, but a *mouse* his size was a frightening sight and caused his prey to recoil. Men twice Tumbler's size cowered in his presence. Few people had ever seen him up close. Most of those wouldn't be telling anyone.

He removed his purple kerchief from his lapel pocket and placed it on the doorknob. Then quiet, like both an undertaker and a mouse, he slowly turned the knob with his left hand. He slid his right hand inside his pants pocket. Warm metal lay against his white thigh—his lily-white thigh that had never known sunshine. With great pleasure, he withdrew the ivory-handled Schrade/Walden pocketknife with the surgical-steel blades. And opened it. If he had to use the knife, he could always tell Kaufman she didn't cooperate.

Tumbler listened as he let his eyes adjust to the light inside the gym. He could hear the shower running and a girl's voice humming. If he could search her locker, he might find enough information for Kaufman that he wouldn't have to hurt her. But eventually, he knew he would get to kill her. Kaufman had hatched the harebrained scheme at the last minute, forcing this daylight foray. It was the girl's fault. She should never have gotten engaged to the Carrington kid.

He glanced down the row of metal lockers. One locker stood wide open. He quickly tiptoed closer. The sweat-soaked orange and white track shorts and shirt she had been wearing lay scattered on the bench in front of the open locker. On the floor lay her muddy shoes. One shoe sat upright; the other lay bottom-side up. Her orange-banded white socks lay curled into a ball on the bench. Draped across the bench hung a large clean, white towel. On the towel lay an apple blossom. When he bent over to look inside the locker, his coattail swished against the blossom, knocking it to the concrete floor.

Inside the locker was as neat as a bride's hope chest and smelled of lilac, fresh sweat, and young girl. A plastic Dairy Queen cup sat in the bottom of the locker, with, of all things, a dozen long-stemmed roses. A long, navy-blue skirt hung beside a white, high-neck frill-blouse. A fresh, white, cotton head-band dangled from the same hanger. At the bottom of the locker sat a blue, plastic bin. Inside the bin lay a neatly folded pair of white lace bikini panties and matching bra. On top of the underclothes lay five quarters and a dime.

Quiet as a mouse, Tumbler poked around in the blue plastic bin with the big blade of his knife, lifting the underclothes, taking care not to disturb anything and to leave no fingerprints. Beneath the lingerie lay a small half-open purse. Using the

56

blade, he seesawed the purse open further and saw four twenty-dollar bills, a few singles, a see-through plastic cosmetic bag, and an Arby's *buy one, get one free* coupon. He listened to make sure the shower was still running. The bathing girl was still humming. It was a church song. Or a folk song. Whatever kind it was, it had such a sadness to it that he wished she would stop singing.

But he got right back to the purse. He still hadn't found a mud-bead necklace. A doubt gnawed at him. He would get the blame if anything went wrong. Kaufman would not tolerate a mistake in the report. Tumbler thought, If I could find a driver's license or credit card, I could learn a lot about her. But he found neither. And most unusual, no car keys. So he kept looking. A new pair of white Nikes sat beside the blue plastic bin, and a chemistry text book was wedged between the shoes and the side of the locker. Still using the big blade, he tilted the book cover and pried it open enough to read the words written just inside the book: Barbara Dare; Cades Cove, Tennessee. That confirmed what the black girl had just told him. Now if he could find that mud-bead necklace, he could be doubly sure he had the right girl. He pushed the hangers and clothes to one side revealing the locker's back wall.

There! There it was! The mud-bead necklace. It was hanging behind the blouse. With the back of the blade—so he wouldn't cut it—he lifted the common-looking necklace, curiously studying it. They *were* mud beads! Mud beads strung onto a homemade, frayed string. The neck was Tumbler's favorite part of a girl's body, and the mud beads offended him. Why would a girl about to marry the son of the richest man in North Carolina—a U.S. Senator and tobacco baron—wear such a common thing? He would know the answer to that question in the morning at 11:05, Washington, D.C. time.

Suddenly the shower went off. Tumbler jumped behind the next row of lockers and listened to wet feet slapping the floor. He got down on his haunches and duck-waddled to the corner and peeped, his knife drawn.

The towel-draped, tall blond, evidently cured of the sad song she had been singing, came skipping toward the locker, swinging

57

her arms like a child on a playground. Now she was singing "Here comes the bride." She'd do well to forget that song.

She was now coming toward him! He jumped back behind a row of lockers, trying not to breathe. At the last instant, she wheeled away from him and headed down another row toward her own locker. As she turned, he peeped out. He was so close her heels splattered a drop of water on the lapel of his suit.

That's when he heard a jingling sound. He searched her up and down with his eyes—she now had her back to him—for the source of the sound. The jingling led his eyes to a set of keys in her right hand. What on earth? Car keys? Had to be. Why would she take keys into the shower?

Just then the gym door flew open and the rest of the team came rushing in.

Tumbler slipped into a janitor's closet. In the darkness, he adjusted his bow tie, felt inside his suit-coat pocket and touched a 3 x 5 card, reassuring himself it was still there. On the card was the private number to the desk of Senator Charlie Carrington in Washington, D.C. At exactly 11:05 tomorrow morning, he would dial that number, the number to Barbara Dare's future father-in-law.

11

Tamika came out of the shower, dried off with a white towel, then tossed it onto the bench. "Did that reporter find you?"

"*What* reporter?" asked Barbara, startled.

Tamika reached inside her locker for her jeans. "Some weirdo."

Tumbler, still hiding in the broom closet, held the door cracked open so he could peep, as well as hear, and gnawed at a fingernail.

"*Weirdo?*" Barbara was already dressed and standing in front of the mirror, brushing her damp hair.

"Yeah," Tamika said, zipping up her jeans. "Odd-looking duck. Looked like a cross between a hedgehog and Mickey Mouse gone mad." She removed a robin's egg-blue T-shirt from the locker and slipped it on. "Talked like an undertaker. Wanted to interview *you.*"

"Interview *me?*" Barbara had finished with her hair and started to toss the brush into the blue bin in her locker.

"Lemme borrow your brush," Tamika said, reaching. "Yeah, like *you* was the one that won."

"No one interviewed me."

"I probably discouraged him."

"Did you see where he went?"

"He was headed this way, but I told him you don't grant interviews."

"Good." Barbara fidgeted nervously as she grabbed her headband and lab book. "Gotta get to chemistry lab. See ya."

"Just a minute." Still barefooted, Tamika took one more swipe through her hair, and tossed the brush into Barbara's locker. "I'm gonna run by the DQ and get an Icee. I'll walk with you to the parking lot." She was still sliding one of her feet into the wide-heeled, wedge shoes as she hobbled to catch up to Barbara. "Wait up."

Tumbler followed. He was still smarting about Tamika's having called him stupid. He was willing to let that remark pass, but calling him a *weirdo*, too. Well that couldn't be tolerated.

At the entrance to the Science Building, the girls parted company. Barbara turned and started climbing the steps to the lab. Tamika kept walking toward the parking lot.

"See ya."

Halfway up the steps, Barbara turned and called back, "Tamika?" She tossed her headband to her, "Pitch this in my car as you go by. I don't want to keep up with it."

"Ain't it locked?"

"Just ring it around the antenna."

"Speaking of rings," Tamika called back, "Set the date yet?"

"I'm calling Todd tonight. Let you know tomorrow."

Barbara disappeared into the building, and Tamika walked on toward the parking lot, Barbara's white, cotton headband dangling from her fingers. As she passed Barbara's old silver-gray Camaro, she tossed the headband around the antenna. "Two points."

That was the last thing she ever said. When Tumbler finished with her, he picked the lock to Barbara's trunk.

The Camaro, an '89 T-Top, had a hatch opening with a cargo hole for a trunk. The cargo hole was covered with a vinyl security cover that worked like a horizontal window shade with hooks. Tumbler had to rearrange the body a few times, trying several positions, until the security cover hooked clean, revealing no bumps.

"Now who's *stupid*?" he asked out loud, slamming the lid. "Now who's a *weirdo*?" Putting the body in the trunk of Barbara Dare's car was an afterthought, and poor pay for not getting to kill her too. But the body in the trunk would unnerve her until he could. Unnerving a target brought great satisfaction.

If a cop stopped her, she'd have some explaining to do. Maybe Kaufman could pin the murder on her. Maybe he, Tumbler, had found some dirt on Miss Barbara Dare after all. Kaufman didn't say he couldn't *toss* the dirt on her.

Tumbler knelt and wiped the black girl's red blood off the silver blade of his ivory-handled knife on the green grass beneath the rusty bumper of the silver-gray Camaro. With the knee of his purple suit captured in the mix—if Mickey had been there he would have had some *orange*—he paused for a fleeting moment, admiring his homemade rainbow. Daylight had at least one good thing going for it, he thought, You can see colors. Then he scurried off into *his* realm...the fast-coming night.

Panting hard, the mouseman climbed into the backseat of his mouse-mobile and sped away. Mickey asked no questions—that was what he liked best about Mickey.

The trappings of the day's track events were still up, including the orange and white crowd-control ribbons used to close off Widower-Maker Hill for the marathon. The ribbons fluttered in the soft, hot breeze. Tumbler burst through the barrier, just as he had planned, then took the back roads toward the Great Smoky Mountains. One of the ribbons clung to the front bumper and tapped urgently against the back panels of the Mercedes.

"Sounds like a ghost runner," Tumbler said to Mickey, practicing his undertaker voice, "trying to get out of a...trunk."

The thought of what he had done to the black girl's throat gave him a choking sensation and made his neck hurt, so he reached up to unbutton the top button of his shirt, and that's when he realized that his purple polka-dot bow tie was missing!!

12

Barbara Dare, all refreshed, walked into chemistry lab, the clean smell of gym-shower still on her.

She was still wearing the navy-blue skirt and white blouse, and, of course, her mud-bead necklace. There wouldn't be time to change after lab, and she wanted to look pretty for her meeting later tonight. When she wore pretty things, she felt pretty. As always, tonight she would change into her disguise, but somehow they would know she had dressed pretty for them.

The air conditioning in the lab felt good and reminded her that her hair was still damp. She would make short work of the private lab lesson, then she would risk it all on the secret mission she must make tonight. Tonight she would find out if there would be time for an apple-blossom wedding before the Death Angel came for her.

"Good race," the middle-aged professor said as she moved toward his desk.

"Thank you, sir," she said softly. She always spoke softly. She wasn't sure if she just had a soft voice or if it was because all her life she had tried to go unnoticed. She strolled over to the peg-board, removed her sky-blue smock, and tied it on. The hardest part was pretending nothing was wrong.

"Your last race?" he asked as he stood and helped her set up the experiment.

"I hope not." She laughed, forcing the humor. Everybody, including her coach, had said it was the biggest race of her life. But they didn't know what she knew. The race of her life waited just outside the door. Any door.

All four years with the Lady Vols Track Team, whether a hundred-yard dash or a marathon, every single race had been to prepare for the time when foot-speed might save her life. But only Grandmother Dare knew what had driven her to the brink of bursting her lungs.

"I meant at UT," the professor said.

Barbara smiled. "Just kidding. I knew what you meant."

The day was coming when she would race the race of her life

all right, but her yet-to-be-named opponent would choose the time and place. There would certainly be no fans cheering her on. And because of the secret, he would chase her to her death.

She shuddered as she half-sat on a white stool in front of a glass beaker, barely able to keep her mind on the experiment. The night was coming. Night was the hardest time. Night was when she had to make her secret mission each month. And tonight was that night.

She now held a slender test tube in her tan hand and poured its contents into the beaker of chemicals. The pot sizzled, a vapor rose, and a sulfur smell filled the room. She held her nose and forced a smile. Her professor nodded approval, then smiled back. Men always smiled back. But she was so in love, she seldom noticed.

"Any news on a job?" he asked.

"A couple of nibbles. Nothing definite."

"I received another call from that lab over at Morehead City, asking about you. It's a cushy position."

"That the one on the coast?" Barbara asked.

"I believe Morehead City is still on the coast," he said a little condescendingly and a little humorously.

"I deserved that. I know where Morehead City is. It's near New Bern. I used to have a friend who lived in New Bern." She still did; *Todd* lived in New Bern. But speaking of the friendship in the past tense was part of her cover. "It's just that I don't want to leave the mountains. Don't you know of any lab jobs in the mountains?"

There was a tap on the door.

"I'll keep my ears open," he said, glancing at the clock on the wall and moving toward the door. "Meanwhile, it's time for my next student."

Lab experiment complete. Private lesson over. Time to go into the night. Tonight's secret mission had taken on new significance in the last twenty-four hours. In the last twenty-four hours she had received and accepted a proposal of marriage. Tonight she would ask permission to marry.

The professor opened the door. A girl wearing cutoff jeans, thong-sandals, and a man's yellow dress shirt with the tail hanging out, sauntered in, acknowledged Barbara, then went to the pegboard for a smock.

Barbara nodded to her, then began removing her own smock. If she could just make it to the car...In her mind she was already running as she carefully cleared her work station, then stored away the lab materials. From the relative safety of the class, she said good-evening to her professor, tucked her lab manual under her left arm, and darted from the room.

She hurried down the empty hall, clutching her car keys like a winning lottery ticket—she always clutched the keys, even when taking a shower. On the key-chain hung a picture of a man. On the back of the picture, hidden by the small frame, were the words "All my love, Todd." Only she and Todd Carrington knew they had ever been penned, for she had taken white-out and further hidden the words.

She loved Todd so much she would die for him. And might have to. But she loved him more than that. She loved him so much she would give him up so he could live. The key-chain picture was her lone breach of security. If *they* caught her, they would demand to know who he was. So she had had her answer prepared ever since her freshman year when she began dating Todd. "He's just someone I used to know," she would say. And such might be true as of this time tomorrow night. They could cut out her tongue but she would never tell his name.

Ever on guard for the slightest out-of-the ordinary noise, she cocked an ear as she hurried on down the hall of the Science Building. The only sounds were the squeak of her shoes on the hardwood floor and the swish of the flowing hem of her skirt against her bare legs—long tan legs.

That *weirdo reporter* Tamika had mentioned...Wonder if he was one of those men Grandmother Dare had said would be coming for her one day? She would be extra careful tonight.

At the exit, she stopped and peeped into the fast-gathering twilight—all directions.

All clear. She shot out the door.

Once in the grassy open, she sprinted toward the parking lot, constantly glancing over her shoulder, ready to toss the lab book if she had to launch into an all-out race. Her long blond hair kept swinging into her blue eyes each time she glanced back, looking for anyone out of the ordinary, or anyone out of place, but especially for anyone resembling a *weird reporter.*

She figured she could outrun him, or *them,* on foot. Or if she could just make it to the Camaro, she would once again be somewhat safe. They would never catch her fast car. Even if they had a high-speed vehicle, too, she felt she could lose them, for she knew these mountains like a mother knows her baby's cry. The roads she hadn't driven, she'd jogged the trails that interlaced them. She knew the whippoorwills, bob-cats, and bears by name. This was her turf.

In spite of being fast on her feet and having a fast car, she knew that her best defense was a low profile. They must never know where she was. Every year when the photographer set the appointments to make pictures for the school yearbook, she came up with an excuse to be absent.

Keeping a low profile had exacted other kinds of costs. She had the dubious honor of being the University of Tennessee's only elected Homecoming Queen ever to refuse to accept the honor. When the Homecoming Committee notified her of their selection, she screamed, "No!" and began to weep. Then she begged them not to make a media event of her decision.

Stunned and embarrassed committee members and university officials agreed. Still the news leaked out, at least on campus. When Barbara gave no reason for such a decision, rumors began to fly. Some said she had the big head. Others spouted it was boyfriend trouble. Feminists bragged that she was making a political statement. But the ones who knew her best, the Lady Vols track team who had helped her put together three championship seasons, said they didn't care what her reasons were; they trusted her. All they knew was that she had a burning desire to be the fastest person alive, on foot or on wheels.

The whole Homecoming mess ripped Barbara's heart out, but one thing was sure. She could never reign over the University of Tennessee's Queen's Court, and she could never tell why. She would go to her grave with that secret. Publicity was a luxury she couldn't afford. She knew that if she accepted the honor, long before her coronation, the news would reach certain ears and *they* would descend on the Smoky Mountains like bloodhounds thirsty for a rabbit.

Tennessee was scheduled to play Florida at the Homecoming game in Neyland Stadium in front of a hundred thousand fans. The teams were ranked number one and number four in the coaches' poll, respectively. Halftime festivities would unfold in the middle of the field. Todd would be her escort. But the minute he ushered her up the platform steps to the Queen's throne, it would mean certain death. And not just hers. Everyone in range would go down with her.

Now as Barbara raced toward the parking lot, she thought how Homecoming had come and gone and most of the fuss about her refusal to be crowned Homecoming Queen had died down and now she was about to graduate. Her safety pod, a silver-gray, '89 T-Top Camaro, was now in sight. An orange and white UT sticker on the back window trumpeted her allegiance to her soon-to-be alma mater.

As she got closer, she scanned the parking lot. No one was at the car. She saw nothing amiss, but she had a creepy feeling. Something made her skin crawl. Still, she quickly climbed in. On the bucket seat beside her sat a small plastic bowl filled with scuppernongs, her favorite grape. She turned the switch and revved the powerful V-8 engine. Tires squealed, laying rubber for a block as she headed into the Smoky Mountains.

Soon, the orange glow from the University of Tennessee campus and the city of Knoxville dominated her rearview mirror.

Deep in thought, she popped one of the tough-skinned, silvery amber-green grapes from the plastic bowl in her mouth, rolled it around between her teeth, teasing it with her tongue, then bit into it, exploding its sweet juices, then spat the seed out the window.

All her senses had been honed to accommodate handling the Camaro at top speed. She clung to the wheel and fought the winding road, trying not to outrun her headlights. Expert at the gear-shifting business, she depended on sound to tell her when to slam the stick-shift into a new gear. The whine of the big engine signaled her ear when a curve needed more torque, more juice, or less speed. Being from the mountains, she had the eye of a mountain woman for judging the speed of a bird on-the-wing or the distance a cheetah required between itself and a gazelle, bringing death at seventy-miles-an-hour. And so, judging when to brake for a curve was a snap; she seldom touched her brakes, depending instead on geared-down engine compression. She loved the taste of speed and the smell of burning rubber as she came out of curves at full throttle in broadslide.

A soft voice, a peaches and cream complexion, lacy clothes, and Joy perfume were not usually associated with racetracks and fast cars; she tried really hard not to look and smell like a Hotrod Annie. But life had forced her into the arena of speed, and she had soon discovered that she loved that arena, though not the reason. She would need the fast car tonight, and all her skills, if they came after her in these mountains. In fact, the only place she ever felt safe was at church; surely they wouldn't do it there. But she wasn't at church now.

Nerves on edge, two goals fought for dominance in her brain: to escape impending danger and to complete this evening's secret mission.

This should be the happiest day of her life, she thought. Last night at the dance, Todd had asked her to marry him in *June*, just after graduation—his, a Master's degree at the University of North Carolina, and hers, a B.A. at UT. She had suggested a wedding date next April. No matter, the mission she was on right now, if he found out about it—at some point she'd have to tell him—would put an end to all that.

Todd Carrington had everything. She had nothing. The son of a wealthy senator, Todd also wanted to become a senator. Barbara's family was of a more dubious background, worse than poverty. But she had done well at UT, a 4.0 GPA with a major in human resources and a minor in laboratory sciences. She knew she would be snatched up by some large corporation—she already had four offers—where she hoped to get lost from anyone asking too many questions and where she could shun publicity that might trigger a background investigation. The problem with the four businesses was that none of them was in the mountains.

It wasn't until after she'd said yes to Todd's proposal of marriage last night that he dropped the bomb: He wanted to follow in his father's political footsteps! All along she'd thought he was going to become a political science professor! Now if she married him—his career in politics would thrive on publicity, the tiniest fragment of which the press would scrutinize—the dark secret she held in her bosom would destroy him. As a child, out behind Grandmother Dare's barn, she had watched the death-dance between the Black Widow spider and her mate. She could not, *would not*, play the role of *femme fatale*.

Marriages produce children, she thought as fear continued to dart around and through her every emotion, raiding the nest of her dreams and robbing her of any hope of ever birthing a child.

The night grew darker. Soon the streetlights of the small town of Pigeon Forge came into view. Road signs invited tourists to dine at the Apple Barn and to visit Dollywood. Bigger and brighter signs teased and flirted with the travelers, trying to pull them ten more miles on up the road to Gatlinburg, entranceway to the Great Smoky Mountain National Park.

But in Pigeon Forge, it was time for the first stage of camouflage. Barbara pulled over at a mini-mart, dashed inside, and purchased a peanut butter pie. Not just any pie would do. It had to be made of peanut butter. Back in the car, she set the pie on the bucket seat on the shotgun side beside the bowl of grapes and headed back into the night.

As prearranged, the pie would fulfill two purposes: It would camouflage her mission, thus getting her past every checkpoint, and it would serve as signal to the head-man in case an emergency kept him from their meeting. Lesser lights could study for a thousand years and never decode the message hidden in the peanut butter. It had already cost one life, and, if anyone deciphered its meaning tonight, it would cost her hers. Only one man knew its meaning and he knew it well.

Barbara Dare had made this trip once a month for four years now and no one had found out. Almost to her rendezvous point, she stuffed her long blond hair under a gray, granny-type wig, then reached under the front seat and pulled out a walking cane.

69

She turned off the Camaro's headlights and engine and coasted in tire-on-dirt quietness to the edge of the woods. She grabbed the pie, climbed out, pulling a tattered, gray shawl around her shoulders as she did, then walked with a fake limp the rest of the way in the moonlight, a false name on her lips.

Tucked under her arm she carried the passkey, a badly worn thin book written in French, *La Chanson de Roland.*

13

Later that night at Sagebrush Prison, mountained-in between Knoxville and Gatlinburg, alarm bells exploded and emergency lights flashed. Guards and medics ran down the hall dragging the face-down fat prisoner, bleeding from the mouth.

Once inside the infirmary, as doctors worked on the patient from Cell Block 13, one guard said to the other, "His first day at Sagebrush."

"Prisoners watch TV, too," the other commented. "And they don't forget. Five years of appeals, fighting off coming here, did him no good."

"Yeah. No wonder he wanted a 'walk-alone' sentence. Leader of that child kidnapping ring, I heard."

"That fake 'Friend of Children' has talked his last child into going with him to a *false* safe haven."

"Did they ever find his tongue?"

"Buzzard Mackelroy had it in his pocket."

14

Eleven the following morning, the hearing on regulating nicotine. Out of nowhere, a key Democrat, a woman, jumped up and shouted, "Mr. Chairman, I call for the question!"

Pandemonium broke out.

Charlie Carrington started banging his gavel. "Order. Order. Order."

The pager-vibrator in his pocket went off. It buzzed three times. One buzz meant vote *yes*. Two buzzes meant vote *no*. Three buzzes meant *call a recess*. The tobacco cartel's other five senators also carried similar buzzers.

"You're out of order, senator!" shouted Chairman Carrington, trying to be heard above the ruckus. He gave his ruling an exclamation mark with a hard rap of his gavel.

"Point of order!" shouted the Democrat.

Pandemonium broke out again. Buoyed by the explosive reaction, the woman wouldn't hush. She knew she'd started a fire, and, with TV cameras rolling, immediately threw a bottle of nitroglycerin at the flames. "I call for a ruling on my motion to—"

The vibrator in Charlie Carrington's pocket went off again. Five senators—three Republicans and two Democrats—leaped to their feet in unison and called for a recess.

Senator Carrington abruptly called an early lunch break and stormed out of the hearing, hotter than a pistol. His bluster, for the most part, was for the benefit of the D.C. press corps who were chasing him with cameras mounted like shoulder-fired missiles. They didn't know about his impending retirement. Yesterday he had told his wife. This morning at a power breakfast he had told a few trusted friends, swearing them to secrecy. After no small amount of arm twisting, on their part, he promised to finish out his term.

"It's not *regulation* they're after," Senator Carrington now fumed to the press. "It's *prohibition*!"

This morning, Schubert Morgan, assisted by the six other FDA attorneys, had continued the argument from yesterday that tobacco was a drug and as such should be regulated. But the tobacco lobby knew where that would lead. The fight had spilled-over into the White House and, thanks to the President, the tobacco industry's opponents were about to get their strongest toe-hold: no advertising of cigarettes to teenagers. It was only a step to annihilation of one of the wealthiest and most powerful conglomerates on earth.

Senator Carrington now hurried on down the hall toward his office, his aides vying for his attention, handing him messages, notes, and files as they rushed alongside him. A CNN reporter shoved a microphone in his face. "Senator, what do you have to say about spiking?"

The senator froze in his tracks, freezing his entourage, also. He stared into the cameras. "*Spiking* is a word the FDA made up."

"Your opponents say that where there's smoke there's fire."

"*Fire*! There's not even a *trace* of smoke!" He wheeled around and was off down the hall, the pack still chasing him.

His tall assistant, highest in his staff's pecking order, motioned him to bend down as he hurried. She handed him a folder and whispered up into his ear, "It's the Barbara Dare file."

The senator halted and turned to the press. "That's all I have to say. Now I have to get to work on the President's budget." He slipped through another door and down another hall, leaving the reporters behind. Once out of their sight and sound, he stopped. Only his aides stood near. He glanced over the file, handed it back to his assistant, and whispered as loudly as he could softly, "Shred it!"

At the door to his office, he dismissed his entourage and stepped inside. Alone at last, he gave a deep sigh, pulled the white linen kerchief from the lapel pocket of his dark blue suit, and wiped perspiration from his brow. He began removing his coat, anticipating Kaufman's phone call.

Suddenly the smell of cigar smoke hit him.

"Good job." The voice came from the other side of the room.

Startled, Senator Carrington wheeled around. "Kaufman!"

Kaufman never showed up in person unless there was a

matter of highest urgency, choosing to issue orders over the phone. Kaufman, a distinguished looking rotund man, wearing an expensive suit, sat in the shadows in a motorized wheelchair, chewing on a glowing cigar and rubbing his knees. Krandall Kaufman told the tobacco lobby, and just about everyone else associated with the tobacco industry, what to do and when to do it.

"Didn't mean to startle you, senator. But you did do a good job with those dingbats." In his mid-sixties, Kaufman had a full head of black hair and dark bushy eyebrows, magnified by his black suit. When he did appear from his sumptuous world of shadows, it was usually at the most awkward of times. Like a car repossesser on the prowl.

"Thank you," said Senator Carrington, semi bowing. "Could I get you a drink or something?"

Kaufman waved no with his half-lit cigar. "I'm here to discuss your replacement."

Shocked, and not shocked, the senator said, "News travels fast. I only told a few close associates—"

"That you'd be leaving at the end of your term." Kaufman finished his sentence for him. "I have no problem with your retiring. But we need your help with your replacement."

"I've given you all the help I'm giving you." The senator removed the black pager-vibrator from his pocket and tossed it on his desk with a thud. "At the end of my term, I'm out of here."

Kaufman ignored the comment, took a deep draw on the cigar, rubbed his arthritic knees again with his puffy hands, and sighed, letting the smoke out in little jerks. "It's such a small pleasure. Why are the Democrats making such a fuss?"

Still standing, stiff as a new broom, Senator Carrington leaned over his desk and nervously shuffled some papers, glad he had not brought the Barbara Dare file into the room with him. "It's politics, sir."

"Don't humor me, senator!" Kaufman snapped. "I *know* it's politics."

"I'm sorry." He waited for Kaufman to ask him to sit, but before he got permission, the phone rang. Lady Carrington was calling from North Carolina.

Kaufman reached over and hit the speaker phone button just as Lady Carrington said, "I'm lonely, dear. Please hurry home."

"I'll be there," the senator promised. "I only have a few last minute things to tidy up. I'll be leaving momentarily. I—"

"I thought you would be here by now. You're going to be late; I just know it, and—"

"I won't be late, dear. Don't worry. I'm as excited as you about Todd's engagement."

"You've changed your mind about Barbara? You don't mind now that she's a mountain girl?"

Kaufman squirmed in his wheelchair and stared at the floor as if embarrassed at listening in on the conversation.

"I never minded that she was a *mountain girl*," the senator said, speaking more softly into the receiver, aware and unaware that the speaker phone was still on. "It's just that we haven't learned anything about her family."

"She loves our boy. That's all any mother can ask. Last year, I saw it in her sparkling blue eyes when she played ping pong with him in the game room when she was here for his birthday. She's so pretty, their children will all be beautiful. And Todd is such a child himself; he will make a wonderful father. I want a house full of grandchildren. I hope they have half a dozen. I wanted more myself, you know?"

Kaufman made circling motions with his cigar hand at the senator, as if to say, "Stop prattling and get on with it."

"Todd's enough," the senator said abruptly cutting her off, remembering that Kaufman knew why they had not had more children. The senator reached over and slapped the speaker phone off.

Kaufman popped it back on and stared at him like a schoolyard bully, daring him to turn it off again.

"She's not only pretty," said Lady Carrington, "she's also smart."

76

"I have to hang up now," the senator said, pleading the pressure of time. He didn't know what else she might say and he was tired of playing speaker-phone tag with Kaufman.

"I'll be leaving for home in a few hours. We took an early lunch break; I'll make it a short session this afternoon."

"Don't you think she's smart?" Lady Carrington chatted on, as though she had heard nothing he had said.

"If the truth be known," the senator responded, staring at Kaufman, "she's probably smarter than Todd."

"Todd's plenty smart," Lady Carrington snapped back. "You don't receive a Masters degree from the best university in the South, *magna cum laude* at that, and not be smart."

"There are two kinds of smart, dear, and Barbara Dare is both. All I meant was that Todd has never had to scrap for himself. She's a fighter. You can see it in her eyes. I wouldn't want to walk into a Senate hearing and have her on the other side. And I wouldn't want to be the man who tried to force his will on her."

"Todd said she wants an apple-blossom wedding."

"Isn't that a little rural?"

"If she wants an *apple-blossom* wedding, that's what she's going to have." Her voice rang with command.

"I'll let you know about the wedding after my men finish checking out her family."

"I want her for a friend," Lady Carrington said. "I'm lonely, and I want this house brimming over with grandchildren." Then she made an attempt at humor. "To get them to hurry, I may offer them a farm for each grandchild. I'll hold those babies, and walk them, and love them; then I'll hold them, and walk them, and love them again. I'm so lonely."

"I've let you down, dear," the senator said, softly, wanting to turn the speaker phone off, but knowing that Kaufman would just slap it back on. So he did the best he could. He turned his back, and whispered tenderly, "The Senate has been my mistress. But I'm coming home. For good."

"But when you're home, dear, you're not home. I'm so lonely."

"I'll make it up to you." He felt embarrassed that anyone

was hearing this intimate moment. He wished she would hush, and he wished Kaufman would leave, but both held their ground. He loved her, but when she got all emotional like this, her mind was like a runaway grocery cart in a high wind, and he knew from experience to let it run its course.

Kaufman leaned his head back and blatantly stared at the ceiling, all the while nervously tapping his index finger on the arm of the wheelchair.

"Charlie?" she said, begging him. "This big house is so lonely. And the sea makes it lonelier. This morning when the fog came in, I thought I would die of loneliness. Maybe because happiness was never this close before. Please don't let your men find anything bad on Barbara. Please let Todd marry her. She's my kind of person. I need her more than he does. If they find something bad on her, don't tell me."

"Be reasonable, dear. Politics is politics." He felt his voice harden and wished it hadn't. "If she's got a crazy aunt in an attic somewhere, we need to know before Todd gets in too deep."

"If your men destroy this dream," he could hear the lump in her throat, "like they did ours, I'll walk into that ocean and I'll never come out. Then you'll have all these tobacco farms to yourself. I never wanted them anyway."

Charlie Carrington quietly pressed the speaker-phone button to off, and whispered into the receiver, "I understand, and I love you. We'll talk about it tonight. Good-bye." As he hung up, he turned to Kaufman. "Sorry for the interruption,"

Kaufman swiped an understanding wave with his cigar, but then ordered, "Tell your receptionist to hold your calls."

"Hold the calls," the senator said softly into the phone.

"By the way, what time is that black-tie affair at your house tonight?"

He stared at Kaufman with whipped eyes.

"Eight, and you're invited."

"I told you not to humor me!" Kaufman's voice had ice in it. "I know I'm invited. But Tumbler had to ask you for the invitation."

"I didn't know your address."

"No, and you never will."

Senator Carrington remembered how, when he first came to Washington, he had checked with lobbyists, trying to learn more about Kaufman, but none of them had ever heard of him. At least they said they hadn't. But whether they had or hadn't, they did his bidding; they got their orders from somewhere. And Kaufman was always appearing out of nowhere for key votes.

The senator had remained standing all this time, waiting for permission to sit. Kaufman finally pointed with his cigar toward the wine-colored executive chair behind the massive desk. "Go ahead. Sit."

"Back to politics," Senator Carrington said and quickly sat. "You know the tobacco vote's split right down the middle. Except for my vote. And since I'll be retiring soon—"

"You and your farms have been a good friend to our industry."

"I'm a tobacco farmer; that's all. When I hired-in"—though he had risen to the upper echelons of politics, Charlie Carrington prided himself...no, he strove to maintain the language of the common man, even to the point of working a couple of weeks every year with the field hands on his tobacco plantations— "thirty years ago, I thought I could make a difference."

"You've made a *difference*," Kaufman said with a hacking chuckle, "for the tobacco industry."

Senator Carrington stared at the gaudy red, white, and blue diamond pin on Kaufman's lapel. "I've done your bidding. That's all. I've done your bidding," he said, chasing the demons from his dream.

"We've let you vote your conscience on other issues."

"And that's all that's kept me from going insane." The senator turned and looked out the burgundy-draped second-story window toward the Lincoln Memorial. Silhouetted in the blue sky, the blackbirds were lined up on the phone wires like clothespins. Mist filled his eyes. "I came to Washington right off the farm, all big-eyed, tan, and healthy. Now look at me."

"Handsomest sixty-five-year-old in Congress. And we never had a better friend."

Senator Carrington turned back to face the man who had stolen his dream. "My career is a mockery. I'm just a ghost in this flesh—bought and paid for. But, sir, don't call me your friend."

"We're so pleased with your work that we plan to replace you with someone just like you."

"I feel sorry for the person you wave your skull and crossbones banner in front of. Don't expect any help from me."

"By the way, didn't I hear that your son plans to go into politics sometime soon?"

"Don't joke about Todd."

"It's no joke. Tumbler already has a file on him."

"*A file?* On Todd?"

"We take the long look. A long time ago, our cartel found that it was smart to keep a file on everyone. We even have one on the President—an Arkansas file. I bet you Republicans would like to get your greedy hands on it. Lot of stuff about—"

The senator leaped to his feet. "I won't be a party to obstructing justice!"

"Sit down!"

Silence.

The senator sat, slowly, like an angry Doberman that had been told to sit but wasn't quite sure he would.

Kaufman knitted his bushy eyebrows and stared at him.

The senator stared back from his ready-to-pounce position.

Kaufman tapped his nicotine-stained, manicured fingers on the wheelchair's joy-stick. After an eternity of embarrassing silence, Senator Carrington blinked and eased all the way back in his chair, submissively.

"That's better," Kaufman said, quietly. "Justice," he hooted. "Hogwash."

The two men eyed each other for a stale moment. Finally Kaufman broke the silence. "Back to your son. I'll say this for him; we all think he'll make a fine candidate."

"Please, Mr. Kaufman, not Todd."

"The boy made quite a name for himself over at the University of North Carolina. Got his Masters degree."

"Todd's not your man. He wants me to plant cotton instead of tobacco on my farms."

"*Your* farms? Your *wife's* farms. Let's not forget that."

"I didn't forget," the senator said, meekly.

"You just introduce me to your boy tonight at that big party when he presents his hillbilly bride-to-be to North Carolina's socially elite. Between me and that pretty little darling of the mountains, we'll get Todd's mind off planting cotton."

"I'll introduce you, but you leave Todd out of your night empire. I may be only a ghost of what I meant to be, but ghosts can haunt. I'm warning you!"

"*Warning*! Don't raise you voice to me, senator. You're not talking to the Democrats!"

The phone interrupted them again. Senator Carrington looked at the brass clock on the wall. It was exactly 11:05.

"I told you to hold the calls!" barked Kaufman.

"It might be the President. He's anxious to know how the hearing's going." The senator reached for the phone, but didn't pick it up.

Kaufman nodded.

"Yes?" the senator asked into the receiver. He then handed it to Kaufman. "It's for you."

"I bet it's Tumbler," Kaufman said reaching for the receiver. "I almost forgot about him." Then he spoke directly into the phone. "Yes...Yes...Cades Cove?...I know all about that Cherokee mud-bead necklace! I was the one that told you...Homecoming Queen, huh?" Kaufman winked a knowing wink at the senator, but kept talking to Tumbler. "Turned it down, did she?...Been in school there four years and not a single picture of her in any of the school annuals?" Kaufman put two pudgy fingers to his chin. "Hum...What about her parents?...Well, find out!" He tossed the receiver back to the senator, to hang it up, but as he did, he heard Tumbler yelling something else into the phone. "Hand it back to me," Kaufman ordered the senator. "What are you babbling about?" he asked Tumbler. "You did what!!...I told you not to hurt...Oh. Where is it?...The trunk?...Okay. I may be able to use that."

Kaufman tossed the receive again to the senator. "Tumbler's in Cades Cove."

"*Cades Cove*?"

"Research on your son's girlfriend."

"On *Barbara*!?"

"I believe that's her name. Barbara Dare, isn't it?"

"You leave her alone!"

"Tumbler had no luck finding out about her parents. Know anything about them?"

"Leave her alone!"

"Miss Dare was in a big track meet yesterday over at the University of Tennessee. At Knoxville. Tumbler went. He posed as a press man, but didn't get to interview her. She almost won, but didn't hang around to talk to the media. Wonder why?"

"Please. You don't have anything to worry about. My men have already checked her out."

"*Your* men? Your men are *my* men."

"Not all of them. Barbara's a mountain girl. You'll find nothing on her."

"That's what you said thirty years ago about your wife."

"I love my wife very much."

"Yeah," Kaufman said with disdain, "you showed how much you love her."

"I made the debt and she paid the price."

"But Tumbler found out, didn't he?"

Senator Carrington swallowed hard.

"You're not the only one who ever got caught, senator. I've never told."

"Blackmail. Thirty years haven't dimmed the fact that it's still blackmail."

"You'll think *blackmail* when Tumbler turns in his report on that little hillbilly girl." Kaufman hit the wheelchair's joystick and began rolling toward the door. "Everybody's hiding something, senator. And if that little mountain girl with the Cherokee mud-bead necklace is hiding something, Tumbler'll find it. By the way, you might check the trunk of that Camaro she drives."

"Trunk of her car? Are you implying Barbara's peddling dope or something? You better not have planted—"

"You have a dirty mind, senator. Just think of it as a wedding gift, a reminder of how much we want your son in our corner as the next senator from North Carolina."

15

By daybreak that same morning, Barbara was already headed to New Bern, North Carolina. To see Todd. To tell him. The wedding was off. Todd had to be told. A change of clothes and an evening gown—just in case she didn't arrive until the party had already started—hung on the hanger in the rear of the Camaro. In the seat beside her sat a box of CDs and a small overnight case. A suitcase would have had to go in the trunk, but she didn't plan to be in New Bern long, so she didn't bring a suitcase.

Last night's mission had not gone well; she had missed her contact, the head man. When the front-page story broke this morning, she knew it would be only a matter of time until her name was tied to it. Maybe a month, maybe a year, but one day it would all come out.

So she had made the decision about the wedding without seeking counsel at last night's rendezvous. She knew what the answer would be. What it *had* to be. There was no need in asking. There could be no wedding. Todd had chosen politics. She had chosen anonymity—actually the Dare family secret had chosen it for her. Politics demanded a high profile. The secret demanded she avoid publicity. Politics thrived on publicity. *Publicity* could get her killed. A fish could marry a bird, but one would have to die. And there was something else. Todd would want children, heirs for his plantations. There hadn't been time to tell him that she must never have children. The secret would claim every Dare baby.

Last night she had talked to Todd by phone. He was already in New Bern. He'd flown his dad's jet there. She had called to tell him that she couldn't marry him, but when he answered the phone, his voice so mesmerized her, she couldn't say the words. You just don't tell the man you love that you can't marry him, on the phone. But neither could she stop the social calendar of the most powerful family in North Carolina. The Carringtons were throwing a big party tonight at their coastal mansion, a graduation party to celebrate Todd's getting his Masters degree.

It had been planned for some time. High-profile parties were not her thing, so last week when he invited her, she had refused. He now insisted that she be there.

As her silver-gray Camaro whizzed along Highway 70, she turned on the radio. Vince Gill and Dolly Parton were singing a new arrangement of Dolly's old hit "I Will Always Love You." The duet moved her, but the version of the song that really knocked her socks off was Dolly singing the original. She remembered Dolly telling on TV that she wrote the song when she and Porter Wagoner were breaking up their duet act. In the song Dolly sang about how things could never work out. Barbara knew the same was true of Todd and her. She just wasn't right for him, and she was on her way to tell him such in so many words. But nothing could stop her from always loving him.

Tobacco fields skirted both sides of the road for miles and miles. *Tobacco*, a word that meant millions to Todd's dad, but a word that caused Todd such anguish. Todd wasn't against smoking; he was against *addiction*, but Barbara had no opinion. The top brass from all the big cigarette companies would be at the Carringtons tonight. Barbara didn't care who was going to be there. It would be the last time she would ever see any of them. She cared only for Todd. But it would also be the last time she would ever see him.

Her heart was breaking, but she'd cried up all her tears. She looked down at the lap of her khaki skirt, now spotted with the residue of her grief. She had to get to Todd's home before guests arrived and saw her in this condition.

She wouldn't tell Todd everything, but she would tell him enough. Then she would tell him good-bye.

16

"Not Barbara!" Todd yelled. "You're not doing an investigation of Barbara!"

In New Bern, a little before party time, Todd Carrington tossed his white dinner jacket across his arm, jerked his suspenders over his shoulders, and went bounding down the stairs, two at a time, in pursuit of his father.

Senator Carrington, a few steps below him, had already made the turn in the long, wide, red-carpeted staircase. A cigarette in one hand, a cocktail in the other, and already dressed for the party, he descended with the dignity of one on the way to greet the President.

"You're not doing a security check on Barbara!" Todd argued, respectfully.

Without speaking, Senator Carrington strolled toward the center of the living room, puffing the Winston.

Todd finally caught up with his father under the middle of the three giant crystal chandeliers, the one by the orchestra platform. "I can't let you do it, Father."

"We have no choice, Son." The senator sipped his martini.

"Boys!" Lady Carrington scolded kindly, then went back to scurrying about with a gold decanter, spraying mist-of-gardenia throughout the party area and giving last minute instructions to white-aproned, black-dressed maids. She then hurried over to the butler.

White-haired, white-gloved Samson, the Carrington's tall, skinny, lifelong butler—an African-American—stood by the door, practicing pronouncing the names on the guest list.

Todd's father handed Todd a drink. "Let's go outside. Take a walk."

At the door, Todd tossed his dinner jacket over the mahogany staircase rail. Outside, on the first-floor verandah, his father put his arm across Todd's shoulder and they walked down the steps, past the security gate, on to the water's edge, and then strolled along the sandy shore. Todd knew his father's concern about security, but he cared too much for Barbara to treat her with suspicion.

He paid little attention to the gentle lapping of the waves against the boathouse. But the thing he did notice was that he was finally as tall as his tall father. "Father, she's perfect. You should not concern yourself about Barbara."

"All the same," his father warned, "don't you think we should wait about announcing your engagement? At least, let's not announce it tonight. The background check—"

"I've dabbled in politics too, Father. And if I'm going to follow in your political footsteps—"

"That's another thing. If I would agree to plant cotton instead of tobacco, like you've always wanted, would you be willing to forget politics?"

"I should like to do both."

His father sighed a desperate sigh. "I was afraid you would say that."

"I know I can make a difference in Washington, Father. I have a dream for a better America. I have a plan, a good plan, where everyone has a chance."

"Doing good can be a dangerous occupation, Son." His father paused, tossed the cigarette butt into the water, removed another Winston from a gold case, and flicked his gold lighter. He puffed gently, causing the tobacco to glow in the moonlight. "Nasty habit. Glad you never took it up."

"And so am I."

"Back to your career. I'm not talking about running for class president, Son."

"No, indeed.

"I'm talking about political hardball."

"I'm not naive." Todd laughed, confidently. "Barbara and I have cared for each other since she was a freshmen. Don't you think I'd know if there were skeletons in her closet?"

"Yours is not the only career at stake here, Son."

"Her grandmother, high in the Tennessee mountains, raised and taught her."

"And her parents?"

"I think they're dead. At least she's never mentioned them."

"Family history is important, Son."

"Make no mistake, the Carringtons have nothing on the Dares. They moved into Cades Cove with the Boone party and bought the land from the Cherokee. I've been up to their cabin on several occasions."

"I trust your judgment, but men like us can never be too careful."

"Indeed. But you worry too much, Father. Barbara will make the perfect politician's wife. I'll have trouble keeping up with *her*—and I don't mean just because she runs track; I *surely* can't keep up with her when we jog. She knows when to challenge and when not to, when to talk and when not to. When we move to the Capital, she'll have Raleigh's country club set wrapped around her little finger in no time."

"I suppose too many Senate battles have jaded me, making me naturally suspicious."

"Father, she's a winner, and a fighter. But most of all she loves me. And I love her."

"I know you do. And we love her, too. But this is not a heart decision, alone. Perhaps I should have told you, but—"

"*Told* me what?"

"It didn't matter when you were just *dating* Barbara. But the other night when you phoned and said you were going to *marry* her, our investigators immediately started the security check."

"Already!? On Barbara!? Then, why are we having this conversation? I thought you were asking my permission!"

"Couldn't. Had to leave you out of it."

"Well? Did your goons find anything?"

"Everything seems to check out. Except her parents. We've been unable to learn about them. Those mountain people won't talk."

Todd was smarting. What would Barbara think if she found out? He would have to tell her. And as soon as she arrived, he'd do it. "I can't believe you did a security check on her without informing me. Barbara knows how important publicity is to a politician. She would have told me if there'd been a concern. How would you feel if she started checking *us* out?"

His father laughed. "I'm afraid the media—and my opponents—have already done that."

"Well, I want the investigation halted! Right now!"

"So be it. I did it for your own good."

"But Barbara's going to be the mother of my children."

"And my grandchildren. I'm sorry, but I needed to be sure."

"I believe that, but why do I feel betrayed? And that we've betrayed Barbara?"

"It's the curse of living in the spotlight. Better that we do it than some Democrat. Damage control, you know." The senator paused, then flipped another cigarette butt into the water. "When it's all said and done, you're all your mother and I have that really counts." He turned and looked toward the house. "We'll go ahead and announce your engagement tonight."

Todd couldn't stay mad at his father, so he put his arm across his shoulder. "Nothing could please Barbara and me more."

Senator Carrington looked around, searching with his hard blue eyes. "By the way, where is that belle of the mountains? Shouldn't she be here by now?"

"She's usually very punctual. But I didn't tell her the party was to announce our engagement."

"While she's here, why don't we check the trunk of her car."

"*Check her trunk?*"

"It's a long drive back to Knoxville. Make sure her spare has plenty of air."

"Quite thoughtful of you, Father."

"Barbara may not think so. Some women would take offense. So there won't be any hint of that, your mother and I will wrap a large wedding gift that will fit only in the rear of her car. After the party, you and I will put it in there. While we're doing that, you can accidentally push on her spare tire."

Todd laughed. " Only a politician would think of doing it that way. I have a lot to learn before I go to Washington."

17

Barbara was in a dither. She had hit Raleigh right in the middle of the six o'clock rush hour and was now hopelessly stalled at the interstate split—had been for thirty minutes. An overturned eighteen-wheeler—a milk tanker—lay on its side with milk spouting in all directions and running off the side of the highway in a sea of white. Barbara realized she could never make New Bern by 8:00. Her skirt was a mess from all the crying; and anyway, she couldn't go running into the party dressed so casually. Time for a mid-course correction. She decided, if she ever broke free of the milk-spill, she would stop in Goldsboro, fill up with gas, and grab a burrito and a Moon Pie. She would change into party clothes—and party face—in the ladies room. That way she could subtly get Todd off by himself. And tell him.

It was 8:30 when the valet-guard signaled her Camaro to a halt at the gate in front of the Carrington's waterfront home. The antebellum mansion was located near Tyron Palace, a former governor's residence and New Bern's most famous landmark. Rolls Royces, Mercedes, and stretch-limos—drivers standing beside them—lined the circular drive, license tags boasting "Reynolds 1," "Camels 1," "Raleigh 1," and "I Smoke."

Barbara rolled the window down to identify herself and simultaneously turned down the bluegrass recording. When she did, orchestral music in the distance invited her to a banquet of sweet poison.

She climbed out and tossed a spare set of keys to the valet. She kept her own set. Even when sleeping she clutched the Camaro's keys. The difference between having them in hand and having to grab for them might give her the edge in an all-out escape attempt.

She pulled her shawl around her bare shoulders, tucked her purse under her arm, and hurried along the driveway that ran next to the channel. The stars mirrored in the water made it look like the whole world was turned upside down. "God, o God, o God, o God," she whispered. "I can't do this, I can't do this, I can't do this." But there was no backup in her. She knew what had to be done.

She felt as if her heart had been ripped from her bosom and she was physically carrying it in her hands. She would lay it at Todd's feet and there it would stay forever, for she would never love again.

She jerked up the hem of her pale-green gown so she wouldn't trip as she charged through the yard full of yellow-centered white chrysanthemums and potted bright-yellow tulips. She had chosen the gown because she thought it looked like something Grace Kelly might have worn on such an occasion—during the long cold winter nights, as a little girl curled up in front of Grandmother Dare's fireplace, Grace Kelly had taught her much through her movies on TV. Barbara now thought the pale-green of the dress served best to camouflage the pale-green stains on the palms of her hands, stains from helping Grandmother Dare hull black walnuts last weekend.

Grandmother Dare had six walnut trees that had grown up wild out back of the cabin. The fun part of Barbara's job each fall was to climb the trees, barefooted, and shake the walnuts to the ground. Of course last weekend's hulling had been a basket of walnuts from last year's harvest. The stain had to wear off; it couldn't be washed off. If she kept her palms down, maybe no one would notice.

And no one would notice, especially Todd's father, her mud-bead necklace, tucked under the gown. The last time she wore the mud beads, the senator had commented one time too many on how "unique" the necklace was. And he was right. The mud-bead necklace wasn't for formal wear. But it could be worn to formal occasions, just hidden.

As she climbed the marble steps, her high-heels, already in rhythm with the waltz coming from inside the mansion, echoed like a chisel on a tombstone, reminding her more of the Anvil Chorus than a Viennese waltz. Wanting to go unnoticed until she had told Todd what she had to tell him, she quickly and quietly stole through the front door.

Once inside, she stood quite still, getting oriented. The party was already in full swing. Elegant ladies in evening gowns and men in tuxedos waltzed away, while in every corner, pockets of important looking people—a few whom she knew—puffed on a brand of choice as if giving validity to their business. She knew that most were associated in one way or another with Senator Carrington's political machine, the tobacco industry being his primary supporter. And of course his plantations provided much of the tobacco.

The smell of tobacco smoke, muted by gardenia, greeted her before Samson did. The white-haired black man stood with his back to her, swaying to the music. Momentarily he glanced around, still in rhythm, clapping his hands without letting them touch. At first startled, he quickly greeted her with a smile that went from ear to ear. "Why, Miss Barber. Look at you. Mr. Todd, he been comin' to the door ever' little bit lookin' for you."

"Where is he, Samson?" she asked, handing him her wrap.

"Over by the senator. In front of the band. Waitin' to make that big announcement, I reckon, Miss Barber."

Announcement? Probably about Todd's graduation. Surely not their engagement. She touched the back of Samson's gnarled hand affectionately with her finger tips, then quickly swept past the caviar and the champagne fountain, her eyes searching for Todd.

"Hello, Barbara," came a voice.

"Nice to see you, Miss Dare," called another.

"Beautiful gown," said someone else.

The burrito and Moon Pie were now fighting and sat uneasy on her stomach, yet she nodded courteously to each of the guests who greeted her and kept going. She didn't want small-talk now. They'd die if they knew what she knew. Then she spotted Todd's father towering over a small group of couples. He must have seen her coming across the dance floor, for he stepped up onto the podium in front of the orchestra, then moved to the microphone. He was now pulling Todd up there beside him.

Barbara hurried faster, bumping into the dancers. The deeper into the smoke fog she went, the more nauseated she became.

Senator Carrington signaled the conductor. The music stopped right in the middle of the "Blue Danube." Then he raised his hand. His big mellow voice, full of warm Carolina drawl, boomed, "Folks, may I have your attention. May I have your attention."

Todd, looking as proud as she'd ever seen him look, stood beside his father on the podium. The room became quiet. Smokers snuffed out their cigarettes and bunched toward the stage.

Barbara reached up, grabbed Todd's hand, yanked hard, and whispered, "I've got to talk with you. Right now!"

Todd evidently didn't hear her, for he pulled her up beside him and hugged her. The senator stepped between them, then held each by the hand. "Lady Carrington and I have an announcement."

Oh Lord, he's going to announce it. I'm caught now. She wanted to run, but, with her head swimming and her stomach churning, her feet wouldn't move.

"As most of you know, Todd just received his Masters degree at the University of North Carolina, the greatest school in the country."

Cheers came from the audience.

"Now he tells me, one of these days before too long, he wants to run for the Senate. Fill my shoes, so to speak."

Cheers again.

"Nothing could make me happier. Well, I suppose one thing could, and that's the announcement Lady Carrington and I want to make now." Before Barbara knew what happened, Senator Carrington raised their hands high overhead. "Todd, here, and Barbara are engaged to be married!"

Champagne corks popped as if on signal, the orchestra exploded into "Congratulations To You," news cameras flashed, and the place became a madhouse of cheers.

Barbara dashed for the powder room, hand cupped to her mouth.

18

In a quiet distant corner, Krandall Kaufman applauded courteously from his wheelchair. He signaled Tumbler to him, dismissing his audience of yes-men in the process. "What's in the report?" he asked, "And why are you not wearing a tie?"

"Lost it…at the race yesterday," Tumbler said.

"Why didn't you buy another one?"

"Polka-dot bow ties…are hard to find." His tongue always seemed to stagger for words.

"*Bow ties?*"

"Especially purple ones."

"You should not have come here without a tie," Kaufman scolded. How could such a brilliant man be so stupid about his wardrobe?

Tumbler, who always slumped, slumped even further. "They had two…at that shop where I got the first one. I'll go back and…get the other one."

"What's in the report?" Kaufman asked, disgusted.

Tumbler, who had perfect recall, began to recite in monotone, "'A' student, ran track, wears mud beads—"

"I know all about the mud beads! Her parents! What about her *parents*?" Kaufman liked Tumbler's propensity for details but hated hearing him recite and Tumbler was a reciter to end all reciters.

Tumbler knew everything about the tobacco cartel. But most of all, he knew the hiding place of the cartel's tell-all file. The file held information about spiking, which senators were on the take, and who got paid what and *for* what. And he knew where Kaufman kept the stacks of hundred-dollar bills to pay off those he paid off. So for that reason, Tumbler was the only man Kaufman dared not cross.

"Nothing," Tumbler said. "Her grandmother owns a hundred-acre farm. At Cades Cove. The girl will inherit it someday. Farm can't be sold." Because of his inability to talk in sentences, Tumbler often spoke in lists.

"Can't be sold?"

"Eminent domain. Cades Cove is now part of the Smoky Mountain National Park. As families die off...government pays a fair-market price. Takes over the land—"

"We need to know everything about the would-be senator's would-be wife. Todd Carrington might not be as friendly to our industry as his dad has been. I want to know about her parents."

"Yes, sir."

"The girl doesn't look the mousy sort. Career-minded woman?"

"You nailed it." Tumbler began reciting again. "Major in human resources. Minor in laboratory sciences—"

"Call Dr. Clark. Tell him to hire her as Director of Personnel at our main lab in Asheville."

"*Asheville*? At SIG Labs?"

"Certainly. That way, every now and then she can wear a lab coat and tinker around with test tubes."

"Wouldn't that be dangerous, especially with that Senate hearing in the papers every day, the Medical Association yelling about too much nicotine in cigarettes, the FDA wanting nicotine declared a drug so they can regulate it—"

"There's an old saying," Kaufman said, "'Stay close to your enemies.'"

"Hum."

"Offer Miss Barbara Dare a salary she can't turn down, but one that doesn't arouse suspicion."

"I understand."

"I don't think you do. If she's the woman we think she is, she'll turn it down."

"Wouldn't want to upstage her husband?"

"Now you're tracking. So, over the next three weeks, have three independent sources offer Todd Carrington a high-paying job in some aspect of city government in Raleigh, Winston-Salem, and last, Asheville. Make the most attractive offer in Asheville."

"Ingenious."

"I want Mr. and Ms. Todd Carrington in Asheville as soon as they return from their honeymoon."

"Yes, sir."

Kaufman noticed Barbara coming out of the bathroom. "I think she's regained her composure from whatever upset her. Now take me over and tell the senator to present me to her."

19

Embarrassed, Barbara returned from the powder room, Lady Carrington by her side, comforting her.

Todd and his father were waiting in the hall. Todd put his arm around her. "You all right, honey?"

"I'm fine." Barbara smiled, uncomfortably. "A little red-faced."

"Too much excitement, I suppose," the senator boomed. Then he whispered, "If it'll make you feel any better, all these tobacco fields will belong to you and Todd one day. And to my grandchildren."

"Daddy, she's not interested in tobacco fields right now," said Lady Carrington. "They want to be alone."

"And I'll plow them under straight away," Todd said. "I'll plant cotton or soybeans."

"Sh." The senator looked around. "I know you're only kidding, but don't let our guests hear you say that."

"I'm not kidding."

Just then a fashionable rotund man in a wheelchair rolled up to them. Though the chair had a motor on it, it appeared to be being pushed by a milky-eyed, small man, and, of all things, wearing no tie.

Senator Carrington became flustered. He now focused all his attention at the wheelchair occupant. After strained introductions, the festive mood began all over again.

Barbara thought they said the wheel-chaired man was head of some tobacco group, but she didn't remember his name and didn't care what he was head of. She wanted to be alone with Todd, and so as soon as good manners permitted, she escaped with him to the second floor verandah.

Alone at last, and in the arms of her lover, her lungs searched for the fresh night air. She leaned against the balustrade and stared toward the Carolina moon, shimmering in the harbor. Now lost in Todd's embrace, she was torn between her love for him and the fear of what her secret would do to him. So she decided she could stay a minute longer in the beautiful dream. Then she would tell him. But her heart made her mind race for another solution.

Todd broke the spell. "You haven't commented on my decision to enter politics."

"No I haven't, but I—" Suddenly it hit her. There was one chance, and take it she must. Maybe she could talk Todd out of politics. Maybe he would consider going back to his original plan to teach political science. So she began her assault. "Sweetheart, are you sure that's what you want to do?"

"I've never been more eager about anything in my life."

"But you always said you wanted to teach political science at a small college."

"I did indeed. But now, I feel I have a greater mission. One that involves more people than I could ever impact as a professor."

Barbara grasped at the first straw that came to mind. It was a story she had heard a white-haired minister tell from an all-glass church on TV. It was the story of the "number of seeds in an apple." It seems teacher asked student, "How many seeds are in an apple?" Student guessed six or seven. Teacher responded, "But what if you planted the seeds?"

So Barbara applied the story. "Todd, if you went ahead and became a teacher, your students could take your ideas to the marketplace. Each student would be like an apple seed that becomes an apple tree. Each tree would become an orchard. Each orchard would become a—wouldn't that reach enough people?"

"Capital idea! You're the one who should enter politics."

Good. She was making progress. Maybe there was hope. So she kept composing. "Vicariously, you could plant your political concepts in orchards across the country. Like Johnny Appleseed!"

"Sweetheart, that's brilliant. But I can't live my dream vicariously. Other than my love for you, my dream has become my *raison d'être.*"

His *reason for being.* She lowered her eyes and sighed hard. Her world was slipping away. And so was she. But before she completely released him, she wanted to know what noble cause had stolen him from her. She reached up and touched his hair. "Todd," she whispered, "would you tell me your dream, just one time?"

"Let's see—" Todd, the master dreamer, hesitated and for answer pointed to the sky full of stars. He began to weave his dream. He told her his vision of a better world, a world where everyone had a chance, where color didn't matter, where a person's station in life didn't matter, and of how he needed her help in building the new world. But soon she noticed he was torn too—between his love for his father and his contempt for his father's backers.

"I'd like to keep Father's political machine intact," he added, "but plowing under the tobacco crops will not only alienate the tobacco lobby, it will also force them to the other side."

"Doesn't cotton have a lobby?" asked Barbara.

Todd laughed. "A *cotton* lobby? Indeed. What a really delicious idea. See why I need you?"

In the muted darkness around the curved driveway below, uniformed chauffeurs and guards stood at their stations, cigarettes glowing from their hands like orange eyes peering from the night.

Barbara was coming to a decision. Todd's dream, though somewhat naive, was too noble for her to try further to take it from him. And she'd fight anyone who did.

"And all the media coverage," he said. "Can you imagine how much free publicity tonight's event will generate?"

She began to rationalize. The damage was already done. Even now the media had the announcement on the wire. If she broke the engagement, news hounds would track her down to find out why. So she made a decision. Happiness for a while with Todd would be better than unhappiness forever without him. But she could never tell him her secret. Maybe she could just live with it and hope no one ever found out.

There was a certain dishonesty in her decision. She knew that. She would tell him everything else, but rationalized, surely a fiancée was allowed to keep one secret from her beloved. All these years no one had found out; maybe they never would. She thought of the story she had read about two men hauled before the king to receive their execution dates. One man said, "O King. If you'll stay my execution for a year, I'll teach your horse to fly." The king granted the request. On the way back to their cell, the other man said, "Why did you make such a foolish promise? You know you can't teach the king's horse to fly." The first man replied, "I get to live another year, during the year the king may die, and who knows, by then, the horse may learn to fly."

Barbara knew *her* "horse would never fly." But somewhere deep inside her, doubt and hope were locked in a life and death struggle for her future. Doubt ran back and forth like a caged hyena, ranting and raving, hurling dreadful insinuations. Hope just stood there helplessly, letting the worst of it ricochet off. That night, *hope* won the battle and came storming thought the gate of her young heart. Maybe she had bought another year.

And so, weeping, and trembling like a tuning fork in front of a hopelessly out of tune orchestra, Barbara Dare promised, "Sweetheart, I'll help you build your dream. But you must let me stay in the background."

Todd held her, calming her, but she knew she had just signed her death warrant.

20

The party was over. The guests were gone. The last Rolls Royce was leaving the grounds. Senator Carrington was at last ready to search the trunk of Barbara Dare's car. Carrying a large box wrapped in teal paper, he went to the verandah where Todd and Barbara were cuddling in the swing.

"I hate to interrupt you two love birds," he said, looking at Barbara, "but Lady Carrington and I want to give you your first wedding gift."

"*A wedding gift*!" Barbara sat up and reached to receive the package.

The senator pulled it back, like he was teasing her. "You can't open it until you get back home. And it's a little heavy. If you'll hand me your car keys, Todd and I will load it in your trunk."

Todd was smiling like the canary that ate the cat.

"I'll go with you," Barbara said and stood enthusiastically, then shook the wrinkles from her gown. "Trunk's a little hard to open."

It was a hot, muggy evening and the flies were out. Barbara shooed the flies from around the trunk of the Camaro as she inserted the key.

The senator stood to the side while Todd raised the lid and unhooked the security cover over the cargo hole. The vinyl cover shot back like a window shade with an overactive spring.

Barbara's scream told it all. Her blood-curdling wail echoed out across the water like a ghost hunting a home.

Tamika, wearing the robin's-egg-blue T-shirt and jeans, lay in a pool of dried blood, her long body folded in the fetal position—that's the only way she would fit in the small space— and one of her shoes was missing.

The police came, the coroner came, the hearse came, and the media came. The senator told the press that the family was in shock, unavailable for comment, but to come back in the morning for a statement.

The next morning, the police quizzed Barbara, but soon

dismissed her as a suspect—a murderess wouldn't drive around for two days with her best friend in the trunk of her car.

Later that same morning, on national TV, the senator seized the opportunity to deflect the heat from Todd and his new fianceé. He announced his retirement from the Senate, effective at the end of this term, and blamed Tamika's killing on enemies of the tobacco industry, enemies trying to force him to vote against the tobacco bill now making its way through Congress. He even went so far as to say the murder of Tub Humphry, the Winston-Salem farmer, might be related to the killing of this poor innocent girl. His enemies would stop at nothing to put the tobacco industry out of business.

21

Atlanta, Georgia. Tamika proved to be as *salty* in death as she had been in life. At her funeral, a big controversy broke out on the church steps over whether or not to have women pallbearers, a first in that part of the country.

Barbara and Aunt Maudie, Tamika's only living relative, had planned the funeral like they thought Tamika would have wanted it. The service was held in Atlanta at one of the churches where Dr. Martin Luther King, Jr. had preached. The Atlanta mayor would deliver the eulogy.

Barbara and Aunt Maudie arranged transportation for friends from Tamika's old neighborhood, the one where she outran the MARTA. The buses just kept coming. The church was packed and so was the yard. The singing! What singing! Victorious singing, not burying singing, had already started when the pink hearse backed up to the front steps. The choir was singing, "Shake Hands With Jesus, Sweet Child."

Six women pallbearers reached for the gold-plated handles on the pink coffin to carry Tamika up the steps.

And that's when the trouble started.

"They ain't no women gonna carry no coffin into this church while I'm alive." The words came from a baldheaded deacon, a slender, elderly man, standing defiantly at the top of the cracked and chipped concrete steps.

The singing stopped, the yard full of people froze, and the six women carrying Tamika paused at-the-ready.

The pastor, in his long black robe, hurried to the top of the steps and tried to reason with the man that Tamika would have wanted it that way. "These six girls are her friends, Deacon Jones."

"Not over my dead body," croaked Deacon Jones, loudly and belligerently, his toothpick legs spread wide apart. "It ain't ever been done that way."

A ragged little girl from Tamika's neighborhood ran inside and whispered to Aunt Maudie, who had already taken her place on the front row as the sole family-mourner on Tamika's behalf.

Aunt Maudie, big enough to have played tackle for the Atlanta Falcons, hurried, as fast as a seventy-year-old could hurry, toward the problem deacon. When she got there she was already huffing and puffing. "Joe Willie Jones, you contrary old haint," she barked, staring down into his eyes, "you git!"

"Now, Aunt Maudie—"

"Don't you *Aunt Maudie* me, you wall-eyed weasel." She was flailing the air with both arms. "My niece tryin' to git in there to shake hands with Jesus, and you makin' her and the Saviour both wait. You backslidin' ol' heathen', you! Git!'

"No, ma'am. This ain't woman business. If the Lord had 'a meant it to be woman business, He wouldn't 'a called it *Paul*-bearing, after the disciple Paul; He would 'a called it *Mary*-bearing, or *Esther*-bearing, or some woman name like—"

"My nephew hep'ed build this church," she said, trying reason.

"Maybe yo' *nephew*, but not yo' *niece*. This is man business."

"You ignorant old fool!" Aunt Maudie got right in his face. "I'll knock you down the steps and beat you over the head with yo' shoe—with yo' foot still in it!"

Deacon Jones slipped into the crowd, like a little dog cowering from a big dog.

"Don't you come back!" she called at him. Then she wobbled to the bottom of the steps, and, with a big grin, said to Barbara, "If I likes ya, I lets ya. If I loves ya, I heps ya."

Through tears, Barbara winked at her.

Aunt Maudie winked back. "I loves ya, and I'm gonna hep ya. Y'all bring that girl and come on in. Jesus is waitin' to shake hands with her." Then Aunt Maudie, a dyed-in-the-wool Georgia fan, led interference as six University of Tennessee female pallbearers, close on her heels, lovingly lifted the earthly remains of the fallen Georgia track star and triumphantly walked into the church.

Barbara, Tsu, and Brandi gently carried one side of the pink casket while three girls from Tennessee's national championship basketball team carried the other side. A spray of virgin pink rosebuds lay on top, tied with a matching pink sash that read, "Go Big Orange."

The mayor concluded the eulogy by reading from an article in the *Atlanta Journal* by a local sportscaster. "In high school, Tamika could run like the devil, as if she had wings, and we all thought she would go to college in Georgia. Instead she chose our arch-rival, the University of Tennessee. Sports-wise, at least as to bragging rights, we felt we had lost her. Now she has come home. Now she runs with the angels. Now she belongs to us all."

In death as in life, Tamika Louise Brown had won.

22

When Barbara honeymooned in Paris, it was carried on the news. Grandmother Dare watched it all as she rocked away the hours in the Shaker rocker in her little cabin in Cades Cove, Tennessee.

Tucked away as far back in the Smokies as civilization goes, she prayed to God for Barbara's safety. Already a milky-eyed man had been sniffing around like a hound after a fox.

In this land of the bobcat, the black bear, and the red wolf, she had never been afraid—at least not afraid of the animals. But now, even the wildflowers in her beautiful meadow trembled.

In her day Grandmother Dare, now in her seventies, had been quite a runner. She ran the woods with the Cherokee girls. But one day an uninvited man came calling. She tried to outrun him, but a child in each arm slowed her. Not being fast enough had cost her a daughter and, in the worst way a mother can lose a son, a son. After that she didn't run much any more.

When Barbara returned from her honeymoon, Grandmother Dare would warn her to watch out for a milky-eyed man driving a big white car.

23

At Sagebrush Prison, two guards—one in front and one behind—herded the pale and slender Buzzard Mackelroy from solitary confinement back to Cell Block 13.

As Buzzard walked down the wide halls, enjoying the sound of his own footsteps, he ran his fingertips along the green wall, basking in the touch of anything green and taking great delight that he could stretch his arms all the way out. He breathed in deeply, filling his nostrils with the fresh smell of stale.

The guards escorted him into the community room and then to a card table in the center. Once he was seated, one guard handed him a pencil and a sheet of paper, the priceless courtesies worthy of his ranking in the prison system. The paper was white, and the short-stubby pencil was green with green lead. At Sagebrush prison, all pencils were short and stubby and all wrote green. Prison-green. That simplified monitoring. An inmate caught with a pencil of another color, or paper with writing in another color, got 30 days in the cooler. But that wasn't why Buzzard Mackelroy had been in solitary.

"Anything else, sir?" asked a guard.

He waved them off, then raised an eyebrow, signaling his own two men.

Two large inmates standing against the wall hurried to him but did not sit, and he did not stand. They leaned down into his presence and all three talked in whispers. Buzzard Mackelroy always talked in whispers. Most of the other prisoners sat watching the big screen TV.

Buzzard Mackelroy spoke five languages and had read every book of significance in the prison library. He was also the Building Tender. The Building Tender's job was to see to it that if anybody needed a whipping, they got a whipping. He also handled other discipline. There were no discipline problems in Cell Block 13.

"Did he live?" asked Buzzard.

Clifford, the smaller of his two giant errand-boy bodyguards, pointed across the way to a cell that held a tongueless, fat prisoner.

Buzzard turned and locked his eyes on him. The fat man flinched like he would wet his pants and looked away.

"Want me to finish the job?" asked Axe, the larger of the two big associates.

"Don't let anybody ever touch him again. I want him to live with what he did."

Clifford then handed Buzzard Mackelroy a video and a photograph. "We taped the news about the honeymoon for you. And here's the Asheville newspaper. I think you'll find it most interesting."

Dead silence.

Buzzard Mackelroy studied the photograph. It had been taken from the rear of a tiny church. A bride and groom knelt on a wooden floor before an altar of apple blossoms. The girl wore a long white dress and a single apple blossom in her long blond hair.

"Clear the room."

Axe stood and gave the clear-the-room signal. Prisoners scampered to their cells like mice fleeing a cat. But no eyes peeped from the cells. Cliff shoved the video into the VCR and angled the big screen TV toward Buzzard. Then he and Axe moved next to the wall and crouched at attention as if waiting for an explosion.

Buzzard Mackelroy adjusted his unusually thick glasses that resembled welder's goggles and were held on with an elastic band. With one eye on the TV and the other on the newspaper, he devoured the newspaper. A full-page layout in the Lifestyle section told it all:

Asheville welcomes the Todd Carringtons, fresh from their month-long honeymoon in Europe. Todd Carrington, son of Senator Charlie Carrington, and rumored to be destined for Washington, will apprentice in the City Manager's office. Barbara Dare-Carrington, his lovely bride, a University of Tennessee graduate, will become Director of Human Resources at SIG Laboratories, Inc.

Buzzard Mackelroy sat there for the longest time. Then he glanced at his two executives. He had chosen Cliff and Axe, not only because of their size, but also because of their special skills and intelligence. Cliff was a white man, expert in communications, and especially skilled at breaking codes. Axe, on the other hand, was a black man, a fighter, particularly gifted in clandestine military operations. In the outside world he had been a captain in the Air Force until he cracked—he threw two recruits out of an airplane at 30,000 feet for refusing to obey an order. Loyalty wasn't a factor with Cliff and Axe. Everybody was loyal to Buzzard Mackelroy.

Cliff and Axe now hurried back to Buzzard's table where they stood stiffly.

"Get a dossier on the City Manager at Asheville." Buzzard was looking at Cliff, the communications man, when he gave those instructions. "Also, get a complete file on the head of SIG Laboratories *and* on the man who does his dirty work."

He then turned to Axe, the fighter. "Find out who or what they fear most. Boil it down to one word." He handed him the green pencil and the white paper and whispered, "Bring me the word."

24

Barbara grieved for Tamika for almost three months, then she had married Todd the last of August.

After a near perfect honeymoon, the first thing she did on arriving in Asheville was to check the map to see how far it was to her *secret rendezvous spot* across the mountain in Tennessee. One-hundred-and-ten miles exactly. Two-hundred-and-twenty round trip. Good. She could make the trip in an afternoon. All she had to do was find a time when Todd would be busy.

Meanwhile, she went about the task of getting settled in Asheville as Ms. Dare-Carrington. She had two weeks before she had to report to her new job at SIG Labs.

Their new home wasn't ready, so, while construction was being completed, she and Todd camped out in the posh Executive Suite at the Grove Park Inn Resort. Grove Park Inn, atop Sunset Mountain, with its massive fireplaces at each end of the Great Hall—the work of the finest Italian stonemasons—and touting its AAA Four Diamond Award—had enticed wealthy families of the past: the Fords, Rockefellers, Edisons, and Firestones.

After a week at Grove Park, Barbara and Todd moved into their new home near the Biltmore Estate—the largest private home in America. Barbara's and Todd's home was a Swiss chalet, overlooking the Blue Ridge Parkway, and had an all-glass front, just for looking.

It was late September, and, just as the Smokies were ablaze with fall colors, Asheville's media was afire with football fever. Since Knoxville lay thirty minutes or so inside the Tennessee border, just across "Old Smoky," the sports hype centered on the rivalry between the Vols and the Tar Heels. With season tickets to both universities, Barbara and Todd had the best of both worlds.

Barbara now had one week before she had to report to work. So, dressed in denim cutoffs and a white, orange-lettered, University of Tennessee sweatshirt, she threw herself into getting their new home in order. The first thing was to unpack.

The first thing she unpacked was a gold-framed plaque from her honeymoon. As she held up the plaque, she remembered. They had crossed the Atlantic on the Queen Elizabeth II, the majestic cruise ship of the Cunard fleet, and had flown back on the supersonic Concorde, owned jointly by England and France.

The QE 2 had docked in South Hampton. A private driver met and chauffeured them the one hour's drive into London where the Savoy's honeymoon suite was prepared with special amenities for the lovers. They spent the night in mad lovemaking, and the following morning the passionate loving began all over again. That afternoon, Todd escorted Barbara to high tea at the Ritz. She wore an apple-blossom-white, long flowing gown and wide-brimmed hat, a straw skimmer. During the entire honeymoon Todd showered her with gifts, but it was at the Ritz that afternoon that he gave her what he called "her wedding gift": a Rolex Oyster Perpetual Lady-Datejust watch with 40 square cut rubies on an 18-karat yellow gold bezel and 10 brilliants set on its dial, and a 14mm bracelet studded with rubies and lined on either side with diamonds. It was the most beautiful piece of jewelry she had ever seen, but, even if she had had that kind of money, she was too frugal to ever have considered paying that much for a watch—she still saved coupons. But Todd wanted her to have it so she accepted it and wore it with great pride.

That night they went to the Adelphi Theatre where, from box seats, they enjoyed Andrew Lloyd Webber's "Sunset Boulevard." After the show, they piled up in bed and sipped champagne and ate strawberries dipped in sour cream and powdered with brown sugar, and Todd taught her "a new way to dream."

For a moment there in London, Barbara forgot the *Secret*, and for a moment she was without fear. Then she remembered how "Sunset Boulevard" had ended. And though Norma Desmond, the play's aging star, had "never known the meaning of surrender," Barbara knew the day was coming when she, herself, would.

From the wedding trip, besides a heart full of warm and wonderful memories, and besides personalized stationary, which the QE2 always gave first-class passengers, she had brought home the gold-framed plaque she had just unpacked and was now holding. The plaque framed an old prayer. The memories were for herself, the stationary for Todd, and the prayer-plaque was for Grandmother Dare.

Barbara's cabin steward had brought the prayer-plaque with him when he brought a bottle of gold-sealed red wine, Cella Lambrusco, "Compliments of the Captain." He also told her that the late Commodore John W. Caunce, master of the original Queen Elizabeth, used to keep a framed copy of the prayer on a wall in his quarters, often showing it to passengers. The author is unknown:

Keep my mind free from the recital of endless details; give me wings to get to the point. Seal my lips on my aches and pains. They are increasing and love of rehearsing them is becoming sweeter as the years go by. I dare not ask for grace enough to enjoy the tales of others' pains, but help me to endure them with patience.

I dare not ask for improved memory, but for a growing humility and a lessening cock-sureness when my memory seems to clash with the memories of others. Teach me the glorious lesson that occasionally I may be mistaken.

Keep me reasonably sweet; I do not want to be a saint—some of them are so hard to live with—but a sour old person is one of the crowning works of the devil. Give me the ability to see good things in unexpected places and talents in unexpected people. And give me, Lord, the grace to tell them so. Amen.

The prayer reminded Barbara of a lesson in her psych class: *With the elderly, tact is one of the first social skills to go.* On the cruise, getting the prayer-plaque for Grandmother Dare had seemed such a good idea. But at home, after rereading it, it sounded too "preachy" to just mail to anyone, especially Grandmother Dare who certainly didn't talk too much and was still most tactful. So Barbara decided to hang the plaque over her own kitchen sink, then the first time Grandmother Dare visited her, she would see it and hopefully ask for a copy.

Barbara would then make a copy, but for sure, Grandmother Dare would get the original.

While Barbara finished unpacking, she decided she wanted some music. She flipped on the stereo and a Brahms symphony filled the room. She wasn't in the mood for Brahms—that was Todd's CD anyway—so she touched the radio button. Vince Gill was in the middle of a plaintive wail, his new song about the death of his brother, "Go Rest High Upon The Mountain."

That was too much for Barbara. And so, with misty eyes wide open, as Vince sang his heart out, she breathed her own prayer. "Lord, one way or the other, Grandmother Dare will soon be coming to that 'high mountain' also. You may not recognize her. Her once bright eyes now show disappointment. Her strong hands are wrinkled and her hair has lost some of its beauty. If You still don't recognize her, look for me, for when *they* come for me, they'll come for her, too. Give her my part of Heaven for she's had her own private Hell here on earth. I don't guess she's a saint, but You know her worth. She'll be wearing that old blue gingham dress; I'll see to it."

After the prayer, Barbara finished unpacking then climbed into her Camaro, the one that had entombed Tamika. The police had impounded the car for a while. When they finally released it back to Barbara, she couldn't get the bloodstains out of the carpet in the trunk, so she replaced it.

Today she cruised in the old car from one mall to the next, talking to this designer and that designer and choosing drapes, furniture, and pots and pans for their new home.

She couldn't believe how things had fallen together. She and Todd were enjoying a charmed life. Of his three job offers, Asheville's had been by far the most attractive. And if that weren't enough, she had landed the perfect job in the same city. Yes indeed-ee. Lady Fortune was smiling. Barbara liked Asheville because it was in the mountains. But she liked it best because she could keep the monthly rendezvous just across the Tennessee border. She would never have considered a town that wasn't within comfortable driving range. And what a salary! The two of them made a combined 6-figure income, with Todd's only slightly more than hers. Of course the money meant nothing to him; the Carringtons had more than they could ever spend.

Todd had already reported for work as assistant to Asheville's City Manager. Having been raised in a senator's home, he knew politics from the top down. Now, he would learn from the bottom up.

She checked the time on her new Rolex. 3:30. She headed to Barnes & Noble where she bought a cookbook, using a discount coupon. It felt odd rifling through her handbag for discount coupons while wearing a hundred-thousand-dollar watch. Old habits die hard. And it took forever to find a book with a recipe for peanut butter pie. She would need the peanut butter pie for her next secret trip across the mountain. But she still hadn't found a time when Todd would be away for a whole afternoon. His being at work didn't count; he could call home, or pop in. That would require a heap of explaining.

She dashed out to the Farmer's Market for fresh veggies, and then on to the grocery store for pantry staples. She would still have time to read the cookbook before preparing her first at-home dinner.

Barbara always kept the Camaro in good mechanical condition, so it took the curves on the Blue Ridge Parkway quite well. But the car's days were numbered. They would be ordering a new one soon. Todd had said he didn't care what kind as long as it was American-made. He was so child-like in his belief in the flag, the Star Spangled Banner, and the American dream that sometimes his eyes welled up when he talked about them. She wouldn't think of doing anything that hampered his dream, so the new car would definitely be American, probably another Chevy. What she really wanted was a Corvette. A black one. And after a few pay checks, that's exactly what they'd buy. She loved fast cars and had a natural talent at the wheel. But like it or not, necessity had forced her to develop the talent.

At 4:00 she turned off the Parkway and into the long driveway that circled up the side of the mountain to their home, off in the distance. Her mailbox was on the Parkway, so she got out and checked it. No mail. She hadn't expected any. The landscape man, at her request, was planting a pair of burning bushes, one on either side of the mailbox. In the fall, the bushes would turn a burnt red. She spoke to the man and drove on up to the house and parked.

The Camaro looked like the Beverly Hillbillies' truck; it was packed to the hilt with groceries—including a box of Moon Pies—scented candles, fabric swatches, and carpet samples, and with drapery rods poked out the partially open trunk.

Todd was standing in the newly sodded, steep yard, grinning like a kid who had been in the cookie jar, welcoming her. Lord, he's handsome. Broad shoulders. No waist.

She jumped out and rushed to him, giving him a big hug and kiss. "Miss me?"

"So much I left the office early."

"Good day?"

"Perfect. I dictated the minutes for the City Council's zoning meeting and refereed a dog fight between two neighbors."

Barbara laughed. "Help me unload the car. I have a surprise for you."

"I have a surprise, too."

"Oh?"

Todd pointed the garage door opener at the house and pressed the button. The garage door started sliding open.

Barbara gasped.

Matching Corvettes—one red and one black—sat facing her, sparkling in the sunlight. Overcome, she laughed so hard she went down on one knee and had to grab Todd's arm to keep from flopping down on her bottom, right there in the middle of the driveway.

"I guess that means," Todd was now laughing so hard he had tears in his eyes, "you're pleased."

She stood there staring at him, proud that he was vulnerable to her opinion. "You're a dream," she said, pulling him toward the black car. She climbed in. The smell of new leather shot through her. "Let's try it out."

"Parkway speed limit's only 35."

"Then let's go where it's not. Hop in."

An hour later they returned from the Asheville Speedway. Barbara was still at the wheel. "Now for your surprise," she said.

"Can't wait."

She walked to the Camaro, opened the door, and started handing the groceries to him. "I can't cook."

25

Cell Block 13, Sagebrush Prison.

"He won't pay up," one inmate said of another.

Buzzard Mackelroy was holding court at the card table in the center of the community room. A Styrofoam cup of creamed coffee, still steaming, was the only item on the crippled table. The smell of men too long in the house filled the room.

Buzzard kept an eye on the door. It was time for the mail. "I'll handle it," he said to the complaining prisoner, then stood. "First, I gotta go to the john. Get rid of some of this coffee."

Other than his steel-trap mind, Buzzard Mackelroy had three major talents, but doing life without parole rendered two of the talents useless: He was without equal at the wheel of an automobile, he was good with men, and he was good with dogs. He could make a bad man be good without whipping him, and he could send a pack of dogs after two separate bears. The bloodhounds would eat one bear and lie down beside the other. Buzzard used an old Cherokee technique of sweet and sour smells to tell the dogs which bear to kill and which to befriend.

This morning he had just taken his first step away from the card table, headed for the restroom, when the community room door opened and a guard ushered the prison mailman in.

"Mail call." As was his practice, the mailman walked toward the card table, intending to hand the mail for Cell Block 13 to Buzzard who would inspect it, then disperse it to the others.

Suddenly a loud boom sent everyone scurrying to safety. Nails shot into the ceiling, walls, floor, and flesh. Sawdust peppered the prisoners. Smoke filled the room. It smelled like a July-the-Fourth firecracker shootout.

The mailman lost a finger and the tongueless fat man, hiding in his cell, lost control of his bowels.

While the smoke settled, the stunned guards quickly ordered prisoners to their cells, then escorted Buzzard to the infirmary. He had a face full of sawdust and a nail sticking through his chin.

"Inside or outside job this time?" one of the guards asked him, casually.

Buzzard was holding his shirttail to his chin, trying to stem the flow of blood. "Outside."

"Any idea who might have sent you the mail bomb?"

"Legion."

"That his first or last name?"

"Legion means thousand," said Buzzard Mackelroy, and that's all he said. But of the thousands out to kill him, only one man would be stupid enough to send a so-easily-traceable bomb. Nails and sawdust. The foolish man's name was Baldy. Baldy owned a sawmill. Baldy had more reason than any to kill or maim Buzzard Mackelroy.

In Cell Block 13, the rule of law was an "eye for an eye" and a "finger for a finger." You paid your debts no matter how small. To do otherwise would be seen as weakness, and if the Building Tender didn't mete out justice, the prisoners took the law into their own hands. Such mutiny could soon get the Building Tender-king overthrown. It was well-understood procedure that you didn't let attacks from any quarter go unchecked, even a nail mail bomb. If someone was about to take a punch at you, you cold-cocked him. You didn't wait for his swing. It wasn't boxing, and there was no referee. The man left standing got to live. Somebody else had made the rules. Buzzard just carried them out. He was a survivor. You lean that when you're doing life without parole.

The guards liked a well-disciplined cell block. When accounts were being settled, they found it convenient to look the other way.

Buzzard's reward for keeping discipline? If thirty days passed without any problems on his cell block, he got a special treat. The treat? Ten minutes of sheer ecstasy. Once a month, if he was good, they would usher him into the prison lobby and place him inside an all-glass cage. The cage was about the size of a phone booth and had been built especially for him; he was too powerful and too dangerous to be allowed to associate with prisoners from other cell blocks. But mostly it was for his own protection. Any number of inmates would love to take a whack at him without his entourage around, more especially without Cliff and Axe around.

Three years before becoming the Building Tender, Buzzard Mackelroy had served as assistant to the then Building Tender, Huey Lamb. Lamb was waiting to die in the electric chair. But everyone knew that Buzzard was the power behind Lamb's throne and the heir apparent.

So, even during his years as assistant Building Tender, the guards treated Buzzard as a prince. From his bulletproof, glass, holding tank, the guards would let him watch visitors from the outside world—families, girlfriends, confidants, or what have you—as they interacted with the prisoners. And for three years Buzzard watched an elderly woman teacher schooling Huey Lamb, his mentor, though Lamb would soon die in the electric chair.

There in the prison lobby, with everyone watching, including the guards, and the warden if she wanted to, Buzzard Mackelroy would transform himself into somebody they didn't know. They had found how to pull his chain. He would fight the devil and half of Georgia for that treat. But they had no idea why the ten minutes transformed him into such a genteel man. And he never told them. But to him, the man in the glass cage was the man he might have been, could have been, and was on the way to becoming, until one horrible night. The night a man raped Buzzard's mother.

In his youth, Buzzard Mackelroy had aspirations of racing in the Indy 500 and was on the fast track to fulfilling that dream. But in an instant all that changed. The rapist fled, but Buzzard, then a small boy, got a good look at his scraggly face, his mouth full of rotten teeth, and the warts on his hands. Those warts burned and seethed in his memory.

Vengeance was slow in coming. But every man in the mountains got the once-over from Buzzard's young eyes. Some years later, he and Preecher Kinser—his mechanic and best friend—were doing a road test on a yellow roadster in the mountains near Gatlinburg. Preecher Kinser was trailing in his own race car.

They pulled into the parking lot of a small convenience

store, raised the hood, and, with the engine idling and the muted bazooka pipes slapping the chilly morning breeze with that soft cracking sound that is so intoxicating to a connoisseur of hot rodding, started adjusting the timing on the roadster.

A man came out of the store carrying a steaming cup of coffee in one hand and a six-pack of beer in the other. He walked by the two boys working under the hood, stuck his head under, and goaded them, "Git a horse."

Buzzard smiled and glanced up. Staring him in the face was a scraggily-faced man with bad breath and rotten teeth. Buzzard's eyes shot down to the wart-covered hand that held the six pack resting on the yellow fender.

"That's him!" he yelled to Preecher.

The rotten-toothed man vanished into his mud-splattered pickup and fled.

They chased him home—it was no race; the yellow roadster could catch anything in the Smoky Mountains—and settled the score. Preecher Kinser helped pour the rapist into four towsacks, then Buzzard sent Preecher home; he didn't want his friend taking the heat.

Buzzard Mackelroy wasn't his real name, but he had a two-year-old daughter, whose beautiful young mother had died giving her life, to think about...just in case this thing took a turn for the worst. So, in a flash—he later wondered if it was panic or brilliance—he threw his billfold and all his identification out the window. The name *Mackelroy* just popped into his head. Since he had just returned from Vulture Mountain, the name *Buzzard* did too. Thus was born, "fully-growed," at age eighteen, Buzzard Mackelroy.

He then delivered the four bags to Sheriff Bufford Blankenship over at Alcoa. He introduced himself as Buzzard Mackelroy, and that's the only name he ever gave. Like any young mountain boy was trained to do, he proudly confessed. He told the sheriff that he thought he was justified in killing the man. Sheriff Blankenship thought so too, but the judge didn't. Judge Samuel L. Skillet—the prisoners called him *Frying* Skillet because he had fried more men in Tennessee's electric chair than any other judge in the state's history—threw the book at him.

He said society couldn't survive if mountain people kept taking the law into their own hands, and vowed to make an example of the reckless young hotrodder standing in front of him, even though, so far as they could tell, the trembling boy was a first-time offender.

Now Buzzard Mackelroy was no longer a virgin offender. The prison system had seen to that. Prison had taught him the foolishness of his naive confession to Sheriff Blankenship. The prison system said, do what you need to to survive. Just keep your mouth shut.

Now, the mail bomb. It would have to be answered. Buzzard's enemies were always watching for their chance to seize his throne, watching for any sign of weakness on his part. A plan was already beginning to formulate in his mind.

Baldy's sawmill was located on Vulture Mountain, way back in the Smokies. Buzzard had been there only once. He decided to let him gloat a while, brag to his boys, think he had gotten away with the mail bomb. Then along about Christmas, a visitor would call on him at the sawmill. But he wouldn't be bringing gold, frankincense, and myrrh, and it wouldn't be Jesus, the Messiah.

26

Barbara's first couple of weeks in the beautiful city of Asheville were exhilarating—lovemaking in the early evening, then off to a concert or fancy dinner. She and Todd were the perfect pair bond. It looked like the happy days would last forever. But everything was about to change. Tuesday evening of the second week, Todd took her to the Riverdance Show. Then Wednesday night they went jogging, in the moonlight, up the Blue Ridge Parkway. But when they returned, Mr. Monty Ezell, a local insurance agency owner, called and said the Asheville Country Club's Executive Board had just voted the Todd Carringtons in. On the first ballot. He then invited Todd to play golf with him Sunday afternoon.

Todd turned to Barbara. "Okay if I play golf Sunday after church?"

Bingo! That was the afternoon she was looking for. "Of course," she said, trying to conceal her excitement.

Sunday morning, she and Todd joined the Redeemer Presbyterian Church during the early service. That afternoon, he left to play golf with Mr. Ezell and two city officials.

As soon as he was out the door, Barbara jumped into the Camaro—the Corvette would arouse too much suspicion where she was going—and headed across "Old Smoky" and the Tennessee border for her monthly secret rendezvous. She'd missed last month because she was on her honeymoon.

As a student, she'd chosen the Camaro with the blowout T-Top because of its power and speed. The car wasn't much to look at any more—the silver-gray paint had begun to peel—GM had agreed to re-paint it—but it would run like a scalded dog. Beside her, in the other seat, sat a homemade peanut butter pie, the first she had ever made.

After a successful meeting, she limped back to her car, hidden in the bushes. Then, like Super Woman dashing into a phone booth, she yanked off the "granny" wig and tossed it onto the seat where the peanut butter pie had sat. She shoved the walking cane back under the seat, fired up the V-8, and headed home.

It was late afternoon when she hit the bustling town of Pigeon Forge. Minutes later she sat trapped in the one way, two-mile-an-hour, tourist traffic through Gatlinburg. Once she broke free, she popped out the T-tops and let the wind have its way with her hair. Then she headed into the darkest part of the mountains—the Great Smoky Mountain National Park—ever watchful in the rearview mirror for a tail.

Having tasted the speed of the Corvette earlier in the week, her confidence in the Camaro was now shaken. It wasn't as fast as she had remembered. Speed and a low profile were her only weapons. Now she felt vulnerable. Now she knew she could be caught.

It was twilight as she drove through the steep curves. A canopy of leaf-laden branches—magnificently colored and hanging out over the road—made her think how she'd never seen a more spectacular fall display. Surely no place in the world could be more beautiful than this, her backyard.

Wind-swept, surrendered leaves teased the yellow line and stirred her memory of sleeping laurels and rhododendrons that usually grew up through the damp moss alongside the highway, only slightly softening the painful memory of what might have been and the tragedy that was to come. She couldn't bring herself to wish she had never married Todd, but she knew she shouldn't have.

Then there was the matter of Tamika's murder. It was a commonly held notion that one of the tobacco industry's opponents had had Tamika killed. And that they did it to force Senator Carrington to abandon his support of the tobacco legislation now wending its way through Congress. Barbara held that view, too. She knew it was not one of the men Grandmother Dare had warned her about. Those men would not have killed Tamika and left Barbara alive. They would have taken out every girl in the race to make sure they got her.

Three other things were now clear to Barbara: One, there were too many enemies in the camp. And if that weren't enough, Todd, himself, would soon develop *political* enemies.

128

Maybe already had. It was only a matter of time until one of them got nosey and wanted to interview her. Two, as fast as her Camaro was, it would never stay with her Corvette. An enemy might also have a Corvette, or equivalent. Three, since she could never drive her new car on this mission, she must find a way of making her old car faster.

She would keep an eye out for a mechanic she could take into her confidence. A little.

Monday morning, two Corvettes pulled out of the Carrington driveway and headed in opposite directions on the Blue Ridge Parkway. Todd headed the *red* Vette toward downtown, and Barbara aimed the *black* one at the industrial district.

She watched Todd in her mirror as she shifted gears. He was still waving when he rounded the curve. He was on his way to the mayor's office to solicit his support; the golf game yesterday hadn't been about just golf. The locals wanted Todd to run for Representative to the General Assembly and he had agreed.

Barbara was on her way to SIG Labs, her first day on the job. She hadn't been able to learn much about the company, but, evidently, they preferred to go unnoticed, and she liked that.

She felt great, but she got to thinking that her appearance— black business suit and black car—might appear too somber. Todd had helped pick out the suit. He said it made her look professional without sacrificing her femininity. She had chosen accessories to soften the look: matching shoes, bag, and a gold-plated belt-buckle. She smiled. The black Corvette would have to stay *black*. There wasn't much she could do about it...unless she tied a red bow around it.

Soon she was deep in Asheville's industrial district, all the while hoping she remembered how to find "Industrial Way." The lab was at 4222 Industrial Way. She had only been there once—on the day she interviewed for the position.

She slowed down to read the names of the streets. Momentarily she spotted Industrial Way, but missed the turn because a tree limb partially blocked the sign. She made a U-turn, and then turned left onto Industrial Way, a cul-de-sac.

Number 4222 was the only address on the street. The isolated site was perfect for Barbara. She figured SIG Labs liked the location for the same reason she did: no other businesses were in view. If another business ever moved next door, all they would see was a cluster of old buildings.

A ten-foot chain-link fence, topped with razor wire, surrounded the sprawling complex, which consisted of one tall building and five smaller ones. Housing the executive offices, the tall building was a three-story brick and sat in the center; it was surrounded by five smaller cinder-block structures. Barbara imagined that from a helicopter, the whole scheme would resemble a five-spoked wagon wheel.

Each of the five, finger-like, single-story buildings had a loading ramp in the rear. A smoke-tinted glass walkway with a rounded top connected the five single-stories to the three-story. The whole compound looked like a poor man's Pentagon.

At ten minutes till eight Barbara Dare-Carrington pulled up to the security gate and proudly flashed her Executive-Parking Pass. The uniformed and armed guard courteously tipped his hat and pointed in the direction of her parking spot on the unkempt scrub grass. It seemed deliberately unkempt.

Entering the front door of the main building, she passed through the metal detector and into the reception area. She was immediately struck by the strong smell of chemicals. The reception area stood in stark contrast to the exterior. The interior was quite elaborate.

"Good morning, Ms. Dare-Carrington," said the receptionist, beaming. "Ms. Chastine is expecting you. Please be seated. I'll see if she's ready."

"Thank you." Barbara wandered around the room, absorbing the contradictory visual and olfactory sensations. This was the only part of the interior of the building she had already seen. Last month, when she arrived for the interview, this same receptionist handed her a green plastic folder with a packet of loose sheets inside and said, "Look this over. If you're still interested, here's an application. If I'm not here when you finish, leave it on my desk along with your transcript and vita."

Barbara had left the "interview" thinking it was a lost cause.

But the next day, the headhunter who had booked the interview called her at Grandmother Dare's, where Barbara was staying until the wedding. "You got the job!"

Today, as Barbara wandered around the lobby, she paid more attention. The floor was carpeted. Colored pictures of happy looking, white-coated men and women, apparently doing laboratory procedures, hung from the walls. Also attached to the wall was a gold-leafed framed copy of the company's statement on the importance of "THE CUSTOMER."

The receptionist returned to the door and called, "This way, please."

Barbara followed her through a long corridor of offices to the penultimate door.

"Ms. Chastine, this is Ms. Dare-Carrington," the receptionist announced and then left.

"I'm Sally Chastine." The attractive fortyish African-American woman shoved her hand out hard, but shook hands like a dead fish, her courtesy, at best, strained.

Barbara instantly felt the ice in the air. "I'm Barbara, and I'm looking forward to working with—"

"I've been instructed to show you the ropes." Sally Chastine shoved a green plastic folder to her. "Look this over first."

It was the same folder Barbara had already looked over, but she didn't think this was the time to tell Sally Chastine that. Somehow she had to get Sally on her side. On the desk sat a cruise-ship photo of Sally, a man, and two teenage boys. Maybe if she talked about the picture, the ice would thaw. "Your family?"

"Gene's my husband."

"And the boys?"

"They're mine. Not his." Her words still chilled like water dripping off an icicle. "His first wife shamed him."

Shamed him? Barbara didn't think this would be the best time to ask how she did that, so she asked, "Where does Gene work?"

"At the speedway."

"Driver?"

"Mechanic."

Mechanic. Maybe Gene could help soup-up the Camaro. But if the acid in Sally's voice continued, she would probably never get to meet the mechanic.

Sally snapped, "And he earned it. He didn't need some politician to—" She stopped, abruptly.

What did she mean by that?

"I'm sorry." Sally recovered and smiled as if they were best friends, but there was pain in her voice. "Please come with me; I'll show you to your office."

Green folder in hand, Barbara walked briskly behind Sally, trying to keep up. At the last door on the hall, they went in. The vacant office was twice as large as Sally's and had a large, flourishing peace lily in the corner. If Sally's office had a plant, Barbara hadn't noticed. Sally briefed her on office protocol and showed her the files, the computer, and the telephone system. Then, strangely, she warned her that no one was allowed on the second floor.

"What's *on* the second floor?"

"Dr. Clark is expecting you in ten minutes. His office is on the *third* floor. Would you like coffee before I escort you up there?"

"Yes. And if you'll show me where the break room is, next time I'll get the coffee."

Then, as if to say, "I'll just take you up on that offer," Sally marched double-time in front of Barbara to the break room. She slammed two cups on the counter, jerked the glass carafe off the burner, poured her own coffee, and walked out without comment.

Stunned, and then embarrassed, Barbara froze. She decided she didn't want coffee after all. Alone, she returned to the other end of the hall, thinking, If things get any colder around here, I'll bring ice skates tomorrow.

Back in her office, she laid the green folder on the walnut desk and walked around, studying the room. The whole set-up seemed sterile and manufactured. But what seemed the most unusual was that her one window, also smoke-tinted, was tiny, not much larger than a ship's porthole. She peered out. What a waste, viewing the Smoky Mountains through that tiny window.

But the ambiance of the whole complex was like a hide-out, and that pleased Barbara Dare-Carrington very much. No one would ever think of looking for her here. Her secret was going to be safe. For awhile.

27

Barbara glanced at her watch. In three minutes Sally Chastine would be back to take her to meet Dr. Quebian Clark, Director of Research and Head of the laboratory. What could she do for three minutes? As she paced she wondered, like a child warned to stay out of a cookie jar, what was on the second floor?

She sat at her desk, fidgeting. Then she thought of the family picture on Sally's desk. There would be no pictures on her own desk. But in her handbag was an item that told more about her than any photograph ever could. She removed from her handbag a worn and tattered book, *La Chanson de Roland* (*The Song of Roland*), and placed it between two bookends on the desk. She chuckled. She could see herself now, the picture of success, sitting there in her new suit in front of the big desk with *one* book. The slender little book appeared lonely sandwiched there all alone between those two bookends. She didn't care. The book was in its original language, French. An English translation was scribbled-in below the French in pencil. Grandmother Dare used to read the medieval French epic to Barbara and Mr. Scarecrow. Now an amusing thought came to Barbara. One of those summers that she played tag with Mr. Scarecrow was the summer she tripped and fell into the poison ivy near the bear cave; she spent a week scratching, coated with Calamine Lotion. It wasn't too funny then.

She would loan the tiny book to her desk during work hours, but every night it would go back into her purse. Without the book, she would not be admitted to her secret rendezvous each month.

But back to now. She fidgeted a while longer, tapping her finger on the desk. She scratched a note to herself to bring a scented candle from home to help make peace with the chemical odors. Then she decided to open the green folder. Same stuff the receptionist had given her at the interview. She now knew it by heart, but still she flipped through it again.

The first page stated: SIG LABORATORIES, INC. is an

international network of high quality laboratories, each offering a comprehensive range of testing services.

Testing of:
Groundwater
Soils
Sludges
Cosmetics
Priority Pollutants
Hazardous Wastes
Petroleum
Water and Waste Water

Other Areas:
Stack Testing
Field Sampling
Bioassays
Mobile Laboratory
Pesticide Registration Support
Asbestos
Radiological Analysis

The second sheet listed *Accreditations/Approvals:*
- Food and Drug Administration (FDA)
- U.S. Naval Energy and Environmental Support Activity (NEESA)
- U.S. Army Corps of Engineers (COE)
- U.S. Department of Energy, Hazardous Waste Remedial Action Programs (HAZWRAP)
- U.S. EPA Superfund Innovative Technology Evaluation Program (SITE)
- National Oceanic and Atmospheric Administration, Status and Trends Program (NOAA)
- U.S. EPA Drinking Water and Wastewater Performance Evaluation Program
- National Institute of Standards and Technology/National Voluntary Laboratory Accreditation Program (NIST/NVLAP)

Barbara's cup of tea. It Looked like the syllabus for Environmental Sciences 310 at UT.

A tap on her door told her it was time to go meet the man. Sally peeped in, a Kleenex in hand. "Ready?"

They walked halfway back up the hall to the elevator. Barbara couldn't help noticing the unusually wide hallway, wide enough for a wheelchair race. Inside the elevator, the control-panel showed "First Floor" and "Third Floor," but there was no button for the second floor. Between the two buttons was a place to insert a key, like in expensive hotels and high-rise office complexes.

Dr. Quebian Clark greeted them at the elevator. He was completely bald and had a white goatee; it looked like his head was on bottom-side upwards. Other than that, he looked like she thought a scientist ought to look: wire-rimmed glasses, white lab coat, and scuffed loafers. But curiously, around his neck hung a gold chain with a gold key dangling from it.

"You're excused Ms. Chastine," Dr. Clark said. Then he stood there until the elevator door closed. As soon as the elevator motor started, without speaking, he ushered Barbara down the hall to his office.

His office had walnut paneling on three sides, but one wall was all mirror. There were no windows. Clark nodded to a large leather chair. As Barbara sat, he perched himself on a high, white stool behind his mahogany desk, and peered over his glasses. He looked for all the world like a hoot owl with gas sitting on a fence post.

"Was Ms. Chastine cool to you?"

Shocked, Barbara said, "Distant might be a better word."

"No. *Distant* is not a better word. Cool is the word. Ice cool. Want to know why?"

Barbara didn't answer, but she sure wanted to know why.

"You took her office."

"*Her* office?"

"Sort of. She thought she was in line. To get the job I hired you for. She's excellent at hiring and firing. Your dossier says you are, too." He spoke nervously in short clipped sentences, making Barbara feel nervous too.

137

"I'm glad I have the job, but why me over her?"

"She knows nothing about laboratory procedure. You do. I believe you minored in laboratory sciences."

"That's right, but—"

"No buts about it. You know your way around a lab. She doesn't. So you got the job. She didn't. That's it. End of discussion."

"Yes, sir. But I didn't know I'd be working in the lab."

"You won't. But you could. That's the point. She can't. So there." His head shook from side to side as he talked.

"Oh."

"Tomorrow, we'll tour the laboratories. Introduce you to our doctors. Today, Ms. Chastine will show you around the shipping and receiving area. That'll be enough for now." He nervously stopped talking, stared at her, then bit at a fingernail. When he did, Barbara noticed all his nails had been chewed down to the quick.

She didn't know whether to continue the conversation, to nod, or to leave. When he said nothing more, she eventually stood and began backing out of the office, searching for a closure comment. Finally she said, "Yes, sir."

"Ms. Chastine is not allowed to wear a lab coat," Clark said, his back already turned. "Tell her to get you one."

Barbara rushed to the elevator, anxious to get back to the warmth of Sally's coolness. She understood coolness. She didn't understand insanity, or whatever was wrong with Dr. Clark.

Krandall Kaufman had watched it all. He sat in his wheelchair and stared through the one-way mirror into Dr. Clark's office. He pushed the intercom button. "Come in here."

Dr. Clark dashed out into the hall, ran to the first door, then quickly slipped in.

"Sit," Kaufman ordered.

Clark sat on command, like a dog.

"Now we'll see," said Kaufman, "what kind of wife that would-be senator has married."

Kaufman had arranged three straight-back chairs in the observation room so they faced the window/mirror. Clark now sat perched on the edge of the middle chair; the other two remained empty. A TV monitor and the red glow of the buttons on the electronic equipment provided the only light.

"She doesn't suspect a thing, does she?" Kaufman puffed on his cigar, then adjusted the gold chain and key—just like the one Dr. Clark wore—around his neck. There were three gold keys in existence.

Tumbler, wearing the third key, stood behind Kaufman's wheelchair, making tiny circular motions on a miniature whetstone with his pocketknife, always sharpening the blade. While in the Observation Room, Tumbler usually wore a mouse-gray sweat suit. He had seven of them, one for each day. All mouse-gray. But today he was still wearing the purple suit. He held the knife shaft with a purple kerchief that matched his newly-replaced purple polka-dot bow tie.

Kaufman turned and glanced at his loyal subject standing in the shadows. Tumbler always stood in the shadows. But Kaufman knew Tumbler had reason to be loyal. He might know where the tobacco cartel's secret file was stored, but Kaufman knew how Tumbler used the knife. It was not a friendship made in heaven, but it produced loyalty. Of a sort. And so the gentle sound of metal grinding on rock, especially when Tumbler was behind him, suited Kaufman. It was when he stopped grinding that Kaufman became unsettled.

"No, sir. She doesn't suspect a thing," Clark said. "But Ms. Chastine's hot."

"Good. Turn on the monitor and let's watch the fireworks."

Tumbler flipped the remote. The screen displayed Sally Chastine's office. Barbara was coming through Sally's door in a trot. The two women stared at each other without speaking.

Finally, Barbara said, "I'm sorry."

"He told you, didn't he?"

Barbara nodded as if she didn't know what to say.

"I could take it better if I knew why. I've given my life to this company," said Sally. "Did he give you a reason?"

"Not one I understood. Something about my minor in

laboratory sciences giving me an edge. But that didn't make any sense; I wasn't hired to work in the lab."

"A lot of things around here don't make sense."

Kaufman turned and looked at Tumbler.

"Well," said Barbara, "this won't make everything right, but since I'm in charge now, suppose I turn in a request for a healthy raise for you?"

Sally gulped. "After how I treated you?"

"If he'd done me that way," Barbara laughed, "I'd have let the air out of his tires."

Tumbler rubbed the blade of the Schrade-Walden faster on the whetstone.

Kaufman nodded. "Watch this woman. She's a fighter."

"You're all right, honey," Sally said. Then she laughed. "That'll make the old geezer squirm worse than he already squirms."

"Is he normal?" Barbara asked. "He has difficulty carrying on a conversation."

Obviously embarrassed, Dr. Clark cleared his throat.

"If you don't want to hear it," Kaufman barked, "you don't have to listen!"

The scientist left the observation room.

"Dr. Clark's all right," Sally said. "They brought him here from the Atomic Energy Lab over at Oak Ridge. It's that high IQ. He's brilliant with formulas and research but terrible with people."

"Nobody's perfect. I'm glad he doesn't know my weaknesses."

"Like what?"

Kaufman and Tumbler leaned toward the screen.

"I'll never tell. Oh, Dr. Clark said he wants me to wear a lab coat and that you'd show me where they are."

Sally looked her up and down then began to cackle. "A lab coat over that outfit? And that figure?"

Both women were still laughing as they headed for the lab coat closet. Tumbler turned off the monitor, but the video camera kept recording. It recorded everything in the complex, 24/7. The last thing Tumbler did before leaving at night, and the

140

first thing when arriving in the morning, was to review the recording.

Kaufman turned to Tumbler. "What about her husband?"

"He took the bait yesterday." Tumbler began to recite in monotone. "Mr. Todd Carrington will be...Buncombe County's next Representative to the General Assembly."

"*Buncombe County*? Representing Asheville?"

"Yeah. He's over talking to the...mayor right now."

"The mayor in our camp?"

"Nah. He's a local war hero. But we have a plant in the city manager's office."

"What about the manager?"

"Doesn't know about the *plant*. And Todd Carrington has no idea we're...providing the money for his election."

"Good. Get Monty Ezell hired as his campaign director."

"Piece 'a cake. Ezell orchestrated the...golf foursome yesterday."

"Let me know as soon as it's a done deal."

"If you ask me," Tumbler said, "this boy doesn't look like...senator material."

"The Carrington boy's like any other son of wealth who's partied all his life. This is his first real job."

"You know best. It's your head."

"You looked at any of those other freshman senators lately? Most are just like our boy, handsome rich kids who never worked a day in their life."

"I suppose," said Tumbler. "I better get on over...to see Ezell so he can get him started...dancing down that yellow brick road to the Senate."

"Before you go, what'd you learn from Barbara Dare's grandmother, when you were up at Cades Cove?"

Tumbler stopped sharpening his knife, closed the blade, then dropped it and the whetstone into his pants pocket. After that, he neatly rearranged the purple kerchief in his coat lapel-pocket. "She hasn't talked yet."

"See that she does. Now get on over to Ezell's."

Part of Todd's training was to take notes at City Council

meetings, much as an NFL quarterback, relegated to the sidelines, is required to record the plays. That night there was a City Council meeting—they were rezoning some creek property. Later, there was a big fight over a proposed name change to one of the schools. Monty Ezell was even there. Tempers flared and the fight went on into the night.

By the time Todd got home, Barbara was already in bed, reading a novel, and had a nice surprise for him—She was wearing a white nightshirt, and that's all, with "Lady Vols Track Team" written in orange across the front.

He sat on the bed, loosening his tie and removing his shirt, all the while, telling her about the Council meeting and asking her about her first day at SIG. She told him a bit, but was more interested in being held than in talking about lab coats, a nervous boss, an icy reception that thawed, razor-wired fences, and forbidden second floors. Todd listened but seemed unusually preoccupied. Maybe he was just wound up from the Council fight, so she decided to unwind him. She ran her fingers through his hair, then started teasing him with her skimpy nightshirt. He surrendered.

Later, just before they turned out the lights, she learned why he had been so preoccupied. He told her about his new friend, Monty Ezell. "I'd like to invite him and Carol over for dinner Friday night. Surely we can find a housekeeper by then."

"Carol his wife or girlfriend?"

"Both, I hope." Todd laughed.

She poked him in the ribs.

"Seriously, I'm thinking about asking Monty to handle my campaign."

"Dinner's fine."

"You're good at reading people, sweetheart. I need your opinion of him."

"I'll do anything to support you. Just don't ask me to front anything. I'm not good with the media and those kinds of things."

"You are so. Why, one of these days I'll get you up there on the platform with me and—"

Barbara jumped onto her knees. "No, you won't! And

142

Todd, don't ever tease about that again! I will *not* appear on stage with you!"

"Wow. I struck a nerve. Is this my sweetheart talking?"

"I'll always be your sweetheart," she pleaded, "and I'll mop the floors for you after the campaign is over, win or lose. But you'll make the mistake of your life if you try to force me to the forefront."

Todd's whole mood changed and he became most tender. "I'd rather have you in the *background* than to have Miss America standing up there *beside* me."

"You must never forget that promise."

He pulled her back down close to him and held her in his strong arms. But she shivered, even under the duck-down comforter that Grandmother Dare had made for their wedding.

Now she remembered. She must call Grandmother Dare soon to see if anyone had been snooping around, asking questions.

Again, she shivered.

28

Barbara Dare-Carrington's second day at SIG Labs went smoother, and by the end of the week she had even gotten used to the lab coat. But she still didn't know what was on the second floor. She had gotten to know Sally Chastine well enough to tell her she wanted to meet Gene, her husband, to see if he would work on the Camaro.

They were standing by the water fountain in the hall when Barbara said, "Maybe we could have dinner some evening."

"Fine," said Sally, "just give us a call." She bent over and took a sip of water. "You know I gave Gene the lottery test."

"The *lottery test?*"

"Yep. Even if I won the lottery tomorrow, I'd keep him."

Barbara giggled.

"That's what they say. If you'd keep 'em, even if you won the lottery, you got a good man. I'd keep Gene."

"I can't wait to meet this lottery-test winner," Barbara said as she walked off. By the time she reached her office, she had applied the same test to Todd and had decided she'd keep him, too. But, it wasn't quite the same. Todd had more money than an Amway Diamond.

Since Barbara got off at 5:00 and Todd did too, everyday that week her Corvette raced his home. The prize? Whoever got there first got to choose the CD for the stereo. When *she* won, guitars and throbbing mandolins rang through the chalet all the way out to the Blue Ridge Parkway, with Emmylou Harris or Dan Seals singing some bluegrass song at the top of her/his voice.

But Friday, Todd beat her home. When she walked in, Johnny Brahms had all his fiddlers tuned up, sawing away on one of his symphonies. Briefcase in hand, Todd waltzed toward her. She still got weak in the knees and she still held her breath when he came to her. It was honeymoon time all over again.

Later, lying in his arms, she thought how fortunate she was

to have found Todd. He could do anything, and he could talk her into anything. At the university, he'd played chess, tennis, and golf, the games of a gentleman. He was a gentle man but strong as an ox. He'd never known fear. He'd never had to. But she had. Fear was her constant companion. Todd had tried boxing for a semester; but in a Golden Gloves bout, he won the fight but got a broken nose out of the deal. He didn't sign up for a second dose. He excelled in everything he tried, but there were two areas where she was his superior: She could outrun him on wheels, and she could outrun him on foot. Todd thought it was all a game, but she knew the day was coming when the two talents might save her life.

Suddenly she jumped out of bed and began slipping into her sweats.

"What's wrong?" Todd asked.

"You made me forget. I have to get dinner. We have guests coming tonight!"

That evening the Ezells dined with the Carringtons, their first dinner guests. It was the first time Barbara had met Monty and Carol. Monty, a jock turned politician, had led the successful reelection campaign of the mayor and was now rumored to be a kingmaker in the making. He made a habit of smiling—displaying his piano teeth—whether there was anything to smile about or not. Carol Ezell said very little and her only reason for existence seemed to be to serve as his silent yes man.

When they left, Todd said, "What's your opinion of Monty?"

Barbara was putting the food away and pushing the dining chairs back into position. "As a person or as a campaign manager?"

Todd loosened his tie, then picked up an empty salad bowl and a silver bread-tray and followed her toward the kitchen. "Either."

"He certainly has the flamboyant personality of a politician."

"You're hedging."

"I think you've already made up your mind. I trust your judgment."

"No. I need your honest evaluation of him."

146

"Carol obviously likes him. I like Carol," she said, blowing out the candles, "so I suppose he's all right."

"Now that's a diplomatic answer if I ever heard one."

She didn't tell Todd, but there was something about Monty Ezell that she didn't like. It was his eyes. She didn't trust anyone whose eyes shifted back and forth while looking straight at you. That was it. Monty Ezell had shifty eyes. Maybe all politicians did. But this being Todd's first venture into the real world of politics, she didn't want to burst his balloon, so she decided to let him learn for himself if shifty eyes meant shifty dealings. It was a little lesson. Or so it seemed.

Saturday morning she and Todd washed and polished both Corvettes, then flipped a coin to see which they would drive to the football game over at Chapel Hill. They had first considered flying, but decided that even though it was a long way, they wanted to enjoy the scenic trip from ground level. Barbara flipped the coin and Todd called tails. The red car won, so he tied a Carolina-blue streamer to the driver's side mirror. They went inside and showered, got dressed in their football finery—including matching Coogi sweaters from Neiman Marcus—then started gathering up binoculars, stadium chairs, and a thermos of hot apple cider.

The phone rang and Barbara answered. It was Monty Ezell, inviting them to fly over to the game with him and Carol in the corporate jet—he and Carol were UNC alumni, and some years back, Monty had warmed a bench as a fullback for the Tar Heels.

"Sounds fun," Barbara said, "but here's Todd. Ask him." She passed the phone to Todd.

"Good plan," Todd said. "Just a minute." He turned to Barbara. "What do you think?"

"Go for it." Then she laughed. "Shouldn't we at least offer to let them ride over with us—in the tiny back seat of the Vette?"

Thirty minutes later Monty and Carol pulled into the Carrington's driveway. Monty honked the horn of his company car, a four-door Jaguar. Barbara and Todd raced out and climbed into the backseat.

147

"This whole trip's our treat," Monty said, chewing on an unlit cigar. "I'll charge it off to the agency. I've got one of those joint-lease accounts with a bigger company for the car and the plane."

In almost no time, Barbara sat buckled up in the smoke-colored Gulfstream IV as it roared down the runway at Asheville Airport. Barbara settled back in the butter-soft leather seat, feeling quite at home since the plane was similar to Todd's dad's, the only noticeable exception being that the Carrington jet was white. The Gulfstream IV was a superior business jet, seated 12-16, and cruised at speeds in excess of Mach .80 at an altitude of 45,000 feet.

An hour later, they landed at Raleigh/Durham International where Monty, using his corporate Visa gold card, leased a limo for the short drive out I-40 to Chapel Hill.

At the stadium, everybody knew Monty and he knew everybody. You would have thought the governor had come to the game. Monty was constantly bobbing up and down, shaking hands and waving to well-wishers. He was a handshaker to beat all handshakers. Barbara understood why he was in politics. Obnoxious, yes. But maybe that went with the territory.

Monty signed for their front-row seats on the corporate card—though Barbara and Todd had their own season tickets. He acted like the new rich and seemed to take great delight in flashing the gold Visa around. He even used it to pay the photographer for the photos of the four of them waving banners and cheering on the team. All afternoon he was huggy-huggy with Carol calling her "sweetums" this and "sweetums" that. Carol was less than responsive.

When Miami stopped beating-up on the Tar Heels, the two couples loaded into the limo and headed over to the Capital and had dinner at the Prestonwood Country Club. Again, Monty paid for everything. While they were at the game, the jet's tanks had been topped off, so prior to leaving the Triangle area, Monty charged that, too, to the company card.

But, to Barbara, the strangest thing of all was that Monty never mentioned Todd's campaign all afternoon. Until...

That evening, they arrived back in Asheville, then climbed

148

into Monty's Jaguar. When Monty pulled into Barbara's and Todd's driveway, he turned off the motor, rested his elbow on the seat-back, and spoke to Todd. But stared at Barbara. "I hope this afternoon's little outing has removed any concerns you might have about Carol and me." He then hugged Carol to him and smiled a mouthful-of-teeth smile.

"Most enjoyable," Todd said.

"Does that mean I'm your new campaign director?"

"Let Barb and me go inside and talk about it. I'll give you a call."

"Fair enough," said Monty. "Make it soon. We can still make the Sunday edition."

Barbara felt his shifty eyes come back to her.

"Now, Barbara, I need you in my corner," he said, hugging Carol, but it was more a jostle than a hug. "Don't we, sweetums?"

Carol smiled obediently.

Todd got out and, while he was coming around to open Barbara's door, Monty gave her a friendly wink. "We'll use this little ol' campaign as a warm-up. If you'll trust me, I'll take your man all the way to the U.S. Senate."

The Carringtons waved to the Ezells. As soon as the Jag roared out of sight, Barbara put her arm around Todd's waist and he put his around hers. They walked up the circular walkway without speaking. The lightning bugs helped the Carolina moon illuminate their path.

At the front door, Barbara didn't want to take the somber mood inside, so she thought she should lighten things up a little. "Well, I don't want to pour salt into your wounds, but you've got another problem."

"Yeah?" Todd asked as he put the key into the door and turned the lock. "What's that?"

"UT's going to whip the Tar Heels, too." She giggled and raced for the bedroom, unbuttoning her blouse as she ran.

Hot on her heels, he yelled, "Oh yeah. Wanta put a little bet on it?"

"Ten kisses." She was already turning the covers down on the bed.

149

"I'll take that bet."

After the love making, Todd was all business again. "See what I mean about Monty? Don't you think he's perfect for my campaign?"

"As I told you earlier, I trust your judgment. But I do have one concern."

"What?"

To her, Monty was as obvious as new paint. But she wanted Todd to see this for himself. "I know I shouldn't, but for some reason I felt Monty was trying to get us obligated to him."

"How?"

"By paying for everything today."

"Obligated?" Todd stroked his chin, in deep thought. "Very astute observation. I would never have thought of that little trick. But that's what he was doing, wasn't it?"

"Perhaps it's just politics."

"I think it worked," said Todd, "because now it would be a slap in the face if I didn't give him the job."

"I don't know about a slap in the face, but if that shifty-eyed—" she caught herself. "If he had called her 'sweetums' one more time, I was ready to throw up."

29

Sunday morning, a clean, blue, smoky-haze hung over Asheville, a typical sight in the Smokies.

At his mansion overlooking the city, Krandall Kaufman, dressed in a black silk robe, and winter pj's, lounged by his swimming pool, enjoying his first cigar of the day. A glass-top table with silver legs sat between him and the pool. The table was elevated a couple of inches to accommodate his wheelchair, but today he sat with his feet adjacent to the table, rather than under it. On the table sat a pitcher of orange juice, a carafe of steaming coffee, and a cellular phone.

A crystal ashtray rested on his stomach. Also on his stomach, beside the ashtray, lay a blue envelope speckled with ashes. Inside the envelope was a subpoena from the United States Senate.

The clean smell of chlorine from the pool was pleasant to his senses and, in a way, justified, at least in his own mind, the invasion of the cigar smoke into the otherwise unpolluted setting. But chlorine and nicotine could not squelch the stench of the subpoena. If he had to appear before the Senate, there was going to be a stink.

In pain, the tobacco mogul coughed and cleared his throat. The rheumatoid arthritis that had put him in the wheelchair wouldn't let him alone; his knees hurt all the time. He would soon have to have them drained again. Maybe he could wait until after he had answered the subpoena. He couldn't go up to Washington, D.C., and appear in front of those dingbats all doped up.

He puffed on his cigar. Such a small pleasure to have so many enemies. Why didn't Congress leave the tobacco industry alone and spend its time on hard drugs?

The pool gate clanked.

Shocked at the broken silence, Kaufman turned. Tumbler was sneaking across the sundeck, hiding from the sunshine from under his purple polka-dot umbrella. Tumbler always sneaked. He was wearing a white shirt and the same skinny polka-dot bow tie; Kaufman wondered if he had slept in it. "What are you doing here?" he scolded.

The mouse quickly handed the mogul the Asheville newspaper. "Look at our boy."

Kaufman stared at the front-page picture. It showed Todd sitting at his desk, smiling confidently, while Monty Ezell, displaying a head full of teeth, smiled broadly and leaned over his shoulder: TODD CARRINGTON ANNOUNCES HIS CANDIDACY FOR THE OFFICE OF "REPRESENTATIVE FOR BUNCOMBE COUNTY." MONTY EZELL, LOCAL KING-MAKER, WILL DIRECT HIS CAMPAIGN.

"Good work," said Kaufman. "And let the Carrington boy think he's doing this little piddling campaign on his own. Be sure Ezell keeps good receipts."

"Like these?" Tumbler tossed a large brown envelope on the glass table. Kaufman leaned over but didn't touch the envelope. Tumbler opened it and dumped the pictures and credit card receipts onto the table.

Careful to leave nothing but his thoughts imprinted, Kaufman poked at the evidence with the wet end of his cigar: receipts for four University of North Carolina football tickets, two photos of the Carrington and Ezell couples, one tank of jet fuel, rent of corporate jet and corporate car, and a two-hundred-dollar dinner at the Prestonwood Country Club. The imprint on all receipts said, "Carolina Tobacco Institute."

Kaufman winked at Tumbler. "Scrape them back into the envelope and lock them in the vault on the second floor at the lab."

"Yes, sir."

"Then the day our boy decides to run for the U.S. Senate, he'll already be compromised. We'll have our accountant inform him that we're his partners and have been all along."

"That's an awfully slow process." Tumbler held his umbrella with one hand, and with the other trimmed at his mustache with his pocketknife, testing the blade's sharpness.

"*The years tell us much the days never know*," Kaufman said, quoting Emerson.

Tumbler hunched his already hunched shoulders and stared blankly.

"You forget. We had trouble getting his daddy, old Charlie Carrington, into our camp. But look how many times his powerful voice rescued our industry during those Senate battles."

"That reminds me. There's also an article on page two about the hearings." Tumbler picked up the newspaper from the table, folded it open to page A-2, and handed it back to Kaufman.

Kaufman glanced at the article and coughed. "The tobacco business is in trouble on Capitol Hill. We can't permit Todd Carrington to replace his daddy's voice up there unless his support is locked in."

"These receipts of Monty Ezell's, showing that the tobacco industry financed his first campaign, ought to do that."

"No. The receipts will do little more than *soften* our senator-to-be. For sure it'll make him mad. Since he's a principled young man, he might even come out swinging. Our goal is to get him in our corner and keep him there."

"I thought we were going to do the same thing we did to his daddy," Tumbler said, "find something on his young bride."

"That was my first thought...before we knew this girl. Now I'm not so sure that'll work."

"I believe it will," said Tumbler. "Remember, it was Charlie Carrington's wife who inherited all those tobacco farms at New Bern and Tarboro. And when I found out—"

"It's got to have a different twist," Kaufman said, interrupting him.

"Why?"

"We have a different problem with the boy's wife than we had with the senator's."

"How so?" asked Tumbler.

"The two women are vastly different. The senator's wife is a genteel woman. Operates by the rules of *genteel* society. She'd never think of causing a stink."

"Barbara Dare-Carrington *now* lives in a genteel world."

"But she is not *genteel*. She's a mountain woman thrown into a special set of social circumstances. We can't push her, and we sure can't control her."

153

"So we're back to square one.   How do we make Todd Carrington kneel...and stay knelt?"

"Fortunately, we have a little more time, now that the senator has said he'll finish out his term."   Then, in deep thought, Kaufman leaned back in the wheelchair. "It's becoming clear to me," he said stroking his chin with his thumb and index finger. "It's not Todd Carrington we need to make kneel—"

"Oh?"

"It's his wife!"

"I don't get it?"

"Don't you see? Suppose we force the boy into our corner. As soon as we turn our backs, he runs home and tells his mountain mamma."

"Kablooy! She blows sky high."

"I don't think she'd blow up," said Kaufman, "but she certainly wouldn't let him sacrifice his career for some indiscretion she might have committed."

"If not an indiscretion, what?"

"I don't know. But it's got to be more than a school girl prank, or an act of passion, or...We've got to find her fault-line."

"What if she's clean?"

"I'm thinking!" Kaufman scolded. "I'm thinking!"

Tumbler took a step back toward the pool.

"Let's say she's clean," Kaufman mused.

"Nobody's really clean."

"*Clean* is relative. Suppose she cheated on a test. We can only make so much out of *cheating on a test.* But maybe...that's it."

"What?"

"If you can't find any *real* dirt on her, find out who or what she cares about more than life itself."

Tumbler started pacing excitedly. "And when we find 'who' or 'what,' we offer her the option of kneeling or having her 'who' or 'what' removed."

"You got it."

"She's close to her grandmother. Maybe the old woman's the key."

"Perhaps. Perhaps not."

154

"How hard can I push the bride?"

"Until she kneels."

"And if she won't kneel?"

"Then I don't want her standing. We can't let that pretty little hillbilly wreck the tobacco industry's thirty year investment in the Senate."

"I think Cades Cove holds the secret."

"Then why are you standing around here?"

30

Barbara awoke Sunday morning concerned about speed. As for herself, she was as fast as she was ever going to be. She just needed to stay in shape. But her Camaro was another matter. The car was fast, but it had to be faster. Much faster. Before the day was out, she had to put the wheels in motion to get the job done. But she had to do it without arousing suspicion from Todd, or anyone else for that matter.

Before breakfast, and while Todd was getting his Nikes on, she strapped to her palm the orange band of her yellow Walkman, draped the earphones around her neck—she was already wearing her mud beads—and stuffed her drivers license and Visa card into the pocket of her white shorts. Because she often ran so far, she carried the documents for identification in case of an emergency. Then she and Todd went jogging back into the mountains. He took the three-mile loop and she the seven.

As they parted, she waved bye, then positioned the Walkman ear-phones on her head—she cherished their time together so much she would never block out his voice when he ran beside her. Even without him, though, she always took care to leave one ear uncovered, listening for danger.

Near the end of her run, she broke out of the mountains and headed for downtown Asheville. She jogged through the main square, past Governor Zebulon Vance's statue. She paused at the Radisson Hotel Giftshop, across the street from the Thomas Wolfe Home, long enough to charge to her platinum Visa card with no credit limit a copy of Thomas Wolfe's novel, *Look Homeward Angel.* Then she trotted home, anticipating an afternoon of solitude in the hammock while Mr. Wolfe told her his tale. When she got home, she found Todd couched-out in front of the TV reading the *Wall Street Journal*, watching cartoons, and sipping a saucered cup of black coffee. She liked cream in hers and usually drank from a mug—no saucer.

She and Todd were both voracious readers, but their tastes in the printed word differed widely. He liked newspapers and she liked novels. Everyday he reviewed four national papers, especially happenings in D.C. Right now he was keeping up with the two big political fights on Capitol Hill: balancing the budget and whether or not to regulate nicotine. His father was caught in the middle of both squabbles, fighting as hard *for* the President's budget as he did *against* regulating nicotine.

Now famished, Barbara and Todd ate breakfast in the backyard gazebo: orange juice, bananas, and low fat granola. He was as conscious of nutrition as she. Then they showered and went to the late service at Redeemer Pres. After church, they dined at the country club as guests of the mayor, the bank president, and their wives.

The mayor arrived late. As he hurried to join his guests in the smorgasbord line, he said, "If my Baptist preacher doesn't shorten his sermons, I'm joining you Presbyterians."

Barbara laughed along with the others. At the luncheon, it seemed to her that everybody got what they wanted from the meeting. The city fathers wanted the influence of Todd's name in attracting new industry and he wanted their support in his campaign.

It was a warm sunny day, so that afternoon, while Todd watched the Cowboys whip the Eagles, Barbara took *Look Homeward Angel* out back and lay in the hammock. The hammock was tied to an oak tree on either side of the tiny stream that ran through their back yard. As the hammock swung back and forth, she tried to read the Thomas Wolfe classic about characters who lived in an Asheville boarding house. A horsefly landed on the calf of her leg. She swatted it away. It came back. Then a leaf—a bright golden leaf—fell in her coffee. And then another. Between the horsefly and the leaves, she gave up and went inside. Her mind wasn't on the novel anyway. Her mind was still on her Camaro and its speed. Or lack of it. So she came up with a plan.

At halftime, she got Todd's attention away from the football game long enough to run part of her plan by him—the trigger mechanism part. Todd agreed. So she called Sally and Gene Chastine and made the same proposal to them, "After the game, let's run down to Shoney's for a sandwich. I have something I want to run by Gene."

Gene, himself a black belt heavyweight, was watching a kick-boxing match on TV. But they agreed. They would meet her and Todd at Shoney's. After the game/match of course. And before the NFL's night game kickoff at 8:00.

At Shoney's, Todd and Gene hit it off. As soon as they shook hands and were seated in the back booth, Todd said, "Barbara tells me you're into karate."

"You bet," Gene said. "And Sally tells me you're into politics." He leaned back, comfortably, in the booth. That's when Barbara noticed that he wore on his left thumb a metal clamp with a screw through it, like a ring—a smaller version of a radiator clamp. Almost in the same breath, Gene added, humorously, "My first wife ran off with a politician, the dogcatcher."

Todd chuckled, but before he could speak, the waitress, an elderly lady wearing a hairnet and with *Betty* on her name tag, walked up carrying four glasses of water on a brown tray. She propped the tray on her hip and tossed four giant menus on the table. "Hello, Barbara."

"Hello, Ms. Goodner."

"See you brought your man back." Her coarse, alto voice sounded almost as low as a man's.

"He likes your cooking," Barbara said, then gestured her hand toward the other side of the booth. "These are our friends Sally and Gene."

"I know that one," Betty said, pointing at Gene. "We've banned him from our food bar. Eats too much." She winked at Sally.

"You got that right." Gene patted his washboard stomach—not an ounce of fat on him—as everyone laughed. Gene weighed 185 pounds—not that big as "big" goes, but Rocky Marciano didn't weigh but 182 when he was Heavyweight Boxing Champion of the World. Marciano was never defeated.

"Y'all havin' the bar," Sally said, "or you want it *a la carte*?"

Todd looked at Barbara, as if asking her to decide.

Barbara glanced at Gene and Sally, and, seeing no objection, said, "We want to visit. We'll order from the menu."

"It's yore money," the waitress said, mothering Barbara, "but the bar's cheaper."

"I'll have a Reuben and a Diet Coke," Barbara said.

Todd and Sally ordered cheeseburgers—no onions—and fries and Cokes. Gene ordered chicken-fried steak smothered in onions and gravy and a large glass of buttermilk.

The waitress wrote it on her pad, but as she left, repeated, "Bar's cheaper."

As soon as she was gone, Todd, accustomed to servants speaking when spoken to, said, matter-of-factly, "Rather talkative, wasn't she?"

Barbara gave him a love poke in the ribs. "She's just being neighborly."

"By the bye," Todd said, taking a sip of water. "Where were we? We were talking about—"

"Karate and politics," Barbara said. "You and Gene were talking karate and politics.

Todd turned to Gene. "What first aroused your interest in karate?"

"I couldn't whup nobody. What got you into politics?"

"I shall not let you off so easy," Todd said with a chuckle. "We can't both tell at once. Please go first."

Gene smiled, leaned back, and crossed his legs. "You won't believe it, but when I started to school—what schoolin' I took—I was little. The big kids used to beat up on me. I couldn't whup nobody. I swore if I ever found anybody I could whup, I'd go get him outta bed and whup him."

Everybody laughed.

"Now what got you jazzed on politics?" Gene asked.

"I couldn't whup nobody either," Todd said in his cultured, rich Carolina drawl, laughing as he spoke.

"You used to be a fighter?" Sally asked, cajoling Todd.

"Not really, but at the university I tried my hand in the Golden Gloves. The first chap I fought broke my nose. That was the end of my boxing career."

"And that's what throw'd you into politics?" Gene asked.

They stopped talking when Betty arrived with the food and drinks. When she left, Barbara picked up her sandwich and looked at Todd to see how he might reply to Gene's question.

"I suppose so," Todd said, squeezing mustard on his cheeseburger.

Gene, in the process of drowning his chicken-fried steak in black pepper, slapped his thigh. "And you thank nobody won't take a punch at you in politics?"

Todd laughed. But Barbara didn't. Gene might be uneducated, but he was smart, and most of all he was a man's man; she could tell that Todd liked him. So she relaxed and munched on her Reuben sandwich, all the while looking for an opportunity to bring up the matter of her Camaro.

She had just taken the last bite when Sally asked her, "You always hold your keys while you eat?"

Barbara blinked. "Habit."

True. But it wasn't just habit. As long as she had known how to drive, when out of her car, Barbara had clutched the keys, eating or not. And when she went into any building, she always took note of the exits. And she always sat with her back to a wall, ever ready for a fast getaway. Now self-conscious from Sally's question, she flopped her hands into her lap, causing the keys to jingle. But she didn't turn loose of them.

Sally winked at her. "What's this big deal you want to talk to my man about?"

About that time three men, construction-worker types, walked in. They were dressed in white jump suits with clean dirt on them. "Acme Brick" was written across the vests. The largest of the three large men was arguing loudly into his cell phone as the three were being ushered to a booth. "It ain't my fault," he was saying. "Yes, you will pay!"

Betty seated them in the booth next to Barbara's booth. The boisterously-talking man's back was now almost touching Gene's back. The man hung up and immediately redialed. From his tone, Barbara surmised it was his secretary who really caught heck. He began blaming her for some mix-up. He cursed her out, soundly. And loudly.

Betty came back and tried to make a joke to calm him, but the man was way past being calmed, so he cursed her out, too.

Gene turned to the man and put his finger to his pursed lips as if to say, "Sh," but didn't. Instead, he whispered, as diplomatically as possible under the circumstances, "Hey bud, ladies present."

Red-faced, the considerably larger man, turned and stared at Gene as though he had poured hot coffee down his shorts.

Gene, one karate-developed muscle, smiled at him and went back to eating his chicken-fried steak.

Todd mouthed the word, "Thanks," to Gene.

Mr. Loud-Curser sat there heaving and snorting and still talking abusively, but now under his breath, to his two buddies. But he didn't make any more loud phone calls.

Barbara gave Gene an appreciative wink, and then took up where Sally had left off. Barbara wasn't going to let any bricklayer derail her purpose in getting the four of them together. "Gene, do you think I could bring my Camaro by and let you take a look at it?"

"You bet. What's wrong with it?" he asked between bites.

"It won't outrun my Vette."

"Humor her, Gene," Todd said with a laugh. "I don't understand either."

"Okay. Me and Sally'll follow you home, and I'll just take it on out to the garage right now. How's that sound?"

"Great." Mission accomplished.

Todd paid the bill, and the four walked out to the parking lot. Barbara and Todd climbed into the low swung red Vette, and Gene, still saying goodbye, pushed Todd's door closed for him, saying, "See you at your house."

Just then Barbara saw the loud-curser and his two buddies come storming across the parking lot in a lope.

It all happened in a flash. The three of them surrounded Gene.

Mr. Loud-Curser got right in his face. "*Now* tell me to be quiet, big boy."

Todd was coming out of the Vette.

162

Sally had already climbed up into their green wrecker, and was looking out the rear window, over the boom and tow-cable pulley, like she knew what was coming.

"Let it lay, bud," Gene said, and turned and started walking toward the wrecker.

And that's when Mr. Loud-Curser made his big mistake. "Why you black—" He grabbed Gene by the shoulder and tried to jerk him around.

Gene spun and cold-cocked him with a roundhouse back-fist to the neck.

Mr. Loud-Curser hit the asphalt like a yard dart. His two buddies picked him up and wobble-walked him toward a white pickup with "Acme Brick Co." printed in red letters on the door.

A crowd started pouring out of the restaurant, coming to the fight.

Gene shoved Todd into the Vette. "Get outta here before somebody calls the cops. The media would love this show."

31

Later that evening, and still shaky from the scuffle in the parking lot, Barbara made a determined effort to think about something else. That brought her thoughts back to the Camaro. Other than the incident with the three men from Acme Brick, her plan had worked. Gene and Sally had taken the Camaro home with them, and a nice little serendipity had come her way: Todd and Gene were becoming good friends. Wonder how long it takes to soup-up a car? she thought.

But now she faced a new problem. A fast car would do her no good if the men who were coming for her slipped up on her. Grandmother Dare might have seen or heard something. She had to get Todd out of the house so she could call her.

Barbara looked at the kitchen clock and saw that it was fifteen minutes before the NFL night game. One football game a Sunday was plenty for *her*, but Todd was all set to watch it. Fifteen minutes would be all she needed.

She grabbed at the first straw. "Would you run to the store for some potato chips?"

"*Potato chips*?!" Todd blurted. "The game's com—"

"Not for fifteen...fourteen minutes." She was pushing him toward the door. It was for his own good. "We're completely out. Get Lays."

Once his taillights made the curve, she went back to the kitchen and dialed Cades Cove. After she told her grandmother how happy she was with Todd, she told her that he was running for a state office, Representative to the General Assembly.

"Can't you talk him out of it?" Grandmother Dare asked.

"Asking my sweetheart not to run for office would be like your asking the butterflies to stay out of your valley of wildflowers. Now that his dream has taken command, it's as though he was born to politics."

"You know they'll come after him."

"Anyone been coming around?" Standing barefooted in the kitchen, Barbara pulled a stool to her with her toes.

The wooden stool used to belong to Tamika. Tamika had

bought it at a garage sale in Atlanta and painted it her high school colors. When she came to UT, she painted it UT colors: the seat and rungs orange and the legs white. After the funeral, Barbara helped Aunt Maudie pack up Tamika's things, and asked if she could have the stool as a keepsake.

Grandmother Dare now answered Barbara's question, "Nobody but those fool Slocum boys. Every time they get drunk."

Barbara propped a knee on the stool. "They still race their logging trucks through the Cove?"

"Like the trucks could make someone talk."

"Grandmother, those boys have done that as long as I can remember. They aren't smart enough to come in out of the—"

"No, but their daddy is. Too much inbreeding. He shouldn't have married his cousin."

Barbara pulled back the yellow curtains and peeped out the window, watching for Todd. She saw headlights coming down the Parkway. "Besides the Slocum boys, has anyone else been snooping around?" The headlights went on by.

"Yes," Grandmother Dare whispered into the phone.

Barbara gasped, then whispered back, "When?"

"He first came while you were on your honeymoon—"

"On my *honeymoon*. Why didn't you tell me!?" She gave the stool a kick, shoving it back toward the sink.

"Didn't I tell you?"

"No, Grandmother."

"Guess I forgot."

"Has he been back?"

"Back this afternoon."

"Mountain man or newsman?"

"*Newsman* I reckon. Says he's with the Tennessee Historical Society. But he's not."

"What makes you so sure?"

"He didn't go out and look at the old water wheel and mill, the grinding shed, or the barn or anything. He didn't even have a camera."

"What kind of car?"

"Child, I don't know. It's white and big."

166

"Tennessee tags?"

"North Carolina."

Uh, oh. "Was he by himself?"

"There was a driver with him, but he stayed in the car. One of them rode in the front seat and one of them rode in the backseat."

"The one who talked to you, what did he ask?"

"About your parents."

"What else?"

"He's talked to everybody in the Cove. And you're the only one he's asked about. I just hope he never comes around while those Slocum boys, with their log-chain-rattling, fenderless trucks, are cutting their 'figure-eights,' slinging mud a mile high in our valley of wildflowers."

"What could the *Slocum boys* tell him?"

"They could tell him plenty if they ever figure out who you are—"

Grandmother Dare was becoming overexcited and anyway Barbara knew enough not to pursue that subject. "What's the stranger look like?"

"He's a small, mousy kind of man."

"That could be anybody, Grandmother."

"He carried a purple umbrella."

"*Umbrella*?"

"Polka-dot. Like he was hiding from the sun."

Umbrella. A man carrying a polka-dot umbrella. That was something to go on. But Barbara didn't want to further alarm her grandmother, so she said, "Let's talk about something else." She pulled the stool back over and sat down on it, trying to relax. "Todd and I are thinking about coming to see you Christmas."

"Could we go over to Gatlinburg and see the lights?" Grandmother Dare asked, cheerfully.

"That's a promise. We might even take in Pigeon Forge, too. Todd hasn't seen *any* of the Christmas lights. Maybe it'll be snowing."

"I'll uncork a jug of cider and bake you a pecan pie."

"Good. And let's have some of the neighbors over so Todd can meet them."

"I'll try, but child, you know how mountain folks are about new people. They have to watch them a while."

Barbara laughed. "Well, invite them anyway and they can sit and stare at him a while."

When she hung up, she sat there perched on Tamika's stool, both feet propped on the rungs. She racked her brain trying to think if she had seen a small, mousy-looking man with a purple polka-dot umbrella and a large white car with a chauffeur. No one came to mind. She understood about Grandmother Dare forgetting to tell her that the man had been there before; her memory wasn't what it used to be. But if the mouseman knew with whom he was messing, he'd stay out of the Smoky Mountains. Before Mr. Mouseman knew what had happened, it would be too late for him. But it would also be too late for Todd Carrington.

The tears started coming at her hard. But what could she do? There was *one* thing she could do. And she decided right then and there to do it. Tomorrow she would call Gene Chastine at Asheville Speedway and ask him to hurry with the Camaro. She had to be sure she could outrun the mouseman in his chauffeur-driven big white car with North Carolina tags.

When Todd got back with the potato chips, he asked why her eyes were red. Had she been crying? She told him she had just talked to Grandmother Dare and was sad about her living alone up there in the mountains. "She said she'd break out a jug of cider if we'd come to see her Christmas."

"Then that's where we're going. Maybe we can celebrate New Year's in New Bern with Mother and Father."

"That's a deal," Barbara said.

"Mother might break out a six-pack of Brad's Drink." He laid the potato chips on the coffee table, then sat down on the couch and started looking for the TV remote control.

"*Brad's Drink?*"

Todd laughed. "Brad's Drink was invented by a druggist in New Bern. Only now we call it Pepsi Cola." He was feeling around under the couch cushions. "You seen the remote?"

"It was on the couch a moment ago."

"Oops. Here it is. Sitting on it." He clicked on the TV.

Barbara was standing directly in front of him. He was leaned back, peeping around her at the TV. She didn't move. She had to start preparing him for what was coming. "Todd, do you love me?"

"*Love you*?!"

"Do you love me?"

"Sweetheart, I'm sorry I acted that way." Still sitting, he waved his arms in surrender, then picked up the potato chips and rattled the bag. "Honest, I didn't mind going to the store."

"I'm not talking about potato chips!" She grabbed the bag of Lays and tossed them on the carpet.

All big-eyed, Todd leaped to his feet.

Now she was flustered. That wasn't the emotion she meant to show. She turned her back to him...to give herself time to regroup. When she turned back she asked again, "*Do you love me*?"

"With all my heart." He took her in his arms.

"If someday I did something that embarrassed you," Barbara said, looking up into his eyes, "or say, if somebody told you something real bad about me, would you still love me?"

"I'll love you forever. I wouldn't be anything without you. What's this all about, love?"

She stayed in his arms. And shook. Then she said, "Could we go out and sit on the front porch?"

On the big-screen TV, Hank Williams, Jr. was singing, "Are ya ready for some football?" and the Denver Broncos were running onto the green field at Mile High Stadium. Todd clicked off the TV.

He took her hand and led her into the cool night air. She sat there on the steps in the moonlight, arms locked around her lover's waist, head resting on his shoulder. The lightning bugs competed with the stars for their attention, the whippoorwills and bullfrogs set the mood, and the sweet smells of autumn drifted on the breeze.

Barbara looked into the stars, but spoke to his eyes. "Remember that night on the verandah at your parent's home, the night your dad announced our engagement?"

169

"Happiest night of my life," Todd said. "How could I forget?"

"That night you told me your dream of a better world...of how *you* see the world." She swallowed back the tears. "Would you tell it to me just one more time?"

Todd stood—he couldn't sit when he talked about his dream—and looked into the sky full of stars. Before saying a word, he strolled back and forth on the damp grass, collecting his thoughts. Then, in his deep rich voice, all full of ethos, he began his "I SEE A WORLD" speech: "I see a world where children can...I see a world where mothers can...I see a world where plumbers and carpenters and farmers can—" Suddenly he stopped and asked most sincerely, "Do I sound like I'm on a soapbox?"

Standing there, handsome as a movie star, again he was vulnerable to her.

"No sweetheart. You sound like a man possessed." He did sound a little soapboxish, but she was so proud of him, she didn't care. And she didn't deny that he was naive about certain things. But the naiveté was part of his boyish charm. His sincerity was so devastatingly disarming. The United States of America was about to meet a politician the likes of which it had never known: a man who had everything and who truly wanted the best for his country, expecting nothing in return. America had better watch out. Before long there might be a new man on the nickel.

Todd winked at her and kept going, "I see a world where a tired old veteran can wave the flag without being..."

The more *he* dreamed, the more *she* trembled. The darkest part of the night was coming.

32

Monday morning in Cell Block 13, Buzzard Mackelroy watched the big hand on the clock on the wall. Two minutes till nine. At nine o'clock, Axe would bring the results of his weeks of research on SIG Labs. Buzzard had instructed him to boil his findings down to one word.

Buzzard's chin wound had almost healed from the mail bomb, but a nasty scar would probably linger. He now wore a bandage just below his left elbow where a prisoner had knifed him during a dinner attack two days ago. Axe had removed the knife from the prisoner, breaking both of the man's wrists in the process. The man had not been seen since. Some said Axe flushed him down the toilet.

While Buzzard waited for Cliff and Axe to arrive, he did his lesson. Today's lesson was on *touching* and *hearing*. He ran the elastic band on his goggle glasses between his thumb and forefinger, *feeling*, forcing his mind to remember what things on the outside *felt* like: a feather, a leaf, a raspberry. And then he forced himself to remember certain *sounds*: a baby's cry, a dog's bark, or a carpenter's hammer. This was his daily ritual. Every day he forced new memories on each of his five senses. They had only imprisoned his body, not his mind.

At exactly 9:00 on the dot—no one was ever late with a report to Buzzard Mackelroy—Axe burst through the community room door and hurried to the card table. "Regulation."

"*Regulation?*" Buzzard whispered.

"Regulation."

"Regulation is the word they fear most?"

"Yes, sir."

"Of what?"

"Nicotine."

"What about Asheville's City Manager?"

"He's clean."

"And the mayor?"

"Clean, too."

"Who owns SIG Labs?"

"Tobacco cartel."

"Who heads the cartel?"

"Krandall Kaufman."

"Who's his henchman?"

"Tumbler."

"What's their weapon of choice?"

"Kaufman wears a coat-sleeve derringer. Tumbler carries a pocketknife."

"Who wants to regulate nicotine?"

"The FDA."

"Why?"

"They say tobacco companies are spiking cigarettes, purposely making addicts of consumers, and thus the nation."

"Where's the battle taking place?"

"Congress. Senate hearing."

"Who's leading the fight to keep them from regulating nicotine?"

"Senator Charlie Carrington."

"What's his interest?"

"I suppose same as the tobacco cartel. Money."

"No. That senator has money. Must be something else. Bring me all the videos and newspaper clippings of the Senate hearing."

Cliff had now arrived. He moved to the table. He picked up Buzzard's goggle-glasses from the table and started cleaning them on his shirt-tail. He was holding an Asheville newspaper in his armpit. When Axe stepped to the side, that was Cliff's signal to move forward, which he did, and in the same process handed the glasses and newspaper to Buzzard.

Buzzard slipped the elastic band over his head and adjusted the goggles. He then buried himself in the article about Todd Carrington's running as Asheville's Representative to the State General Assembly. When he finished he looked at Clifford. "Who's Monty Ezell?"

"Political pimp."

"Is he clean?"

"We didn't check *him*."

Buzzard raised an eyebrow as if to ask, "Why?"

"We'll take care of it. What about the senator?"

"Watch him."

"And his boy?"

"Anybody lays a hand on him, I'll cut his heart out and scatter it across Vulture Mountain."

That night Barbara couldn't sleep. She was beside herself over how to warn Todd of impending danger, so he wouldn't get blindsided. She couldn't tell him when the trouble was coming or who would be bringing it. She didn't even know. But it was coming.

She began to reason. If she told Todd now, it would be the end of everything. At least if she didn't tell him, he would have what politicians call "plausible deniability." He could say he never knew. And if she were still alive after it all came down, she could support his denial. But if they let her live, Todd wouldn't want her anymore for she wouldn't be the same person she was now. And at the very least his political career would be over. She finally slept, but the clear crisp mountain morning brought no relief to her anxiety.

So, most every evening that week, after dinner, she lay in the hammock beside Todd and listened as he gave wings to his campaign dream, ever watchful for a way to subtly warn him.

If America ever had a patriot, it was Todd Carrington. But he naively believed that everyone wanted the best for the country, and she wouldn't be the one to tell him different. Monty Ezell had offered a room in the back of his insurance company for Todd's campaign headquarters. Buttons, banners, and posters were being printed, and he and Todd were yellow-marking a map, plotting the route the campaign would take across their district. Monty took a billiard game approach to politics. He said that one office positions you for the next office, just as a cue ball positions the next shot. So he not only wanted Todd to cover the district, but also the entire state, meeting big wigs, power brokers, and fund-raisers. Monty also made arrangements with the city manager's office for a leave of absence for Todd until after the election.

Barbara knew the day was at hand when Todd would no longer be hers alone. She would soon lose a large portion of his time to a nobler cause. And she knew she couldn't hide forever in his arms in the hammock under star-filled skies out on Blue Ridge Parkway. So she held him closer and relished every second of the lull before the mounting storm. Todd wanted them to start their family right away, but there would be no children born to this marriage. She'd never bring a child into the Hell that raved in her heart. So she very carefully monitored the birth control pills, and told Todd, "Let's wait."

Finally, a plan began to form in her head on how she could warn him. She and Todd both had birthdays coming up and they had agreed to give each other *personal* gifts, but gifts that would enhance their home. She had just the gift in mind. She would never part with the item, but since it was to be kept in their home, it might work.

Having been raised in a senator's home, Todd was wise beyond his years in politics and was afraid of nothing, sometimes foolishly so. But life had made her an expert on fear. Maybe she could impart her expertise, vicariously, and at the same time begin to explain her deadly secret to him. She knew a book that paralleled so much of her own family's story. Different playing field. Similar circumstances. Same results. After Todd had read the story, she would walk him through the bloody minefield step by step.

And so, Friday afternoon, as was her daily custom, she brought the thin little book home from the office. While Todd played a round of golf with Monty Ezell, she reread the brave little story. When she finished, she wrapped the well-worn book with the finest purple paper in all Asheville and tied it with the manliest ribbon she could find, careful that no tears fell on it.

That evening, for his birthday, she gave Todd, *The Song of Roland*, the copy that Grandmother Dare had read to her and Mr. Scarecrow when Barbara was little. Todd had many of the noble qualities of Roland, the book's hero, and in many ways, he and Roland shared the same innocent, but deadly dream: There were those standing at the ready, and help only needed to be summoned. But there was one major difference in Roland and

Todd. Todd's nobility and dream had never been tested in the fire. Roland's had. And still it cost him his life.

Barbara's and Todd's birthdays were one day apart, though he was three years older. Saturday afternoon he asked her to play tennis at the country club to celebrate her birthday. She quickly slipped into her white tennis skirt and blouse; she was already wearing her mud beads.

The string that held the earth-colored beads was made of straw. It had been tied back together in several places. A Cherokee Chief, a friend of Grandmother Dare, had made the necklace for Barbara. Once, when Todd had quizzed her about the well-worn necklace, she told him that the frayed straw was her rebellion against her own desire for order.

Now, as she walked into the living room, carrying her tennis racket, Todd was waiting with her birthday gift, his gift for their home.

"A Renoir!" she exclaimed.

He then helped her hang the painting above a table beside the sofa.

"I finished *The Song of Roland* today," he said.

Good. Now let's see if the lesson took. "Did you know it's the most famous of the French *chansons de geste*?"

"War songs?"

"*Touché.*"

"That's about all I remember from French 201." Then he asked, skeptically, "Your grandmother read that book to you as a child?"

"Yes, she did." Barbara's eye for texture, shape, and order wasn't quite pleased with the effect of the Renoir, so she searched the room for an object that would provide the perfect balance and complete the total focus. Beside the front door, on a tall marble-top table, sat a ginger jar from the same Impressionist period. She picked up the fragile treasure and held it as they talked.

"Pretty gruesome tale," Todd said.

"Aren't most fairytales?"

"I suppose."

175

"No worse than *Jack And The Bean Stalk.* Or *Hansel and Gretel.*"

"You must have forgotten what Roland's uncle did to the villain who killed Roland."

"No. No. I didn't forget. But that's not the point."

"What point?"

"Roland made the mistake of thinking that everyone wanted for his country what he wanted."

"What's wrong with that?"

"Nothing. Except when Roland called for help, no help came." Barbara was still holding the ginger jar, but she was thinking of an unopened jar of peanut butter. And she was still plotting.

"But do you remember what Roland's uncle did to the villain?" Todd asked.

"He rounded up the four 'finest steeds in the land,' tied one to each hand and one to each foot, then said, 'Giddy up.'"

"He quartered him!" Todd said.

"Roland's uncle was no one to mess around with."

"I should say not."

"I know parents who would do the same under similar circumstances," Barbara said.

"I don't. No matter what anyone ever did to me, my father would never do anything like that."

"Mine would."

"But you have no father."

Barbara walked back and forth in front of the Renoir. Yes, that spot would be perfect. She sat the fragile ginger jar on the table under the painting, then turned her eyes on Todd. "Then I would."

"*You* would?" He laughed. "You mean, if somebody did to me what Ganelon did to Roland, you'd get four horses and—"

"Hey, this is getting way too serious," Barbara said, laughing. She'd almost said too much. "I thought we were going to play tennis."

"We are. With Monty and Carol. Let me grab my racket."

Monty and Carol? Barbara tried to hide her disappointment. She thought she was going to have Todd to herself. Monty and

Carol. Monty and Carol. She could just hear Monty, as soon as the tennis match was over, "Why don't Carol and I take you out for a little candlelight dinner? Celebrate Barbara's birthday in style." Barbara liked Carol, but she'd had just about enough of Monty Ezell's horning in.

As Todd drove toward the club, Barbara noticed the bronze tan of his big hands wrapped around the red Corvette's black leather steering wheel. Todd had a cannon in either fist, yet to her knowledge, neither had ever been exploded in anger.

He glanced over at her. "Back at the house, I thought for a minute you were serious about getting four horses and tying one to each arm—"

"I might have been." She laughed. "Only, I'd use four stockcars." Mission accomplished. That would be enough for now.

On Monday, Todd and Monty hit the trail in Monty's Jaguar; Todd left the red Vette at campaign headquarters. It was the first time Barbara had been separated from him since their wedding. Soon she was as lonely as a coach's wife.

She tried filling the hours by lying in the hammock, reading books, and eating Moon Pies. The first story she read was Hemingway's *Snows of Kilimanjaro*. When she finished she said, "Thank you," not because the little twenty-nine page short story was brilliant—although it was—but because, after having heard so much about Hemingway, and it being her first piece of his to read, she felt she had just met him and that he had personally told her the story. Besides, there was no one else in the house to thank.

Before long, reading wasn't enough and the loneliness bore down on her. She went through the house lighting the scented candles, then blowing them out. She put fresh linens on the bed. Fifteen minutes later she couldn't remember if she had or not, so she put fresh linens on the bed again. Then she paced the halls. She walked the floor all through the long night hours. The next night walking the floor wasn't enough. She began to despise politics, but because she believed in Todd, she was forced to believe in his dream.

Friday morning of that week, in the kitchen, she pressed the lever on the water-purifier and filled two Evian water bottles, her way of recording when she'd consumed her day's quota. It was a ritual she and Todd did every morning, but Todd wasn't there, so she filled the bottles alone. Then she went jogging. It was a ritual she and Todd did every morning, but Todd wasn't there, so she jogged alone. When she returned, she showered. It was a ritual. But Todd wasn't there, so she showered alone.

So lonesome she could die, she dressed for work and was heading out the door when the phone rang. It was Sally. "Gene's on the extension. Your Camaro's ready."

"Hello, Gene."

"Got yo' hotrod ready."

"Will it outrun my Vette?"

"It'll outrun anything in these parts. Just turn the key and stomp the gas. Want me to bring it to yo' house or the office?"

"Bring it here to the house, Gene. I'll—"

"Do it on my lunch break."

"I'll try it out after work this afternoon."

"Give you whiplash if you goose it. Oh, and I put bigger tires on it."

"*Bigger tires?*"

"Racin' tires. Had to. Street tires unravel at 120."

"Thanks, Gene. Just leave the keys under the mat. I owe you one. Send me a bill."

"How 'bout if you and Todd just take me 'n Sally coon huntin' over at Cades Cove?"

"Deal. We might even stop at Ol' Rocky Top and go clogging."

"How 'bout Maggie Valley? Cloggin' Capital 'a the World."

"You call it."

"Whew doggies! Hey, I thought yo' man wuz a waltzer."

"He is," Barbara said, chuckling, "but he needs to learn to clog."

"Make it on a Saturday night. Black man lives for Saturday night."

Barbara laughed and said goodbye, but the rest of the day, as she went about her work at the office, her mind was on the Camaro and the monthly rendezvous. Sunday she would make the secret trip, the perfect time to try out Gene's work. And with Todd out of town, she wouldn't have to make up an excuse to slip off. Just after closing, she tore out of the parking lot at SIG Labs, the black Corvette slinging gravel into a rooster-tail. When she pulled off the Parkway, she saw her old silver-gray Camaro sitting in the driveway just as Gene had promised.

But the red Corvette was there also. Todd was home! She dashed across the yard.

Then it hit her. Something was wrong. No Johannes Brahms coming from the CD player. The house was quiet as a tomb. She slowly opened the front door and tiptoed inside. Todd stood in the middle of the living room, holding her granny wig in one hand and her walking cane in the other. Oh, Lord. He found out!

"What's this?" He held out the evidence.

Struck dumb, she blurted, "Where'd you get them?!"

"Gene found them in your old car."

"Oh." She stalled, trying to let her mind clear. "Let's go try it out. See if it's as fast as he says."

Todd didn't budge.

She avoided his eyes.

"Barbara, what's the meaning of this?"

"It's nothing." She had to think fast. "Since you're going to be on the road so much, I was thinking of joining Asheville's Little Theater."

"Oh." Todd put the wig on, then poking the cane into the carpet, limped around the room, a campaign button on his suit lapel. "Maybe they'd audition me, too."

He bought it. She had narrowly escaped. Weak from the emotional swing, she flopped onto the couch and pretended to be entertained by his antics.

When he finished the tap-dance clowning, he came to her. "How about a welcome home kiss?"

179

But self-preservation was stronger than desire. She gave him a peck on the cheek. "Later." She grabbed the wig and cane from his hands, dashed out the door, and yelled back, "Right now, I wanta try out the Camaro."

33

"I'll be right there," Monty Ezell said, hanging up the phone at his country club estate.

He snatched up his Hartmann briefcase, then confidently strolled out the door. He slid his long frame into the Jaguar and cursed the cold leather seats as they crackled in the frosty Saturday morning air. Careful not to attract attention, he drove through the streets of Asheville, lighting a Philip Morris with the dashboard lighter as he headed into the industrial district, feeling proud of how far he had come financially.

Monty Ezell was a wife-tamer. Carol was his third wife; he had tamed two before her. Carol didn't know about the waitress over at Tarboro. Ezell had made his money early as a salt-car trader. Up North, he had bought cars eaten up with street-salt; the cities used the salt to melt snow and ice. Ezell hitch-pulled the salt-cars to western Carolina, patched the rust with Bondo, painted them, rolled back the odometer, and sold the cars as low-mileage one-owners. Two of his associates got caught and went to prison for the practice, but Ezell turned state's evidence and copped a plea. He parlayed his salt-car money into an insurance agency and was now a respected member of Asheville society. Todd Carrington's file on the seat beside him would bring more money than a year of selling salt-cars.

Ezell drove one street past Industrial Way, then, watching that no other cars were in sight, made a sharp right into an alley camouflaged by overgrowth. He parked in the hidden underground garage, then, with excitement overtaking him, he trotted through the well-lit tunnel, past several armed guards. At the private elevator he punched "three." The rest of SIG Labs was locked down for the weekend.

He strutted into the darkened Observation Room. Kaufman was in the wheelchair watching the TV monitor that displayed the garage and tunnel Ezell had just come through. Tumbler was standing in a corner behind Kaufman, sharpening his knife as usual. He was wearing the same purple polka-dot bow tie. Red buttons on the electronic equipment reflected off the pocketknife's steel blade.

Monty Ezell, who was used to high protein football-player food, vitamins, and an everyday workout, had seen Tumbler in the light only once. Tumbler looked and acted like a mole. His pale skin gave the appearance of a man who, as a child, had suckled cokes instead of milk. But in spite of his small size, he still scared Ezell.

Tumbler never acknowledged Ezell.

Kaufman turned from the TV monitor. "Let's have it."

Ezell unzipped the briefcase, removed a stuffed, brown 8 1/2 x 14 clasp-envelope and offered it to Kaufman.

Kaufman backhanded the envelope onto the floor. "Not receipts, fool. We've got receipts!"

"But I thought—"

"Don't ever hand me a piece of paper again. I don't want my fingerprints on your filth. All your reports to me will be oral. If you bring writing, hand it to Tumbler."

"Yes, sir."

Tumbler kept sharpening and never looked up.

"I want to know where Todd Carrington's head is? Who's he plan to use for his backers? Who's he talk to? What's he lie about? What's he brag about? What are his plans for all those tobacco farms he's about to inherit?"

"He's the absolute worst kind of politician there is," said Ezell, "a good man with high ideas."

"What about his wife?"

"He seems in love with her. What man wouldn't be… that luscious Barbie Doll figure and—"

Kaufman gave him a critical glance. "Who's he flirt with? When he's out on the road?"

"No one. He's true blue."

Kaufman slammed his fist on the arm of his wheelchair. "Ezell, stop aggravating me! Tell me something I don't know."

"Yes, sir."

"You've been riding around with him all week; surely you've learned something. What about her parents?"

"Todd thinks they're dead. He said he used to ask about

182

them, but the subject seemed to make her uncomfortable, so he quit asking."

"Keep trying to find out about her parents. He ever say anything about her we might use against him?"

"There *is* one thing."

Kaufman leaned forward and Tumbler stopped sharpening.

"Barbara is deathly afraid of the camera, being on stage, or anything to do with publicity."

Kaufman glanced at Tumbler. When he looked back at Ezell, he asked, "More than just stage fright?"

"She has a phobia about anything to do with publicity."

"You may be on to something."

"I told Todd that people will start talking if she doesn't begin to appear in public with him. But he said, 'let them talk. Barbara's not part of what I'm giving my country.'"

Kaufman smiled. "That may be the chink in her armor."

The mood in the room changed, and Ezell relaxed, enough to make an attempt at a joke. "She's a *good* girl. You know what they say about *good* girls.

Kaufman looked at him, puzzled.

"Good girls get to go to heaven and bad girls get to go everywhere." Ezell laughed a nervous horselaugh, but when no one joined in his attempted jocularity, he froze.

"Let's force the issue," Kaufman said. "Schedule a TV interview for Ms. Dare-Carrington."

"That'll get me fired! Todd told me to keep her out of the press at all cost."

"Hmm. What do you think, Tumbler?"

Tumbler began his monotone recitation. "Leave Ezell out of it. Give him a denial route. *I'll* arrange the press conference. To throw her off, we'll invite wives of two or three other up-and-coming politicians."

"Good plan," said Kaufman.

"When?" Ezell asked, pulling out his pocket Daytimer.

"Saturday. Week from today."

"Perfect," Ezell said, marking his calendar. "Todd and I will be over on the coast, at Morehead City that weekend. I'll leave

Barbara a schedule for the week, but I'll make sure it's off by a day or two. So she can't call him."

Kaufman said, "I'll prepare a list of questions for the TV anchorwoman—What's her name?"

"Dolly. Dolly Dauber."

"That's her," said Kaufman, "and the first question will be, 'Ms. Dare-Carrington, are your parents in politics?'"

"Oh," Ezell said as he started for the door. "I have Todd convinced that he should run for the U. S. Senate as soon as he wins this local election. He's going to tell his father New Year's Day."

"Fine," said Kaufman. "Good work."

"But there's one little problem."

"What's that?"

"He plans to tell his father that he wants no help from the tobacco lobby. Say's he's going to plow those tobacco fields under and plant cotton."

Kaufman looked at Tumbler. "Call New Bern. Get Charlie Carrington on the phone."

34

Barbara waited for death to knock her front door down. As she waited, she became concerned about her mental well being. She was afraid the constant threat of dying would make her lose her mind. So she began looking for low-profile opportunities in the community in which she could become involved—anything to give relief to her emotions. So when Todd suggested they take ballroom dance lessons, she jumped at the chance. It was a trade off—she would take ballroom lessons and he would take clogging lessons. Saturday night they would take their first lesson—the waltz and the rumba. Actually, it was a dance *class*—one hour, followed by a two-hour practice party.

Todd wore a navy blazer, khaki trousers, and a white Ralph Lauren button-down shirt, no tie. She wore a red party dress with spaghetti straps. On the way to the dance class, she began to feel a little overdressed, but Todd reassured her. He was right. When they walked in, everyone else was all dressed up, too. But there was one odd thing. Most of the dancers, men as well as women, carried little black bags. She immediately became curious as to what was in the bags.

She didn't have to wait long to find out. The dancers quickly sat down, opened the bags and removed dance shoes. Then, almost in unison, they each took out a steel brush and began scuffing the suede soles. Next they removed battery-operated, hand-held fans, turned them on, and began to cool their faces and necks. They looked like mannequins mimicking one another, and sounded like a mosquito convention.

The warm-up music began—a waltz. Then the all-business herd of hoofers charged the dance floor. It soon became obvious to Barbara that this wasn't a beginner group. The instructor came over, introduced himself, and explained that he would teach an advanced class after the beginner class; that way the beginners would learn from the "pros." A practice party would follow the lessons.

The class went okay—the waltz and the rumba. Todd knew how to lead, so Barbara picked up both dances rather quickly.

She already knew the basic steps, but not the styling. Todd was especially proficient with the waltz—his tall frame, arched back, and broad shoulders gave him the appearance of a god come to life. But Barbara took to the Latin rhythm of the rumba far better than he. The rotating hip movement was made for her.

She soon learned that the dancers, though friendly, were all business. At the party, a small man from England, obviously of modest means, stole the show with his European manners and international dance style. Hitching up his pants, he strolled over to Barbara and bowed. "May I have this waltz?" As he led her to the floor, he pulled a faded white handkerchief from his coat pocket, placed it in the palm of his left hand, then held it against the small of her back. When she asked why the kerchief, he replied, "So I won't soil your dress."

She introduced the little Englishman to Todd, explained that Todd would be on the road a lot, and asked if he would be her partner while Todd was gone.

"But no flirting," Todd joked.

The elderly little man blushed. "Maybe a wee bit, old chap."

On the way home, Barbara reminded Todd that now he owed her. Tonight she would call Gene and Sally Chastine and book a trip to Maggie Valley for a clogging lesson—for Todd.

The dance class was fun, but still Barbara longed for something more meaningful to fill the hours while Todd was on the campaign trail. Her opportunity came on Sunday morning. After the worship service, she and Todd lunched in the fellowship hall with the congregation. The luncheon was to celebrate the pastor's anniversary. From the head table, the pastor made a joke about Todd's being a politician, but he didn't mention Barbara. At Barbara's request Todd had explained to the pastor that she would be willing to help with the Ladies Auxiliary, the nursery, or most anywhere she was needed, but preferred to work behind the scene.

After lunch, the pastor came to their table. He shook hands with Todd but spoke to her. "Your husband explained that you might volunteer to help at church."

Barbara nodded.

"I think I have just the job for you. You would make an excellent hugger."

"*Hugger*?" responded Barbara. "I beg your pardon."

The dignified minister smiled. "Hugger. Our church sponsors a program at the hospital for newborn babies. Some are orphaned, some are addicted to drugs, and others have AIDS. We go twice a week for a couple of hours just to hold and hug the babies."

"How wonderful."

"Something tells me you will make a first-rate baby hugger, Barbara. Would you like to try it?"

"Oh, yes. So very much."

"Call my secretary Monday and we'll adapt a schedule to yours."

A hugger. A baby hugger. That was perfect. Between the dance class and the hugging opportunity, she was set.

It was a sunny afternoon, so when they got home, while Todd sat in the gazebo and worked on his campaign speech, Barbara lay in the hammock and did her Christmas shopping from an array of catalogues, every now and then glancing up to admire his broad shoulders or to wink at him.

She chuckled to herself as she thought of their coming visit to Grandmother Dare's for Christmas. Grandmother Dare had warned her that it might take a while for neighbors to warm up to Todd, his being a stranger to the mountains. So Barbara came up with a plan to break the ice. She would tell the neighbors that Todd was hard of hearing, then tell Todd that the neighbors were hard of hearing. After a few minutes of yelling at each other, she would let them all in on the joke.

"See anything in those catalogues *you* might like for Christmas?" Todd asked as he stood and stretched.

"I like them all," she said with a giggle, and pulled him toward her with a flirty "come-hither" wiggle of her forefinger.

"I meant your present from me," he said as he strolled toward the hammock. The hammock straddled a small stream. "I don't know what to get you."

187

"I like memories better than things." She took his hand, swinging it. "Let the trip to Grandmother Dare's be my gift from you."

"Besides that." He sat beside her, his feet at water's edge and his long legs rocking them.

Barbara knew she was speaking with one with whom money was no object. Anything she asked for, he would get it. But she didn't want that much. There was one thing, though. "I've always wanted to go to Salt Lake City."

"*Salt Lake City*?"

"The Mormon Tabernacle." She tossed the catalogues onto the grass.

Todd laid back in the hammock beside her. "We're not Mormon. We're Presby—"

She adjusted his arm under her neck. "I've always dreamed of hearing the Mormon Tabernacle Choir live. Especially their Christmas concert. Grandmother Dare and I used to watch it on TV."

"I'll take you!" he said like a little boy and so full of excitement that he sat up on the edge of the hammock. "Front-row seats."

"I'd settle for a dressed rehearsal." She gave him a sexy wink.

"Want to take your grandmother?"

"No. Just you and I. But let's not go this year. This year maybe just a CD of them singing the 'Pilgrims' Chorus.' I love how, at the climax, they sound like they're climbing the mountains, bringing the pilgrims home. Besides, with your campaign, we have enough going on."

"Next Christmas, then?"

"Deal," she whispered, then added, as she pulled him down on top of her, "Now let's practice my hugging."

He kissed her long and hard.

Later, spent from the raucous love making—hammock style—she remembered her monthly rendezvous. It was scheduled for this afternoon. Of course she would postpone it since Todd was home. She would make the border-trip next

Sunday while he and Monty Ezell were over at Morehead City lining up support for Todd's future national campaign.

"I'll go inside and get us a coke," she said, raising to her elbow." Just then the hammock broke, spilling them into the cold stream.

"Good timing," Todd said, laughing.

"The best," Barbara said, splashing about in the shallow water.

As they walked arm-in-arm toward the bathroom for towels, she thought about *timing*. So far, no one had found out about her monthly mission.

35

Monday morning Todd and Monty left for another week of campaigning, and Barbara left for work.

That morning she made the rounds through the lab's five white buildings, talking with scientists. As she did, she began to notice an unusually large number of panel trucks parked near the loading ramps; the trucks had no windows and bore the markings of major tobacco brands. She decided to find out why.

She remarked to one of the scientists whose name tag read, Dr. Edith Trybyszewski, "Most of our work is environmental. Why all the tobacco trucks?"

Dr. Trybyszewski responded with a Polish accent. "Call me Treby. Everyone else does."

"All right, Treby. Why all—"

"I wondered that too when I came here three years ago. But no longer. Now I wonder about a lot of things."

"Such as?"

"The tinted windows throughout the complex, and—."

"Dr. Clark said the tint was to keep sunlight from compromising lab experiments."

"*Tinted*, yes. But *bulletproof!*"

"*Bulletproof?*"

"Please forget I said that." Treby's eyes blinked with fright, and she rubbed her hands, nervously.

"All right, but tell me about the tobacco trucks."

"Every Monday morning, just like clockwork, those trucks pull up to the ramps and unload." She kept glancing over her shoulder as they talked.

"Tobacco?"

"What else," chimed Treby.

"Where do we store it?"

"My area's cosmetics. I've learned you last longer around here if you don't ask questions that don't relate to your field. The people on the third floor know everything, and the tiniest whisper can send you packing."

"*Third floor?* You mean Dr. Clark?"

"No."

"I thought Dr. Clark was the only one on that floor."

"Humph." Dr. Trybyszewski gave a suspicious stare. "I've said too much." She walked back to her lab station.

Barbara hurried over to her, then whispered, "Do you know what's on the *second* floor?"

The scientist's eyes bulged. She looked around the lab, like she was searching for a stoolie. "We all do. At least all the scientists do. We know part of the story. But we're sworn to secrecy."

"Sworn to secr—"

"At the risk of losing our positions. Or worse yet, the threat of being blackballed with authorizing agencies."

"*Blackballed.* What on earth?" Barbara asked.

"You know about Mr. Puff, don't you?"

"*Mr. Puff?* Is that a joke?"

"I've said too much. I thought they had told you. Especially you having such a high position with the company."

"I handle all non-scientific personnel. I know nothing about a *Mr. Puff.*"

"You're going to get me into a lot of trouble. Please don't ask any more questions." Treby trotted out of the lab and down the glass-domed hall, her skirt-tail and lab coat swishing nervously.

Late that afternoon when Barbara got home, she darted through the door, tossing her lab coat, skirt, and blouse aside. She slipped into sweats, pulled a UT ball cap over her hair, dashed to the Camaro, and headed to the Asheville Speedway. The day Todd had found her wig and cane, she had been too distraught to give the Camaro a *real* workout. But not today.

Once on the track, she let the hammer down. The Camaro's front wheels came off the ground. The power surged through the entire car frame and all the way down to her toes, pinning her shoulders to the seat. The car laid rubber for a quarter mile. The loud roar brought Gene and other mechanics out of the shops to watch. Traveling the fastest she had ever traveled on land, she touched the blue button that let loose the bottle of nitrous oxide. "Lordy!" The speed doubled. Gene hadn't overstated the Camaro's dig-out power or speed. Let them try to catch me now, she thought.

On the way home two teenage boys in a yellow Porsche pulled up beside her, honked, and revved the engine, challenging her. She smiled, but dared not accept their challenge. The Camaro wasn't for joy racing. And besides, she didn't want to embarrass them; they had a girl in the jump seat.

When she got back home, the phone was ringing. It was Todd telling her how the campaign was going, that he and Monty were working their way across the state to the coast, and that Monty was the kind of friend every man dreamed of. "He's like Roland in the book you gave me: loyal, capable, and trustworthy."

Barbara didn't know where Monty Ezell fit into *The Song of Roland*, and he might be able to act the part, but no matter what Todd thought, Monty was no Roland. If she were casting the play, she'd cast him as Ganelon, the villain. It was Ganelon who told the enemy army to attack Roland from the rear, killing him in the process. She could spot a wolf in sheep's clothing and Monty Ezell was no sheep. But perhaps it was an innocent enough lesson for Todd to learn, so she decided to let him attend "the wolf in sheep's clothing school" on his own.

"Hope to be home by Wednesday week," said Todd. "And I love you and miss you."

It was the first time they had talked that long on the phone in some time. Perhaps because he wasn't there to distract her, she noticed how his deep voice resonated with that warm rich Carolina/Virginia coastal accent. How she wished he was there to distract her. She longed for him to be there to hold her in his arms, but she said, "Love you too, sweetheart."

She had never discussed SIG Labs with Todd—he had enough on his mind. So she didn't that night either. But she wanted to. When she hung up, she couldn't get over how frightened Dr. Edith Trybyszewski had been when Barbara had asked her about the second floor at SIG Labs. And who else, besides Dr. Quebian Clark, was on the third floor? And who was Mr. Puff?

Barbara took an early leisurely bubble bath, went to bed, and read from John Grisham's *The Client.* When sleep was about to overtake her, she made a mental note that tomorrow she would quiz Treby again about the second floor. Then clutching the keys to the Camaro, she said goodnight to another safe day.

Tuesday morning when she arrived at SIG Labs, the place was abuzz with flashing lights and sirens. Ambulances and police cars were all over the place. Dr. Edith Trybyszewski had committed suicide. She had cut her own throat. The handwritten note found in her blood said so. A Schrade/Walden pocketknife still lay in her open hand.

Thursday, Barbara attended Treby's funeral at the United Methodist Church. The scientists and staff were there. Dr. Quebian Clark gave a glowing eulogy that would have taken anyone else five minutes, but in his short clipped sentences, he finished in sixty seconds. Barbara would like to hear him play "The Minute Waltz."

After the funeral she went to the Asheville Hospital and hugged newborn crack-babies for two hours. Each baby in its own hell, the job was as painful as watching a thousand infants tossed overboard at sea. As she rocked, she vowed anew that there would be no babies born to her marriage.

The Dare secret was like the old joke Grandmother Dare used to tell: "What is it nobody wants, but if they had one they wouldn't take a million dollars for it?" Then she would laugh and answer, "A bald head." That's how the Dare secret was. She hadn't wanted it, yet now that she had it, she wouldn't take anything for it. But she would never pass it on to a child. Holding a thrashing crack-baby in her arms was no substitute for her instinct to hold a baby of her own in her arms. But it helped.

When she got home, she moped around, wishing Todd was there. The house had never seemed so empty, and she had never needed him as she needed him now. So much had changed since he left Monday. She had tried to call him several times since

Treby's suicide, but he and Monty were evidently off-schedule, for she kept missing him. She sat on the bed, toying with the white buttons on the high-collar black dress, and trying to decide how she would spend the hours till bedtime. So she did what she always did when she had serious thinking to do. She put on her UT track shorts, T-shirt, and sneakers, and wearing her mud beads, headed into the mountains. She didn't take her Walkman; she would do some *serious* running today.

As she ran, tears streamed down her cheeks and she didn't know why. She raced through the oak, hickory, and maple trees, and while the birds sang and the squirrels skedaddled, she ran until she had run it out, whatever it was that was bothering her. Twenty-six miles later she wearily climbed the steps at their chalet. But the house was as empty as when she had left. One thing, however, was now clear that had not been before she went running: Dr. Edith Trybyszewski did not commit suicide. But if she didn't, who killed her? Barbara didn't know the answer to that question yet, but she figured it had to do with what Treby almost told her—about whatever was going on on the second floor of SIG Labs.

Suddenly a bolt of horror shot through her. No one else was present during her conversation with Treby. Barbara didn't tell, and Treby was too scared to tell. But somebody told. Or heard. That meant only one thing. Treby's lab station was bugged! Maybe all of SIG Labs was bugged!

But why? One thing was sure. From now on, she would watch what she said around the office, and she would warn Sally. She would trust Gene and Sally with her life. Might have to someday.

Since Treby died soon after she told her about Mr. Puff, maybe Mr. Puff killed her. Even if he didn't, why was he hiding out on the second floor? Barbara began plotting a way to get onto the second floor to meet this Mr. Puff. Tomorrow would be Friday. Tomorrow she would ask Sally to have dinner with her, some place away from the lab.

But as soon as she arrived at work the next morning, Dr. Quebian Clark called her to his office. "A reporter wants to ask you some questions."

"*Questions?*"

Clark handed her a note card. "You will show up at this address tomorrow. At 10:00 AM."

"Oh. About the suicide?"

"I suppose. Maybe an obituary report."

Obituary report? After the funeral had already taken place? It sounded stupid but she wasn't going to tell her superior that. Maybe Dr. Clark meant a follow-up to the death notice. "Couldn't someone else do it?"

"If someone else did it, why would we need you?"

"Yes, sir." Barbara left his office. She didn't like the assignment, but thought it would be all right. She could certainly express the sympathy of SIG Labs on behalf of a faithful employee. As for details of the tragedy, she would refer the reporter to the police and coroner reports. She'd be in and out of the reporter's office in five minutes. Then on Sunday, she would read the obituary column where she expected her interview to be buried.

As she walked by Sally's office, she popped in and casually asked, "Would you like to have dinner with me this evening?"

"Sure. Gene, too?"

"No. Just girl talk. I'm missing Todd more than I want anyone but you to know."

"I'll leave Gene a TV dinner. Where you wanna eat?"

If someone were listening, Barbara didn't want them to know where they would be dining. "Some place casual. I don't know what I'm hungry for yet; I'll come by for you around 6:30. We can decide then."

She closed the door and nonchalantly walked to her own office to work on the Trybyszewski file for the interview.

Krandall Kaufman didn't bother calling Dr. Clark to his office. He and Tumbler had watched it all through the one-way mirror. On the TV monitor, they now watched Barbara leave Sally's office. When she entered her own office, Kaufman turned the monitor off. "That was easier than I thought it'd be."

"Couldn't have planned it better," Tumbler said, always sharpening his blade.

"New knife?"

"Yes, sir. I only use them once."

"Aren't those Schrade/Waldens collector editions?"

"All the more pleasurable, sir."

"Barbara Dare-Carrington is going to that interview in the morning," Kaufman said, "thinking it's about poor ol' Edith Trybyszewski's suicide."

"Dolly Dauber, that buzz-saw reporter, will cut her to shreds."

"No. I don't want her *cut to shreds*. I just want Dolly to get her shook up enough that she tells who her family is. You gave her my list of questions?"

"She's chomping at the bit to get at the rising politician's wife, especially his being the newest board member of Asheville's biggest bank."

"Now, inform Dolly Dauber that we won't need the wives of the other two politicians in the interview."

"Let the two of them go at it one on one, huh?"

"If Dolly sticks to my list of questions, Barbara Dare-Carrington will spill the beans about her parents."

About that time the phone range. It was Ezell. Kaufman hit the speaker phone button. "Yeah?"

"I don't know if this is important or not, but this afternoon Todd told me that if he gets elected to the Senate, he's already picked out a bodyguard. It's Gene Chastine, Sally's husband."

"Who?"

"Sally that works for you."

"I know who *Sally* is. Why's that important?"

"It seems that there was a scuffle in the parking lot at Shoney's a week or so ago. The two couples had just come outside from dinner and three men jumped them. Gene Chastine gave the biggest of the three a karate chop and that was the end of it."

"So?" asked Kaufman.

"Todd said Gene Chastine shoved him into his car and told him to get gone before the cops and the press showed up."

"Interesting," said Tumbler. "Very interesting."

"Good work," said Kaufman. "We'll take it from here. Wait a minute. Any idea who the men were?"

"Todd said they had 'Acme Brick' written on their work-vests."

"Good job, Ezell." Kaufman flipped off the speaker phone and, in the same motion, turned to Tumbler. "Find out who owns Acme Brick Company."

36

At 6:30 that evening, Barbara pulled up in front of Gene's and Sally's home next to the Asheville Speedway and honked the black Corvette's horn.

Sally came running out, wearing jeans and a red sweater and carrying her jacket. She climbed in and bubbled, "Okay, Miss Lonely Heart, your love counselor is reporting for duty."

"Do you know an out-of-the-way restaurant?"

"Depends on how hungry you are. Want a 'meat and three?'"

"Meat and three?"

"A meat and three vegetables."

Barbara smiled. "No. Just some place where we can talk privately."

"How about the Esmeralda?"

"Is it private?"

"You bet. Clark Gable, and a whole bunch of other movie stars, used to use it as a hideout."

"Perfect. Which way?"

"Straight ahead. Catch 74-A toward Chimney Rock."

"Just tell me when to turn." Barbara pulled away from the curb.

"Okay, what's up?" asked Sally.

"We need to talk. And it's not about love."

"Uh oh," groaned Sally. "Do I smell divorce on the horizon?"

"Heavens no. It's not about me and Todd. It's about murder."

"Murder!?"

"I think Treby was murdered."

By the time they arrived at the Esmeralda Inn & Restaurant, Barbara had told Sally all about her conversation with Treby and about her suspicions that SIG Labs was bugged.

While they waited to be seated, Sally whispered, "Have you told the police?"

"Too much publicity. And it's only a suspicion. I don't

want to look like a fool. I can just hear some police reporter now, 'Candidate's wife claims Dr. Trybyszewski was murdered!'"

"That certainly wouldn't do Todd's career any good. What are you gonna do?"

When the hostess came to seat them, Barbara pointed to a dark corner. "May we have that table by the fire?"

The hostess ushered them through the half-empty, candle-lit, room to the table and handed them two menus. On the front and back of the gray menu were historical sketches, printed in red, of the inn, built in 1891. A list of movies that had been filmed there was included, along with a note that Lew Wallace finished the script for *Ben Hur* in room 9.

Barbara hid behind the menu, then peeped out to see if she recognized anyone in the restaurant.

Sally peeped too, then giggled. Her eyes got as big as silver dollars. "All clear, Sherlock?"

"I suppose."

"Well then, can we order? I'm hungry."

Barbara nodded to the waiter. When he came, she asked his recommendation. He suggested, as an appetizer, the Baked Brie in a Puffed Pastry for two.

"What's that?" Sally asked.

"Baby brie cheese and raspberries baked to a golden brown," said the waiter, "but you have to allow extra time."

Sally smiled an agreeable smile.

"We're in no hurry," said Barbara. "We'll have the brie for two."

"May I suggest for your entree the *Salmon Au Poivre*?"

"Salmon?" asked Sally.

He smiled. "It's pan-seared with a peppery brandy sauce."

"Go for it."

Barbara nodded agreement. "And two glasses of white wine. Your house wine will be fine."

As soon as the waiter left, Sally asked, "Why do you think the lab's bugged?"

"Has to be. No one was around when Treby and I talked about the second floor. I didn't tell. And she's dead."

"You know, I've always suspected a stoolie. But I never thought about the place being bugged."

"Oh?"

"Dr. Clark has an uncanny way of knowing information I've told only my closest associates."

"Um hum."

"One time a group of us got together and discussed the Employee Christmas Bonus. Later, Dr. Clark knew as much about the meeting as I did. Since he hadn't been there, I asked how he knew. He said it was just my woman's intuition in overdrive."

"You ever heard of a Mr. Puff?"

"*Mr. Puff?*" Sally cackled. "Sounds like a cartoon character."

"It's no joke."

"Go on," Sally said, waving her off.

"There is a Mr. Puff on the second floor, and Treby died before she could tell me what he does. But whatever it is, it's top secret."

"You're scaring me."

"I'm scared too. Mr. Puff may be the one who killed her."

"No way," said Sally, insecurely.

"Who besides Dr. Clark offices on the third floor?"

"No one."

"Yes there is! Treby told me so."

"She say who?"

"She started to, but then she ran away."

Sally began to shake. "What does Todd think of all this?"

"He's out of town," Barbara said, breaking a cracker. "And what's to tell?"

Conversation stopped when the waiter arrived with the wine and cheese. He spoke into the silence, "Enjoy," then left.

"Tell him that a Mr. Puff is on the second floor and that others have offices on the third—" Sally began to laugh. "That does sound pretty stupid, doesn't it? Gene would ship me off to the funny farm if I came home with a tale like that."

"It may be nothing, but I want you to help me find a way to get onto the second floor."

201

"How?"

"Dr. Clark wears a key on a chain around his neck. That may be the key that makes the elevator stop on the second floor."

"He'd fire us, if—"

"Not if we put him to sleep."

"*Put him to sleep?*"

"Sleeping gas from the lab."

Sally laughed. "I always wanted to be a detective. When do we do it?"

"On a Saturday. While the lab is closed—"

"*Saturday?*" Sally gulped in the middle of a sip of wine. "Tomorrow's Saturday!"

"Not *tomorrow*. In the morning I'm meeting an obituary reporter about Treby. But some Saturday soon. While the lab's locked down and no one's eavesdropping."

"How do we get Dr. Clark there on a weekend?"

"I haven't figured that out yet."

"What if they leave the eavesdropping equipment on over the weekend?"

"We'll jam it."

"How?"

"I haven't figured that out either."

"How should I act at work?"

"Act natural."

"I always wanted to be an actress, too."

"Just remember, someone is probably listening to every word we say at the office."

"I'd like to give that Dr. Quebian Clark an earful."

"I don't think it's Dr. Clark," Barbara said. "It's probably Mr. Puff."

The waiter arrived with the tasty-smelling entree, and poured more wine. When he left, Barbara and Sally continued to plan their assault on the second floor of SIG Labs. They devoured the *Salmon Au Poivre* as if it were the Last Supper.

"Memory," from *Cats*, played somewhere in the background, making Barbara wish the same wish as Grizabella, the scraggly old cat from the musical. If by some magic touch, she could be reborn...If the weight could be lifted...If she and Todd could go to the land of beginning again—

Sally interrupted her musing. "When we find this Mr. Puff, what do we do with him?"

"'To make tiger stew,'" said Barbara, "'first you must catch the tiger.'"

Tumbler and Mickey sat in the white Mercedes in the dark bushes across from the Esmeralda. Tumbler trimmed his nails with his pocketknife while he waited for Barbara Dare-Carrington and Sally Chastine to come out. An hour later, the two women came through the door. Arm in arm, they strolled across the wooden porch and down the stairs to the parking area, giggling like girls who had been naughty in Sunday School.

Tumbler loved their giggle. The throat, ah, how it thrilled him. He held his fingers up in the moonlight to check the work on his nails. One nail irritated him, so he began to cut at it until the blood came. A shaft of light, captured on the cold steel, glistened, bringing even more pleasure as he watched the women's hair vanish inside their car. His excitement mounted.

"Let's go, Mickey."

The white Mercedes followed the black Corvette home.

37

Saturday morning, Barbara woke up thinking about Mr. Puff
and the second floor of SIG Labs. But she soon dispatched that
venture to the back of her mind. She had other business today—
the interview about Treby with the reporter.

She walked into the kitchen in her sky-blue, silk pj's—short
sleeves, short pants—and pressed the radio button. It wasn't
even Halloween yet, but the Yuletide Strings started playing a
Smoky Mountain version of "Do You Hear What I Hear?" It
seemed every year advertisers started hawking Christmas earlier
and earlier. Barbara began moving her hips in Cuban motion to
the rumba rhythm. She opened the cabinet doors and peeped in,
trying to decide whether she would have granola or raisin bran,
all the while dancing with the cabinet doors, gently swinging
them back and forth, one in each hand.

After breakfast, she made a peanut butter pie, then set it in
the refrigerator. She would deliver the pie tomorrow when she
made her monthly secret rendezvous across the Tennessee
border.

Todd's tour schedule was taped to the refrigerator door. It
caught her eye, reminding her to try again to reach him; the
schedule was Monty's doing. Barbara dialed the number where
Todd was supposed to be, but he wasn't there. Earlier, he hadn't
been at the other motels on the list either. If she didn't know
better, she would think he was avoiding her.

She glanced at her Rolex. Time to get ready for her 10:00
interview with the reporter. She went to the bedroom, showered,
got dressed in her black suit, grabbed her purse and the
Trybyszewski folder and strolled out to the garage. She fired up
the Corvette, then headed up the Parkway to the downtown
address Dr. Clark had given her. She would make short work of
the interview and be back home in no time and try calling Todd
again. Now she wished they had an answering machine. But
Todd didn't like answering machines. They were too
impersonal. So they didn't have one.

On the way to town, as she cruised along the scenic Blue

Ridge Parkway, she decided she would like some music. So she touched the CD player. The Mormon Tabernacle Choir began to sing Wagner's "Pilgrims' Chorus." That Todd. He had given her her Christmas present early. But how did he get it in the Vette without her knowing? I love you, Todd.

All the world seemed at peace this morning. On one occasion, just for fun, she and Todd had driven the Blue Ridge Parkway's full 470 miles. The Parkway began at Cherokee, south of Asheville, and wound north along the highest ridges into Virginia's Shenandoah Valley. To Barbara, it was the most beautiful drive in all the world. But today, like commercial airline pilots who fill long hours in the cockpit, planning what they would do in this emergency or that—where they could land if—Barbara played out every conceivable emergency she could be trapped in, and not just in a car, and plotted escape routes. She had memorized every turn-around spot on that part of the narrow Parkway she customarily traveled.

The Mormon Tabernacle Choir was now coming to that magnificent climax of climaxes in the Pilgrims' Chorus. When the giant pipe organ began the hill-climbing crescendo, soon overpowering the singers with its marching sound, walking the pilgrims home, Barbara broke loose from her earthly bonds and, for one brief moment, went soaring up there with the jets and the angels and the pilgrims.

The anthem soon ended and she crashed back to earth. She knew that sooner or later, with Todd in politics, as surely as the sun comes up in the morning, as surely as pilgrims long for home, one day a reporter would run up and shove a microphone in her face. She had an escape route for everything, but she didn't have one for that.

Now her attention was only slightly on the irritation of having to use a precious Saturday morning with a newspaper obituary reporter. At 9:50 she arrived at the address Dr. Clark had dispatched her to. It was a television station! An alarm bell went off in her head and perspiration broke out in her armpits. She checked the address again, but her hand shook so she could hardly read the note. The address was correct. She grabbed the file on Treby and dashed inside the building where she handed the receptionist her business card. "I'm from SIG Labs; here to see a Ms. Dauber."

"Yes. Oh yes," said the receptionist with an over abundance of excitement in her voice. "This way please; Dolly's expecting you."

Barbara followed her through a maze of crisscrossing halls and electronic equipment, all the while taking note of exit signs.

The receptionist finally stopped in front of a solid door. Above it, a red light glowed. "We can't go in while the light's on."

"I believe there's some mistake," Barbara whispered.

The light went off.

The receptionist jerked the door open and quickly ushered Barbara into a room full of cameras, set up like a living room. "Here's your ten o'clock, Dolly."

Dolly Dauber, a buxom peroxide blond with a Pentecostal hairdo and a too-short, black-leather skirt, leaped from the couch and beamed as she stuck out her hand. "Ms. Todd Carrington. What a special treat. I'm Dolly Dauber."

"Two minutes, Dolly," a camera woman said.

"I'm afraid there's been an awful mix-up, Ms. Dauber. You see, I'm the one Dr. Clark sent to tell about Dr. Edith—"

"And that's what we're going to talk about, honey." She guided Barbara to a wing-back chair by the couch. "Hold that thought just a moment. Would you like coffee?"

"No thank you. But—"

"Just relax. Wasn't that dreadful what happened to the lady scientist out at your company? Did you bring some information on her?"

"Yes, but for an obituary column. Not for TV." Barbara sat, nervously, on the edge of the chair, her right foot bouncing like a sewing machine.

"Honey, just read from your notes. My mouth's big enough for both of us. I'll do most of the talking."

Barbara gasped. "I'm not going on television!"

"But Dr. Clark said *you* are in charge of personnel," Dolly said with a bumfuzzled look. "Let me get him on the phone." She reached for the receiver.

"Wait."

"There's not something about that woman's death you don't want to talk about, is there?"

"Of course not. It's not anything like—"

"Ten seconds, Miss Dolly."

Dolly patted Barbara on the knee. "Relax and leave everything to me. Just watch the red dot."

"Silence." The camera woman counted down with her fingers: 5, 4, 3, 2, 1.

Dolly broke into a big smile and stared into the camera. "Good morning, good morning, good morning. This is your Saturday, 'Hello Asheville Show.' And do I have a surprise for you. The town is abuzz with talk of the political promise of Todd Carrington, son of Senator Charlie Carrington."

Barbara glanced at the monitor. The camera began to fan out so that it had found her and now included her in the scene. She peeped inside the folder to be sure she had Treby's birth date correct.

"I have pulled the coup of the season: the first reporter in Asheville to land Mr. Carrington's beautiful—but elusive, I might add—wife." Dolly winked at Barbara.

Barbara quickly stared back at the file in her lap. If she didn't respond, maybe Dolly would hush and let her go.

"Ms. Dare-Carrington, we know a great deal about your husband's family, especially about Senator Charlie Carrington of New Bern, but we know nothing of your family."

"While I appreciate," Barbara said, smiling, "and even respect your interest and curiosity about me and my family, I came here today to talk about, and perhaps pay tribute to the late Dr. Edith Trybyszewski, who worked for SIG Labs for over three years."

"That's old news, Ms. Dare-Carrington. Our audience wants to know about *your* family."

O, Lord. Here it comes. Barbara began to shake with fright. She was trapped. The newscaster had no way of knowing she was sending her to her execution. So she decided to put her best foot forward during the massacre. She opened the file, and with her head down began to read. "Dr. Edith Trybyszewski was born on July 6, 1974. She is survived by—"

"We already know about poor Dr. Trybyszewski, honey." Dolly patted her again.

Barbara felt like a fool.

"As I said, we want to know about *you* and *your* family."

"My family came to Cades Cove, Tennessee, with the Boone Party and purchased land from the Cherokee."

"Not your *ancestors*, honey, your *parents*." Dolly held a cue-board with a sheet of questions clipped to it and she was going down the list.

Trapped, Barbara began fidgeting and couldn't stop. Maybe this was the day the stars would fall. She glanced up. "I was raised by my grandmother."

"But your parents? Who is your father?"

The phone beside Dolly's chair rang. "I better answer that. We have a call in to Monty Ezell. That may be him."

"*Monty Ezell*?"

"He's managing your husband's campaign, isn't he?"

Barbara licked her lips. "Yes, but—"

Hanging up the phone, Dolly said, "I must say you're acting mighty jumpy about the death of that scientist...like your company might be hiding something." Then she turned to an assistant and said, "That wasn't Mr. Ezell. Keep trying to get him. And try to get Mr. Todd Carrington on the phone with him."

Barbara knew she should run. But Dolly had her cornered, what with the accusation that Barbara might be hiding something about Treby's death, and that Monty Ezell, and maybe Todd, was going to be interviewed by phone any minute now. She was trapped.

"Before the call, I asked who your father is, Ms. Dare-Carrington."

It was now a demand. Barbara felt she had to tell her a little. "I lived with my grandmother until I went to college, then I lived in an apartment in Knoxville—" She shouldn't have said that. She was saying too much.

"So your parents are dead?"

209

Dolly had crossed the line now. Barbara could bite a nail in two. She spat out, "I didn't say that."

"But your father's dead?"

"I...Er...I thought you were going to ask me about Dr.—"

"Ms. Dare-Carrington, the jumpy way you're acting about that dead scientist, and the suspicious way you're refusing to discuss your father...Oh...Oh my." Dolly froze, as if a great revelation had just become apparent. "The two, heaven forbid, are not related in any way, are they?"

"That's insane." Her voice cracked.

"Oh?" Dolly said with a shift of tone. "Then what's your father's name?"

Barbara smelled a rat. This was no funeral interview. It was a setup. She had to shut this down quickly and get out of the building.

Dolly became even more demanding. "Your husband is a potential senator. Our viewers have the right to know the name of his wife's father."

Barbara turned around, her eyes searching for the exit door. "My family is from Tennessee."

"Your *father* is from Tennessee?"

"I didn't say that."

"Does your father work?"

"Yes. No—"

"Is he on Welfare? That's nothing to be ashamed of."

Barbara had said all she was going to say. So she smiled pleasantly, lowered her eyes, and stared at the dead scientist's folder in her lap.

"Let's talk about something else then. Barbara—It's all right if I call you Barbara, isn't it?"

Barbara nodded, trying to wipe the anger from her face.

Dolly signaled the camera girl to zoom in for a close-up of Barbara's face. "The entire state is saying that your husband will take the fast track to Washington."

Barbara forced a smile.

"Has your husband ever beaten you?"

"*Beaten* me? Todd?"

"That temper of his, you know."

"*Temper.* Todd is the mildest mannered man I—"

"That's not what Bill Cooper said."

Barbara blinked. "I don't believe I know Mr. Cooper."

"Bill Cooper's daddy, William Cooper, Sr., owns Acme Bricks. The senior Mr. Cooper said your husband and another man attacked his son in Shoney's parking lot with a tire tool."

"Why…Why…that's not at all what—"

"Here's a picture of the young Mr. Cooper in a neck-brace." Dolly held up an 8 X 10 glossy for the camera. "A picture's worth a thousand words. Do you still deny that your husband—"

Barbara could feel herself squirming, ready to explode. "I most certainly—"

"Never mind." Dolly cut her off. "There's a lot of talk going around that Todd Carrington is living off his father's money and reputation. You don't deny that, do you?"

"What son or daughter doesn't?" Barbara replied, quietly.

"Rumor around Asheville is that the reason you never appear in public with your husband is that your marriage is in trouble."

That hurt. "Todd and I are very much in love. But politics is not kind to a tag-along wife. So he has his career and I have mine."

"Ms. Carrington—"

So it's Ms. Carrington again, is it? thought Barbara.

"Career politicians are saying that there is nothing to Todd Carrington's speech. It's all fluff: Mom. The flag. Apple pie. How do you answer those critics?"

She'd goaded her too far. Barbara couldn't take that. But she tried to remember what Grandmother Dare had taught her about a soft answer turning away wrath. So she stared Dolly in the face. Then she whispered, "You and the critics may be right. And perhaps Todd is naive in his belief that flying the flag is important, that every person should have a chance, and that the American dream is alive and well." Then she turned and looked into the camera, her soft blue eyes on fire, and showed why she'd made an "A" in Speech 401. "And I may be foolish for keeping the home lights burning while he's out there fighting for his country, but even if you threatened to cut my throat, I'd never be the one to tell him to stop believing in his dream."

211

The camera crew applauded.

Dolly Dauber adjusted her short black skirt and cleared her throat.

The crew kept applauding.

Dolly's phone switchboard began to light up. "Then why are you so ashamed to tell us about your father?"

Barbara exploded. "I'm not *ashamed*. My father did nothing any other man wouldn't have done under similar—" She quickly hushed. Oh, Lord. I've done it now. She stood and jerked the mike cord from around her neck.

"Break. Break. Go to a commercial!" Dolly laid down the clip-board with her list of questions on it.

Ready to bolt for the exit, Barbara glanced at the ten questions:

1. Who is your father?
2. Who is your father?
3. Who is your father?
4. Who is your father?
5. Who is your father?
6. Who is your father?
7. Who is your father?
8. Who is your father?
9. Who is your father?
10. Who is your father?

When she walked through the door at home, the phone was ringing.

Todd screamed, "Sweetheart, you were great."

"Todd!"

"Why didn't you tell me you were going on TV?"

"Todd, where have you been!?"

"Complications. Monty had to change the schedule. I'll tell you when I get there Wednesday. But the wire services picked up your interview and you're on all the national news."

"Please come home," Barbara begged, tearfully.

"It's not much longer until Wednesday."

"I *need* you."

"I miss you too, sweetheart. But the campaign—"

"Please, Todd, you must come home."

"Let's split the baby."

"What?"

"*Split the baby*, Todd said laughing. "It's political slang."

"I don't think it's funny."

"It means 'split the difference.' Monty's teaching me how to manipulate words, campaign speak-ease so to speak. He said I need to talk more like a politician."

"I like the way you talk. Please don't let him change you."

"I won't. But I will still *split the difference* with you. Monday, we have a meeting we can't get out of; I'll leave as soon as its over. Deal?"

"All right," she whispered. But it wasn't all right. Monday might be too late. All her years of keeping a low profile had just been erased. Somebody had set her up and now somebody else was about to knock her down.

Sunday morning Barbara staggered into the late service at Redeemer Presbyterian in a daze. The whole service seemed surreal, like she was suspended somewhere outside the sanctuary and outside herself. A young couple sat on the pew in front of her, the wife balancing a checkbook. Dead-faced ushers passed brass offering plates up and down red-velvet-cushioned pews, and sunlight beams, coming through the stained-glass windows, danced off the high-gloss brass plates and off the chandeliers and raced each other to the ceiling, like a mirror-ball gone mad. Finally the congregation observed the Last Supper. Barbara ate the flesh and drank the blood and clutched her car keys so tightly her hand almost bled into the holy cup. She had never prayed so hard in all her life. And while she was at it, she asked God to forgive her for the hatred that had begun to fill her heart—hatred for Monty Ezell. She didn't remember the sermon title, but she thought the soprano sang, "What Wondrous Love Is This."

After church, she picked up a Kentucky Fried Chicken dinner, took it home and nibbled on it in the gazebo. She had made birdhouses out of gourds and had hung them in the mulberry trees along the backyard boundary line. The birds lived there rent-free. Now showing their appreciation, they sang their hearts out. But today, all their songs rang in a minor key.

When she finished lunch, she went to the living room and picked up *The Song of Roland*, lying on the table beside the ginger jar that sat under the Renoir. She put it inside her special *granny* purse. She then went to the kitchen and took the peanut butter pie out of the refrigerator. Dirge-like, she carried it to the Camaro. She backed out of the garage, pulled onto the Parkway, and headed across Smoky Mountain to her secret rendezvous. They all would have seen her blunder on TV yesterday.

38

When Barbara arrived at her destination, she parked in the bushes, pulled the granny wig on, picked up the pie and purse, and limped up the dusty road with her walking cane, toward the massive concrete building. She climbed the steep steps out front, moving one foot up to a step, then pulling the other foot to the same step. Straining at each step, it took her two minutes to get to the top. Then, cradling the pie in the crook of her arm and against her slender waist, she moved granny-like down the long corridors past the guards, her purse banging against her hip and her cane echoing on the concrete floor.

At the Control Center desk, she handed the guard the pie and a brown piece of paper torn from a grocery sack. She knew the pie would reach its destination. On the paper was the name of the man she'd come to see. It was a needless gesture; they all knew whom she'd come to see. But it was part of her senility routine. And being this close, she didn't speak for fear her youthful voice would give away her age.

The guard smiled. "He missed you last week, ma'am. Just a moment, please."

When the guard returned, he ushered her to the Inmate Visiting Area. A long table ran the length of the room. The guard pulled out a chair and seated her. When he left, Granny Barbara hung her cane across the chair's crest. A glass-screen ran down the center of the table, separating her forever from the man she had come to see. She removed *The Song of Roland* from her purse and laid it in her lap. Ready for French class.

Momentarily, two guards with weapons drawn entered the room. She knew the routine. These two armed guards would be followed soon by two other guards whose job it would be to restrain him.

She heard the chains before she saw him.

Suddenly, a most pleasant-looking man with intelligent eyes, and smiling from ear to ear, was led into the room. He was handcuffed and a belly-chain ran down to his shackled feet. The two usher-guards placed him inside an all-glass cage and strapped him into a straight-back chair facing her.

"Ten minutes," said one of the guards. "Now be good." He locked the door to the cage, then all four guards stood a few feet away at attention.

The man encased in the glass tomb now sat directly across the table from her. At eye-level, there was a hole about the size of a Moon Pie for him to speak through. And listen through.

Once the guards were out of hearing distance, she opened the book and began to read, in French.

"Hi, Baby," he said.

Without looking up, she traced her hand along the words, pretending to be reading. "Hello, Papa. The guard has your pie."

"Thanks, sweetheart."

"Sorry I couldn't come last week," she said softly.

"You don't need to explain, honey."

She glanced up at him. That's when she saw a new scar on his face. It had been covered by a bandage on her last trip. She touched her own chin at the spot where the scar appeared on his face.

"Same old, same old," he whispered.

They were always trying to kill him. And they would kill her if they knew she was his daughter.

"But how did—

He waved her off, and his chains rattled. They only had nine minutes left and he didn't want her asking questions she already had answers to. She knew that.

"Papa, I'm in trouble!" she blurted out.

"I know. I saw it on the news."

She began to weep. "They tricked me. It was a setup."

He smiled kindly. "There, there, don't cry. Some people are like that."

"But the reporter had a list of ten questions. I saw her sheet. All ten questions were the same: 'Who is your father?'"

"Did Dolly Dauber say where she got the list?"

"No."

"Well, you let me worry about that."

216

"Now everybody'll know."

"We always knew someday they would," he whispered. His voice was soft like hers.

"But Todd and I were so happy. Now, he's a marked man."

"You must be even more careful. As you know, I have many enemies in here as well as on the outside. Some have served their time, and more than one has vowed to get even as he walked through the freedom gate. You're the only way they can get even with me. As long as you come here dressed like an old schoolmarm, teaching me French, they won't suspect who you are."

"But after the TV interview this morning, any one of them can put two and two together."

He nodded.

"You would never tell me before, but, now that it's out, is there anyone in particular I should watch out for?"

"They're all bad. I recently got a sawdust-and-nail bomb from the one who probably hates me most."

"Who?"

"Baldy Slocum."

"*Slocum?*"

"Baldy Slocum and his boys."

"Those crazy Slocum boys...the ones in the logging trucks?"

"They're the ones."

"Why?"

"It happened when I was a boy. I fought Baldy Slocum's daddy to the death for what he did to my mother—"

"To Grandmother Dare?"

"Yes, sweetheart. Over at Slocum Sawmill on Vulture Mountain."

"I knew part of that story. But I didn't know who."

Grandmother Dare had told her that when she was a young mother with two small children, a man from Vulture Mountain broke into her cabin. She grabbed the children and ran, but he caught her. He locked the children in a closet, then ordered her to his log truck. She pleaded, saying that the children would starve, or die of thirst before anyone found them, as far back in the mountains as they were. So the man shoved a bucket of

217

water, a jar of peanut butter, and a spoon into the closet. Then he took her away for a while. A week later, she broke free and ran home. She jerked the closet door open. The little girl was dead and the boy was unconscious. They had been unable to get the lid off the peanut butter. When the boy got big, like mountain folks do, he avenged his mother. Now he was doing life without parole.

"Do you have a fast car?" Barbara's father now asked.

She smiled through her tears. "Yes, Papa. Gene Chastine, head mechanic at Asheville Speedway, souped it up for me."

"If it's not fast enough, call Preecher Kinser over at Alcoa Speedway. He owes me a favor."

"Thanks, but my Camaro's plenty fast."

"Time's up," the guard called, tapping on the cage.

"Bye, darling. I love you more than life, and I'm proud of that husband of yours. Tell him to keep waving that American flag for the ones of us who can't."

"I'll tell him. Happy Halloween."

"Please know I'm there with you when you celebrate Halloween, sweetheart. Only my body is imprisoned by these walls. Every night my mind takes flight."

She watched the guards remove him from the glass cage, then lead him away. He always walked so erectly, but today she thought she detected a limp. He was still waving when they slammed the metal door at the end of the hall.

Barbara limped down the corridor, out the door, and down the stairs. Whether she came to the prison or not, every thirty days the guards ushered their most dangerous prisoner into the glass cage for his ten-minute treat. There he kept up the ruse, playing like he was on the outside and pretending to become the gentle man he had meant to become.

As for herself, the guards thought she was just a kind old lady who had taught French to Professor Huey Lamb until he died in the electric chair. Huey Lamb preceded her father as Building Tender. For three years prior to Lamb's electrocution—ever since she reached sixteen and got her driver's license—Barbara had dressed up in her granny outfit and visited the condemned man each month, bringing him a pie.

218

Her father had worked out the plan. He and Mr. Lamb were best friends and he let Mr. Lamb keep the pie for playing the part.

For three years, her father sat in the glass cage, near the death-row inmate and, without giving the slightest hint he knew the teacher, looked falsely up and down the lobby and listened as she recited from memory to the condemned man in French, *The Song of Roland*.

The guards often commented, "The old biddy doesn't know the fool will never get to use them French lessons."

After Mr. Lamb was electrocuted, the old woman, at the request of the warden, began teaching French to the prisoner sitting in the glass cage—no one ever visited him. Before long she had transferred all her doting onto that prisoner, even bringing *him* a pie each month like she had brought Mr. Lamb. What a kind person. The crippled old woman was occasionally sick and could not make her monthly lesson with the dangerous inmate, but if he was especially good, they usually accommodated her request to see him, even when she was off schedule, her being old and all.

Back at her Camaro, Barbara now headed into the Smokies.

In a rare Sunday afternoon work session, at 4:00, Krandall Kaufman and Tumbler sat glued to the monitor, playing over and over again the interview between Dolly Dauber and Barbara Dare-Carrington. Like coaches reviewing last Sunday's game, they backed up the video, fast forwarded it, paused it, and searched every nuance in Barbara's voice for any hint of over-excitement, nervousness, or slip up.

Finally Kaufman said, "Her father has done something so bad, she doesn't want anybody to know—"

"And whatever it was," Tumbler said, cutting in, "she thinks he was justified in doing it."

"So she's protecting him."

"Maybe hiding him out somewhere."

"Do a computer search of welfare rolls, jails, halfway houses, and—"

219

"Wouldn't it be easier to just make up a story on her father and spread it around?"

"That would only cost Todd Carrington votes. We want him elected. It's *his* vote we want."

"I see."

"Search the master files on computers at state headquarters for a man named Dare who might have requested a name change."

"Tennessee or Carolina?"

"Both. And check her student loan papers over at the University of Tennessee. See if there's anything on there about her old man."

"Already did. She didn't get a loan."

"Hmm. Tumbler, if we find her father, we've found the crowbar for influencing our next voice to represent the tobacco industry in the Congress of the United States of America for the first quarter of the next millennium!"

"Unless the public gets its way on those term limits."

"Congress will never let that happen."

"What about that Y2-K bug they're all talking about?"

"Bug?"

"A year from now when the computers roll over to 2000."

"I'm not worried about any bug. Find her father!"

"Now that we know she has one...and she's hiding him somewhere...I'll find him."

"We're closing in on her. I may get my first good night's sleep in a long time. *Now* that pretty little hillbilly will kneel."

"Why don't I just take her out in the bushes and make her tell where her daddy is?"

"Not yet. Tail her. Follow her everywhere she goes."

"Yes, sir. By the way, it was that list of questions you had me give Dolly Dauber that did the trick."

39

At 5:00 that same Sunday afternoon in Cell Block 13, prisoners, including Cliff and Axe, stood in their cells, facing the opposite direction from the Community Room.

In the center of the big room, Buzzard Mackelroy sat all alone at the card table, weeping and eating a peanut butter pie. The only sounds were the scraping of metal-on-metal as his fork hit the tin pan and the "ping, ping, ping" of his tears tapping that part of the pan where he had already eaten the pie.

The right leg of his blue pants was rolled up above his pale knee. His shin was blue all the way to his ankle, and he couldn't stand for the cloth to touch it. A guard, hired by someone on the outside, or a fellow inmate, had whacked him on the leg with a metal pipe while he was sleeping. It was probably a guard, aiming at his head, since most prisoners knew that he slept one night with his head on the pillow and the next night with his feet on the pillow—that gave him a 50% chance of survival. He figured he could survive a blow to his feet. Last night he had beaten the odds. But the would-be-assassin got away in the darkness; someone had removed a fuse from the fuse box.

When Buzzard Mackelroy finished eating the pie, he sat and cried a while longer. Then he signaled Axe to him. "Tell Preecher Kinser to take Dolly Dauber coon hunting."

"Yes, sir. When?"

"Tonight."

"Why?"

"I want the name of the person who gave her the list of questions for that TV interview."

"Want the coon skinned?"

"No need to harm her. Just take her coon hunting."

40

Since Todd wasn't home and wouldn't be until tomorrow evening, Barbara went to bed early that Sunday night. Clutching the keys to the Camaro, she tossed and turned, even more than usual. Any one of her daddy's enemies might already be on the way. And if they had TV that far back in the mountains, and if Baldy Slocum had watched her interview this morning, and if he had figured out who her father was, he and his boys would already be coming out of those mountains in their logging trucks with their saws and axes. One night soon they would burst through the chalet doors like Baldy's daddy had on Grandmother Dare. But they wouldn't put Todd in a closet with a jar of peanut butter.

Sleep finally came in the form of a nightmare on Vulture Mountain: the battle between her father and Baldy Slocum's father. In the bloodiest part of the fight, Barbara screamed. Her scream awoke her.

She sat up in bed.

A noise.

Someone was coming though the garage door. Oh Lord, God.

Holding the keys to the Camaro, barefooted, and wearing only her UT track shirt, she dashed down the hall, headed for the front door.

Abruptly the lights came on.

She raced faster.

She fumbled with the key to get the door open.

A hand came down on hers.

"Sweetheart, what are you doing?" Todd asked.

"Oh. Oh. Oh." She collapsed in his arms, knowing he heard the sigh she almost gave. "You scared me. I thought you were a burglar."

As he held her, he explained that after he found out about Dr. Edith Trybyszewski's death at SIG Labs, he had told Monty to cancel his Monday meeting.

"Oh, Todd, I'm glad you're here. Hold me closer. I was having a nightmare."

They talked into the night and she brought him up to date on all that had happened—all that she was allowed to tell him. And he told her what a good job Monty Ezell was doing, and how well the campaign was going, except that Monty had gotten the schedule all mixed up—the schedule Todd had left with her.

Finally Todd went to sleep, but she couldn't. She slipped into her apple-green robe and walked the floors. After a while, Todd came looking for her, tying the belt to his royal-blue robe and yawning as he did. "What are you doing?"

"Checking the door and window locks."

"Sweetheart, I never saw you so wound up. Let's go to the kitchen; I'll fix us a cup of hot tea."

Barbara drank the "cozy" chamomile tea, but its sedative claim to be as "soothing as a field of daisies," did little to halt her shivering and shaking. She couldn't tell Todd that her secret was about to get him killed. Maybe the dishonesty of not telling him was her fatal flaw. So she began to consider her options. She was coming to a dreadful conclusion. The only way she could save Todd was to leave him. But that was her mind talking. Her heart said she'd rather die. Either way, her options were growing slimmer and slimmer.

She led Todd back to the bedroom and laid down in his arms until he was asleep. Then she sat on the edge of the bed and beheld him. What a man. Handsome as a young lion. Yet how innocently he slept and how naively pure his dream. If she thought it would do any good, every night for the rest of her life, she would wear a sign hung around her neck that said, "I'll go with you willingly if you'll just let Todd live out his dream."

Her next trip to see her father would fall on Thanksgiving week-end. She couldn't wait to discuss her options with him. But if she could get at Dolly Dauber right now, she'd scratch her eyes out.

41

Buzzard Mackelroy had turned nineteen on the last day of his trial. The trial lasted only a few days. It happens that way when you confess. The jury foreman, an African-American railroad signal man, reacting to the harsh sentence, later said on TV, "What else could we do? The boy confessed. The judge told us we *had* to find him guilty. We thought, because of the circumstances, and it being his first offense, he'd get off with a light sentence. Maybe even probation. None 'a us figured on *life without parole*."

Judge Samuel L. Skillet, a white man, unfazed by the criticism of the sentence, was quoted in the *Knoxville News Sentinel*: "At the sentencing hearing, the District Attorney joined the defense in a request for clemency. I think the boy's a mad dog killer. I wanted to give him the chair. Time will prove who was right."

News travels fast in the prison system, especially in Cell Block 13. Everyone at Sagebrush Prison knew that Buzzard Mackelroy, the kid who stupidly confessed to murder, was coming their way. And they knew it was his birthday. The party was all planned.

Cell Block 13 was where the warden kept her meanest and most violent prisoners. The highest rank in Cell Block 13 was that of the Building Tender. The Building Tender, an unofficial, though very real position, handled discipline problems. So long as he did, the guards looked the other way while discipline was meted out. The Building Tender got to be the Building Tender, not by vote, but by hook or crook. As long as he could stay on the throne, he was treated as a quasi-king. But one slip, one bit of bad judgment, one night of sleeping with both eyes shut and the king would be washing the feet of some new king.

Such was the situation when Buzzard Mackelroy, age nineteen, arrived at Sagebrush Prison.

Harry Hancock, a violent and ruthless giant of a man, was

the Building Tender back then. As was Hancock's custom, each new prisoner was thoroughly beaten and forced to drink a prison cocktail. The cocktail was a glass of water from the commode, after Mr. Hancock had just used it of course. The whipping was to show who was boss. The cocktail was to teach humility.

Buzzard Mackelroy, the brash young teenager, stepped up before the giant to take his beating like a man. His lack of fear insulted Harry Hancock. When the whipping was over, Buzzard Mackelroy had a broken jaw and two broken ankles. When they dipped the glass into the commode and handed it to him, the kid drank the urine in one gulp as if it were Kool-Aid. That made Building Tender Hancock even madder. He boomed out with his big bass voice, "Do his wrists."

Four men threw Buzzard to the floor. While they held him face down, two others stomped his wrists. They left him lying in a heap beside the commode, twitching.

After the king and his henchmen strolled off, Huey Lamb, a fellow prisoner, came to the boy. He cradled him in his arms and carried him to the community room exit. He kicked on the metal door, rattling it. Ten minutes later two guards showed up with a gurney and casually unlocked the door. Huey Lamb refused the gurney, opting instead to carry the boy to the infirmary. The guards nonchalantly rolled the stretcher alongside, zigzagging it like in a cartoon, unlocking gates and joshing with prisoners, "He'll learn."

When Buzzard finally came to, and before the doctor arrived, Huey Lamb leaned over and whispered in his ear, "It's okay to show them you're a man, but don't be stupid about it, boy. Hide that youthful arrogance."

An hour later the doctor arrived. He asked Buzzard how he got hurt. The two guards stopped talking to each other and listened as Buzzard answered, "I fell down the stairs."

The news went through the prison like a dose of salts. "The kid has guts."

A week later, Huey Lamb rolled Buzzard Mackelroy into the cafeteria, in a wheelchair. It was Buzzard's first trip to the cafeteria. Both ankles were in casts, both wrists were in casts, and a bandage stretched from the top of his head to under his jaw.

The men all stood, except for Building Tender Hancock and his cronies.

Huey pushed Buzzard up to his assigned seat at one of the long tables. Once he was in place, the men sat. No one touched his food, not even Harry Hancock. When Buzzard Mackelroy took his first bite with his crippled hand, then, and only then, the men began to eat.

Harry Hancock looked chagrinned, but he never touched Buzzard Mackelroy again.

The Lamb—that's what the prisoners called Huey Lamb because they said he was gentle as one—shot his eyes across the cafeteria at the ruthless Building Tender. "I aim to take him."

"Tonight?" asked Buzzard.

"No, no, no. Patience. Patience, my young friend. First, I have to get you mended and trained. You're going to be my second-in-command."

From his first night in prison, Buzzard Mackelroy and Huey Lamb became pals forever...or at least until Huey's execution. For ten years, the Lamb taught Buzzard Mackelroy patience, and the first lesson was on how to survive in prison and, just as important, how to tolerate it.

Huey Lamb had been a tenured professor and head of the Business Department at a prestigious Tennessee university, not the one in Knoxville. But he had an affair with a female student—the Governor's daughter. The political heat got Lamb fired and run out of town. He turned to alcohol. Then he turned to bootlegging. In a drunken stupor, he killed a still operator who sold him some bad booze. At his trial, Huey Lamb, too, had the bad luck of coming up against Tennessee's "frying" judge, the Honorable Samuel L. Skillet. But the D.A. didn't speak on *Huey's* behalf.

The Lamb had already been on death row for three years the night Buzzard Mackelroy took his birthday whipping. Appeals would stretch out for another thirteen years, but a date certain was coming.

Days turned into weeks, weeks into months, and months into

years. All the while, Huey Lamb was becoming a rising star among the inmates. He taught Buzzard everything he knew about computers, networks, accounting, and administration. Before life as a professor, the Lamb served his country as a Navy SEAL. His expertise was breaking enemy codes, an expertise he taught to Buzzard. Obviously aware of the boy's gifted mind, the Lamb encouraged him to spend time, a lot of time, in the prison library, developing the gift. Buzzard Mackelroy was a good student and did exactly as instructed. He set himself a goal to read every book of significance in the library.

Meanwhile, Harry Hancock continued to rule Cell Block 13 with an iron fist, beating the men into submission, every now and then killing one of them. But after years of beatings for no rhyme nor reason, Hancock was starting to lose his power base. The men understood force, but would not long accept *unjust* force.

All the while, Huey Lamb's winsome personality was "winning friends and influencing people." *His* power base was expanding, in no small part due to his young right-hand man, Buzzard Mackelroy.

One day the Lamb said to Buzzard, "You've spent enough time in the library, boy. Your *mind* is not enough. Sometimes you have to *whip* a man. Now, get over to the gym."

Buzzard headed for the gym. He took up weightlifting, wrestling, and boxing. There he learned the finer points of low blows, eye-gouging, and the use of steroids. But it soon became obvious he would never whip some of the prison giants. And that's when Huey Lamb accidentally discovered Buzzard Mackelroy's greatest talent: his natural ability to lead men.

"You have a way with men," the Lamb said to him. "You can whip a man and make him like it. That's because you are fair about it. Men, even prisoners, respond to fairness. They respond to loyalty. And they respond to respect."

"Yes, sir," Buzzard whispered.

"But some men respond only to force. Yet if force is your only tool, like Harry Hancock, and if you cut enough people, you might drown in their blood. So use force sparingly."

"Explain?"

"If you have enough power behind you, a raised eyebrow will get the job done. Walk softly and carry a big stick."

"How do you get enough power behind you?"

"By building a network of men, men loyal to you."

Back to the library. There Buzzard found a book on networking. He studied the difference between a *wide* network and a *deep* network. He decided to incorporate both concepts.

He soon had a network of *frontline* men, men loyal to him. Under each frontline man, he built a *deep* network of men several levels down, each level responsible to the level just above its own level. The concept would work to infinity, but ultimately each man was responsible to Buzzard, and that's where the power came from. And he shared the power; he encouraged his downline to build their own networks under themselves. The men liked this, and the only danger, the networking book said, was that one especially good at networking might become too powerful. But since all the networks were under him anyway, Buzzard decided to cross that bridge when, and if, he came to it.

As part of his fledgling network, Buzzard now had two personal bodyguards—before Cliff and Axe. Of course all of Buzzard's network was first-level to Huey Lamb, but primarily loyal to Buzzard.

"The night we take down Harry Hancock," Huey Lamb said, "is the night we'll join our two networks."

"When?" asked Buzzard. "I've been training for ten years."

"Soon, and very soon."

"I'm ready to do it tonight. I was ready the first night."

Along about midnight of that very evening, Buzzard's two bodyguards were slaughtered while taking a shower. The guards spread the rumor that the killings came on orders from outside the prison.

Buzzard knew who had drawn the blood.

When the men came down to breakfast the following morning, Harry Hancock was hanging by his feet, stark naked, from the highest rafter. Tied to each of his wrists was a rope that dangled the mutilated bodies of Buzzard Mackelroy's two bodyguards, still dripping blood.

Cliff and Axe, Buzzard's brand-new bodyguards, stood at attention underneath the spectacle.

The slaughterhouse-smell of fresh meat froze the incoming men in silence. The only sound was that of the rope sawing into the wooden rafter. Creaking...creaking...creaking.

Other than the swinging, the only movement was *former* Building Tender Hancock. Twitching...twitching...twitching.

Word went out from the Lamb, the new Building Tender, that the three men were to hang there for twenty-four hours. The next day they cut down Harry Hancock, the man with the big bass voice. Both his shoulders were dislocated, and the rest of his life he walked with a limp and talked like a soprano.

The midnight massacre *did* alert Buzzard to the danger that could come from outside the prison, so he put himself to work on developing a network on the outside for the sole purpose of handling acts of retribution.

After becoming the new Building Tender, the Lamb, ever so meekly, though he was now king, asked the guards if he might take French lessons. "Before you take me for that last walk, I want to learn French."

That request was granted, and they soon made arrangements with a retired schoolteacher to come once a month to teach him French. Lamb's second request was that his second-in-command, Buzzard Mackelroy, be rewarded with a ten-minute visit to the "prisoner visitation room" once a month.

"Why?" the guards asked. "In ten years, he ain't had a visitor."

"That aside," said the Lamb, "it would please me greatly if you could make such arrangements."

"He's much too dangerous."

Professor Huey Lamb raised an eyebrow. "Perhaps you could build a portable glass cage just for him and just for when he's out of his cell."

And that's when the all-glass, bullet-proof cage was built for Buzzard Mackelroy's monthly visit to the prisoner visitation room.

Professor Huey Lamb held the position of Building Tender for three years. Buzzard and his fast-growing network remained loyal to the Lamb right up to the night they led him the few feet down the hall to shake hands with "Old Sparky." That night Buzzard Mackelroy ascended to the throne of Building Tender and inherited the Lamb's vast network, along with his elderly French teacher. Buzzard said he, too, had always wanted to learn French. Reluctantly, the elderly schoolmarm, obviously eaten up with arthritis, agreed to make a stab at it, weather permitting. Every thirty days for three years she had brought a peanut butter pie to Huey Lamb, perhaps as a reward for his being a good student. Now, she brought Buzzard a peanut butter pie. Old habits die hard. The crippled old woman with the little girl voice was Buzzard Mackelroy's first visitor in thirteen years.

After the respectful three days of mourning, Buzzard Mackelroy got right to work blending his network and Huey Lamb's, both inside and outside prison. The combined database would rival that of major corporations. Buzzard kept the records on a floppy disk and kept the disk stored in a vault under one of the pit stops at Alcoa Speedway in Alcoa, Tennessee, about an hour from the prison. Fourteen years in the making, his *outside* network was about to deliver its first act of retribution.

Preecher Kinser owned Alcoa Speedway. Preecher drove the chase car that fateful morning he and Buzzard caught the man who had raped Buzzard's mother. Preecher Kinser just now received the email message, in code: Take Dolly Dauber coon hunting.

42

Later that night, Preecher Kinser got all dressed up in his coon hunting duds—overalls and clod-hopper brogans. He climbed into the little yellow roadster and headed for Asheville, North Carolina. Dolly Dauber was about to get her comeuppance.

Preecher ran the Speedway in Alcoa, Tennessee. Alcoa was the home of Alcoa Aluminum, not far from Maryville. Maryville lay just south of Knoxville.

Preecher Kinser, a beanpole of a man with gaunt hollow cheeks and hypnotic eyes, hadn't always been in racing. At age 10 he "got the Call" and his handlers bought him a revival tent. An Oklahoma faith-healer had started the tent fad some years earlier when he brought his big tent through East Tennessee, filling it every night with people and filling washtubs with money. Soon everybody in East Tennessee had a revival tent. Some of the new tent-preachers were converted car dealers and the like—men and women who had a way with people and words. By age 13, Preecher was the biggest draw between Knoxville, Tennessee, and Roanoke, Virginia. But also at age 13, his preaching began to lose some of its fervor; the pleasures of the flesh were just too enjoyable for him to come down so hard on sin. And so, without anything to preach against, he soon lost his crowd. Then the money dried up. Then he lost his handlers. Then he backslid.

Preecher served a stretch at Sagebrush Prison for "lifting an offering" without permission and for "testing the speed" of cars that didn't belong to him. After he was paroled, he tried his hand at preaching again, but he just didn't feel it. So he got baptized again, but that didn't help. Used to, he could pack out a massive tent; now he couldn't fill a phone booth. So in desperation he got baptized some more. And some more. He got baptized so many times he knew every frog in the creek by name. Eventually, he gave up on preaching and opened the racetrack at Alcoa. He had always liked fast cars.

Preecher's men-friends kidded him about how ugly he was,

but women flocked around him like bees after honey. And he flocked back. He considered himself a right handsome ugly man.

But most important, Preecher Kinser drove the chase car that morning fourteen years ago when Buzzard Mackelroy went after Baldy Slocum's father for raping his, Buzzard's, mother, Grandmother Dare.

As Preecher now raced though the Smokies, he popped in a cassette, and some gospel group cut loose on "Give Me That Old Time Religion." Preecher turned the volume as high as it would go, almost drowning out the roar of the yellow roadster.

By 11:00 PM, Preecher had found the address he was hunting and now his long and lanky frame sat crouched down in the idling roadster. Waiting for a silver Porsche.

He didn't have to wait long. His tuned-ear soon heard the whine of the engine even before the lights of the Porsche came into sight. That would be Dolly Dauber coming from the cocktail party. Preecher hoped she ran. The Porsche wouldn't stand a chance against the roadster.

Dolly pulled into her boyfriend's driveway, opened the door, and climbed out. She was wearing spike heels and a short, tight-fitting green party dress.

Preecher floorboarded the yellow coupe. The engine noise exploded like a noise-bomb. The tires shrieked and the exhaust pipes spat blue fire.

Dolly Dauber froze in the headlights like a bug-eyed deer.

Preecher Kinser slammed the brakes, the bumper inches from her short green skirt. He leaped over the hood, grabbed her, and gently threw her, kicking and screaming, into the shotgun seat, then roared off into the mountains.

"What do you think you're doing?!"

"You'll have to speak up, ma'am. I can't hear you over these bazooka pipes."

"What are you doing?!"

"Takin' you coon huntin'."

"*Coon hunting*?! I'll be taking you to jail!"

"Coon huntin' against the law in yo' state?"

"This is kidnapping."

234

"No it ain't." Preecher laughed. "This is show and tell. I show you a coon; you tell me a name."

"*Name*?"

"Name."

"What *name*?"

"Name of whoever give you that list 'a questions for yo' TV show yesterday."

"If Ms. Todd Carrington sent you to—"

"That the name of the housewife you had on yo' show this morning?"

"Barbara Carrington."

"Never heard of her."

"Then who sent you?"

"If you guessed a thousand years, you'd never get it right. Just tell me the name."

"It's not ethical for a reporter to reveal a source."

"*Ethical*, huh? And you think what you did to that housewife on yo' show was ethical?"

"All I did was ask about her family."

"I got you figured out, missy. You're the kind a person who'd say she went to church, and didn't. Seems like we need to have us a little lesson in ethics tonight."

"If you don't stop this car, you'll think ethics."

"All that buzzin' ain't gonna do you no good." Preecher dug around in his box of cassettes, trying to find his favorite tape. "You know what you are?"

"I'm the anchor woman at—"

"Dauber's a good name for you. You a mud dauber."

"*Mud dauber*?"

"Yeah," Preecher said, still searching through his pile of tapes. "All you do is go around trying to find some mud to daub on somebody."

"You call it mud. I call it news. Everybody's hiding something. It's my job to find out *what* and tell."

"'Fore the night's over, you may want to find a more honorable profession."

"*Honorable.* I'm going all the way to the top of my profession. People say I've got the looks. Some even say I look like Dolly Parton. She made it big. She's from these parts."

Preecher Kinser glanced over at the buxom blond. "No offense, ma'am, but to match up to Dolly Parton, you'll need more 'n peroxide and paddin'."

"Why, you sorry excuse for a—" She smacked him right in the mouth.

Preecher cocked his fist but remembered, preachers don't slap women. Besides, slapping her wouldn't get what he wanted from her. He shifted gears as he took a new curve. "You ain't bad lookin'. You just need to stop pretending to be somebody you ain't."

"I suppose you expect me to say thanks."

"I don't expect you to say nothin' except that name. But I reckon you ain't ready to do that yet. So just sit back and enjoy the ride. You won't be hurt nor nothin'. All I want's the name of the person who set that housewife up. Soon as you tell me, we'll call off the dogs."

They were now in the darkest part of the Smokies.

"*Dogs*? I don't see any dogs."

"Don't see no bears neither. But me 'n you both knows they's bears in these mountains. Bobcats too."

"I'm not scared."

"No need to be. I'll be right beside you. Most 'a the time. Here's you a flashlight."

"You'll think *flashlight.* Just wait 'til I turn the TV spotlight on—"

Preecher found the cassette he'd been hunting, and waved her off. He shoved the tape into the tape deck and turned the volume as high as it would go. Dolly Parton and Porter Wagoner, guitars in hand, and dressed in their best sequined finery, dashed out on the Grand Ol' Opry stage and began to sing, "Daddy Was An Old Time Preacher Man," drowning Dolly Dauber's threats. Preecher tapped his left hand in rhythm on the dashboard.

After a while he turned off the highway onto a gravel logging road. A few miles into the most dense part of the forest, he took another logging trail, forded a creek, then followed it a ways. At trail's end, he pulled to a halt.

"Git out."

Dolly didn't budge.

Preecher strolled over to a portable metal cage he had left earlier in the evening and let loose three blue-tick hounds. "Sick 'em, Blue."

Blue and her two boys dashed into the night.

"Come on." Preecher said, pulling Dolly Dauber with him into the pitch-black woods.

Soon the long-eared hounds began singing up one holler and down the other.

Still clasping Dolly's hand, Preecher led her along, zigzagging and circling until he knew she couldn't find the roadster again. Suddenly, Blue's voice changed and she began to yelp and holler in one constant roar.

"She's treed."

"A coon?" Dolly asked.

"Or a bear."

They raced to the tree. Preecher shined his light up into the branches. Two eyes stared back from the top limb.

Preecher grabbed a stick and slung it, knocking the coon out of the tree. The dogs jumped it. Preecher grabbed the animal by the tail, put his right brogan on its head. Then he got down and spoke directly into the coon's ear. "Tell me the name of the man who gave you that list of questions."

But the coon didn't answer. So he gave a hard yank on its tail. The coon lay lifeless as the dogs bayed.

"You killed it. Why'd you do that?" Dolly asked.

"The coon didn't answer my question."

"You're crazy. The coon didn't know the answer."

"I didn't know that."

"You're nuts. A coon can't talk."

"You can."

"But you said you wouldn't hurt me."

"Ethics, ma'am. That's when I thought you'd tell me what I wanted to know." Then he looked into the night. "Go git another 'un, Blue."

237

The three long-eared hounds lit out through another holler, after another coon.

Preecher turned his flashlight off. He looked at Dolly and pointed. "You go that way, ma'am; I'll go this. Meet you at the coon." And with that he ran into the night.

"Wait. I don't know the way back."

He hid behind an oak tree and peeped while she wandered around in circles through bushes and trees until the batteries on her flashlight gave out. She sat down on a stump, removed her spike heels, and sat there banging them against each other. Then she began to shake and cry. Then she told Preecher what he wanted to know.

At 8:00 the following morning, the yellow roadster pulled up in front of Dolly Dauber's TV Station. Her green dress tattered and torn, her hose ripped to shreds, one shoe heel missing, her hair a mess, and the smell of the hunt all over her, she climbed over the side of the car where a door ought to be.

"If you ever tell anyone what I asked you," Preecher said, "we'll go coon huntin' again. Only next time, I'll *skin* the coons. All of 'em."

Dolly stood in the cold morning fog and stared at him.

"Have a nice day, ma'am. If you ever get tired 'a that rich boyfriend, give me a call. Bye."

With that, Preecher Kinser and Old Blue and her two sons blasted off down the road in Buzzard Mackelroy's yellow roadster; he had to get back to Alcoa, Tennessee, for a race tonight.

He turned the tape to full volume and let the song ring throughout the Smokies, "Daddy Was An Old Time Preacher Man."

43

Always-nervous Tumbler stood in the always-dark Observation Room, making his report to Kaufman. "For a week, I've tailed Barbara Dare-Carrington everywhere she's been in that black Corvette."

"Yeah?" asked Kaufman.

"Nothing."

"*Nothing*?"

"Nothing yet."

"Tumbler, there's something mighty peculiar going on with that woman."

"What's that, sir?"

"Get that video out and let's play it again."

"The Dolly Dauber interview?"

"No, I've got that one memorized. The one with her and Dr. Trybyszewski talking about the second floor."

Tumbler typed the word "Trybyszewski" into the computer, then hit the video-retrieve button. In seconds, the video loaded itself into the VCR. Tumbler punched another button, and Barbara and Treby began their conversation in the lab. When the scientist abruptly ended the conversation and trotted down the glass-domed hallway, the screen went blank.

"Play it again," Kaufman ordered.

The scene started over.

"Shut it off." Kaufman turned to Tumbler. "I've got a bad feeling about little Ms. Carrington."

"I don't get it."

"What woman would listen to Dr. Trybyszewski's comments and keep silent about it?"

"Uh oh. You mean she's told someone?"

"Worse yet," Kaufman said, "She hasn't. If she had told, the police would be out here going through this place with a fine-tooth comb. Doesn't it seem odd that she hasn't mentioned the second floor to Sally Chastine, or anyone else at the lab?"

"Wait a minute. Maybe she has."

"Oh?"

"The week before I started tailing her every move, I followed her and Sally Chastine on a little trip over to the Esmeralda."

"*The Esmeralda?*"

"You know. The Esmeralda. It's an inn & restaurant, back in the mountains—"

"Don't lecture me! I know what it is. But why did they go all the way over there?"

"You can bet it wasn't just to eat fish."

"The Esmeralda isn't a fish—"

"No, but that's what *they* ate. They were whispering like detectives. And that was right after the killing."

"Think she's told Sally Chastine?"

"Wouldn't doubt it," Tumbler said. "They're thick. Their husbands too; they go fishing together."

"Hmm."

"Don't you know she's dying to get on that second floor," Tumbler said.

Kaufman turned and bent into the moment, a freakish grin on his face. "Well why don't we just let her do that."

"Sir?"

"Let's introduce her to Mr. Puff."

"*Mr. Puff!* Isn't that dangerous?"

"We'll tell her a little. I'd rather have her know a little, than suspect a lot. Only get Dr. Clark to make the intro—"

"While we watch her reaction on the TV monitor." Tumbler rubbed his palms excitedly. "But what if it gets out of hand, and I have to dash down there—"

"Then we'll have to cut our losses and find another way to pry loose the vote of Mr. Todd Carrington, the widower. If you have to come on the scene, I want you to be the last thing she ever sees."

"But I don't think I can get this girl to write a suicide note."

"Fool! I don't want two killings here at the lab! Drag her into the mountains."

Monday morning when Barbara showed up for work, Dr.

240

Quebian Clark summoned her to his office. She slipped into her lab coat then headed down the hall toward the elevator. As she passed Sally Chastine's office, she started to pop in and say good morning, but didn't. She took the elevator to the third floor, ever mindful that no button would make the elevator stop on the forbidden second floor where Mr. Puff worked. She and Sally had been working on a plan to get on the second floor. The plan was almost ready to be put into action.

When she walked into Dr. Clark's office, he blurted out, "Today you will meet Mr. Puff."

"*Mr. Puff?*" Barbara gulped, trying to curb her excitement. Then anxiety hit her. Treby was the only other person who had mentioned Mr. Puff. Just before she was murdered. Now, Barbara wished she had told Sally she was on the way to Dr. Clark's office. At the time, she hadn't been concerned. She was concerned now. If push came to shove, she knew she could get away from Dr. Clark, the crotchety old scientist. But she didn't know about Mr. Puff. Mr. Puff must have been the one who slit Treby's throat.

"Come with me." Dr. Clark, in his white lab coat, led the way to the elevator. Once inside, he inserted the ever-present gold key into the elevator button-pad.

The elevator stopped on the second floor. Barbara held her breath.

Dr. Clark pointed, and she stepped off. He exited right behind her. The elevator door slammed. She realized it was just her and him in the dimly lit hall. Dr. Clark walked ahead of her, past doors with no knobs. A ways down the hall he stopped in front of one of the doors. Written on the door, like a celebrity's dressing room title, was the name, "Mr. Puff."

"Top secret. You must never tell anyone what you see here today." Clark inserted into the lock the same key he had just used to make the elevator stop on the second floor. Then he ushered Barbara inside.

It was a large room, brightly lit, and smelled of ammonia.

Then Barbara saw the most spectacular sight she had ever seen. In the middle of the lab-room sat a sealed glass cage. Inside the cage sat a chrome-plated robot. The robot sat in a straight-back chair, smoking one cigarette after the other. Hooked to his cage were cables, wires, and hoses of all sorts, ventilating the smoke to individual animal pens that held white rats, rabbits, guinea pigs, chickens, monkeys, and such.

"What on earth?!" asked Barbara.

"Meet Mr. Puff." Clark pointed at the shiny robot.

Barbara couldn't respond. All of the contracts she had seen for SIG Labs were for environmental projects. No contracts revealed anything to do with tobacco testing. Something was catawampused here, and Treby had died trying to tell her what it was. Barbara also knew the place was bugged and that someone was probably listening right now and might even be watching. She began to play dumb in order to gather as much information as possible.

"What's that for?" She pointed to a giant computer, hooked up to all the apparatuses.

"This is the biggest computer IBM makes. Amway and the Mormons have the next two largest sizes. This is the greatest computer ever made. It measures and manipulates. The effect of nicotine. On all sorts of species. Including humans."

His short clipped speech irritated her. "I know of a computer that calculates the information faster and more accurately," she said.

"Oh?" Clark jerked a pen and pad from his lab coat, ready to copy the name of some company with better equipment. "And who might have such a machine?"

"Everyone. It's the human body."

Clark peered over his horn-rimmed glasses at her as if to say, "Cute, Ms. Dare-Carrington. Cute." But he said nothing.

"Dr. Clark, I thought our laboratory only did environmental testing. Why are we involved in nicotine testing?"

"The tobacco industry requires the best. The best testing facilities available. They know we have the best. But they want it done discretely. Especially these days. And most especially with that Nicotine hearing going on in Washington. They asked us to do this, how should I say, behind the scenes project for them. As you know, these are tight financial times. The tobacco industry has financial resources. Such financial resources are unavailable to the environmentalists."

"I see."

"The tobacco industry makes up the financial difference we lose to environmental projects. It's all legal and aboveboard. It's just secret."

"Let's see if I understand," said Barbara. "We do testing for environmental agencies, and we do testing for the tobacco industry. We just don't tell the environmentalists. Is that correct?"

"I could not have said it better," said Clark.

"So, it's a matter of the bottom line."

"You do see." Clark smiled.

Innocent enough as Clark explained it—innocent, maybe legal. But for sure, unethical—and she believed he was telling her the truth as he knew it. She pointed to the hoses that delivered the cigarette smoke from Mr. Puff to the animals. "Why this experiment?"

"To study the damage of nicotine. On the liver, the lungs, the heart, and the kidneys."

"Why?"

"Ms. Dare-Carrington, I've seen your transcript. I know you're not stupid. We apply what we learn about the effect of nicotine on animals to the effect of nicotine on humans."

"Let's see. You pump smoke into the chambers that hold the animals so you can see the damage nicotine does to them, thus to humans?

"Now you've got it." He grinned confidently.

"But if Mr. Puff is the one doing the smoking, the animals are getting what I believe is called *auxiliary* smoke."

"Exactly. Those vials at the top of Mr. Puff's head are filled with nicotine. We adjust the amount to get the desired effect on the rats."

Barbara glanced to where Clark pointed. When she did, she also saw a large cigarette-filled-"Y"-shaped machine with a glass front. The machine fed cigarettes to Mr. Puff. "So you're testing how much nicotine you can add to the cigarettes before the mice die?"

"Heavens no. I would never permit them to kill anything. Don't you read the papers? We're measuring how much nicotine we can take out and keep the rats hooked?"

She must not show shock. "This must be quite an expensive operation."

"The tobacco industry spends millions annually to protect the public."

"Why don't you just unplug Mr. Puff?"

"Why. Er. Why. Er. We—" Clark caught himself, then grinned a most respectful grin. "Why Ms. Dare-Carrington, I do believe I'm going to have to keep an eye on you. You see, if Mr. Puff didn't puff, we'd be out of business." He abruptly stared at the ceiling and cleared his throat.

Then as if whoever was watching had somehow signaled him—Maybe he was wearing an ear receiver—Dr. Clark blurted out, "What are your thoughts on Mr. Puff?"

It was a loaded question, so she thought for moment, then chuckled. "He certainly is a heavy smoker."

But Clark didn't laugh. "Lesson over."

As they left, Barbara observed rows of black file cabinets that lined the walls. She started toward them. "What are these?"

"None of your concern," he said, nonchalantly.

She tried to read the labels, but couldn't without getting closer.

"Come along. The elevator is waiting."

Barbara walked as slowly as she could, studying the whole layout, but she knew she would be back to the second floor. And soon.

Later that evening, with Todd off on the campaign trail, she took Sally Chastine back over to the Esmeralda, so they could talk and not be overheard by SIG Labs eavesdroppers. As they sipped Cabernet Sauvignon and dined on Brace of Quail, she brought Sally up to date on Mr. Puff.

When she finished she said, "I have our plan all worked out to get on the second floor and search it. Everything except one thing."

"What's that?"

"When."

44

Tumbler tailed Barbara for three weeks. It was finally time to give Kaufman a report. It was the Wednesday before Thanksgiving when he and Mickey drove the white Mercedes into the hidden underground parking lot at SIG Labs. Tumbler hurried through the tunnel, past the guards, then took the secret elevator to the third floor.

Kaufman was waiting for him in the Observation Room. "Well?"

"Nothing."

"*Nothing*?"

"Nothing." Tumbler began to recite in monotone, "Monday through Friday…she goes to and from work. Two Sundays ago went to church alone…while husband out of town. This past Sunday had lunch with husband and the mayor at country club. Saturday, went with Sally Chastine to Folk Art Center on the Blue Ridge Parkway. Husbands went fishing—"

"Stop reciting! Summarize. What did you find out that we can use on her?"

"That's it. I even did a little dumpster diving. But her trashcan had no *personal* mail."

"You've followed her for three weeks and that's it?"

"There is one peculiar thing," Tumbler said, trimming his fingernails with his pocketknife.

"What?"

"She and her husband both have new Corvettes, and—"

"I know that. Tell me something I—"

"Here's what's unusual."

"She kept her old car."

"*Kept her old car*?"

"Kept it."

"Wonder why?"

"Camouflage?"

"She ever drive it?"

"No, sir. The Camaro just sits there in the driveway. The mileage hasn't changed since I started tailing her."

"Drives the black Corvette?" asked Kaufman.

"Yes, sir. Maybe the Camaro is her father's car, and—"

"No. She wouldn't be that foolish, her trying to keep anybody from locating him." Silent for a moment, Kaufman fiddled with the joy stick on his wheelchair. "I have an idea. Tell Monty Ezell to send a used car dealer out to act like he wants to buy the Camaro. See what she says."

"Yes, sir. Want me to keep tailing her?"

"First, let Ezell find out why she's so fond of that old clunker."

45

Early Thanksgiving morning, Barbara sat at the kitchen table, slicing apples—the housekeeper hadn't arrived yet to start the holiday dinner, and Todd was still asleep. She was wearing her orange and white UT sweatshirt and black sweatpants. On the floor between her legs sat a bushel of gala apples she had purchased over at Hendersonville, apple capital of North Carolina. Sally and Gene had gone with her. Gene insisted they go in his green wrecker, so they did. They made a day of it, stopping at Flat Rock to visit the home of Carl Sandburg, then having lunch in Cashiers and dinner in Highlands.

Now, while Barbara peeled and sliced the apples, she dialed Grandmother Dare on the cordless phone to wish her happy Thanksgiving. After the greeting, she asked, "Doing anything special today?"

"I reckon I'll just work on that jig-saw puzzle you sent me. The one of the pilgrims' first Thanksgiving."

"You'll never guess what I'm doing." Barbara tucked the receiver under her chin and kept peeling.

"What?"

"Slicing apples."

"Making a pie?

"Making dried apples."

"*Dried apples?*"

"Like you used to. Only I can't remember what to do after I get them sliced."

"Why, child, just put them on a board and leave them out in the sun for three days."

"That's all?"

"No, you have to bring them in at night."

"*Bring them in?*"

"Keep the dew off."

"I forgot about the dew. Isn't there an easier way?"

"I reckon so. Find an old car and put them in it for three days. The sun'll do the rest."

"Well, I have an old car, so I think that's what I'll do."

After she hung up she went to the garage where she found a wide paneling-board, laid the sliced apples on it, and started for the Camaro.   There she met Sarah, her part-time cook and housekeeper, coming through the garage door, so she set the apples on a bench in the garage, forgot them, and jumped right into preparing Thanksgiving dinner. Then, of all things, while she mixed the turkey stuffing, and while Sarah fixed the trimmings, Monty Ezell called. He had a friend in town who collects Camaros and wanted to bring him out to see hers.

"I guess it's all right, Monty," Barbara said. "Todd's still asleep."

"Too much celebrating?"

"I suppose."

"Don't wake him. We'll only be there a minute. My friend just wants to take some pictures of your Camaro for his collection."

"Come on out. Sarah's liable to put you to tearing lettuce for the salad."

In a few minutes, Monty and his friend arrived, but stayed in the driveway. Barbara met them at the Camaro. "Monty, how did you get out of helping Carol with Thanksgiving lunch?"

"We're dining at the club."

"Oh."

His jovial words dripped with syrup, but his eyes danced a cold and calculating dance, making Barbara's skin crawl. For Todd's sake, she hoped she was wrong about his campaign manager.   Maybe being two-faced went with the territory. Monty's friend didn't seem to know much about Camaros, but he showed a great deal of interest in the history of her car.

Monty bent down like he was inspecting the wheels. "Why such large tires?"

Without batting an eye, she answered, "I hear it snows a lot up here."

Ezell's dummy friend looked at her dumbfounded.

She chuckled and started back in the house. "You men go ahead and kick the tires all you want. I have to get back to the kitchen so Sarah can show me which end of the turkey to stuff."

"Just a minute, Barbara." Monty opened the driver-side door and peeped toward the odometer. "My friend here can't understand why an executive, who owns a new Corvette, would keep an old car like this...why you haven't sold it."

Barbara smelled a rat. "I didn't hear him make an offer."

Monty gulped.

She walked inside, then came right back out, this time through the garage, carrying the board laden with sliced apples. She popped the button to the hatchback lid with her elbow, and laid the board in the trunk. Monty and his friend looked puzzled.

Barbara stared at the hot sun. "I keep the Camaro to dry apples in."

Monty shook his head, laughing.

She went back to the kitchen. As soon as she heard Monty's Jag fire up, she peeped out the window and watched them go around the curve and out of sight. Then she went to the bedroom to check on Todd. He had slept through it all. Yesterday, he had won the election as North Carolina's Representative to the General Assembly by a landslide, and she had celebrated with him into the night. Before they had gone to bed, he told her that Monty wanted him to announce his candidacy for the U.S. Senate right away. But first Todd wanted to discuss the decision with his father. He would do that New Year's Day.

Barbara went back to the kitchen and looked out the window at the Camaro's trunk full of sliced apples. That was Thursday. The apples needed three days to dry. Perfect. She would remove them on Saturday, then on Sunday she would drive the Camaro across Old Smoky for her visit to Sagebrush Prison.

Four days had passed and it was now the Monday after Thanksgiving at SIG Labs. At 6:00 o'clock in the morning, Tumbler raced down the hall to the Observation Room, carrying a map in his hand.

"What's the emergency?" Kaufman asked.

Out of breath, Tumbler blurted out, "The Camaro has 220 new miles on it!"

"Since Ezell checked it Thursday?"

"Yes, sir."

"How you know?"

"Every morning since Thursday, at exactly five o'clock, on my way in to do a read out on the TV monitor, I went by and checked the mileage. One hour ago, that speedometer showed 220 new miles. She had to have put the miles on there yesterday!"

"What do you make of it?" asked Kaufman.

Tumbler ripped open the map that showed Western North Carolina and East Tennessee. He located Asheville on the map, then pulled out a compass and drew a circle with a red marks-a-lot. The circle took in 110 miles in any direction. Then with all his force he drove the big-blade of his little pocketknife right through Asheville, all the way into the wooden desk. "Somewhere in that radius is our next senator's father-in-law!"

"Good work. Now all we have to do is plot when she's going to make that trip again and follow her," Kaufman said, studying the blood-red circle on the map.

"Christmas," Tumbler said.

"*Christmas*?"

"Christmas weekend."

"Why then?"

"What loyal daughter wouldn't go see her father for Christmas?"

"You may be right."

"Also, it's four weeks to Christmas," said Tumbler. "We tailed her for three weeks; add this week plus those three and that makes *four*."

"Hmm."

"She never moved the Camaro during those first four weeks."

"By George, I think we've got her, Tumbler."

"Christmas weekend, I'll just fall in behind the Camaro, and we'll take us a little trip."

"And New Year's Day, when Todd tells his senator father that he doesn't want the tobacco industry involved in his campaign, we'll produce his long lost relative."

"His wife's daddy!" Tumbler yanked his knife out of the wood, and put it, the map, and compass away.

250

"Tumbler, if you pull this off, it'll be the best Christmas present I ever received. Keep your car gassed up; you might even get a tune up, and once she climbs in that old clunker, don't let her out of your sight."

"Duck soup. A new Mercedes can overtake an old Camaro any day of the week."

At eight that same morning Barbara Dare-Carrington reported to work at SIG Labs a lot smarter and a lot wiser. Yesterday she had visited her father at the prison. She never asked her father where he had gotten his information—she knew not to—but she now knew that a man named Tumbler had delivered the list of ten questions to Dolly Dauber for the trick TV interview, that Tumbler was the henchman for a man named Kaufman, that Kaufman was head of the tobacco cartel, that he had an office at SIG Labs, and she also knew their weapon of choice.

She now remembered meeting Kaufman. Todd's father had introduced her to him in New Bern the night her engagement was announced. And she remembered that he was confined to a wheelchair. The wheelchair would explain the extra wide halls at SIG Labs. But she had never seen Kaufman at the lab. He and Tumbler must be the ones Treby was talking about who officed with Dr. Clark on the third floor. Then it hit her. Since she had never seen a wheelchair come through the lobby or go up the lobby elevator, there must be another elevator in the building. Maybe it also led to the second floor.

At the prison yesterday, her father had also told her that Kaufman and Tumbler were involved in the fight in the U. S. Senate hearing over whether or not to regulate nicotine. That might also explain Mr. Puff and all the un-invoiced tobacco deliveries in those panel trucks every Monday. But she still had no idea why the tobacco cartel was so interested in knowing who *her* father was. Her father had nothing to do with the tobacco industry. She had a sneaky suspicion she would find the answer once she gained access to those file cabinets on the second floor.

A terrible gnawing in her stomach warned her of what she

didn't want to admit. The tobacco cartel was probably after Todd. Maybe they were promoting a political opponent who wanted to release a negative story about him to the press. Todd's being married to the daughter of a notorious prisoner would certainly give the press plenty to write about. But politically speaking, Todd was a small fry. At least for now. Perhaps they were after Todd's father, the senator. No, the senator was already on the tobacco industry's side. None of it made sense. But whether it made sense or not, Tamika and Treby got their throats cut by somebody fighting the tobacco war.

One other thing was clear. Tumbler and Kaufman were obsessed with learning who her father was. So she had to find out why. If she could find out why, she might be able to stop them in time.

It was obvious that Tumbler and Kaufman were not enemies of her father; they didn't even know him. They'd be more careful if they did. But their meddling could cost Todd his political career and get her slaughtered. So they had to be stopped, or at least thrown off track.

She began to plan. She figured the second floor at SIG Labs would probably tell her what she needed to know on Tumbler and Kaufman. So cracking the second floor mystery, at first a curiosity, now became a top concern. But when could she do it? The best time to break in would be when there was the smallest amount of activity going on around the lab. When would that be? Christmas! The week before Christmas things would begin to grind to a halt. But when to break in? The Christmas Decorating Committee! She would appoint herself and Sally Chastine as the decorating committee. Then at night, they would sneak up there and...

46

December 19, the Sunday before Christmas, Tumbler called Kaufman. "I'm in Gatlinburg! Get over here fast!"

"What is it!?" Kaufman rushed.

"She's here!"

"Where?"

"Just hurry. I don't want to lose her. I'll wait for you at the big entrance sign to the Park, the one coming out of Gatlinburg."

"I don't want to drive to Gatlinburg in this snow."

"I'll show you where her daddy lives," Tumble teased.

Two hours later, Kaufman drove though the Great Smoky Mountain National Park entrance/exit gate, just outside Gatlinburg. His wheelchair-equipped Ford van was also equipped with car-phone, miniature computer, and in general, everything required to link him to his office. A heavy snow was falling.

Tumbler climbed into the van and began dusting off the snow. "Get ready. She should be coming through here any minute."

Kaufman held his breath.

The lights of Barbara Dare-Carrington's silver-gray Camaro came into view.

"There she is!"

Almost as quickly, Barbara roared past them and out of sight, splattering slush everywhere.

"Where's she been?"

"Sagebrush Prison."

"*Prison*? Why?"

"To see her daddy."

"Who's her daddy?"

"Buzzard Mackelroy."

"*Buzzard Mackelroy*!? The notorious killer?"

"That's him."

"Fantastic. No wonder she didn't want anyone to know who he was. Tumbler, you've earned your pay this time."

"Want me to go catch her?"

"Not now. Let's talk about our New Year's party."

"Want me to arrange a *Bowing* Ceremony or a *Kneeling* Ceremony for her husband?"

"This calls for the Kneeling Ceremony. Like the one we gave the boy's daddy years ago. Tell the captain to have the yacht on standby New Year's Day. Then call Senator Charlie Carrington. Tell him to bring his boy on their yacht and sail up the Neuse River a way."

"Where do you want to meet?"

"Somewhere along the Atlantic Seaboard. I won't announce the exact spot until the last instant. We've got to get him out of North Carolina though; everyone in the state knows his daddy and might recognize him."

"Why not Savannah?"

"Georgia?"

"Sure. Savannah would give us a little distance. It's far enough away, but not too far to bring in some of our heavyweights."

"Tumbler, you're right. Savannah it is. Anything this important needs a show of force. Who's our man in Georgia?"

Tumbler punched a few buttons on the van's computer. The name "Stoplight King" began to blink on the screen.

"*Stoplight?* That his real name?"

"Doesn't say."

Kaufman said, with some disgust, "Where do these guys get these crazy names: Buzzard, Stoplight—"

"I just asked one of the guards back at the prison the same question. At first he was scared to talk, but I stuck two one-hundred-dollar bills in his uniform shirt pocket and he said that prisoner Mackelroy had slain a man on Vulture Mountain and that's how he got the name Buzzard. I don't know about Stoplight King."

"No matter, what's his front?"

Tumbler punched another button and King's credentials began to scroll across the screen. "Real Estate. Says here he has only one arm. Specialty—buys abandoned commercial buildings and restores or converts to another use."

"I can read!" Kaufman barked. "Get in touch with King.

254

Set up the Kneeling Ceremony at some fancy dining place in Savannah Harbor. If that port's not suitable, go on down the coast to Sea Island and book THE CLOISTER."

"You want the works?"

"Yes. Let's bring in the year right. A seven-course dinner to precede the ceremony."

"Then take him to the boat?"

"You got it."

Tumbler reached for the car-phone. "I'll call King now."

Kaufman jerked the receiver out of his hand. "Don't call. Go. You and Ezell take the jet."

Tumbler gave a happy look. "To Savannah? Right now?"

"As soon as you can get to the Asheville Airport."

"Want the ceremony on New Year's Day or the day after?"

"Better keep the date flexible. We might not be able to hold off that long. Tell King to go ahead and get everything set up."

"Got it."

"I can't wait to see the face of the senator's boy when we tell him we're going to run his campaign for the Senate."

"Then ask for his vote?" said Tumbler.

"Not *ask*. I may let Mr. Todd Carrington carry on for a while with his 'do-good dream this' and his 'do-good dream that.' Then I'll make him kneel right there on the yacht. Right in front of his two-faced daddy."

"What if the boy won't kneel?"

"You mean once we've exposed our hand?"

"Yeah. What's to keep him from—"

"Harpoon a shark and tie him to the back of the boat. Get him good and hungry. Todd Carrington will either kneel or we'll toss him to that hungry shark."

"And his father?"

"We'll arrange for him to have a heart attack."

"Shark attack. Heart attack. Good plan," said Tumbler. As he climbed back out into the snow, he asked, "Want me to drive you over to the prison…see her daddy's house?"

"I can drive myself. You get on down to Savannah."

At five minutes after midnight, a smoky-black Gulfstream IV stole down the icy runway and into the snowy skies over Asheville. At the controls was Monty Ezell, campaign manager for senator-to-be Todd Carrington. Tumbler, the night man, flew copilot. Destination: Savannah, Georgia.

47

Kaufman couldn't have chosen a more beautiful city for his ugly deed. Savannah sits on the Georgia-South Carolina border, 12 miles inland from the Atlantic Ocean. Of Savannah, *Conde Nast Traveler* says, "One of 10 top U.S. cities to visit"; *LeMonde*, Paris, France, calls it "The most beautiful city in North America"; *Walking Magazine* says, "One of the top ten walking cities in the U.S."; and the President of National Trust for Historic Preservation says, "Savannah is one of the best preserved historic communities in the nation."

That said, at 6:00 AM a bag man shuffled down Martin Luther King, Jr. Blvd, north toward River Street. He was wearing a ragged, black overcoat—no buttons—and carrying a brown grocery bag in his arms.

The man crossed against the light and turned right onto Oglethorpe Avenue. Huge, moss-draped oaks towered over the street and the fog hung in the moss, creating a ghostly scene, like some macabre movie. The smell from the paper mill made its presence known and the foghorns from the freighters talked back and forth to each other on the river.

The bag man made his way past elegantly decorated homes whose front porches bore plaques designating them as part of the proud city's rich historical past. Soon the man turned left and walked toward York Street. Momentarily, he stopped under a light pole and set his tired-looking bag by the curb. He knelt and began carefully and deliberately removing the bag's contents, laying everything beside him on the wet grass. He took out an empty Hunt's tomato can with a fresh, bright red label, a purple wrapper from a Tootsie Roll Pop, a foot-long yellow rope, the stub of a worn-out broom, a lady's green sneaker with a hole in the bottom, and other such grabbings from this morning's scavenger tour of the city's alleys. Everything had been carefully chosen for its appeal to his eye for decorating.

Then, from the base of the lamp pole, he just as carefully removed similar items from yesterday's display and placed them inside his grocery bag. After that, he arranged his new decorations around the base of the lamp pole and stood back admiring his work. This was the self-appointed job which he did seven days a week, 365 days a year, rain or shine. Town people took great delight in driving out-of-town guests by to either watch him work, or to see the results of his labor.

Across from the decorated light pole, near Wright Square, stood another tourist attraction: a giant oak, claimed by the old timers to be the oldest tree in Savannah. Its massive limbs hung so low to the ground that a reasonably tall person could back right up to it and sit down. The giant tree was a child's delight.

When the bag man finished decorating the lamp post, he shuffled across the street and sat down on the dirt under the low-swung giant tree—the grass had been worn away from all the foot traffic. This hour of the morning, people were seldom around and he liked it that way. However, this particular morning, a small man was in the tree, straddling its lowest limb and smoking a cigarette, his feet dangling, not quite reaching the ground.

The bag man got comfortable on the ground, stretched his legs in a v- shape and deposited the bag between them. He then began taking stock of the items just retrieved from the light pole, laying each on the ground beside him, checking to see if he could use any of them again tomorrow.

"Your name Neal?" the bag man asked.

"With a 'K'," came a voice from the tree.

"King's the name here. Stoplight King."

The bag man had his back to the trunk of the tree. They talked without looking. The man in the tree gave no name and the bag man knew not to ask for one.

"That's some disguise you got there," said the small man in the tree.

"The man who usually does this, I paid him five bucks and gave him the day off. His bag cost me an extra ten."

Suddenly the bag man was in the clutches of the small man and felt a cold knife at his throat. Yet he had heard no sound.

"You're not King."

"I thought I was." The bag man said, trying to remain calm.

"King has one arm," came the voice that sounded so much like that of an undertaker.

"Is that all?" said the bag man, laughing. "If you'll remove that knife, I'll show you."

The little mouse-looking man released him and leapt around in front of him, the knife glistening from the condensation of fog-droplets on the blade.

King stood, pulled a mannequin arm from his overcoat sleeve, hand and all, and offered it to the mousy-looking man holding the drawn knife.

The mouseman didn't smile. He folded the knife and put it in his pocket. "It looked real."

"I found it in a trashcan out back of Penney's." King then pushed up the overcoat sleeve and scratched his sawed-off elbow with the fiberglass hand.

The mouseman looked him up and down. "You always had one arm?"

"I used to have two, but I also used to have a habit of hanging my left arm out the car window. One day a tobacco farmer in a two-ton truck sideswiped my BMW at a stop-light and took my arm, Rolex and all. Ever since I've been called Stoplight King."

"I don't care anything...about your arm....I don't care anything...about your Rolex....I don't care anything...about how you got your name. Where's a good place for the...ceremony?"

"Bowing or kneeling?" asked King.

"Kneeling."

"Wow!" said King, scratching his stubbed elbow again. "I won't ask who, but the Marina Restaurant and Grill should fit the bill. It's not far from the Convention Center—right off the Savannah River—and there's plenty of room to dock all the yachts. As you know, our airport can handle the private jets."

"Yeah, I checked that out when my pilot landed while ago."

"Then the Marina Restaurant it is. I'll make all the arrangements. What date?"

"Soon after New Year's Day. Maybe before."

Usual number of guards?"

"Yes. No, double it."

"Anything else?"

"Yes," said the mouseman. "Take a boat out in the deep waters of the Atlantic, into a shark-infested area. Capture one of those big man-eaters. Don't feed him until the night of the Kneeling Ceremony."

48

That same Monday morning, the temperature dropped to 18 degrees in Asheville. And it was still snowing.

Barbara had made peace with the kitchen and was making a serious effort at learning to cook. She finished stacking the breakfast dishes in the dishwasher, prepared two pear and almond tarts—Todd's favorite desert—for dinner that evening, then got all bundled up and headed for work.

Tonight would be the night. Tonight she and Sally Chastine would "Watergate" the second floor at SIG Labs. The scheme was that today they would decorate part of the lab for Christmas. They would purposely leave the job incomplete, then tonight they would come back under the guise of finishing.

When Barbara got to the office that morning, "Deck The Halls," a recording by Mannheim Steamroller, was exploding down the halls. Sally, wearing a pert Santa hat, was standing in the middle of the lobby in a pile of decorations, barking instructions to helpers. Another group of employees, in a high state of excitement, stood around the drinking fountain, speculating on the size the annual bonus might be when presented at the Christmas party on Wednesday.

Once in her office, Barbara studied her calendar. Christmas would fall on a Monday. Her holidays would start after the office party, the Wednesday before Christmas. She would be off until January 2. She and Todd would celebrate Christmas in Cades Cove with Grandmother Dare, and then go to New Bern to celebrate New Year's with his parents. That's when Todd would tell his father his plans to run for the Senate.

But already those plans were in jeopardy. Barbara knew Tumbler and Kaufman were on the verge of finding out who her father was. If they hadn't already. Those files on the second floor would tell her why the tobacco cartel wanted to know who her father was. And tonight, if she survived the break-in, she would know what was in the files.

She had two more details to take care of. First she took the elevator to the third floor and to Dr. Quebian Clark's office to make arrangements for him to meet her and Sally at 8:00 tonight at the lab's front door to let them in. Then she went to one of the labs and, screening herself from view with her lab coat, grabbed a bottle of phenobarbital, slipped it into the pocket of her lab coat, and nonchalantly strolled back to her office.

Late that afternoon as she prepared to leave work, she stuck her head in Sally Chastine's door and announced to the whole world, or anyone listening in, "I'll come by for you a little before 8:00 tonight."

"You got it," Sally called out. Then as planned, she asked, "Hey, how do we get in here at night?"

"Dr. Clark's meeting us. Wear your work clothes. We've got to get the decorations finished."

"I reckon so," Sally said in her best actress voice, "especially with the party being day after tomorrow."

Outside, the snow had turned to mist and the only white lay in patchy snowbanks alongside the road. The skies looked threatening and news on Barbara's car radio predicted sleet. She stopped at a convenience store and purchased a quart of eggnog. Back in the car, she poured the phenobarbital into the eggnog. Now she was ready to give Dr. Clark a couple of hours sleep.

When she arrived home, Todd's red Vette sat in the driveway, the motor running and the windshield wipers dancing. He came hurrying out of the house, a suitcase in his hand.

"Sweetheart," she asked, "where are you going?"

"New Bern. Emergency," he said hugging her. "I was stalling until you got home."

"*Emergency?*"

"Father just called. Said for me to get there as quickly as possible."

"Something happened to your mother?"

"Nothing like that. It's a business or political emergency. Father said there was some kind of ceremony about to come down that involved our family in a most serious way. But he wouldn't say anything else. Monty's flying me over there."

"In this weather? Sleet is—"

"I have no choice."

"Do I need to go with you?"   She reached up and

straightened the collar of his camel hair topcoat, letting her fingers touch his cheeks as she lowered her hands and stepped back.

"No. Hope to be back by tomorrow. I'll surely be here by Thursday so we can go to Grandmother Dare's for Christmas." He kissed her, then drove off into the storm. Only the fragrance of his Lagerfeld aftershave lingered. As soon as she got inside, she began to tremble. Had Tumbler and Kaufman already found out who her father was? That would explain why Todd's father wouldn't tell him what the emergency was.

At six o'clock on the dot, Sarah, the housekeeper, set dinner for one and candles for two on the long dining table. But Barbara only forked the blackened red-fish, doused in Pontchartrain sauce, from one side of the plate to the other and stared out the window toward the city of Asheville. In her other hand, she clutched the keys to the Camaro. Why couldn't I have been born to a normal family like anyone else? What she'd give now if by some act of magic she and Todd could be transported to a new life where they each had a blue-collar job working nine-to-five at some North Carolina textile mill. She'd sooner board a prison ship anchored in some distant harbor than face what was coming.

After a while, Sarah came to the table, carrying the two pear and almond tarts. "Want me to save this until Mr. Carrington gets back?"

"That will be fine." By 6:30 Barbara forsook the dinner. She ambled down the hall to the bedroom. There she laid out her black nylon sweat suit with hot-pink trim, a pair of white socks, and her favorite running shoes. That's what she would wear tonight to finish decorating SIG Labs with Sally. Nope. She changed her mind. She didn't like the outfit. Real athletes despise fancy "sweat suits," and she did too. So she hung the new outfit back in the closet and laid out her old jeans and UT sweat shirt.

But right now she was still wearing the white wool business suit and pink blouse she'd worn to work. She'd been too devastated by Todd's sudden departure to change. Dazed, she removed the suit-coat and sat on the end of the bed, kicked off her heels, and began removing her pantyhose.

The phone rang, jolting her out of one nightmare and into one far worse. "Hello."

"Barbara Dare?"

Dare? "Yes. This is Barbara." She tossed the pantyhose onto the floor where they now lay in a puddle between her high heels and tennis shoes.

"Urgent message. Your phone is bugged. Go immediately in your fastest car to the Asheville Bus Station. In front of the station is a bank of phones. So the call cannot be traced, I will dial one of the phones."

"Who are you?"

"There is no time. This message is from the man who likes peanut butter pies."

Papa! But that wasn't her father's voice.

The caller hung up.

Barbara jerked on her socks and running shoes—without tying them. Still wearing the white skirt and pink blouse, she dashed to the Camaro. On the first straight away, she punched in the high-speed afterburner. In no time she pulled into the Asheville bus depot. The third phone of the ten was already ringing.

She sprinted to it. "Hello. Hello. This is Barbara Dare."

The snow had now turned to sleet. On the roof of the metal phone booth, ice pellets, harbingers of onrushing tragedy, pinged out a coded message she didn't understand.

"Barbara, this is Preecher Kinser. I'm your Dad's best friend."

She gasped, trying to catch her breath. "I know about you. You have the racetrack at Alcoa where Dad's yellow roadster is warehoused."

"That's me," Preecher said with a proud laugh in his voice. Then he got deadly serious. "Listen fast. Krandall Kaufman, head of the tobacco cartel, knows who your father is."

"Oh, no." She wilted.

"And we now know why he wanted to know."

"Why?"

"Please. Just listen. They want Todd's vote when he runs for Senate."

"Todd'll never vote with the tobacco industry."

"He might. You see, they already have the Kneeling Ceremony planned."

"*Kneeling Ceremony*!?"

"On Todd's daddy's yacht for New Year's Day."

"Todd will never bow to that bunch."

"He wouldn't for himself. But he'll kneel for you."

She began to shake with such fright she thought she would wet her pants. "They might as well kill him. Todd can't live without his dream."

"I have to go," Preecher Kinser said. "I was instructed to deliver this message so you can protect yourself. Your father has powerful friends, but along with that comes powerful enemies. Watch yourself."

Then Barbara remembered Todd's emergency call. "Wait a minute, Preecher. Todd got an urgent call from his father moments ago to hurry to New Bern—"

"Tell him not to go!"

"He's already gone. Monty Ezell flew him."

"Ezell!?"

"Todd's campaign manager."

"Monty Ezell works for Krandall Kaufman and the tobacco cartel!"

"*Tobacco cartel?*"

"Yes, and that Ezell's as sly as a casino rail-thief."

"Oh Lord." All her life Barbara had known this night was coming. Now that it was upon her, she still had no idea which way to run. "Preecher, if you were me, what would you do?"

"If you were my daughter, I'd say git outta town."

"I can't run any more."

"Then I'd hide."

"I've hidden out all my life. I won't hide again. I must face this."

"I have to go," Preecher said, "and report back."

"When will—"

The dial tone came on, and for the first time she noticed the smell of diesel from the bus station. And the night grew colder.

She drove home, slowly. She was so frightened, she could hardly keep the Camaro on the Parkway. Todd was in immediate danger. Then she became furious. She could wring that double-dealing Monty Ezell's neck. He was so mean he ought to be forced to wear a tick collar the rest of his life. She never had trusted him. But Ezell was small potatoes. Kaufman was the kingpin. All her life she had known that one of her father's enemies would someday come for her, but she had never considered that one of Todd's might.

Once she got home, she picked up the phone—bugs or no bugs— and dialed the coastal mansion in New Bern to warn Todd his father was being forced to sacrifice him on the cartel's kneeling altar. But there was no answer. The phone kept ringing, and the answering machine never clicked on. Somebody had already unplugged her from Todd.

What to do? Go to New Bern. Stop that Kneeling Ceremony. Yes. That's exactly what she'd do. She started for the car. Halted at the garage door. How? she asked herself. She couldn't stop the cartel. She had no weapon for such a fight. She would tell Todd to run. Yes, that's what she'd do.

She started for the door again but stopped again. Todd would never run. And he would never kneel. But...Preecher Kinser was right: "Todd won't kneel for himself, but he will for you." Either way, the Todd Carrington she had known was a goner.

By now, the cartel had told him everything, especially who her father was. It was all over. Todd wouldn't want her now. He *couldn't* want her now. There would be no Christmas dinner with Grandmother Dare at Cades Cove. And she and Todd would never ride the lights in the snow at Pigeon Forge and Gatlinburg. Having destroyed Todd's career, she could never look him in the eye again. She began weeping, shaking so hard that one of her contacts washed out. As she put the lens back in, reason began to return.

This was a watershed moment, like Roland's noble ride in *The Song of Roland*. Time to risk it all. The cartel was taking her down, but they wouldn't take her down without a fight.

There was one noble thing left that she could do before she slipped into oblivion. Maybe. The one thing that Todd cared most about, other than her, was his dream. Maybe she could save his dream.

But how? The solution lay with Krandall Kaufman and the tobacco cartel. The first answer came to her as a simple question. What could she trade to the cartel for Todd's dream? What did the cartel want—or need—more then Todd's future vote in the U.S. Senate? And what did the cartel have to hide? Ah. There was the answer! The second floor. SIG Labs. If there *was* a way to stop Kaufman and the tobacco cartel, the answer would be found on the second floor. If she could find out what they were hiding, she might also be able to save Todd.

She became more determined than ever to get on that second floor. There would be no stopping her now. Searching the second floor had started with curiosity over who killed Treby. It had then progressed to trying to stop the cartel from learning who her father was. Now it was all-out war. Now they knew who her father was. It was too late for her, but not for Todd. She would storm the second floor and she would dump every file onto the floor until she found the file that told what Kaufman and the cartel were up to. Maybe she could make Mr. Puff talk. If she could decipher that coded printout from his computer...Then she would dash to New Bern and...

Christmas decorations! Now she remembered that she and Sally Chastine had an 8:00 appointment tonight. She grabbed the phone and dialed. During the two rings, her life flashed before her. The cartel would have no qualms about telling all her father's enemies, including Baldy Slocum and his boys, *who* she was and *where* she was. They would all be coming. Probably already were.

Then a calmness came over her. For the first time in her life she was no longer afraid. Let them tell. Let them all come. Without Todd, life no longer had any meaning, and so her own life was no longer precious to her. Nothing could ever scare her again. Right now, her only reason for living was to save Todd's dream.

Several days ago her dad had warned her that a man with a

knife watched every movement at SIG Labs on a TV monitor. She didn't care. Even if the man was walking the halls at SIG Labs, his knife drawn, SIG Labs is exactly where she was going. Within two hours, Todd's dream would be saved or it wouldn't. Either way, it would all be over in two hours.

Sally answered on the third ring, and Barbara said, softly and calmly, "I'm on the way to get you to finish the Christmas decorations."

"But it's only 7:30," Sally chuckled.

"I'm on the way to get you." Knowing that one woman understands another woman's silence, Barbara Dare-Carrington said no more.

She went to the black Corvette, removed the bottle of spiked eggnog, and took it to her Camaro. After she breached the second floor of SIG Labs, she would need her fastest car tonight to make it to New Bern in time; the Corvette would never be fast enough. On the way to Sally's she topped off both tanks on the Camaro.

Still wearing the white skirt, pink blouse, and running shoes, she started blowing the horn as she came around the corner near Sally's house.

Sally dashed out, dressed in pressed jeans, a Christmas-green sweater with a thick turtle neck, and a long red-leather coat. Climbing in, she gave Barbara the once over. "You making a fashion statement?"

"Hurry!"

49

Earlier that afternoon, at about 4:30, Tumbler and Ezell had gotten back from Savannah. As soon as they landed at the Asheville Airport, Tumbler had instructed Ezell to go get Todd and take him to New Bern, immediately.

"I'll dash in the terminal and call him."

"He's probably in there…waiting for you."

"You called him?"

"His dad did. If he's not there…call him on the phone. Tell him to get on out here."

Ezell left the jet idling while he went inside to check on Todd. Meanwhile, Tumbler left for SIG Labs. At least he pretended to. But he didn't trust Ezell, so he sneaked the white Mercedes into a clump of bushes at the end of the runway and waited for him to return. He wanted to watch Todd Carrington take his night flight.

By 5:30 it was dark and had begun to sleet. Tumbler started growing impatient. The jet's roar hurt his ears and Ezell was taking too long. He didn't like Ezell anyway; he talked too much. And he knew too much. Soon Ezell would have to go, too. But that was for another night.

Tumbler climbed out of the car, opened his polka-dot umbrella and began to pace in the snow-mixed sleet. He would rather be in his own kind of darkness, back at his surveillance monitor at SIG Labs.

At 5:45, through night-vision binoculars, he watched a red Corvette pull up to the terminal. A tall man got out and walked with another tall man toward the jet and they climbed aboard. It had to be Todd and Ezell. The running lights came on and the plane began to ease over to runway Number Nine. Soon the jet screamed into the sky. Ezell would drop Todd off in New Bern and be back later tonight. After that, Mr. Ezell would be of no further use to the cartel, so Tumbler began to formulate a plan for permanently silencing him.

As soon as the jet bore into the clouds, Tumbler closed the parasol, climbed back into the Mercedes, turned on the defroster, and drove to SIG Labs. He didn't like being gone from his duty all day—too many video tapes to catch up on. He would rather watch live action on the monitor than a video of that same action. Sometimes at night, as he kept vigilance at his monitor, he fantasized about catching bandits slipping down the halls at SIG Labs, trying to escape his detection. But that was too much to hope for. No one could ever breech the security, especially of the second floor.

And so, a little before 8:00 PM, Tumbler sat in the darkness of the observation room, reviewing the day's videos on one screen and keeping an eye on the live monitor. This was his favorite time of day—no people or sunlight around to irritate him. On the floor beside him sat a hand-woven basket. In the basket was his dinner. In the privacy of the Observation Room, he always made a formal ritual of his evening meal.

Fastidiously clean, Tumbler removed from the basket a white linen cloth and spread it over the work space. Then he removed a watercress sandwich, a bottle of mineral water, and a can of sardines packed in olive oil. He set everything on the white tablecloth.

Without taking his eyes off the monitors, he removed his pocketknife and began to cut open the can of sardines. Then he sliced the sandwich into fourths and carefully laid the knife, pointing away from him, on the tablecloth. Now, from the pen pocket of his suit coat, he removed an ivory toothpick. He speared a sardine with the toothpick, sucked it off, then took a bite from the watercress sandwich and began to chew. He took a sip of mineral water, leaned back, and, for a careless moment, closed his eyes. What bliss.

He slowly opened his eyes and...Clark!

Dr. Quebian Clark was coming through the front door of SIG Labs, turning the lights on! What's that fool doing here this time of night?! Tumbler hit the button that displayed on the monitor the entire front of the building. A car was pulling into the parking lot.

Two people got out and began to sing, enthusiastically, "Jingle Bells." Sounded like women. Then the lights came on in front of the lab. Clark must have done that.

Yes. They *were* women—a black woman and a white woman carrying garlands, strings of lights, wreaths, all kinds of decorations. And a milk bottle! Eggnog. Had to be eggnog, and they had evidently had a little too much. They were all over the yard, dropping things, staggering, drinking straight out of the jug. The black woman was carrying a step ladder...Black woman...Sally Chastine and...Barbara Dare-Carrington! What were they doing here this time of night?!

Tumbler held his breath as he listened. And watched.

"Good evening, ladies," Dr. Clark said in a most serious tone as Barbara and Sally came through the door.

"Have a drink." Barbara—a strand of Christmas lights now strung around her neck—shoved the half-empty bottle toward Dr. Clark, sloshing it.

"No thank you. Just hurry up and get the decorating completed."

"Ah, come on. Be a sport." Sally grabbed a cone cup from the water fountain, poured a little eggnog into it and handed it to Dr. Clark. "Just a swallow. Show us you're not mad because you had to come out on this snowy night to open up."

"Oh, all right."

Clark drank the Christmas cheer, tossed the cup into the trash basket, and almost immediately fell to the floor, sound asleep.

Barbara dropped her arm load of decorations, jerked Dr. Clark's head up and yanked the gold chain and key from around his neck. "Let's go."

They're not drunk! Tumbler thought. Still at the monitor, he rubbed his hands and licked his chops as the girls ran down the hall toward the elevator, dangling the gold key and chain.

Exhilarated beyond belief he carefully and deliberately put away his dinner finery, savoring the moment, like a cat watching a mouse rush headlong into his trap. There would be no escape. First, he wiped his ivory toothpick on the linen tablecloth, then returned it to his coat pocket. Next, he closed the knife and dropped it inside his pants pocket, feeling it slide down his upper thigh.

He switched the monitor to another camera.

The women were now on the elevator. Salivating, he watched them insert the gold key into the second-floor key-pad that would take them to a place from which they would not return.

So excited he could hardly breathe, ever so gently, he laid the empty mineral-water bottle on its side beside the empty sardine can. Then he took the four corners of the linen cloth and tied them into an elaborate knot.

The girls were now on the second floor, racing down the hall, jerking on locked doors, almost to Mr. Puff's room.

Lifting the linen cloth that held the aftermath of his banquet, Tumbler tossed it all into the trashcan beside the surveillance monitor.

The girls had now breached the door to Mr. Puff's room, and while Sally gawked at Mr. Puff, Barbara sprinted from file cabinet to file cabinet.

Now for dessert! Tumbler shot out of the Observation Room.

"I don't even know what we're looking for," Sally said, still gawking at Mr. Puff.

"Secrets," Barbara yelled, slinging files everywhere. "There's got to be something in here the tobacco cartel doesn't want anyone to know. When we find that—"

Suddenly distracted by a new noise, Barbara stopped in mid-sentence. Constant electronic chatter was coming from somewhere. She dashed over to Mr. Puff.

As before, Mr. Puff sat in his glassed-in room, puffing away, while all the hoses, tubes, and wires connected to him still fed second-hand smoke to caged mice and other critters. But above the noise the animals made was a new noise—electronic chatter—and the chatter grew louder. The sound had not been present the day Dr. Clark had introduced her to Mr. Puff.

Barbara looked behind Mr. Puff and found the source of the sound. A computer hooked up to him rolled forth an endless print out. She studied it. All in code. She could make neither heads nor tails of the information.

Sally called out, "Here's a file cabinet marked, 'Mr. Puff.'"

Barbara dashed over to where Sally was standing. "This may be what we're looking for."

But the cabinet was locked. Barbara tried the gold key. No luck. She looked around for something to force open the cabinet. A short 2 x 4 lay next to Mr. Puff's glassed in room. She grabbed the board and pried at the metal cabinet. No luck.

"Move back." She put her arms around the tall black cabinet and tried to rock it.

"What are you doing?" asked Sally.

"Flop it on the floor. Maybe it'll burst open."

They both tugged and pushed on the secret cabinet. But it wouldn't budge.

"We gotta get in it." Barbara took a quick step backward, got a running start, and leaped on top of it. She hiked up her winter-wool white skirt and straddled the cabinet like a cowgirl in a barrel race. She started rocking it. Finally she tumbled it over. It popped open, and drawers—with files attached to a guide wire in the bottom—slid out. But the files stayed intact.

Barbara flipped through the labels. Nothing. She yanked out the second drawer. Nothing. Third drawer. Same thing. Bottom drawer. Nothing...Wait—

Hidden behind the last file was a thick red folder labeled "Mr. Puff, Top Secret." It stood out like sunlight coming through a crack in a dusty door. She began speed-reading: spiking, ammonia, addiction, regulation, political payoff sheets—then it trailed off into code. She noticed an 8x14 envelope lodged inside the folder. She pulled the clasp and dumped its contents. Two pictures spilled out. Pictures of her and Todd! With the Ezells at the North Carolina ballgame! And receipts for the photos, the Jaguar, the jet, the country club dinner, and...All paid for by the North Carolina Tobacco Institute! "This is it! This is what we're looking—"

"The door!" Sally whispered loudly. "Someone's at the door!"

Barbara turned. Through the fog-glass top of the door she saw a shadow fiddling with the door lock. Assuming it was Dr. Clark, she said, "I should have given him a stronger dose."

"Look out!" Sally screamed.

A mousy-looking man came through the door, his knife-hand in the air.

Decision time. Save herself or save Todd's dream. Barbara jerked on Mr. Puff's file, but it wouldn't come loose; the guide-wire held it securely. She stood. Jerked on it again. She had to have that file.

Sally was now screaming as the mouseman chased her through the rows of filing cabinets.

Barbara thought, Dream or no dream, I can't let a friend go down like this. Diversion. She jerked up the board she had used on the file cabinet and slung it through the glass cage that housed Mr. Puff. Glass splattered everywhere. The smell of ammonia hit the air.

Mr. Puff kept puffing.

The mouseman had Sally by the throat.

Cigarette smoke filled the room.

Barbara jerked the wires loose from Mr. Puff and spilled the animal crates. White mice, rabbits, guinea pigs, monkeys, and all sorts of creatures began running wild. And screaming. Almost instantly the sterile room smelled like a barnyard.

The mouseman froze in horror. "Hey. You can't do that."

But that was enough time for Sally to break free. Barbara grabbed the 2 x 4, now resting between Mr. Puff's legs. She leaped over the spilled file cabinet and began chasing the mouseman who was chasing Sally.

There was no race to it. In no time the University of Tennessee track speedster was within striking distance. She whammed the mouseman across the back of the head with the 2 x 4. He crumpled to his knees. She yanked the gold chain and key off his neck and yelled to Sally, "Go!"

But Barbara still didn't have what she came for. As she ran past the spilled files, she bent over and yanked one more time on Mr. Puff's red folder. She jerked so hard the guide-wire broke. Files flew everywhere. But when the dust settled, she was holding the prize, Mr. Puff's red file.

Sally stood frozen at the door.

In the chaos, Barbara bolted across the room. She crashed the door, shoved Sally out into the hall, and hotfooted it toward the elevator.

"If we can make it to the elevator, he'll never catch us; he has no key." Barbara punched the elevator door. And waited. And waited. And waited for the slow door to open.

Smoke, like that at a smoker's convention, spilled into the hall. The mouseman staggered through the smoke-fog, toward them in slow motion, his knife drawn. But the elevator door was in slow motion too. Cigarette smoke was now in the elevator. The fire alarm went off and bells began ringing like crazy.

Ever so slowly the elevator door started opening. Barbara shoved Sally in. Fumbled with key. Get it in key-pad.

The mouseman was within striking distance.

There. She turned the key and the door began to close. Slowly. The mouseman, still dazed, and with blood oozing down his neck, started in. Barbara kicked him in the stomach, sending him backwards. The door was almost closed. The mouseman shoved his knife-hand into the crack, but the closing door forced him to remove it.

On the first floor, Barbara and Sally shot out of the elevator, through the lobby, and leaped over the sleeping Dr. Quebian Clark—

Huh oh. Dr. Clark was lying in a pool of blood.

They raced faster.

By the time they reached the parking lot, the alarm bells had stopped ringing. The mouseman must have turned them off. He wouldn't want to alert the fire department. Or the police.

Once in the Camaro, and speeding down Industrial Way, Barbara said to Sally, "I'll drop you off at your house. You get Gene and go to New Bern. Tell Todd not to kneel for anyone. And not to give up on his dream. Tell him I've got the tobacco cartel's secret file."

"But we don't know what's in the file," Sally said. "We can't even decipher most of it."

"Maybe not, but I know who can."

"Who?"

They turned the corner on two wheels and Barbara screeched to a halt in front of Sally's house.

Gene had just returned from the gym. Obviously aroused by the commotion, he came running out to the porch, barefooted and still wearing his white karate suit. "What's up with you girls?"

"Hi, Gene," Barbara said, waving to him, as if nothing was wrong.

"Git out 'n come in where it's warm," he called.

"Come in and tell him!" Sally begged.

"You tell him. That mouseman with the knife is probably already on my trail." Barbara tossed the keys to her Corvette into Sally's lap. "Go by the house and get my other car. It's fast."

Sally tossed the keys back. "Gene won't drive nothing but that green wrecker. But it'll outrun most street cars."

"Just hurry."

"What do I tell Todd?" Sally asked.

"That Roland's Army is on it's way."

"Who?"

"*Roland.* He'll know."

50

Barbara dug out, and the silver-gray Camaro went screaming off into the night. Then it hit her. There was no hurry. The prison wouldn't open until daylight—eight hours from now. So she blinked her lights to dim, locked the Camaro in low gear, and cruised the streets of Asheville, just inching along in the sleet. Her goal now became to survive the night.

The high-speed-Gene Chastine-souped-up, powerful engine was traveling at the speed of a funeral and vibrated with such force, Barbara could feel the power running all the way from the axle to her sun-cracked-leather, black bucket seat. She poked along through the heart of downtown, past the governor's monument, past the Radisson Hotel and Gift Shop, and past the Thomas Wolfe home, her old jogging haunts. But she usually jogged faster than the Camaro was now traveling.

She kept an eye on her rearview mirror and both side mirrors and every few minutes elbow-checked the door lock.

She now had one mission. Get Mr. Puff's file to Sagebrush Prison. It was a two-hour trip, so that left six hours to kill. All she had to do was keep herself safe for eight more hours—Todd's dream depended on it. After that it wouldn't matter whether she was safe or not.

But right now, she needed a place to hide out and rest for six hours. She measured her choices, never once considering going home; the mouseman might be waiting there. Maybe she could hide out in her church. No, it was late and the church would be locked. That left only one place of safety, the Camaro. No one could catch the Camaro, but she would have to keep it moving. She looked at the fuel meter, glad she had topped off the tanks on the way to pick up Sally earlier in the evening.

So she made a decision. She would head on over to the prison and drive around in their giant parking lot until daybreak. That assumed that no one would follow her and that if they did she would know it.

She'd made the trip a hundred times, so the route out of town was not in question, and before she realized it, she was on the

Blue Ridge Parkway; that's the way she always went. This route would take her by home, and that was okay because she could glance in the driveway and see if perchance the red Corvette was there. If it was, Todd was back.

She knew not to turn into the driveway where she could be trapped. Theirs was a long driveway that circled up to the cliff-side chalet, about a hundred yards from the Parkway. The automatic timer on the lights would already have the house and yard lit, so seeing would not be a problem. She would ease past the house and then, if Todd's car was there, turn around and come back.

The Blue Ridge Parkway was full of curves and, to her, that was part of its charm. But charm or no charm, the problem with curves is that you can't see what's waiting around the bend.

She was tooling along in second gear, just fast enough to keep from getting rammed from behind. One more curve and her driveway and home would come into view on the right side. Her headlights were now marking that curve. She came around the foggy bend, and glanced up her driveway. The red Corvette was not there. She hadn't expected it would be. Still disappointment beat on her.

Look out!

She rammed the Camaro into low and hit the brakes. The car began sliding sideways on the wet pavement. While her brain caught up with her reflexes, a man changing a tire on the side of the road had come within an inch of death. Her car now sat crossways on the Parkway, a coat of paint from the man's hips.

The man did not move. Instinct told her not to.

His parking lights were on and the trunk lid was up. She couldn't tell if anyone else was in the car. The engine was idling—a telltale trail of vapor rose from his tailpipe and curled into the sleet-fog. He was a small man and was crouched by the rear wheel on the driver's side. At least two feet of his car was out on the pavement of the narrow two lane, as if inviting someone to tag him.

Maybe he was deaf. Barbara blinked her lights to bright in an attempt to get his attention; obviously, he wasn't hurt.

He kept fiddling with the tire tool.

Now she noticed that it was a large, white Mercedes, a four-door, like the one Princess Diana died in. And it had North Carolina license tags.

It seemed like an eternity, but only two seconds had passed since she arrived on the scene. She revved her engine, still trying to get the man's attention. But he didn't move.

North Carolina tags. Something wasn't right. She was starting to smell a rat. Get out of here! Get out of here!! Get out of here!!!

She slipped the Camaro into reverse and started easing backwards, like a little dog trying to escape a big dog.

Suddenly the man—"Oh Lordy, it's the mouseman"—was at her window. The tire tool was drawn back in striking position.

She stomped the gas pedal to the floor. The Camaro left so fast that the tire tool, already in mid-swing, took out her left taillight instead of her window.

As she rounded the next curve, she saw the Mercedes coming after her. The trunk lid was still open and flapping up and down like the eyes of a flirt on a barstool.

It was still sleeting and the Parkway was slick, hindering the Camaro's speed and power on the curves. She had to get to a highway so she could turn her spirited machine loose. No. The big Mercedes was fast too. It was built for cruising the European autobahns at a hundred-and-sixty and was also built for handling curves, even the Alps.

Her best bet was to stay in the Smoky Mountains. She knew them. So she lit out across Old Smoky. The Mercedes stayed after her; she could see its lights making the curves below.

By the time they reached Gatlinburg, the town was shut down. She took him through downtown Gatlinburg at a hundred-miles-an-hour. Once out of town, she hit her first four lane. Pigeon Forge and Dollywood lay in her path.

The Mercedes was now on her bumper and actually trying to ram her.

It was time to give the mouseman a lesson in speed. She reached down and hit the blue button that would let the genie out of the bottle—the nitrous oxide. Her front wheels came off the ground and the big Mercedes looked like it was tied to a fence post.

By the time she reached Pigeon Forge, the Mercedes was nowhere to be seen. But the night was new. She now had to make a mid-course correction in plans. She was too close to Sagebrush Prison to go there; the mouseman might have already guessed where she was taking Mr. Puff's file.

Finally she decided where she would go. She had just the place in mind and wondered why she hadn't thought of going there first. It was a place like no other. She had jogged to the lovely spot on many a pretty day. But to get there, she would have to go back into the Smokies. So she forsook the city lights and turned back into the mountains.

There was no need to drive fast now, so she backed off to the speed limit. Besides, she needed to save the magic juice. She only had enough left in the bottle for one more good race.

All through the long hours of the night, she drove the Camaro through the Smokies. Up one holler and down the other, across one creek then another. She had to assume that the mouseman was still after her. To do otherwise would be to court death. He might have an army of mousemen with him now.

The snow stopped, but the sky still looked angry. The moon darted in and out of the racing clouds. Once on the logging trails, Barbara ran with her lights off most of the time and let the moonlight guide her. She forded streams and creeks and buried herself deeper into the forest and higher into the mountains.

By two in the morning, exhausted and hardly able to hold her eyes open, she wound her way around and through the backwoods of the forest to her destination: Clingmans Dome, the highest peak in the Great Smoky Mountains.

From her eagle's-eye perch, she crawled out of the Camaro and looked down the mountain and off into the woods. She watched a single pair of headlights crisscrossing the area below. Maybe it was the mouseman. Maybe it wasn't.

She couldn't do anything until morning, and she had to have some rest. But just in case Mr. Mouseman got lucky, she prepared a welcome for him.

First, she positioned the Camaro so he couldn't hem her in.

Then she searched for a rope, or a vine, but found none. She remembered that some of the Christmas decorations were still in the Camaro's trunk. So she improvised. She tied a double strand of Christmas-light wire from two trees, across the entrance to where her car was parked. She then dangled her car jack and lug wrench from the wire at a height that would take out the mouseman's windshield. Next, she removed all four hubcaps and dangled them together, hoping that if he hit them, they would crash into each other like a cymbal or a wind chime, and awake her.

She then curled up in her safety pod and hoped for morning. If morning came, she'd be the first guest at Sagebrush Prison.

51

Morning brought a drastic change in the weather. The sun came out, the thermometer shot up to 40, and Barbara Dare-Carrington, granny wig and all, sat across from her father at Sagebrush Prison. Mr. Puff's red folder was hidden in the large black patent purse resting in her lap.

"Hi, sweetheart," he said from his glass cage.

"Hello, Papa." As was her habit, she removed *The Song of Roland*, from the purse and pretended to read from it.

"I love you."

"I love you, too, Papa."

"Did Preecher Kinser call you last night?"

"Yes, but it was too late. They had already come for Todd."

"I was afraid of that."

"I rushed to the second floor of SIG Labs to try to find something on the tobacco cartel—"

"And?"

"I found a secret file, but I got caught, Papa."

"Who?"

"The mouseman. And he had a little bitty knife."

"That would be Tumbler," Buzzard Mackelroy said. "Did he hurt you?"

"No, but he chased me all night. I think he killed Dr. Clark, my boss."

"*Killed* him?"

"While Sally and I were searching the second floor."

"Sally Chastine went with you?"

"Yes. While the mouseman—or Tumbler or whatever his name is—tried to cut her, I hit him in the head with a board, and we ran."

"Sally got free, too?"

"Yes. She and Gene are gone to New Bern to warn Todd."

"You trust Sally and Gene, don't you?"

"They're our best friends. And Gene can take care of himself. You know he has a black belt in karate."

"I have a video of one of his fights. And I think you're right on both counts. Gene Chastine can take care of himself and you can trust him."

"But, Papa, somehow I've got to get back on that second floor, but I don't know how much good it will do me."

"Oh?"

"I got the file, but most of it's in code." She cracked her purse and pulled the corner of the red file enough that she knew he could see it. "There were too many rooms I couldn't enter, too many codes I couldn't break, and too much equipment I didn't understand. I would have to have been an architect, an engineer, a chemist, a code specialist, an accountant, and a human fly to have conquered the lab. I don't know what to do."

"Why don't you leave that to me."

"All right, but there's something else, Papa."

"Yes?"

"Even if I'm successful in saving Todd's dream, I'm afraid he won't ever want to see me again. The tobacco cartel may have dealt a death blow to our marriage."

"Not if Todd Carrington's the man I think he is."

"I hope you're right, but—"

"You run on home and wait for Todd. Let me worry about the second floor at SIG Labs."

"I don't think I'll go home; they're probably watching the house. I may go over to Grandmother Dare's and spend the night. Todd and I were supposed to go there tomorrow, but he won't want to go now. The cartel has ruined everything between us."

"We'll see."

"Want me to tell Grandmother Dare anything?"

"No son ever caused a mother more grief. Tell her her worries will soon be over."

"What's that supposed to mean?" Barbara tugged nervously at her mud-bead necklace. It was Grandmother Dare who had given it to her.

"Just tell her. She'll know what it means. And leave Mr. Puff's file with the guard."

"Yes, Papa." She understood about the guards, and if she had been foolish enough—which she wasn't—to try to hand the

284

file directly to him, she couldn't have. The window and the cage barred her from even reaching to touch him.

He nodded at the book in her lap. "Tell Todd to remember *Roland's army.*"

"Already did. Actually, that's what Gene and Sally are on the way to tell him."

"Time's up," the guard called.

"Come back in the morning," Buzzard Mackelroy whispered. "I'll have the file decoded by then."

"Will the guards let you come back to the lobby so quickly?"

"I've been especially good, lately." He winked at her. "As for all that *coded* equipment on the second floor at the lab, don't give it another thought."

After saying good-bye, she stopped at the pay phone in the lobby and tried to call Todd in New Bern. No answer. Answering machine still off. She started dialing home. Instinct said stop. Hang up. Home phone is probably bugged. Call can be traced. She wasn't ready to be found, but she did call the Asheville Children's Hospital and told them she could not keep her afternoon hugging date with the new-born babies.

Then she headed to the Camaro. Not sure who, or what, might be waiting at home, she was pleased with her decision to go on to Cades Cove and spend the night with Grandmother Dare. It was peaceful there and it would give her time to plan her next move. She would come back in the morning and pick up Mr. Puff's decoded file and then race to New Bern and hand it to Todd. Oh, Todd. She might just fall at his feet and beg him to forgive her for destroying his career.

Tumbler and Ezell watched Barbara Dare-Carrington's Camaro slowly pull away from Sagebrush Prison. They fell in behind her, keeping a few cars between them.

Tumbler's purple suit was all wrinkled and his eyes bloodshot from hunting her all night. His polka-dot bow tie lay on the backseat floor between his legs. Last night, after he slung the tire tool at her, he drove around hunting her. This morning he had gambled that she might run to daddy. He soon spotted her Camaro, with the broken taillight and no hubcaps, in the prison parking lot.

"We have to stay…out of sight," Tumbler said. "If she spots us…she'll take off and lose us."

Ezell laughed a laugh of mischief. "Who you kidding? That old thing can't outrun this big Mercedes?" Ezell, back from delivering Todd to New Bern, was riding beside Tumbler, but behind Mickey. Ezell had ridden with Tumbler before so he knew all about the rear-seat drive and about Mickey. But today, Mickey, chauffeur cap and all, had a new pumpkin head, only two days old.

"Maybe it can't," declared Tumbler, "but it did. That's how I lost her last night. She tore out so fast she threw the hubcaps off."

"No way."

"All four of them. You don't see none on it do you?"

"I can't see her wheels from back here."

"You can on the next curve."

"Well that explains two things," said Ezell.

"What's that?"

"Those big tires aren't for driving in the snow, and she doesn't keep that old clunker to dry apples in."

Tumbler looked at him as if to say, "Make sense, fool," but said nothing.

At Pigeon Forge, Barbara casually turned south at the major intersection, instead of continuing east.

"Whoa," said Tumbler. "She's not going across Old Smoky!" Then a red-light trapped him.

"She's sure not headed home," Ezell said, adjusting his tie. "What do you think's up?"

"No idea…wait," said Tumbler. "Cades Cove."

"*Cades Cove*? What's that?"

"Where her grandmother lives."

"We've got her now."

The light turned green and Tumbler aimed the white Mercedes at Cades Cove. "There's an eleven-mile loop into the Cove. One way in. One way out. One way bridge!" Tumbler got so excited, his words came in gasps. "Get ready…We'll trap

286

her on that bridge...She'll bolt and run...Got your running shoes on?"

"I'm ready." Ezell flexed his muscles, lit a cigar, and leaned back to enjoy the ride through the prettiest part of the world. "Soon she'll be mine."

Tumbler shot a scowl at him. "You'll keep your hands off her." Tumbler had other plans for the girl. Barbara Dare-Carrington would kneel tonight. Then *Todd* Carrington would kneel. And he'd stay knelt. Now, he would have no objections to participating in the tobacco cartel's Kneeling Ceremony.

Later that afternoon, in Cell Block 13, Buzzard Mackelroy sat bent over the card table in the Community Room. On the table lay a stubby pencil with prison-green lead, a blank sheet of white paper, the Asheville newspaper, and the red file that the girl had brought him—Years of hiding her out wouldn't permit him to even think her name. So he always referred to her, even in his own mind, as *the girl.*

The newspaper was new and smelled of ink. It lay open to Page Two. Dr. Quebian Clark's picture appeared there along with an article explaining the tragic accident. They had found him lying on a snow bank in his backyard, his new Sears riding mower, still running, on top of him. The coroner ruled it an accident, but didn't explain why he was mowing his yard in December—it being obvious he was trying out his new mower. The article also noted that Dr. Clark was Chief Scientist at SIG Labs. But of particular interest to Buzzard Mackelroy, nothing was mentioned about SIG Labs being burgled.

He opened Mr. Puff's file. With the stubby green pencil in hand, and only the white sheet of paper—he had the ability to reduce complex information to its simplest facts—Buzzard Mackelroy began tracking Krandall Kaufman's tobacco empire. The bloody path began to unravel. Financial and political payoffs led to and from the doorstep of several major tobacco companies, the U.S. Senate, Wall Street, large and small tobacco farmers, and finally the White House.

Buzzard kept going. Spiking! Ammonia! The Y-1

Formula! Just as he got to the "Y-1" Formula, the code shifted and he couldn't decipher it. Some codes were mixed together—some even in Chinese—leaving significant blank spots in the unfolding information. Krandall Kaufman was a smart cookie. No wonder the tobacco industry had been able to double-talk Congress so successfully all these years. But Huey Lamb, the defrocked business professor, had taught his young protégé, Buzzard Mackelroy, that money leaves a trail. So Buzzard Mackelroy decided to follow the money.

He stood, intending to request a blue-card from the guard on duty; the blue-card would grant him passage to the prison library, his home away from Cell Block 13.

Suddenly another guard—a new man—came rushing through the Community Room door and informed him that he had a visitor in the prisoner waiting room.

Most unusual, Buzzard thought. In fifteen years, other than his elderly French teacher, he had never had a visitor. He nodded to Cliff and Axe, signaling them with his eyes in case he was being led into a trap.

Cliff and Axe walked with him to the exit to the community room. That's as far as they could go, but he knew they could see down the hall. That's where he would die if this new guard had been hired to kill him; he couldn't afford to do it in a public area.

But this guard didn't kill him. He ushered him down the hall where some other guards were waiting. They shackled and cuffed him, just like he was going for one of his ten-minute treats, and led him to the prisoner/visitor waiting room. They sat him in the chair in his all glass cage that sat behind the wire-mesh glass divider. He had been good in all his visits to the visitor room, and, though they still left him chained, they had stopped strapping him to his chair. He could stand and move about the phone-booth-size cage.

Across from him sat a mousy-looking man. Smoke curled upward from the end of an ivory cigarette holder clenched between the man's teeth, exposed by his thin lips.

Tumbler. Buzzard recognized him from the videos Axe and Cliff had provided him from SIG Labs. He gave Tumbler a dead-man stare.

Tumbler fidgeted, clutching something in his right hand. "We got your daughter."

Buzzard Mackelroy never flinched. "You're bluffing of course."

Tumbler tossed a necklace onto the window ledge, a one-of-a kind mud-bead necklace.

Buzzard stole a glance at it. It was the girl's all right. Weeping inside, he asked, "How did you catch her?"

"We tricked her," Tumbler bragged.

"Figures." Buzzard Mackelroy's steel-trap mind slammed shut on Tumbler. It was over for the mouseman. But Buzzard had to have those mud beads lying on the freedom side of the wire-mesh window—not an easy task since the glass wall ran from ceiling to floor and from wall to wall. The bear dogs would need the *sweet* smell of that mud-bead necklace.

"We hemmed her in on that little one-way bridge going into Cades Cove. She jumped and ran. Ezell caught her."

"Not on foot, he didn't." Already a plan for taking the mud beads from Tumbler was coming into play. Only Buzzard's body was imprisoned, not his mind; he had tried to teach that point to the girl.

"Yes, he did." Tumbler laughed, nervously. "She's got a weakness."

"Oh?" He forced himself not to look at the necklace still lying on the ledge.

"Ezell chased her up one mountain and down the other. Finally she disappeared. We knew she was hiding, so he called out that he had come to take her to her husband; that Todd wouldn't kneel so they had had to knock him in the head, and that when he came to, he was calling her name. Your little girl came out of that bear cave whimpering like a puppy."

Buzzard Mackelroy kept smiling, but he knew the mist in his eyes betrayed him. "What do you want from me?"

"We can make Todd Carrington kneel, but we can't make him like it. We want your daughter to make him like it."

"How?" he whispered.

Tumbler gave a confident gloating look.

Good. He was falling into the web he was weaving for him. Let him gloat.

"Earlier last night," bragged Tumbler, "your daughter got into trouble. So when Ezell came back from New Bern to get her, to take her to the Kneeling Ceremony, she ran."

"You said *trouble*?"

"Theft and murder. She robbed SIG Labs and killed her boss."

"*Killed her boss*?" That's not what the Asheville paper said.

"In cold blood. Dr. Quebian Clark. Clark caught her stealing from the lab, so she murdered him."

"Did you call the police?"

"Can't do that. You see, she stole a very important file."

"What's in the file?"

"Really, that's none of your business. But basically, the file contains coded material...it helps my client sleep better at night. He didn't sleep too good last night...he wants it back."

"Give him a sleeping pill."

"They don't make sleeping pills...that strong."

"That's his problem."

"No. There's some spillage. It's now your problem, too."

"My problem?"

"I believe Todd Carrington, the senator-to be, is your daughter's husband. If my client doesn't...get that red file back, he won't need the boy's vote. If he doesn't need his vote, we might *really* have to knock him in the head, or cut him...cut him out of our plans. Get my drift?"

"I still don't see what you need from me," Buzzard whispered, "You're holding all the cards."

"We need your help in getting the file that your daughter stole!"

"Why don't you just take it from her?"

"She doesn't have it on her. Ezell searched her real good. And since you're the last person she talked to, we think she told you where the file is. You will help us, won't you?"

"Why should I help you?"

"Your daughter is tied to a tree in the woods near Cades Cove. You know about bears and wildcats in the area, don't you?"

"Yes, sir, I do," said Buzzard Mackelroy, the Building Tender King, most respectfully.

"And you know about Baldy Slocum, don't you?"

"Yes, sir, I do."

"Well, right now Monty Ezell is gone to Slocum Sawmill, over at Vulture Mountain. He'll tell Baldy Slocum we've got your daughter. You did say you remember Baldy Slocum, didn't you?"

Good. Tumbler was getting cockier and cockier. Buzzard Mackelroy said, ever so politely, "I know him, sir."

"And if Baldy Slocum doesn't want the job, I bet you have some other enemies who would, don't you? The media would have a field day, and I imagine there are some ex-cons who don't think too kindly of you. Cons who might want to spend some time with that pretty little hillbilly daughter of yours. Don't you think so?" Tumbler seemed quite proud of himself as he sat there in his wrinkled purple suit, wrinkled white shirt, and no tie.

Nice suit to be buried in, Buzzard thought. He smiled, but kept his eyes locked on Tumbler, careful not to glance toward the necklace, but measuring Tumbler for a coffin, nonetheless. Now he would lead Tumbler into another strand of his web, setting him up. "You men live above the law, don't you?"

"We're like lawyers," Tumbler gloated. "We live *beside* the law, not *above* it. But *you're* a convicted murderer. Who are you to preach to us about the law?"

"A man raped my mother. I killed him." That ought to keep Tumbler's mind off the necklace. "And in my youthful foolishness, I proudly confessed. Now my lifestyle is dictated by others." He locked his eyes on Tumbler. "But you're free. To stay alive, you didn't *have* to kill Dr. Clark."

"Kill? Clark? Me?!" Tumbler leaped to his feet. "You've got twenty-four hours. I'll be back at noon tomorrow. Same time. If you don't tell us where that red file is, we'll turn Mr. Slocum loose on your little girl."

Buzzard Mackelroy remained seated, but looked up at his

tormentor. He was ready to spring the trap. The mud-bead necklace was almost his! "You said the girl will be safe for twenty-four hours, sir?"

"That's what I said."

"Thank you, sir." He was now quite sure of Tumbler's measurements. He would order a coffin with four compartments. And he would return the mud beads to their rightful owner.

"But sometimes I lie." Tumbler laughed with a tease in his voice, flaunting his presence.

Buzzard Mackelroy quietly stood, smiled, started to step to the back of the cage, but stopped. With blood in his eyes, he turned and whispered, like a striking adder, "If the girl is harmed, you will never father a child!"

Tumbler grabbed his crotch, squeezed his legs in horror, and made a hasty exit.

The mud-bead necklace still lay on the ledge. Thirty seconds later, a guard brought the necklace to Cell Block 13.

52

That afternoon, Buzzard Mackelroy went over the wall. But only in his dreams.

53

Topless sawmill trucks roared, log chains rattled, axes banged and clanked, and tires slung mud all through the cold damp woods around Vulture Mountain. Snaggletoothed Baldy Slocum and his three long-necked, cousin-marrying boys were on the loose, squirrel rifles by their sides. Searching for Barbara Dare-Carrington-Mackelroy. Or whatever her name was.

Slocum was a fat man. Not counting the sawdust in his overall pockets and brogan shoes, he weighed 321 pounds. And he slobbered a lot. His three boys were long and skinny bean poles. They slobbered a lot too.

A man who called himself Ezell, an athletic-looking young man in a blue suit, had said only that Buzzard Mackelroy had fathered a daughter. For Baldy, that was too good to hope for. And her staked-out to a tree somewhere between Vulture Mountain and Cades Cove. Easier than wringing a chicken's neck.

Baldy had always known his daddy raped a mountain girl, but didn't know which one. The name of the victim was not revealed at Buzzard's trial. Baldy had always suspected that Mackelroy was a fictitious name to protect somebody. And that old Dare woman had been living right under his nose all these years. And her granddaughter was Buzzard's girl! "Hee, hee, hee."

Baldy Slocum knew these mountains and he had to have that girl. The score would finally be settled. Buzzard Mackelroy would now pay for killing Baldy's daddy—never mind that he deserved killing. Right or wrong, mountain people had to avenge a killing. It was the code of the hills.

From his command post in Cell Block 13, Buzzard Mackelroy whispered war-orders to his two commanders, Cliff and Axe. "Dispatch two teams. One to the mountains. One to the city."

"To do what?" asked Cliff.

"The Mountain Team will find the girl. The City Team will devour SIG Labs, Inc."

"And?"

"The Mountain Team will be mountain men. And their dogs. The City Team will be city men: the finest architects, scientists, engineers, electricians, and accountants that can be found. Spare no chits. Go through our network and call down anyone who owes me a favor."

Buzzard Mackelroy then turned to Axe. "You draw up the plans for the Mountain Team. Cliff, you draw up the plans for the City Team."

"Yes, sir."

"Fax your plans, in code, to Preecher Kinser over at Alcoa Speedway. I want him to coordinate both teams."

"Any special instructions, sir?" asked Axe.

"I want *bear dogs*. Dogs trained on both *sweet* scents and on *sour* scents. Any hunter who asks what that means, don't use him."

"Yes, sir."

Buzzard then handed a small plastic freezer bag to Axe. Inside the bag was the mud-bead necklace. "Preecher Kinser will need this. Send it by special courier."

"And the City Team?" asked Cliff.

"I want the floor plan of every square inch of SIG Labs, a diagram of the location and the function of every piece of equipment, and the names of their top ten customers."

"When?"

"Six in the morning! When the community room opens."

All three men turned to the clock on the wall. 1:01 in the afternoon.

"Operation Code name?" asked Axe.

"Call it *Operation Roland*. Oh, and one more thing. Have one of the guards bring me some honeysuckle vine."

Cliff and Axe dashed out of the room.

Buzzard Mackelroy headed for the library to the sections marked *Code* and *Decode*. Mr. Puff's red folder was tucked under his arm.

296

Preecher Kinser took the call from Axe. After Axe explained Operation Roland, he asked Preecher, "Did you get the fax?"

"Looking at it right now."

"Any questions."

"Where's the necklace?"

"Polo Kiwanda should be pulling into your place about right now."

"The ex-boxer?"

"That's him."

"He still drive that baby-blue Lamborghini?"

"Said he did."

Preecher glanced out the window. "He just parked out by the track, and he's coming in." Preecher hung up from talking to Axe and got right to work on Buzzard Mackelroy's request, calling on his lieutenants.

"Operation Roland" began to weave its way across Tennessee and North Carolina, beckoning the most talented and mightiest from both states. By dark, the lieutenants began pulling in the net.

In Johnson City, Tennessee, the head of Broomfield Architectural Firm closed his speech to the Chamber of Commerce, walked off the stage in his tuxedo, excused himself, and went toward the bathroom, when...He would draw up the plans for the *first* floor of SIG Labs.

In Raleigh, North Carolina, the new owner of Raleigh Architectural Firm was taking a jog through Nash Square Park. He exited on Martin Street when...He would pencil in the *second* floor.

In Knoxville, Tennessee, the elderly owner of Tall Timbers Architecture relaxed in his smoking jacket at his gated-estate on Silk Stocking Row when the doorbell rang...Tall Timbers would map the *top* floor.

In Oak Ridge, Tennessee, where the atomic bomb was made, Dr. Allien Shirley, the chief scientist at the Regional Laboratory for Genetic Testing, was comparing the DNA of a murder suspect and a purported victim...Dr. Shirley would analyze the data from the nicotine experiments going on at SIG Labs, especially with Mr. Puff.

In Charlotte, North Carolina, the chief engineer at Charlotte Laboratory Equipment Mfg. Co. was barbecuing in his back yard...He would prepare a statement regarding the use and purpose of each piece of laboratory equipment.

In Chattanooga, Tennessee, the newest partner in the old, prestigious Chattanooga Accounting Firm was attending his son's Little League Party at the Children's Museum on Chestnut Street when the helicopter landed beside the building...He would search out who had paid off whom.

In Shelby, North Carolina, the head of anesthesiology at Shelby Hospital had just put a patient under...He would give the guards at SIG Labs a good night's sleep.

On and on went the message until all the experts required for Operation Roland were rounded up. Mission: Devour SIG Labs, Inc.

The bark on the tree Barbara was tied to felt icy against her thin blouse. By twilight, she thought she might freeze. All she had on, except for her running shoes, was what she had worn to work yesterday morning: a pink blouse and white skirt.

Sometime during the day the sun had come out, sending the temperature up to 55 and melting the snow. Now the night was coming on and the temperature was dropping fast. If Ezell didn't kill her the weather would. Even the stars had turned against her.

Monty Ezell sat on a stump a few feet away, looking down the barrel of his pistol, cocked and aimed right at her.

Barbara was so thirsty she thought she would pass out, and she needed to go to the bathroom. She felt naked without her mud beads; Tumbler had yanked them off while Ezell intimately frisked her. There would be no escaping and there would be no calling for help; they had bound and gagged her with a roll of plastic, refrigerator tape.

She felt Ezell's eyes—Ezell who had dined at her table—feasting on her and heard the click as he spun the bullet chamber, playing with the Colt45 as he was playing with her in his mind. But she knew he would touch her only with his eyes; she had seen the fear in his face when Tumbler warned him to keep his hands off her, saying, "Baldy Slocum wouldn't want damaged goods."

Tumbler was still gone and Monty had just returned from Slocum Sawmill. "You better hope Tumbler finds Mr. Puff's red file."

From her prison tree Barbara stared stonily at his shifty eyes.

"I told Baldy Slocum and his boys that Buzzard Mackelroy had a daughter," Monty said. "And that she was staked out in these mountains. Boy, did he get excited."

From the ridge, and from the oak tree she was tied to, she could see Grandmother Dare's isolated cabin way off in the distance. Behind the cabin, and slightly to its right when facing it, stood the barn and the mill house. In front of the cabin lay the meadow of sleeping wildflowers. Past the meadow, and nearer to the woods where she was tied, was the cornfield. A lone scarecrow, her playmate as a child, stood guard right in the middle of the field. The one-way bridge, where Tumbler and Ezell had trapped her, spanned Mill Creek. Mill Creek ran alongside Mill Road that skirted the cornfield and the edge of the woods. Her high-speed Camaro sat on the bridge, still and silent, the driver's side door open.

Barbara's hand felt empty without the ignition key to bruise it. It was the first time she could remember being without the key. What a helpless feeling.

Even the night birds had stopped singing. Two wolves called back and forth to each other from some yonder hill, warning of things to come, but telling only the direction the trouble was coming from: Vulture Mountain.

Suddenly the wolves stopped howling and a new sound began to rumble through the mountains. She cocked her ear. Logging trucks. No mufflers. Grating sound. Searching the mountains. Each crisscrossing pass grew louder and louder, bringing the trucks closer and closer. It was only a matter of time until Baldy Slocum and his boys looped the area where she was bound and gagged.

299

She was angry at herself for getting caught, and she was angry at herself for falling for another of Monty Ezell's tricks. Maybe she could do a trick of her own. He had tied only her body. Her eyes and ears were free. And her brain. They could not tape her brain. Papa had taught her that. Her mind paced to-and-fro like a tigress on a chain. Plotting. Plotting an escape.

She looked at Monty Ezell, the master betrayer who had planted the *Judas kiss.* He would be dead before the week was out. And Tumbler, the Mouseman, would suffer the same fate. She could see them now, drawn and quartered, a stock car chained to each foot and hand—the yellow roadster leading the charge. She almost felt sorry for them. But not quite. Buzzard Mackelroy had read *The Song of Roland,* too, and had *heard* it read once every thirty days for four years. In fact, it was *his* copy that Barbara had given Todd as the house present on his birthday.

Finally she came up with a plan. And she wouldn't have to fake it. She had to go to the restroom. She could hardly hold back her bladder. Maybe Monty would let her go behind a tree. But first she had to find a way to signal him, her mouth being taped.

So she began to groan and rub her knees together, begging with her eyes.

It worked. Ezell removed the plastic tape on her mouth. "What?"

"Please, Monty, I have to be excused."

"You know I can't let you loose."

"Please. If you don't let me go behind a tree right now, we're both going to be embarrassed."

Ezell looked around at the trees and bushes. "Oh, all right. But you better not try to escape!"

"You can shoot me if I do."

"Okay." Ezell cut loose the strapping tape and removed the rope. He then made a hangman's noose and tossed it around her neck. Holding the other end, he yanked on it, jerking her head, then let the rope go slack. "Go behind that tree over there."

Barbara rubbed her wrists and ankles as she scampered behind the tree, feeling the rope around her neck go taut.

Monty watched.

"Please, Monty," she scolded. "I can't go while you're watching. And don't pull so tight on the rope."

He turned his head and let the rope around her neck go slack. "You better not try anything. You know Tumbler wants to silence your Grandmother anyway. So don't make him angry. He'll go after her, too."

In the tenth of a second the rope was slack, Barbara slipped the noose over her head, then cat-like leaped into the bushes. Her first goal was to get out of pistol range, then she would get out of rifle range; then she would get out of log-truck range.

Two tenths of a second passed. She glanced back, Ezell was pulling on the rope, obviously to make it taut, and to assure himself she was still there. But it was too late.

"Stop!" Ezell yelled.

But she didn't stop. She turned on the speed for the hundred-yard dash that had won so many medals for the Lady Vols at the University of Tennessee. A bullet zinged past her head, then she heard the shot. But she was already gone, running like a dog the first time it had ever been free of its chain.

Ezell fired again, but she was already out of pistol range. He would have to use a rifle now, but he'd have to fire in the next three seconds. This was her turf. She could hear Ezell cursing as he chased her. And she could hear logging trucks. They were coming from all directions across mountain trails. The mountains sounded like a war zone.

Her legs enjoying the chance to stretch, she now backed off to her cross-country pace. Twenty-six miles. Further if she had to. Almost to the bear cave where they had tricked her into surrendering, she saw a large hornet's nest hanging from a sourwood tree. She was now a lot wiser and a lot smarter. But Monty wasn't. He would stick his nose right back in the bear cave. She would be ready. And she would make sure the black bear hibernating in there with her two cubs was ready too.

And she would also make sure Monty fell into that patch of poison ivy by the cave—the same one she had fallen into as a child. It was winter, but she figured the poison patch might still work its magic. She'd give Monty a dose of mountain justice.

She jerked a dead honeysuckle vine from a bush, doubled it, then tied it a foot high between two trees, right in the middle of the poison ivy.

She waited until Ezell was in sight. Then she hiked up her skirt and shimmied up the tree the way a bear would. She gently broke off the limb that had the hornet's nest on it, then quickly slid back down.

Ezell was closer but hadn't seen her. He had been teaching Todd *political* talk. It was time Ezell learned *bear*-talk.

At the last second, she slung the hornet's nest, bouncing and banging, into the bear cave. Buzzing like crazy echoed from the cave. Then a low moaning growl roared from within. She knew the hornets had bit mama bear's tender nose. Mama bear was looking for someone to bite back.

Barbara hid and watched.

Ezell tripped over the honeysuckle vine and fell right in the middle of the poison ivy and rolled around in it trying to get untangled. When he got up, he raced to the front of the cave where he had caught her earlier in the day. He paused, then tip-toed in. But he wasn't tiptoeing when he came out.

The hornets must have gotten him, for he squealed and bolted out of the cave, the slow-moving mama bear, half asleep, in somber pursuit.

Barbara lit out. When she glanced back, she couldn't tell if Ezell was fleeing the hornets and the bear or chasing her. Either way, his speed had picked up considerably. He was really "pickin' 'em up and puttin' 'em" down. But she began to pull away, putting even more distance between them. Soon he was completely out of her sight.

Then a horror came across her. She froze in her tracks. "Tumbler wants to silence your grandmother," Ezell had said.

But something else was wrong. Now it dawned on her what it was: the forest had gone silent. Deathly silent. She listened for clues. The only sound was the wind walking in the leaves. Whispering. Warning.

Then it hit her. Logging trucks. There was no roar from the logging trucks. That meant only one thing. Baldy Slocum and his boys had parked their trucks and were now on foot running

302

through the woods. Maybe they had met up with Monty and he had told which way she ran.

The Slocums might be idiots, but they were born and bred in these mountains and, like all Smoky Mountain men, decades of hunting and tracking flowed in their veins.

Oh no. Now it dawned on her. They may have gone for Grandmother Dare. To use her as ransom. Now she faced a new decision. What to do? There was no decision to it. She would go into the jaws of death for Grandmother Dare.

She figured she had a little time. They wouldn't go straight to the cabin. Tumbler might. But the others wouldn't. She knew Ezell was scared of Tumbler and would search the mountains, at least for a while. He would be in a heap of trouble when Tumbler got back and found she had gotten loose.

So Barbara began to plan. A new idea came to her. She had once watched a mother quail do it when a hawk tried to rob her nest. Barbara turned and raced headlong toward the onrushing enemy. Once she had them in sight, she took care to stay out of rifle range.

There they were, five men: Monty Ezell in his suit and tie— still brandishing his pistol—and Baldy Slocum and his three idiot sons, dressed in turned-backward baseball caps and overalls. All toting squirrel rifles. One carried an axe.

Tumbler was not with them. She didn't know where he had gone. Or when he might be back. He might already be at Grandmother Dare's cabin.

Barbara watched the men, running and zigzagging through the woods toward her, gasping for breath. Ezell was scratching as he ran; the poison ivy had started to work.

Now for the mother-quail ruse. Barbara pushed over a small dead maple, causing it to crash, then screamed as if she had been hurt from tripping over it.

"There she is!"

"Git 'er, boys!"

Here they came.

Barbara limped off—always away from the cabin—but stayed just enough in front of her pursuers, teasing them and running them into the ground.

303

On through the night she ran deeper and higher into the mountains. Eventually, Ezell and the Slocums sat down on stumps and panted. She let them rest awhile. Then, making sure she was in their line of sight, she purposefully stumbled into some leaves, screamed, then got up and trotted off—luring them farther away from the cabin.

The men took off after her with new vigor. She heard their curses and rifle shots, but knew the bullets couldn't reach her. Then she sped up. Closer and closer to Vulture Mountain where the original slaying had taken place. Soon she stood at the spine of the peak, taking care not to silhouette herself.

Vulture Mountain got its name because vultures hung around it, but she didn't know if the vultures hung around because the Slocums did or if the Slocums hung around because the vultures did, both wanting to be near their kind. She looked off at Slocum Sawmill. The smell of gas, oil, and sawdust drifted up from the place. Her father slew Baldy Slocum's father down at that mill because of what he did to Grandmother Dare. They had to bury him in four sacks. And that's what the Slocums would do to her if they caught her.

She decided this was far enough to lead Monty Ezell and the Slocums away from Grandmother Dare. Now, with the scent of blood on the breeze, it was time to complete her plan.

It was time for the race of her life.

She changed directions, turned on the afterburners, and made a beeline for Grandmother Dare's cabin, hoping Tumbler wasn't sitting in the living room with his knife open, waiting for her.

At 10 PM, long and lanky Preecher Kinser sped up I-40, coming down hard on Asheville, North Carolina. He had a tight schedule tonight—a 10:00 meeting in the city and a midnight meeting in the mountains.

He careened onto Biltmore Avenue on two wheels and headed downtown. The yellow roadster screeched to a halt in front of an abandoned theater on Woodfin Street, near the Thomas Wolfe Home. The Wolfe Home was across the street from the Radisson Hotel. SIG Labs, Inc. sat in the shadows, sixteen blocks away.

Preecher grabbed his squirrel rifle, vaulted over the roadster's door, and dashed up the old theatre steps. Inside, all the experts for "Operation Roland" sat attentively, awaiting his instructions. Beside each expert, sat a Cell Block 13 alumnus. The Alumni Army could handle photography, locks, and inventory, but did not have the expertise for the specialized information needed for SIG Labs. So they had rounded up experts.

It was now two minutes after ten PM.

Preecher Kinser stepped up in front of the group as if he were about to deliver a tent sermon. He was wearing overalls and a black shirt; his exposed skin was smeared with black grease-paint. He gestured with his rifle. "Remove their blindfolds."

He then explained the mission and their options.

The architects, accountants, scientists, electricians, and engineers quickly agreed to the mission. They very obediently slipped black coveralls over tuxedos, pajamas, dresses, business suits, or whatever they'd been wearing when they were shanghaied. Then they donned black tennis shoes and applied black grease-paint to faces and hands.

Buzzard Mackelroy's vicarious night team then loaded up and headed to SIG Labs.

Preecher Kinser led the first wave as they scaled the walls at SIG Labs, using grappling hooks. The first two goals: give the guards a good night's sleep and jam the video/audio recording equipment.

Two minutes passed.

A whistle from the roof.

A wink from a flashlight on the ground.

The top floor was secure.

The second wave hit the wall. On their shoulders hung cameras, rolls of drafting paper, electrical tools hanging from belts, and backpacks filled with architecture pens, compasses, slide rulers, handheld calculators, miniature computers, film, and a military, magic box for high-speed decoding.

Three rope-ladders came cascading from the roof for experts not expert in wall-climbing. Huffing and puffing, out of shape men and women from the professional community, struggled to the top.

Roland's City Army was now in place.

54

Once the City Team breached the walls of SIG Labs, Preecher Kinser turned the rest of that mission over to Polo Kiwanda, the lieutenant who earlier in the day had delivered the mud-bead necklace from Sagebrush Prison.

Polo Kiwanda, a boxing champion from Uganda, had spent time at Sagebrush Prison for beating up a boxing judge who rigged a fight. He beat up the judge's brother too; the brother was the manager of his opponent in a championship match on Tuesday Night Fights.

Knowing that the City Team was in good hands, Preecher Kinser rappelled off the roof, jumped into the yellow roadster, and headed to Vulture Mountain to meet the Mountain Team.

The Mountain Team would be gathered near Slocum Sawmill. Preecher Kinser's three bear-hounds rode shotgun. The rumble seat was piled full of lanterns, and the car smelled of coal-oil and hound. At five minutes after midnight, he came upon his mountain army.

The night was eerily-quiet.

Fifty overall-clad men stood at-the-ready alongside leashed bear dogs, dogs bred to keep bears away from livestock. Each man held a firearm of choice: a double-barrel shotgun, a squirrel rifle, or a repeater.

No man spoke. No dog spoke.

Preecher started handing out lanterns, though most of the master-trackers had brought one. "Any you men don't wanta use a gun can carry two lanterns."

He squatted and opened a small plastic bag. "Now pet your dogs as you let 'em smell this." He held out the sweet-smelling Cherokee mud-bead necklace. The dogs bunched up next to him, nudging and sniffing as gentle as house pets. "So they'll know she's a friend."

Roscoe Firestone, leader of the Mountain Team, stepped up. "I gave them your instructions, Preecher. We already cased the residence. No one there, and all four trucks are gone."

Preecher looked toward Slocum Sawmill. In the daylight it

was a beehive of activity, but now it sat silently in the moonlight. "Let's go down there."

The men and dogs moved down and tiptoed through the sawmill like ghosts stepping over graves. The gigantic saw had a long wide rubber belt that wrapped around a giant wheel at one end and a small wheel at the other. The big wheel turned the saw that trimmed slabs from logs that came out the other end as 2 x 4s, 4 x 4s, or some measure thereof. Off to the side was a tree-high pile of sawdust. To the left of the sawdust lay a mountain of slabs. Axes, chain-saws, a come-to-me, and all manner of other logging equipment lay scattered on the ground.

"Now make your dogs mad," Preecher said, "and sic 'em on this sawmill scent."

The night turned into a thunderous bloodthirsty, yelping roar. Dogs pulled and jerked at the leashes, dragging their masters through the mill, imprinting the sour stench of the Slocums on their memories.

Preecher held up his hand. The men silenced their angry killing machines, bred for one purpose.

"Now pet 'em," he said.

The mountaineers did as instructed.

"One more time let 'em smell this necklace. We don't won't no mix-ups."

The bear-killers whimpered and begged like children as they drank in the sweet odor of Barbara Dare.

"Keep the dogs quiet until I tell you to loose them," Preecher said, dropping the necklace into his pocket. "Now light your lanterns and fan out."

A stone's throw between each man, Roland's Mountain Army moved out, quiet as a corpse. Neck-hair on the bear dogs stood on end, nerves taut as violin strings.

The smell of blood was in the air.

It was a night like no other. Barbara broke out of the woods and trotted alongside Mill Creek in the moonlight.

She had to make it to Grandmother Dare's cabin. The cabin was in view. How she wished she were wearing something besides her white skirt; it would glow like a lantern when she lit out across the cornfield.

As she trotted, she planned. If she could just get Grandmother Dare to safety, she would then make a mad dash to New Bern and fall into Todd's arms. Hopefully, her father had been successful in decoding the file from SIG Labs. Surely Gene and Sally had found Todd by now and had warned him his dream was in danger of going up in flames.

Suddenly she heard a new sound! A distant muffled roaring.

She glanced over her shoulder, wiping windswept hair from her eyes as she ran. On a far ridge, she saw one of the Slocum trucks, coming after her; they must have parked the other three trucks because two of the boys were hanging off the running board, each holding a squirrel rifle in an outside hand. A third straddled the hood, riding it like a bull. She saw the white from the rifles and figured this would be the last night she would ever spend in Cades Cove.

Between her and the cabin lay the cornfield and the wildflower meadow, though the flowers were dormant this time of year. To rescue Grandmother Dare, she would have to expose her position. Risk it all. Her sides bursting—Ezell and the Slocums had chased her all night—she now had to take the chance.

Out of Monty Ezell's pistol range, but in the Slocum's rifle range and view, she scampered across the creek, splattering the icy water, then ran like a rabbit toward Mr. Scarecrow standing in the middle of the cornfield. She tagged him on the shoulder as she zipped past, as she had done so many times. As a child when she played "last tag" with him, Mr. Scarecrow always let her win. But she might not win tonight.

Soon she was in the valley of wildflowers. She smelled the smoke coming from the cabin's chimney, her weary legs reaching. She could now hear the Slocums, shouting and shooting; she couldn't let them catch her.

Closer. Closer. Closer.

Closer to her goal, she flew past the corn-crib, the water wheel, and the old mill, coming down hard on the front yard. A gray-speckled Dominiquer hen and her brood of chicks, obviously awakened by all the excitement, went cackling and scampering across the dirt yard underfoot.

Barbara Dare was now climbing the steps of home. Suddenly lightning exploded inside her. She felt the deep burning pain go through her side before she heard the shots. The last thing she saw was her own blood splatter the cabin door.

55

Gene and Sally Chastine drove all night in the green wrecker, trying to make it to New Bern in time to warn Todd. But when they arrived, Todd Carrington was already gone. Sally explained to Ms. Carrington that they were friends of Barbara and that it was urgent that they speak to Todd immediately.

"Has something happened to Barbara!?" asked Lady Carrington.

"Yes...no..." Sally didn't want to upset her, but she was on a mission, and this was no time to be timid. "Where's Todd at?"

Lady Chastine said, in her aristocratic tone, "I'm not sure I should tell—"

Gene blurted out, "Ma'am, this ain't no time to pussyfoot around. The tobacco cartel is about to force your son into some kind of kneeling ceremony. And your husband's in on it!"

"I'll get my handbag. I'm going with you."

The wealthiest lady in North Carolina climbed up into the high-speed green wrecker and rode shotgun to one of the prettiest cities in the South, Savannah, Georgia. At a hundred-miles-an-hour, its chrome exhaust pipes, one on either side, sticking up over the cab, and with the muffler caps wide open, the loud-roaring big green machine was a force to be reckoned with. Sally rode in the middle and operated the emergency lights and siren when the traffic bottlenecked.

Earlier that morning, Todd had left New Bern, and was now lounging on the yacht beside his father as they sailed along the Atlantic Seaboard. They had boarded the yacht in Charleston, South Carolina, because that's where the senator had bought the boat and it was in for its first major checkup. The senator's personal pilot had flown them from New Bern down to Charleston.

Todd wore white pants and a heavily-starched long-sleeve shirt with horizontal blue and white strips and Ralph Lauren deck shoes. His father wore his usual blue blazer, with the New

Bern Yacht Club ensign, and white pants. They wore matching Greek fisherman hats. Both were men of the sea and superior helmsmen.

Before leaving New Bern, Todd had a big fight with his father. His father had tried to talk him out of going into politics. He even ordered him not to. But Todd's mind was made up. Too many people were counting on him.

And so now, Todd toyed with the spinnaker as the yacht ran before the wind, its large head-sail set for Savannah, Georgia. His father and friends were throwing a big banquet there tonight to announce Todd's candidacy for the U.S. Senate. Monty Ezell had hurried back to Asheville to get Barbara. He would fly her on to Savannah to meet him. But there was one thing that bothered Todd: Why would a man from North Carolina, running for the Senate, be asked to make his announcement from Georgia? When he expressed this concern, his father explained that U.S. Senators work for the good of the whole country, not just their own state; this announcement would have national implications. The banquet, originally planned for New Year's, had been moved up to tonight. "You have to strike when the iron's hot," Senator Carrington explained.

Also before leaving New Bern, Todd had tried repeatedly to get Barbara on the phone to tell her that Monty would bring her to him in New Bern. At first Todd had refused to sail for Savannah without her. But as the hour grew late, the clock finally made the decision for him. Monty had called from a highway phone, told him he had located Barbara, was on his way to pick her up, and would fly her on to Savannah. Finally, Monty assured him they would be there long before the yacht laid anchor in Savannah Bay. He said he would have Barbara dressed in the black evening gown and white pearls, as Todd had requested.

There were not many men Todd would trust his wife to, but Monty Ezell had proven to be such a loyal friend that he not only trusted him to direct his national campaign for the Senate, but he also trusted him with his greatest treasure, his bride.

Few men could stand in her presence and not want her. But Barbara could take care of herself. In his arms, she purred like a kitten, but he suspected that the wildcat inside her would hurt any man who ever tried to corner her. The memory of her now mixed with the salty taste of sea spray and the warm touch of the setting sun. Those full pouting lips, soft blue eyes, and that infectious smile that so often broke into full scale laughter, often teasing laugher, were all disarming. She could turn little disasters into comical situations, often laughing at herself. She loved him so much she wanted none of the spotlight; she wanted him to have it all.

Then he thought of his life before Barbara. It had been one big social event after another. But Barbara was a mountain woman. She had brought the fire into his structured high society lifestyle, fire he had never known. But she had also brought the ice. The laughter in her voice had a sadness to it and she seemed to like sad songs best. He could tell that somewhere deep inside her, a sad person lived. Something from a long time ago caused her to cry at the drop of a hat. He had come to the conclusion that whatever it was that caused her to weep so easily had to do with her parents; they must have been killed in some horrible accident, for every time the subject came up, her eyes misted over and she went somewhere far away in her mind. Other than her deep sorrow, they were a perfect pair bond. How he longed to ease the hurt. He would give all he owned, his entire inheritance, to the physician who could prescribe a potion to ease her pain. But he knew no such physician and he knew of no such potion.

He had come to a further conclusion. Since he didn't know what caused the wound, he would ignore the scar. So he stayed away from the subject of her parents.

Maybe someday she would tell him what tortured her so, but until then, he would hold her close, kiss away her tears, and try to make her proud she had placed her trust in him. He would die before he would disappoint her. Tonight she would stand by his side when he told everyone his dream of a better world, the dream he had dreamt so often in her arms.

A deep longing for her overtook him...the way she tossed her head...the way her long hair cascaded off her shoulders. He trembled in anticipation of her nearness. There would be no

313

tears in their bedroom tonight. He'd brought pretty flowers and had laid them on their bed down in the hull of the ship. Tonight, after the banquet, his father would fly back to New Bern with Monty. Then he and Barbara would sail out to sea and let the waves rock their cares away.

And so, carefree as a beachcomber, and believing his sweetheart had already taken to the skies, Todd Carrington sailed into the storm, his father at the helm.

Meanwhile, Polo Kiwanda, leader of Preecher Kinser's City Team, raced down the halls of SIG Labs, leaping over sleeping guards. Black-all-over men and women ran behind him, carrying flashlights, lap-top computers, calculators, compasses, cameras, reams of architect paper, cans of pencils with blue-lead, slide rulers, T-squares, formulas, lock-picks, pens, Manila folders, and the high-speed code decoder.

Each expert was accompanied by an alumnus of Cell Block 13. Skilled in locksmithing, ex-inmates opened doors, files, and vaults, carefully handing folders and files to their partners, expert in accounting, machinery, or in unraveling all kinds of scientific formulas. Two men carried a battering-ram for difficult entries. When they came to Mr. Puff's room, they broke down the door. The room was in a mess: cabinets tipped over, files all over the floor, and animals running everywhere.

The team plugged in that high-speed decoder, and Mr. Puff began to talk and wouldn't hush. He told everything.

In forty-seven minutes flat, the City Team walked out the front door of SIG Labs, Inc., toting Mr. Puff.

Mission accomplished.

Polo Kiwanda, the City Team leader, leaped into his baby-blue Lamborghini and raced to Alcoa, Tennessee. Mr. Puff rode shotgun, his shiny chrome frame glowing in the moonlight. His giant computer, still attached, sat in the back seat. On the floorboard lay five cardboard blueprint tubes and a brown, two-inch-thick expanding folder.

The tubes contained detailed drawings of every inch of SIG Labs, Inc. The brown folder held, among other things, the

314

names of SIG Lab's top ten customers, the names of individuals on the take, including six Southern senators—four Republicans and two Democrats. The folder also contained information about the secret plant, Y-1, which produced twice the nicotine, and finally, the locations of the farms in Brazil where they were growing it.

At 3:00 in the morning, Polo Kiwanda arrived at Alcoa Speedway, ready to hand over custody of the five gray-speckled tubes, the brown business folder, and Mr. Puff. But Preecher Kinser wasn't back from the mountains yet. Polo climbed out of the Lamborghini, flexed his muscles, and strolled over to the guard-rail fence. The racetrack sat empty and silent.

Any minute now, he expected the Yellow Roadster to come roaring down the highway with Preecher Kinser at the wheel.

Polo Kiwanda was as high-strung as the high performance engine in his world-class automobile, and he soon got bored. Just for fun, he strolled back over to the Lamborghini, revved the engine, and pulled onto the race track. He turned her loose. In the moonlight, he won every lap. And on every lap, he imagined the yellow roadster pulling up beside him, ready to take on his baby-blue mean machine.

But most of all he wondered if Preecher Kinser's Mountain Team had turned the bear dogs loose yet on Baldy Slocum and his boys.

56

Staggered through front door...Fell to floor...Warm...

The oak floor felt warm to Barbara. In the fireplace, hickory embers glowed and crackled softly. The cabin smelled of Christmas potpourri.

Sit up.

Try to stand.

Nausea.

Hurry.

Stop the blood.

She looked around for something to use as a bandage. On a corner table by a Shaker rocker sat an unfinished jigsaw puzzle. Beside the puzzle lay Grandmother Dare's spoonbag. As a child Grandmother Dare had let her play house with the spoonbag and had told her that in the olden days, neighbors often only had enough silverware for themselves, so when they went visiting, they carried their utensils in a spoonbag. Barbara now grabbed the bag and held it to her side to stem the flow of blood. When she wiped away the red she saw that the bullet had gone all the way through.

Holding the spoonbag to her side, she climbed the stairs to the loft and found Grandmother Dare fast asleep in the feather bed. She shook her gently and grabbed her by the hand. They'd known for years this night was coming, and now without speaking, Barbara, badly limping, led her precious grandmother down the stairs, through the family room, and quickly out the back door.

Back out across the field of wildflowers they ran. Out where the Camaro was parked. The moon peeped between the clouds blowing across Cades Cove, showing the way. It was a night different from all others. Grandmother Dare, wearing her long, flowing, white flannel nightgown, looked like a ghost-angel as she ran through the wildflower meadow, and moved surprisingly well for the age on her.

Barbara knew that Monty Ezell and the Slocums were hiding, ready to jump them. Perhaps at the Camaro. Surely they had spotted her and Grandmother Dare running in the moonlight. Even, if they weren't at the Camaro, she knew they had their guns trained on it.

But she had no choice. The Camaro was their only chance. She had to risk it. If there was a God in Heaven, surely He wouldn't let them die here. Then she thought about it. She'd rather die in this valley of wildflowers than go where the Slocums would take her. And she knew Grandmother Dare would; she'd already been there and it had cost her her only daughter and, in an even crueler way, her son.

Still in flight, Barbara breathed a prayer. Maybe her last. One of two things was about to happen: either they would make it to the Camaro or they wouldn't. If they fell before they reached the car, another means of transportation would be coming for them—a heavenly chariot of some sort would carry them to a more beautiful valley.

But this was no way to end it all. At least she would no longer be an albatross around Todd's neck. Todd! Now she remembered Todd. Oh, Todd—

Suddenly she saw a most spectacular sight. Lights! Hundreds of them! An army of lights—had to be lanterns— coming across the rim of the far mountain. Running to and fro, they looked like giant fireflies on the way to a Christmas candlelight ceremony. They were coming in her direction.

Ezell and the Slocums had to be somewhere between her and the swarming lanterns.

Suddenly gunfire exploded.

She thought she'd been shot again, but felt nothing.

Maybe she and Grandmother Dare had already died and those were night-angels coming for them. Maybe she had died on the porch when they first shot her, and Grandmother Dare had already been killed, and they were merely ghosts running for the skies. Maybe that's why she didn't feel anything.

She heard bloodhounds yelping in the distance.

Oh no! The dogs weren't ghosts. They had turned the dogs loose on them. She could outrun the men, but she couldn't outrun the dogs. And Grandmother Dare certainly couldn't.

By now she and Grandmother Dare had made it through the

valley of wildflowers and were racing past Mr. Scarecrow in the center of the cornfield. They had to make it to Mill Creek Bridge where the Camaro was parked.

Then everything broke loose.

More guns exploded, more dogs barked, and men yelled. It sounded like a war raging in the woods at the edge of the meadow, and soon the smell of gunpowder drifted on the breeze.

All at once the lantern-army froze and the guns stopped. But the hounds didn't. The bear dogs had treed; she could tell they were bear dogs by the deep roar of their song once they had treed. Grown men screamed bloodcurdling screams and begged for mercy.

Soon the bloodhounds stopped yelping. Then all was quiet. The lanterns went out. The Candlelight Ceremony was over.

Barbara didn't know whose side the fresh army was on, but she wasn't about to stay around to find out. It might even be *Roland's Army* coming to her rescue, but like Roland, that was probably only wishful thinking; it was more likely that Tumbler had brought reinforcements.

She and Grandmother Dare had now reached the Camaro. They climbed in. The keys were still in the ignition.

Barbara tossed the bloody spoonbag on the floorboard, revved the engine, and stomped the pedal. Grandmother Dare smiled like an angel, her long gray hair blowing in the cold night air. Barbara started rolling the windows up.

Suddenly Monty Ezell leaped out of the woods. He stood right in the middle of the narrow road. Trapped in the headlights, he waved his pistol at the windshield.

Barbara hit the super-charger blue-button, releasing the nitrous oxide. The Camaro reared on two wheels. She would split him wide open. The bumper almost in his britches, Ezell dived off the road and fired at the vanishing blue streak.

Grandmother Dare adjusted her specs. "Child, I think you've been in my cider. You almost hit a deer."

"Wasn't no deer, Grandmother. That was a skunk."

With Grandmother Dare now safely out of the cabin, Barbara turned her attention to Todd...to getting Mr. Puff's decoded file into his hands— not her personally getting it to him, she didn't know if she should ever try to approach him again, but certainly getting the file to him. In the morning she would pick up the file from her father at the prison. Somehow she would get it to Todd.

For now though, Grandmother Dare was tired. Barbara had to find a place to rest till morning.

57

A little before 8:00 that evening, Todd and his father had sailed into Savannah. When they cruised under the Tall Ship Bridge, what they saw looked like an armada of yachts and tall ships. The city was celebrating Christmas on the River with its Lighted Boat Parade. Historic Riverfront was alive with continuous entertainment, music, food, and fun. Everyone was there for the Lighting of the Christmas Tree.

But Barbara wasn't waiting at the dock.

Todd raced through the festive crowd, feeling River Street's cobblestones at his feet.

He hurried into the Marina Restaurant and Grill, carrying a white boutonniere in one hand and a yellow corsage in the other; he had brought the flowers from New Bern. He peered inside the banquet hall. The tasty smell of lobster came at him. They must have arrived late for the room was filled to capacity and the guests were already eating. But he didn't see Barbara in there, so he dashed to a pay phone, called the Savannah International Airport, and had her paged.

"We have no passenger here by that name," came the answer.

Todd's father paced back and forth in the lobby beside him. The senator had been unusually nervous all afternoon. Now Todd assumed he was worried about Barbara, too. Then Todd noticed all the security people in the lobby. Guards with sidearms stood at the entrance to the banquet room, checking identities and invitations.

All the security bothered him, but at least Barbara would be safe when she arrived. He figured the extra guards went with moving up in politics, but made a mental note that when *his* time came, he would scale-down the security, or at the least make it more discreet. He dialed the airport again and asked to speak with someone in the tower.

"Maybe they ran into weather trouble," said the tower operator.

Suddenly his father grabbed his elbow and rushed him

toward the dining room. In a grave voice, the senator said, "It's time, Son."

The house-lights dimmed, a drum roll exploded from somewhere, and the music from "2001 A Space Odyssey" blared from speakers, announcing that someone important was about to enter the room.

Todd and his father stepped into the banquet hall and stood at attention; they had changed into tuxedos on the yacht. Dueling spotlights searched the crowd like a prisoner had just gone over the wall. The spots came to rest on Todd and his father. The crowd broke into applause.

For a moment Todd was pleased. Tonight his dream would climb up on the high wires and dance for the world as the national media sent out emails, faxes, telegrams, and phone messages. Tonight his dream would finally take flight.

The spotlight guided the two tall men through the darkness. They strode side by side down the aisle. Todd was still pinning on his boutonniere when he reached the head table; he had waited until the last minute so Barbara could do it. Pinning on the boutonniere was a little thing, but it was something she liked to do.

He sat, but his father didn't. The senator walked along the head table, bending over and whispering to this person and that person. Todd looked for Barbara's place card so he could lay the yellow corsage at her seat. There were two empty chairs at the head table, both to his left; one had to be for Barbara.

Between the two empty seats sat the table-lectern and microphone. The first place card, the one beside Todd, read, "Senator Charles Carrington." The table-lectern blocked his view of the other name. So he leaned back and peeped behind the podium to get a better view. That's when he noticed a wheelchair ramp that led up to the speaker's mike. He leaned back further, almost spilling over in the process, still searching for Barbara's name card. It had to be hers; it was the only seat left. Suddenly he got the shock of his life. The card didn't say Barbara Dare-Carrington at all. It said, "Krandall Kaufman." Krandall Kaufman!?!

Todd felt angry and insulted at the same time—*angry* that

322

Kaufman would even be at the banquet, and *insulted* that Barbara had been slighted. No. Maybe she had told his father that she would rather sit in the audience; that would be like her. So he laid the corsage by his own name card. When she walked in, even if he was right in the middle of his dream-speech, he would stop, march down the aisle, pin the flower on her, and give her a big kiss, right in front of everyone.

Todd was still angry about the tobacco mogul...and seated at the head table no less. What was his father thinking? He turned to motion his father to him. But his father didn't see him. Or ignored him. His father was now pacing back and forth even more than he had in the lobby and was perspiring so heavily that Todd became concerned he might have a heart attack.

Another drum roll. The music began again and the applause began again. But this time everyone stood. Krandall Kaufman rolled into the spotlight. The light followed him down the aisle to the head table.

Todd refused to stand. Then he became concerned the gesture would embarrass his father, so he stood. As he did, he jerked on his father's coat sleeve. "Explain!"

"Kaufman raised the money for my campaigns all these years."

"Sir, I made it quite clear I don't want the tobacco cartel involved in *my* campaign."

"Kaufman knows that. But he asked if he could present you tonight. I couldn't ignore him after all these years."

The applause stopped and the crowd sat. Todd's father was also sitting, but Todd was still standing. And still talking. "As long as he understands that!"

"Sit down!" the senator whispered, yanking on Todd's coat sleeve.

Todd sat but kept talking. "Father, I would never be rude to one of your friends, but if Krandall Kaufman makes one move tonight in front of the press, even a hint that he's backing me, I'll kick him and that wheelchair off the pier and into the Harbor."

"Shake hands with him and shut up!"

Shut up? His father had never spoken to him in that tone of voice. Todd turned to shake hands with Kaufman. As he did, he smiled his practiced smile—the one Monty had taught him—for the cameras he knew would be waiting.

But no camera flashed. Something was cockeyed.

Kaufman spoke to Todd. "Congratulations, senator. Your father has told me a lot about you."

"Thank you, but I'm not a senator."

"Oh, but you are...if you play your cards right. We simply have to let the clock run until your inauguration."

Todd's father started to stand and got halfway up—

Kaufman jerked something out of his coat sleeve.

Todd's father sat back down, but he was trembling all over. Whatever it was that Kaufman took from his tuxedo sleeve, he laid it in his lap and covered it with the white linen napkin. Todd assumed it was a box of cough-drops, for it was that size and Kaufman coughed a lot.

"Let's get this Ceremony started," Kaufman said, hitting the joy stick on his wheelchair arm. He began rolling toward the ramp and to the microphone at the center of the head table.

Todd thought, Who does he think he is? It's *my* campaign. So he grabbed at the joy stick. "Wait a minute, Mr. Kaufman. My wife is coming; she'll be here momentarily."

Kaufman slapped Todd's hand away and kept going. "Ezell'll take good care of that little bride of yours."

"You know Monty Ezell?"

Kaufman ignored him and kept rolling toward the speaker-mike.

"Father," Todd said, turning to his father, "you tell him! Let's give Barbara another minute. We've got to stall." Then he noticed that the audience had finished eating, but he had been too concerned about Barbara's arrival to be concerned about lobster on the half-shell.

"We can't stall any longer, Son. It's got to be done. Now."

Todd had never heard his father speak in such somber tones.

The spotlight followed Krandall Kaufman up the six-inch ramp to the speaker's podium. The wheelchair came to a halt at the center of the table, slightly elevated above the other chairs. Kaufman cleared his throat into the mike. The house lights came up as he welcomed the guests and told a stale banquet joke.

For the first time, Todd could see the guests. All men! Not a woman in the room! Rough looking men, smoking and coughing. They all wore tuxes, but they certainly didn't look like pillars of society. He began to smell a rat. Something was wrong. What was it? Then it hit him. There wasn't a newsperson in the—He jerked around and whispered as loudly as he could, "Father, there's not a camera in the room!"

Kaufman turned his bushy-browed eyes on Todd's dad, then jiggled whatever it was he was hiding under the napkin in his lap. The senator didn't respond to Todd's comment. But he still trembled.

Kaufman introduced the program. "And now for the Ceremony."

The house lights dimmed and a stage behind the head table became visible. At the front of the stage was a scrim. A yellow spotlight shined through the semitransparent curtain onto an altar. Two black-hooded priests in black robes were kneeling in front of the altar. There was a place for a third person to kneel between them. Todd couldn't tell if the priests were real or if they were statues. Over the altar were the words, *And Abraham...bound his son and laid him on the altar. Genesis 22:9.* The scrim made it all appear like a ghostly scene from some sacred opera.

Todd whispered, "Father, that's a most impressive backdrop, but what does it have to do with me and my candidacy?"

Charlie Carrington began to stammer. "I'm sorry, Son. I...I...tried to...Your mother and I—"

Kaufman coughed a warning cough. That's when Todd saw what looked like a gun barrel—or a silencer!— sticking from under the napkin on Kaufman's lap. The tiny gun, or whatever it was, was aimed right at Todd's father.

The senator suddenly jumped up like he was in some terrible pain. Straining and sputtering, he blurted out, "Son, it's not a...It's not...It's a Kneeling Ceremony!—"

"He's having a heart attack!" Kaufman yelled. "Grab him, men, before he falls!"

Four men grabbed Senator Charlie Carrington and dragged him kicking and screaming from the room.

Todd, already on his feet, rushed to his father's side.

"Get him to the hospital," Kaufman yelled.

Suddenly there was a loud commotion in the back of the banquet room. Todd looked over his shoulder as he followed his father whom he believed was being taken to a hospital.

At the back of the banquet hall, a black man, wearing a white karate suit was trying to get into the party. A woman was with him. It looked like...Gene...Gene and Sally Chastine...Todd froze. It *was* Gene and Sally!

Gene was coming down the aisle, kicking his feet and slinging his fists and screaming karate yells, "Aahh! Yeeee!"

The aisle became splattered with fallen men.

Todd rushed toward him. "Hey. Leave him alone. He can come in here. He's my friend."

By now a group of men had Gene pinned to the floor, but Gene was still kicking and yelling.

Sally, wearing jeans and a green sweater, jumped on top of the pile, slinging her purse and screaming. Then her eyes landed on Todd. "Run, Todd, Run!"

"Let him up!" Todd started grabbing men by the collars and tossing them to the side like rag dolls.

Gene popped his bloody head out of the pile. "Don't kneel, Todd! Don't never kneel! Barbara said tell you that!"

Then Todd saw another woman with Sally, also slinging her purse at the heads of the men in the pile. "Mother!!"

Something or someone struck Todd on the head and that was the end of the Christmas holidays for him.

58

At 6:00 the following morning, the "Operation Roland" report arrived at Cell Block Thirteen. It was complete. Except for one thing. Now everything was meaningless.

"Baldy Slocum shot the girl," Axe said.

"Dead?" asked Buzzard Mackelroy.

"The hunters never found her. At the cabin, a trail of blood led from the porch to the sleeping loft. She wasn't in the cabin, and the old woman who lived there was missing too."

Buzzard Mackelroy sat down and wept in front of all the prisoners. After a while, he asked, "What about Baldy Slocum?"

"He'll never trouble you again. The bear dogs took care of him and his boys. Preecher said the hunters just couldn't hold the dogs back."

"So you think the girl and the old woman are really dead?" asked Buzzard Mackelroy.

"Preecher Kinser said they were. Then he said something I didn't understand. But he said you would."

"Yes?"

"The Camaro's missing."

Buzzard Mackelroy stopped crying.

59

Last night, after the harrowing escape from Ezell and the Slocums, Barbara and her grandmother made their way to Pigeon Forge, nearest town to Cades Cove. Unconscious of time last night, her plan had been to lose themselves in the stream of tourists and tour buses gawking at the two million Christmas lights that wrapped the city. But when they arrived, the town had gone to bed.

She soon found a tiny motel off the beaten path, not far from the Apple Barn, so Grandmother Dare could rest. Once she got grandmother tucked in, Barbara drove to an all-night pharmacy where she purchased medicine and bandages for the gunshot wound. Back at the motel, between fits of sleep, she spent much of the night peeping out the window, watching for Ezell, the Slocums, and the morning.

Morning exposed a new problem: what to do with Grandmother Dare while she went to the prison to pick up Mr. Puff's decoded file for Todd. Then she remembered. She had just the place. After a couple of stops for clothes and toilet articles for Grandmother Dare and herself, Barbara drove to the Bus Depot and bought a ticket to the Esmeralda Inn and Restaurant. Grandmother Dare would be safe there.

Between announcements of arrivals and departures over the depot loudspeaker, Bing Crosby sang "White Christmas."

Grandmother Dare waved goodbye from the bus window, and Barbara thought, This isn't how we had intended to spend the Christmas holidays. She and Todd were supposed to...now she thought of Todd. Wonder if Gene and Sally reached him before the Kneeling Ceremony?

She must hurry. She headed for the prison.

Granny wig and all, Barbara limped up to the guard—the bullet wound in her side meant she didn't have to fake the limp today—and asked in a quivering voice, "May I see Mr. Mackelroy?"

While she waited, she went through her routine of getting out the book for the French lesson. Soon her father arrived and was locked in his cage. He looked her up and down, as if satisfying himself that Tumbler hadn't hurt her.

"Preecher Kinser's holding Mr. Puff's file for you," he whispered. "It's all decoded. And it's dangerous. If Todd can get it into the hands of the right people, a lot of tobacco executives are going to jail."

"Who should he give it to?"

"Not his daddy. We're still not sure whose side he's on."

"Preecher said as much when he called. Sally and Gene are supposed to have already told Todd that."

"Tell him to personally hand it to Morgan J. Schubert."

"Who's he?"

"The FDA's top lawyer."

Barbara wrote down the name.

"But here's the bombshell," said Buzzard. "According to Mr. Puff, some of the larger companies have a secret tobacco plant. It's genetically engineered to have twice the normal nicotine, and its leaves are already being used in cigarettes now on store shelves. The secret plant's name is 'Y-1,' and they are growing it on farms in Brazil."

"No wonder they were—"

"That's not all your Mr. Puff revealed. Remember the strong ammonia smell you told me about when you slung the 2x 4 through Mr. Puff's cage and broke it—when Tumbler was chasing you and Sally?"

"The ammonia gagged us," said Barbara.

"They were adding the ammonia to the cigarettes as an impact booster—the ammonia freed the nicotine from the tobacco so it could be inhaled in smoke."

"And that's why they had Mr. Puff hooked up to all those animals—"

"*And* to manipulate and measure the effect of Y-1 and ammonia on nicotine and on their guinea pigs. All those wires that were hooked up to Mr. Puff's computer measured how much to add and how much to take out."

"And to keep a record of it," she guessed.

"Yes. And here's Mr. Puff's biggest bombshell: Krandall Kaufman was blackmailing the tobacco companies with that information."

"*Blackmailing the tobacco companies.* Why?"

"To enhance his stock position. He had almost complete control of some of the larger companies."

"So, if Mr. Puff had not talked," Barbara said, "Kaufman might have gotten away with it."

"And may yet. So don't trust Mr. Puff's file to anyone but Todd."

"I'll get it to him," she said.

"Tell him to put Mr. Puff on the witness stand at that Senate hearing. He can tell the whole story."

"I will. Anything else?"

Her father's mood changed. "Baldy Slocum and his boys are dead."

"I thought they might be," she said. "What about Tumbler and Monty Ezell?"

"They've gone to sea."

"Drowned?"

"Nothing like that. Our men are searching the Atlantic Seaboard for them. But now back to you. You must never come here again."

"What?!"

"*You must never come here again.*"

"But you said Baldy Slocum was dead."

"And so he is. But there are thousands of *Baldy Slocums.*"

"I'll never stop coming here."

"Then I'll refuse to see you."

"I can still run and I can still hide. I don't have to be seen in public with Todd."

"That would never work. Todd is a public figure. He always will be. He needs a wife to stand beside him, not one continuously hiding in the shadows."

The inevitable decision was coming down hard on Barbara. Either she must never see her father again, or she must never see her husband again. "But Papa, my not coming here won't stop your enemies. Or the media."

"You're right, sweetheart. But there is a way to stop them."

"There is?" she said full of hope.

"Don't you understand, sweetheart, you and Todd can never live, really live, as long as Buzzard Mackelroy lives."

Suicide! Now it hit her what he was proposing. "No. Not that, Papa. Not that!"

"There's no other way." He stared at her for what seemed forever. A tear rolled down his prison-pale cheek from under his goggle-glasses. He pulled the ragged elastic band over his head and held the glasses in his hand. "I want you to have these. I'll send them around to you by the guard."

"No. Don't do it!"

"Sh," he said, quieting her. "If Todd is to survive, Buzzard Mackelroy cannot. You know it's him or me. And my life doesn't count. His does. Your leaving Todd won't stop my enemies. Only one thing will stop them, and you and I know what that is."

Barbara began to weep. "I won't agree to that."

"It's not your decision, sweetheart." He stood. "You've seen Buzzard Mackelroy for the last time."

"I'll never stop coming here."

"Then I'll refuse to see you. Remember, I love you more than life itself. Try to think of the few good times we had, especially at the races. You were tiny and probably don't even remember, but, for old time's sake, it would mean a lot to me if some Saturday night, you would go over to Alcoa to Preecher Kinser's Speedway like you and I used to do. Take the goggles and let me watch through your eyes. Maybe you can get Preecher Kinser to let my little yellow roadster race around that track one last time."

"No! Give me twenty-four hours!" she begged.

A guard tapped on the cage. "Time's up."

Her father stood, stepped out of the cage, then walking backwards, smiled at her as they led him down the hall, his chains rattling louder than she'd ever heard them.

"Let me talk to Todd!" she screamed in a whisper. "I'll leave him before I'll let you do that!"

He was still waving when the metal door clanged shut.

332

Momentarily a guard came around and handed her the goggle-glasses.

That was the last time she would ever see Buzzard Mackelroy.

Barbara was holding together pretty well as she limped down the long hall of Sagebrush Prison. She clutched the faded elastic band of the goggle-glasses in one hand and the walking cane in the other. The glasses hung down, jostling loosely, like a man dangling from a gallows. Then her nerves began to unravel. She poked the concrete floor nervously with the walking cane, reaching for balance. But the gentle tapping of wood on concrete echoed down the long corridor. The tap, tap, tap grew louder and stronger and began to sound like someone hammering nails into a scaffold. She started walking faster, then moved to a trot, and then into an all out race, trying to outrun the sledgehammer crescendo engulfing her.

Gasping for air, she fell against the front door of the prison, and staggered outside. The door slammed shut, releasing the giant crescendo with an explosive thud...like the slamming of the lid on a coffin. Once she reached the Camaro, she broke down and sobbed uncontrollably. Lost in thought, she was halfway back across Old Smoky before she realized she was still wearing the granny wig. She jerked it off and laid it on the seat.

She tried to pull herself together. She needed her best thinking right now. She couldn't choose Todd over her father's life, and she couldn't choose her father over Todd. But when it all boiled down, that was the decision: her husband for her father—her marriage for her father's life. The secret had cost Todd his career; it would now cost her her marriage. But the decision was a no brainer. There was no other way.

She tossed the wig and cane out the window then hurried home to write a farewell note to Todd. She only hoped her father honored her request for twenty-four hours.

On the way back to Asheville, she drove by Alcoa Speedway and picked up Mr. Puff's file from Preecher Kinser. He showed her Mr. Puff and told her that he was now talking and he wasn't talking in code. He told her that whoever took custody of the Red Folder should also take custody of the robot. Barbara told him her father had given her the same advice. She asked

Preecher to help her load Mr. Puff and his computer into the Camaro. Mr. Puff rode shotgun back to Asheville.

When she arrived in Asheville, she stopped at an office supply store and picked up some standard legal forms. That night she filled in the blanks on a Quit Claim Deed on their chalet, a Divorce Proceedings Document, and a Blanket Bill of Sale, granting ownership to the house and all its contents to Todd. She then packed a suitcase and lit a candle—she thought better in candlelight. She sat down on the bed and began to write:

Dearest Todd,

When you didn't come back, I knew it was because you couldn't. I don't blame you for not wanting to see me again. And I understand. Forgive me for not telling you about my father. You will never know how many times I tried and how much I wanted/hated to tell you. If you could only have known him. Except for one event, he, too, could have been a senator.

On the bed are two folders. One is Manila. One is red. Inside the Manila folder are legal papers that I have signed. The keys to the Vette are on the pegboard in the kitchen. The red folder holds the key to your dream. You must personally hand the folder to Morgan J. Schubert at the Congressional hearing on nicotine. Schubert is the FDA's top lawyer. But be careful on your way there. There are many who want the folder destroyed. Your father may be one of them. Take Mr. Puff with you. He's the man sitting on your side of the bed. Just plug him in and turn him on. He'll talk and he knows plenty.

And now my beloved. From some distant star, I shall watch, with great delight, your star rise. Make it shine brightly for the both of us and for what might have been. I never believed more than I do now in your dream for our country.

Try to forget me. But when you do think of me, try to remember me fondly.

> *All my love, always,*
> *Barbara*

Then she slid the soft-blue paper inside a soft-blue envelope, sealed it with a kiss and laid it on the soft-blue satin pillowcase. She blew out the red candle and walked toward the living room, removing the keys to the chalet from her key ring as she moved. At the front door, she laid the keys and her Visa card on the marble table, under the Renoir painting.

She picked up the suitcase she had left at the door, walked outside, and climbed into her old Camaro. She headed up the Blue Ridge Parkway, and over the hill. To where, she knew not. But some place where she could observe the funeral of all her hopes and dreams.

In her mind, North Carolina would always be the state that gave America the airplane, the Pepsi, and Todd Carrington. But it would never be her home again. She must find a new place to hide.

61

Christmas came and went. A few days later, Monty Ezell flew Tumbler back down to Savannah in the jet. During the flight, Tumbler confided in Ezell that Todd Carrington had refused to kneel and that he was on the way to finish the job on him.

When they landed, he ordered Ezell to take the jet back to Asheville and wait further instructions, all the while cautioning him in his graveyard tone, "Don't tell anyone my mission."

Ezell was scratching like crazy and said that suited him just fine because he needed to see a doctor. He had to find out what was making him itch so. Tumbler told him it looked like poison ivy, but to take his word for it, the itch wouldn't last long.

Then Tumbler deplaned.

Stoplight King, the one-armed man, was standing on the tarmac beside a limo holding the door open. He drove Tumbler to the Savannah Waterfront, lined with over a hundred shops and galleries, high-class restaurants, seductive nightspots, and out-of-this-world inns and hotels. They grabbed a couple of sandwiches to go, boarded a cigarette-company owned jet boat, and slowly headed down the Savannah River to the deep waters of the Atlantic.

Tumbler stood in the open boat, chewed on his lettuce and tomato sandwich, and stared into the afternoon sun. Momentarily, he heard the thunder, then saw Ezell's Gulfstream IV climb into the skies. He glanced at the second hand on his wrist watch. Along about now the high-altitude plastic explosives should cure Ezell's itch.

Suddenly the jet exploded! One giant fire ball. Monty Ezell wouldn't be itching any more and he wouldn't be talking any more.

Tumbler motioned to Stoplight King to shove the boat to full throttle. King leaned on the throttle with his elbow stub. Thirty minutes later they climbed aboard Senator Carrington's yacht, anchored at sea. Todd Carrington, the would-be senator, lay unconscious on the floor.

When Todd finally came to, he was at sea. He didn't know where he was nor how long he had been unconscious. He was still wearing his tux and had a beard with what appeared to be several days growth. The yacht was rocking up and down like crazy, slapping the sea and making his head hurt. Surely he was in a storm.

But when the bow of the yacht dipped, he saw the sun on the horizon and noticed that the ocean was calm. There was no storm. But what was causing the violent jerking and sloshing?

He struggled to stand, but couldn't, and his head hurt worse. Then, for the first time, he realized his wrists and ankles were bound with rope and that his pillow was a block of concrete. A chain was wrapped and tied around the block of concrete. The other end of the chain was clamped to his neck.

He raised his head and peeped over the stern. A giant shark with a bloody mouth was tied to the ship, jerking the yacht around like a toy, trying to get loose. The hundred-foot rope was whiplashing the water and popping it like someone cracking a whip.

When Todd rolled his head around, he saw a small man, with almost no neck, descending the ladder from the tuna tower. He came and stood over him. Todd had enough presence of mind to pretend to still be unconscious.

A one-armed man came from somewhere and spoke to the little man. "Tumbler, I think the shark is getting hungry."

"All right, Moby Dick!" Tumbler yelled to the man-eater. "This looks like as good a spot as any!"

It dawned on Todd that the little man named Tumbler was up to no good and might even be planning to feed him to that giant shark tied to the yacht! All doubt was removed when Tumbler grabbed a crowbar and began prying at the concrete pillow under and chained to Todd's head, struggling to hoist it over the port side.

Todd almost screamed. But he didn't. He had one chance. He had to take it. He took a deep breath, pulled his long

340

powerful legs to his chest, and kicked the little man where it would do the most good. Right in the crotch.

Tumbler went sailing overboard, head first. The shark lunged for him. But he grabbed the rope that tied the dinghy to the yacht and pulled himself into the small boat, then headed toward the shore.

The one-armed man froze.

Todd grabbed the crowbar and stabbed at the rope around his ankles and wrists.

The one-armed man dashed down into the cabin, and came back up the steps holding a spear gun. He was trying to cock it one-handed.

Todd now had freed his own hands. He dived at the weapon, crashing the one-armed man to the deck. He banged the man's head on the floor, then wrapped the slack in the chain around his neck and jerked. The fight went out of the one-armed man. He started sobbing and begged Todd not to throw him to the shark.

"Where's the key to this clamp around my neck?"

"My pocket."

Todd secured the one-armed man, finished freeing himself, then called the Coast Guard on the ship-to-shore phone. By the time the Coast Guard arrived, Todd had found his mother and Gene and Sally bound and gagged in the engine room. He asked about his father and they told him they thought the senator was with him. Gene and Sally told him Barbara's story. After getting their promise to escort his mother home, Todd went running to *his* home.

When he got there, he found Mr. Puff sitting on his bed, he found the red folder, and he found the blue envelope, but he didn't find Barbara. He walked through the house, saw the Christmas decorations still up, and realized he'd missed Christmas. He immediately called Grandmother Dare's cabin. An electronic voice announced, "This number is no longer in service."

62

Barbara Dare drove aimlessly for days. When she finally turned off the Camaro's engine, she was parked in front of the PREMIUM HOTEL, a cheap rental in the seedy part of Knoxville. A sign out front read: ECONOMY RENTALS, By The Day Or By The Week. The sooty red-brick, a four-story walkup, had been a nice hotel in its day, but a changing neighborhood had relegated it to a clientele of indigents and a highway construction crew of hard hats.

Barbara registered as Cynthia Smith. She peeped from under the brown wig she was wearing as she paid cash in advance. The perfect hideout, she thought. Not even the press would think of looking here for the wife—the ex-wife—of a billionaire politician.

Her third floor room was painted off-white, the plaster was falling off the ceiling, and the wooden floor, partially covered with patchy brown-and-white linoleum, buckled and looked like a mole had been tunneling under the boards.

The furnishings were a bed, a chest-of-drawers—with one drawer missing—a small table-top refrigerator, a washbasin, and a small gas space heater. That was it, except for a box of matches on top of the chest-of-drawers, and the musty smell. Guests, male and female, used the bath on the hall. The room had no phone and no TV and Barbara liked that just fine. Her goal was to unplug herself from society in general and from the media in particular. Her father's enemies would still be after *her*, but at least now, they would leave Todd alone. Her father's enemies would have no interest in Todd.

On her way to Knoxville, she had made a brief stop at Sagebrush Prison, and, expecting that her father would refuse to see her—which he did—left a note for him with the guard. The note told him not to do anything foolish because there was no need; she had left Todd.

Now, hid out in the tiny hotel room, she used an eyebrow pencil to darken her eyebrows to match the brown wig. She entertained herself by staring out the window at the brick wall of the building opposite her room, and by rubbing her fingers over the ragged elastic band of her father's goggle-glasses. That substituted for her habit of rubbing the mud-bead necklace, now gone forever. She ventured out only for an occasional walk to the Seven Eleven for bare necessities, always wearing the brown wig when out of her room.

Her dirty laundry began to pile up, so one afternoon she stuffed it into a white pillowcase, slung it across her shoulder, and wandered across the street to the washateria behind the Seven Eleven. She sat there staring at the window in the washer, like she was watching a western on TV, while the red clothes chased the blue clothes and the blue clothes chased the yellow clothes and the...

Two unsavory-looking characters sauntered in and flopped down across the aisle and stared at her. She soon became aware that it was not her but her $100,000 Rolex that held their interest. She jerked the washer door open, right in the middle of the spin cycle, shoved the wet garments back into the pillowcase, and dashed out the door, leaving a stream of water running down her back and onto the sidewalk. Once back in the safety of her room, she wrung out the clothes in the sink as well as she could and hung them all around on coat hangers.

But her expensive wristwatch was another matter; in this present environment, it invited a different kind of trouble. That was an easy problem to solve. She looked around for something to put it in. The matchbox. She picked up the matchbox, dumped the matches on top of the chest, and placed the Rolex inside the box. She removed the cotton from an aspirin bottle and made a soft bed for the mostly red, solid gold watch, crowned with diamonds and rubies. She found a brown paper bag, tore it open, and wrapped the matchbox. Then she addressed it to Todd. No return address.

Now she realized she had no stamps, but didn't want to go back outside where the two seedy characters might be lurking. She looked at the clock: 5:15. The hardhats from the highway department would be coming home soon. Surely one of them wrote home occasionally and would have stamps. She slowly opened her door and walked to the top of the stairs, watching and

344

listening for the workers. The dusty and sweaty men in their yellow hard hats soon started drudging up the stairs, carrying metal lunch boxes. One after the other shook his head, saying, "I don't write; I call." Finally a bright-eyed young man with a cheerful smile came bouncing up the stairs. In a Scottish brogue, he told her he wrote his girlfriend back in Texas every night and that he'd be happy to *give* her a book of stamps. Barbara tried to pay him, but he refused her money, saying, "May the postage bring *yer* laddie as much joy as it would have my lassie."

Overcome with emotion at the first words spoken to her in days, and remembering when she and Todd were that happy, Barbara gave the boy a peck on his dusty and freckled cheek, then dashed back to her room. She licked the stamps and stuck them on the tiny package. She waited a few minutes for the lobby to clear. When all was quiet, she sneaked down the stairs one at a time. Finding the lobby empty, she sprinted across the linoleum floor and dropped the $100,000 matchbox into the hotel's mail slot.

She dashed back up the stairs, taking them three at a time, and got right back to the business of staring out the window at the wall of the opposite building.

For days, she just sat and stared. Soon she couldn't remember how long she had stared out the window. She began to think she might go crazy, so, on one of her forays to the Seven Eleven, she purchased a copy of the *Knoxville News-Sentinel*. The paper would be her first brush with the outside world in days.

When she returned to her room, she changed from faded jeans back into her green robe, then sat on the bed—there wasn't even a chair in the room—and flipped through the Knoxville paper. Suddenly she got the shock of her life. A second-page article told it all:

BUZZARD MACKELROY, NOTORIOUS PRISONER, COMMITS SUICIDE. Buzzard Mackelroy, a confessed murderer, was serving life without parole at Sagebrush Prison. He donated his vital organs for transplants. The Warden said the organ donation was the only decent thing Buzzard Mackelroy ever did, but that no one wanted his heart.

Under the brief article was a picture of a young man, with a note in parenthesis that read:

(In his late teens, about the time of this photograph, he fathered a child, but, according to courthouse records, the mother and infant died during childbirth. Current photo of Mackelroy is not available.).

Barbara wept. They never knew him at all. He never had a chance. And she would just as soon she *had* died as a baby.

She sat on the bed and cried for a while. Soon a feeling of guilt came over her. Maybe she hadn't done all she could have. A great need to do something, to take some action, grabbed her and wouldn't let go. She searched the room for something to do, some project she could lose herself in. Finally, she decided to polish her shoes. She reached under the bed and pulled out her old, old burgundy penny loafers which she no longer wore. She knew they were out of style—they were out of style when she bought them. But the memories weren't out of style. Style wasn't everything. In some eyes, her mud-bead necklace had been out of style from the beginning. But as for the shoes, she'd kept them because she met Todd the first night she wore them, and because the date on the pennies in the shoe-slots marked her very existence. Having no polish, she spit-shined the loafers with a white sock. As she rubbed the slots that held the two pennies dated 1959—her father's birth year—she came up with an idea. She searched her purse until she found a new penny. She pried out the old penny in the right shoe and replaced it with the new coin. Her left shoe now had a penny dated 1959 and the right shoe had one dated 1998. That's about all she felt like doing now, so she laid down on the bed and took a nap.

While she slept, the crystal ball dropped in Times Square in New York City, ushering in 1999.

The organ harvest attracted widespread attention on the Internet. The same day as the suicide, four private jets from four different states landed at the Regional Airport in Knoxville, Tennessee. Then four taxis hurried four teams of surgeons to Sagebrush Prison for the harvest.

Outside the prison infirmary, the four doctors, each accompanied by an intern carrying a red and white ice chest, lounged in the hall, waiting their turn at the vital organs—eyes, liver, kidneys, and etc.—of the dead prisoner. His heart was already missing; the warden said he never had one.

When the medical teams finished, two guards carried a body bag full of what was left of the prisoner through the prison cemetery to an unmarked grave. The only sound was a gentle Smoky Mountain rain pattering softly on the leaves amidst the eerie mist and fog.

"Feels a little heavy, don't he?" said one guard.

They strained to swing the bag over the hole, then let it drop.

"What do I put on this form about next 'a kin?"

"Didn't have none."

"Can't leave it blank. We gotta write something down."

"Just write:

Here lies Buzzard Mackelroy
Home: Cell Block 13
Survivors: Cliff and Axe."

The two men scooped the dirt into the pauper's grave, slung their shovels across their shoulders, and walked away.

"Who'd they say did it?"

"The paper said it was suicide, but Axe thinks it was the fat man with no tongue."

"'Cause he run?"

"Must 'a run. Anyway, he's missing."

63

It was now the middle of January, and the Senate hearing on nicotine was back in session in Washington, D.C.

Krandall Kaufman, all cool and collected, sat in the hot seat, testifying before the Committee. In the unexplained absence of Chairperson Charlie Carrington, Assistant Chairperson Agnes Kennedy commanded the gavel. The Committee was still trying to determine whether or not nicotine was a drug, and as such should it be regulated by the FDA, and whether or not the populace was purposely being addicted by the tobacco industry.

Krandall Kaufman gave the same old, same old testimony: "I don't know," "I don't remember," "I invoke my rights as a citizen—"

Suddenly the doors burst open. In walked Senator Charlie Carrington, Todd, and Mr. Puff.

The senators turned and stared, confused.

Soon after Todd's ordeal on the yacht, and his return to Asheville, he had received a call from a Preecher Kinser at the racetrack in Alcoa, Tennessee. Mr. Kinser identified himself only as a "friend of the family," saying, "We're close to finding where the cartel is keeping your father." He urged Todd to sit on Mr. Puff's file until Todd's father was freed. It might be a day; it might be a week. The rescue would be dangerous, but certain. Hopefully his father would still be alive by the time they reached him.

Todd did as instructed.

Now as he and his father walked into the hearing, the senator looked like one risen from the dead, and rightly so. He had come straight from his tomb.

Mr. Puff was riding in a wheelchair—the thick red file lay in his lap. Todd was pushing him. Behind Mr. Puff's wheelchair, where a motor might be mounted, sat the computer, hooked up and ready to be plugged in.

Disheveled, unshaven, stinking, and still wearing his

Kneeling Ceremony tuxedo, Senator Charles Carrington thanked Ms. Kennedy and took the gavel. He apologized for his unkempt appearance and for the rude interruption. He picked up the file from Mr. Puff's lap. "It's all in here." He held the file overhead and waved it, then laid it back in Mr. Puff's lap.

Kaufman coughed nervously.

Pale and gaunt, Senator Carrington pointed at Kaufman. "I am as guilty as he. I permitted him to operate." He then briefly explained that he had a witness who had fresh and irrefutable evidence that would impact the hearing in a significant way. He introduced Mr. Puff and plugged him in. The information came out on an overhead screen.

Mr. Puff started naming names and telling tales. He spouted formulas and unraveled thirty years of double-talk as the stenographer read the testimony into the record. And the strangest thing. After smoking 3000 cigarettes a day for twenty years, Mr. Puff coughed nary a time.

When he finished, Senator Carrington handed to the Senate clerk the thick red file from Mr. Puff's lap.

The file had the appearance of an elegant gift, considering the resources available, and looked for all the world like someone was giving Congress a Christmas present. A white label on the red folder had large-typed letters: MR. PUFF. A honeysuckle vine was double-looped around it, and across the front, scribbled in prison green, were the words in cursive: *a trace of smoke.*

Morgan J. Schubert, the FDA lawyer, smiled grimly and nodded approval.

But attorney Maxwell "Bones" Talbert didn't smile. And the heads of the large tobacco companies didn't smile. They were all seized by different stages of coughing, gasping, and carpet watching.

There was no cross examination of Mr. Puff by the defense.

Krandall Kaufman was taken into custody on the spot, the big tobacco companies started tattling on each other, and…

64

From the Command and Control Room at SIG Labs in Asheville, North Carolina, Tumbler watched the Senate hearing on TV. When they arrested Kaufman, and the judge refused to set bail—government lawyers argued he would skip the country—Kaufman started singing. He ratted on the heads of several tobacco companies, admitted, personally, to political bribery, but not to murder. He pointed the finger at Tumbler, blaming all the killings on him.

Tumbler knew the FBI would be at the front door any minute. He started packing. The first thing he packed was two suitcases full of crisp new hundred-dollar bills from the safe where Kaufman kept the laundered cash to pay off senators and the like. A noise interrupted his packing. He quickly glanced out the window. Two unmarked cars were pulling into the parking lot. Had to be the fibbies.

Tumbler slapped the two suitcases shut, splashing bills across the floor. He dashed to the secret elevator that led to the secret entrance/exit.

He climbed into the back seat of his Mercedes and drove off, not sure to where. He would catch a plane to somewhere, change his identity, and hide out the rest of his life. It certainly wouldn't be the Caribbean. He hated the sunshine. He might go to the North Pole where one night lasts nine months. Yes, that's where he would go. He would go to the North Pole. Mickey would like it there.

They would never catch him now. Kaufman could sing all he wanted to, but he didn't even know Tumbler's last name; no one did but his mother, and she wouldn't be talking. Few people, other than Kaufman, had seen Tumbler up close, and lived to tell about it, so he was home free...except!—

There was one loose thread: the girl! She had seen him up close several times. Too close. He had to find Barbara Dare. This time Kaufman wouldn't be around to tell him to keep the knife in his pocket. But the girl had disappeared from the face of the earth. He cursed Ezell for letting her loose. He should have killed her while he had her tied to that tree in Cades Cove. Cades Cove! That's where he'd look first. She was probably hiding in that cabin up there in the mountains. If she wasn't, her grand-mamma would know her hiding place. If he talked real nice to the *old* woman, she might help him find the *young* woman.

When Tumbler arrived in Cades Cove, he eased the Mercedes around to the back of the cabin and parked behind the cantilevered barn. He slithered up to the back porch and reached for the screen door. It was latched, so he took his pocketknife and ever so quietly poked a small hole in the wire, then lifted the latch with his ivory toothpick. The big wooden door was not locked. It creaked as he eased it open. Gripping the open knife, he quickly stepped inside. There was no one in the living area. She must be in the loft, probably taking a nap. He put one foot on the stairs. The step creaked, causing him to ease his weight off and back down to the many-colored throw rug.

The phone rang, startling him.

He froze.

It rang again. He turned and looked at the phone sitting on a table beside a rocker. On the table lay a jigsaw puzzle, half-finished. He heard feet, sidling down the steps.

He hid behind the thick blue drape behind the rocker, and gently scraped the surgical steel blade of the knife against the whiskers of his cleanly shaven face.

Grandmother Dare shuffled over to the rocker and sat down in it.

Tumbler was afraid she could hear his breathing, or smell the piece of cheese in his pocket, or hear the scraping blade. He stayed his hand, momentarily. Only the curtain separated them. If she rocked back, the rocker rail would smash his toes.

Her bony hand picked up the receiver and she said in a fragile voice with age written all over it, "Hello...Oh, hello, Todd."

After the Senate hearing Todd had returned home to Asheville. Just now he had tried the phone at Grandmother Dare's again—for the hundredth time. It worked this time.

"She's not here," Grandmother Dare said.

"Where is she, Grandmother Dare?" He sat down on the blue satin sheets in their bedroom. And remembered.

"She didn't tell me where she was going. She said you would probably call, and she knew I would want to tell."

"Will you tell me now?"

"That's why we had the phone disconnected for a while. She wanted me to stay away longer, but I just couldn't. I'm not much on hotels."

"Did she leave any message?"

"Yes, she said for you to forget her."

"*Forget her*! I can't forget her!" He looked at the wedding picture of them kneeling in the little church in Cades Cove.

"It's chilly in here. Just a minute, Todd...the back door's open."

Todd heard her feet shuffling on the hardwood floor, heard the big heavy wooden door slam shut, then heard her feet coming back to the phone.

"Wind must have blown it open," she said. "Now where were we?" She sighed, out of breath.

"I said I *can't* forget her."

"Barbara said to tell you she would always love you."

"*Love* me!? She's got some way of showing it."

"Her father had many enemies."

Tired of the chitchat, Todd stood and began to pace. "I know all about her father. And I know all about his *enemies*."

"Then you surely can understand. Barbara knew that when his enemies came for her, they would take you, too."

"Dead men silence their enemies."

"Perhaps," she said, lightly.

"In fact Buzzard Mackelroy's a hero in Congress," Todd said. "They used his decoder on Mr. Puff. Mr. Puff told the Congressional hearing all about the tobacco cartel. About Kaufman and Tumbler, and—"

"I know," she said, clearing her throat. "I watched it all on TV last week."

"I'll tell you something you don't know. After the hearing, my father asked Congress to intercede to the powers-that-be to have the original charges against Buzzard Mackelroy dropped, posthumously."

"That means a lot."

"Congress agreed that any man or woman among them would have done what he did if someone had raped their mother, or at least considered doing it."

"No. *Murdering* the rapist is not the answer. Tell them to pass laws that will *convict* the rapist. That's the solution. When my son murdered my attacker, I lost my son also. Now I have lost my granddaughter. That's too high a price to pay for the week I suffered in the cabin of the senior Mr. Slocum."

"You can count on it," Todd said. "Passing new laws against rapists will be my first task if I am elected. But meanwhile, I have to find Barbara. Can you give me a hint on where she might have gone?"

"You might look in Knoxville. Perhaps in some personnel department."

Of course, Todd thought. He reached in his pocket for the keys to his Vette. "Grandmother Dare, why did you decide to tell me?"

"Because my son gave his life so my grandchild could live with you. Go and find her, boy."

"Hugs and kisses, Grandmother Dare. I'll find her. And when I do, she'll never have to hide again. If I have to, I'll let Gene Chastine, our black belt buddy, be *her* full time bodyguard."

Grandmother Dare chuckled when Todd yelled, "I'm outta here."

But just as he started to slam down the phone, he heard her voice again.

"Todd..." She spoke softly, and tenderly, almost in a whisper.

"Yes, ma'am?"

"Todd...er..."

354

"What is it, Grandmother Dare?"

"Just for the record...If you talk to those folks in Congress again...er...It's been so long since I said it...I didn't think it would be this hard to make it come out."

"What is it? What are you trying to tell me?"

"His name was Wayne. Wayne Dare."

After he hung up, Todd dashed for the red Corvette. Knoxville...of course...he should have thought of Knoxville. And of course she would work in personnel; that's what she was trained to do. But in a city the size of Knoxville there would be hundreds of jobs in personnel, especially it being a university town.

He headed across the Smoky Mountains. The trip to Knoxville would take him through Gatlinburg. While he drove, he worked on a plan to narrow down the thousands of personnel jobs. He had to find her. Thanks to her, his dream now had wings, and no one blocking its flight. But without his sweetheart, it was a hollow dream. He would find her and he would bring her home. Now he knew why she hadn't been keen on having children. How naive he'd been about all that. Now he knew why she would cry at the drop of a hat for no apparent reason. How blind he had been. Now they would have a house full of children. And that would make his mother very happy, too.

65

In Knoxville, Barbara had finally taken a job at a small laboratory not far from the university as assistant to the Assistant Director of Personnel. She worked for wages, but didn't care. The job was therapeutic, balm for her brokenness. But after a couple of days, she collapsed at the office. When her supervisor called her in, Barbara thought she was going to fire her. Instead, the supervisor told her to take a few days off.

So Barbara decided to go to the mountains to grieve. The bullet wound in her side had almost healed, but she had other wounds. Losing her father and her husband in one fell swoop was too much. She needed time to let her soul catch up with her body. She had some serious rocking to do and Grandmother Dare's front porch was just the place to do it.

The office where she worked was six blocks from the Premium Hotel, so she walked to and from work. The Camaro stayed parked a block from the hotel-hideout, hidden under some mulberry trees, behind an old restaurant sign that read, "Best Food In Town." The restaurant had fallen down and lay in a pile of crumbled bricks, but the sign still stood. One thing about Tennessee, Barbara thought, we build strong buildings, but our signs are built to last till Jesus comes. Then she thought of the joke Tamika used to make about Tennessee signs. Every time they would pass one of the "Jesus Is Coming Soon" signs posted on a four-inch square of concrete, Tamika would laugh and say, "'Comin' Soon,' written on a concrete post." She missed Tamika. Being back in Knoxville made her miss her more. Was it only May when she and Tamika ran their last race for the university? Now January, May seemed eons ago.

Anyway, beside the still-standing "Best Food In Town" sign, and behind the crumbled restaurant, was a good place to hide the Camaro. License tags can be traced, so she had backed the car into the rubble to hide the rear tag. The car had not been started since she arrived in Knoxville.

Today as she walked from work to the Premium Hotel, she was all full of happy thoughts of going to Grandmother Dare's.

She tried to *walk* briskly, but it wasn't in her. So she *sauntered* briskly. She felt naked without the mud-bead necklace bobbing against her breasts.

Ever mindful that her hideout might be discovered, she stayed on the lookout for new faces, new cars, anything out of the ordinary: a car that went around the block too many times, or a stranger staring too intently at the sooty red brick building that was now her permanent home.

When she reached the hotel, and before going upstairs, she stopped at the pay phone in the lobby, a depressing place, and called Grandmother Dare to tell her she was coming to see her. But there was no answer. She was probably out in the yard feeding the chickens or out at the barn giving Old Ned a hug.

Barbara went on up to her room, removed the brown wig and let her long blond hair breathe. She would try Grandmother Dare again after she packed. Her tiny room had no closet, so she lived out of her suitcase which she kept under the bed. There wasn't much to the packing, other than her toothbrush and bathroom toiletries which she kept in a plastic bucket that sat on her lone windowsill.

Exhausted from the six-block walk from work, she sat on the bed for a moment to catch her breath. As was her habit, now that she no longer had the mud-bead necklace to run her fingers over, she removed her father's goggle-glasses from her purse and sat there holding them in her lap, remembering. That's all she had left of him, the glasses and the memories.

After a while she, ever so gently, placed the goggle-glasses back into her purse. The next time she removed them, she planned to be huddling under a blanket in the rocker on Grandmother Dare's porch. That was the plan.

The frumpy skirt and blouse that she had worn to work that morning had been purchased at the Goodwill store. She changed into jeans and a sweater. She pulled the brown wig back on, then dragged the suitcase from under the bed, laid it on the tiny iron cot, then neatly packed her toiletries inside a gallon plastic freezer bag, laid the bag inside the suitcase, and closed the lid. She carried the suitcase down the hall, and using both hands, because of the wound still in her side, leaned on the rail and bumped it down the stairs to the lobby, then rolled it to the army-green counter.

A sign on the counter read, "Please ring bell for service." She waited a moment then gently tapped the rusty bell.

The day clerk, Ms. Chase, a middle aged lady whom Barbara had purposely ignored—she didn't want to know anyone and she didn't want anyone to know her—stepped through a curtained door behind the counter, a toothpick competing with the gum in her mouth. "Git fired?"

"No, ma'am."

"Ya leavin'?"

"Just paying my rent." Barbara politely laid a $20 bill on the counter and stared at the floor while Ms. Chase wrote out a receipt to Cynthia Smith.

"I'll sell your stuff if you ain't back in seven days. I can do that, you know."

"That's fair," Barbara said, almost under her breath.

"Law's on my side."

"As well it should be." Barbara raised her eyes from the floor. Then, so she wouldn't have to look into the fatty-cheeked woman's bloodshot eyes or at her sagging jowls, turned her head to look through the lobby window out into the street. When she did, she saw a new man, a small man. He was leaned against the lamppost across the street, peeping from behind it. She could swear he was staring up at the third floor, and at her room in particular.

She left the suitcase in the lobby and flew up to the third floor to get a better look. No need going into her room; its one window showed only the brick wall adjacent to it.

There was one window at the end of the long hall on the third floor. She sprinted to it. From there she could see the Seven Eleven, the restaurant sign where her Camaro was parked, and the alley below. But she could not see directly across the street where the man was hiding.

She had to get a better look at him, and the only place to do that was in the lobby. But before she went back to the lobby, she started hunting an escape route. She tried to raise the dingy window, but it would go up only a few inches. She forced her head through and, in that strained position, surveyed the situation. A rusty fire-escape ladder, whose black paint had long ago given up and turned loose, reached down to the second floor and no more. The fire-escape ladder appeared to be weight activated, meaning that she would have to dive out the second story window—if it wasn't nailed shut—grab the ladder, swing out on it, and, hopefully, her weight would take it to the ground. While looking down, she noticed what she believed to be an all-too familiar car. A four door white Mercedes sat in the alley with its motor running. A man in a chauffeur's cap sat in the front seat at the wheel. Oh Lord. There was no doubt. The little man out front was Tumbler.

She dashed back to the lobby, her mind burning with escape plans. Ms. Chase was coming back through the curtain-door, sipping coffee from a Rubbermaid cup. Seeing her, Barbara changed pace and calmly strolled to the corner of the lobby and peeped out from behind the ragged window curtains. Dust from the curtains billowed, making her sneeze.

"Bill collector or a ex?" asked Ms. Chase with a cackle.

Barbara ignored her and looked at the little man. He was wearing a purple suit. There was no doubt. It was Tumbler. But how did he find her? There was only one way. Only one person on earth knew where she was. She dashed to the phone, dropped in a dime and a quarter and dialed Grandmother Dare.

Still no answer.

She wanted to cry. Not for herself, but for Grandmother Dare. Grandmother Dare wouldn't have told Tumbler where she was even if he had threatened to cut her tongue out. He must have found something in the cabin that gave him a hint as to her whereabouts. There was little doubt what he had done with Grandmother Dare. Now Barbara was even more glad she had left Todd, for had she not, the two of them might now be at home in bed, in each other's arms, unaware that Tumbler was already racing down their hallway with his knife drawn.

Barbara breathed deeply and pulled herself together. None of this was new to her. All her life she had been planning for this day. All her life she'd been planning escape routes. She had one now.

But she needed to make one more phone call. She checked her pockets and had no more change. She walked to the desk, laid a dollar bill on it and said, "May I have four quarters, please?"

Ms. Chase shoved the dollar back at her. "Change machine's at the Laundromat down by the Seven Eleven. We don't give change."

"Please. It's an emergency."

"They're all emergencies," she said as she lifted her fat cheeks up to the three-legged stool, trying to straddle it. "Sorry."

Barbara looked at her. What could make a person that callous? What events in life had turned her that hostile? For a moment it was almost funny. She wished Tamika was here right now. She'd let her "shove her down the steps and beat her over the head with her shoe." How she missed Tamika.

Barbara hurried back to the phone. She would call collect. It would be the first collect call she had ever made. "Operator, I'd like to make a person to person collect call to Preecher Kinser in Alcoa, Tennessee."

She quickly explained her situation to Preecher. "If it were just me, I could run," she said. "But it's Grandmother Dare. I'm afraid he's hurt her."

"Has your Camaro got any of that joy juice left in it?"

Barbara knew he was talking about the nitrous oxide in her spare tank. "Enough for one good race. If the race doesn't last too long."

"Can you get to your car...without him catching you?"

"I'm a pretty good runner, Preecher. He can't catch me."

"I don't want him to even *see* you until you're in your car. Can you handle that?"

"I can swing down the fire escape."

"Okay. Here's the plan." Preecher stopped talking for a second and she heard him say to someone in the office, "Get Polo Kiwanda on the other phone—he's down at the Spudnut shop—and tell him to get that Lamborghini revved up. I'm coming his way right now and I need him." He then came back to Barbara. "Polo Kiwanda's coming with me—he's a

361

heavyweight boxing champ—just in case Mr. Tumbler brought help."

"Okay," she said, pacing so much she thought she might pull the phone cord out of its socket. "But what's the plan?"

"Here it is. Get in your car. Act like you don't suspect a thing. Drive slowly past Tumbler. Make sure he sees you, but don't give him any idea you know he's there. As you drive by him, do something to attract attention. Stick your head out the window and flirt with some man walking down the other side of the street. Anything. Just make sure he sees you."

"I've never been much of a flirt, but I'll think of something. Then what?"

"Lead him out onto the interstate. Once on the four lane, drive the speed limit. He won't try to stop you till he gets you on some side road. That's when you'll need that afterburner tank. Since he'll soon figure out you're on the way to your grandmother's, he'll probably fall back two or three cars and wait to jump you in Cades Cove."

"I can do that."

"Me 'n Polo Kiwanda are about the same distance from Cades Cove as you, but we'll be pourin' on the coal. If you'll take it slow, we'll be there to greet Mr. Tumbler when you escort him into the Cove."

"Just one thing," Barbara asked. "What'll you be driving?"

"Your dad's yellow roadster—it's got the speed. Polo Kiwanda will be driving a baby-blue Lamborghini. The plan is to let you lead Mr. Tumbler onto that loop-road that encircles Cades Cove. If all goes well, we'll trap him there on that bridge. Be careful. Don't let him force you off the road, and don't get out of that car until you see the whites of my eyes. A movin' car's safer 'n a stopped car."

"Thanks, Preecher."

"Lord bless you and keep you safe, girl. This is one trip your dad would have wanted to make. I wish he'd lived to see the fireworks."

"So do I," she said, wistfully. "So do I." And she knew how much Preecher meant it. He had been her dad's best friend.

She hung up, peeped out the window at Tumbler, then ran

full-speed across the faded yellow linoleum floor toward the stairs, abandoning the suitcase.

"See," said Ms. Chase, "wasn't such a 'mergency after all, was it, girly?"

"No, ma'am," Barbara said, one foot already on the stairs and both hands on the banisters.

"Hold it right there," Ms. Chase said, walking out from behind the counter, still holding the coffee mug in her hand. She pointed at Barbara's Louis Vuitton suitcase. "You can't leave your belongings in the lobby. Five dollars extra for storage."

Barbara had had enough. She turned and walked right up to her, so close she could shake hands with her, and said, with more force than she realized she was capable of, "You keep the suitcase, Ms. Chase. It's all yours. And you may have that plastic bucket in my room to keep your drinking water in. I used it for a slop bucket!"

She then tore up to the second floor and dived out the window, hoping to catch the fire escape swing-ladder in midair.

66

On his way to Knoxville, Todd had never traveled so fast through the Great Smoky Mountains. He was almost to National Park Headquarters, not far from Gatlinburg. By now he had thought of a way to narrow his search for Barbara. He knew one person who had a master network list on his computer: Preecher Kinser.

Preecher Kinser, at Alcoa Speedway, had led the raid on the graveyard where Todd's father had been entombed alive, had led Roland's Army, had given Mr. Puff to Barbara, and had been most helpful during the hearing. Todd decided to ask him to put his vast network in gear to find which company in Knoxville might have hired a new woman in their personnel department in the past weeks. No use looking under the name Barbara Dare or Barbara Dare-Carrington. If she truly wanted to become lost, she would have been too smart to have used her own name.

At Park Headquarters, Todd pulled over, dashed inside to the pay phone, and dialed Preecher Kinser.

"Call back later, whoever you are," Preecher yelled into the phone, his voice all full of hurry. "Gotta go!"

"Preecher, it's Todd," Todd yelled back, just as hurried.

"Todd, my boy. That you?"

"Preecher, I need your help in finding Barbara—"

"She just hung up," Preecher said. "Me 'n Polo Kiwanda are on the way to meet 'er in Cades Cove."

"*Cades Cove*? I thought she was in Knoxville."

"Wuz. But Tumbler's chasin' her."

"*Tumbler*?"

"Yeah. She's gonna lead 'im into that loop-road that circles the Cove."

"I know it well."

"We'll trap him on the bridge by the meadow. Shor' could use a fourth car."

"I'm your man."

"Won't be a pretty sight. Barbara thinks Tumbler's done something with her grandmother...she don't answer her phone."

Preecher then quickly explained the situation and how they planned to spring the trap.

"I'm at Park Headquarters," Todd said. "You know a shortcut? I hate to get caught in that Gatlinburg traffic—"

"Take the River Road."

"Where do I catch it?"

"Right where you're standing. It's a direct shot from Park Headquarters to Cades Cove. Lots of curves, though."

"I can manage curves."

"That means you'll be coming from the east, me 'n Polo'll be coming from the west, and yo' wife'll be bringing Mr. Tumbler in from the north. All trails merge just outside of Townsend. Only way in to Cades Cove."

Todd dashed back to his car. He was on the outskirts of Gatlinburg; Barbara, coming from Knoxville with Tumbler hot on her tail, would come through Pigeon Forge, but turn right before Gatlinburg; Preecher and Polo were just leaving. Since Todd was taking the River Road shortcut, he figured to be the first into the Cove.

His tires screamed and his Corvette fishtailed as he tore out. Then a horror went through him like a bolt of hot metal. For the first time, he suspected Tumbler might have been in the cabin while he, Todd, was talking to Grandmother Dare. All along he had figured Grandmother Dare knew where Barbara was. Out of loyalty to her, she had given him only hints, but enough to find her. Tumbler probably forced her to tell *exactly* where Barbara was.

Todd was all over the road—he knew he wasn't the driver Barbara was. Maybe he could get to the cabin while Grandmother Dare was still alive. He knew Tumbler's *modus operandi*—he would have hurt her—and Todd thought, I should have tied that cable around his neck when I had the chance back at the yacht...let him swim alongside that hungry shark.

Then all thoughts of revenge faded. If he lost Barbara, he didn't care what happened to his dream or anything else. So he hurried through the mountains toward the valley of wildflowers to dance the dance of death.

67

Barbara climbed into her Camaro, parked behind the old restaurant sign. The high-performance engine started on the first turn of the key. She popped out the T-Tops to get rid of the musty smell.

As she drove past the front of the Premium Hotel, a neatly-dressed young African-American mother came around the corner, pushing a baby in a pink stroller. Perfect. They were directly across the street from the lamppost where Tumbler was still hiding. As Barbara came up beside them, she leaned out the window and called out loud enough for Tumbler to hear, but not so loud it would seem phony, "Gone to see Grandmother. Don't worry. Be back tomorrow in time to baby-sit for you."

The surprised mother shrugged and kept walking.

Two blocks later, Tumbler's Mercedes did what it was supposed to: follow her with two or three cars between them. When Barbara reached the Interstate, Tumbler stayed a respectful distance behind her.

At Pigeon Forge, she turned South. Next stop: Cades Cove.

Few cars were on that road, so Tumbler's chauffeur stayed a curve behind her, only occasionally creeping closer.

As she cruised along, she starting putting two and two together. Tumbler was an odd-looking duck. Then she remembered Tamika telling her about the reporter, an "odd-looking duck," just before she was killed. If Tumbler was that *odd-looking duck*, he may have been the one who killed Tamika. But she couldn't think about Tamika now.

Soon, Barbara turned onto the eleven-mile loop road into Cades Cove. One way in. One way out. Mr. Tumbler was about to get his comeuppance.

The chauffeur turned too. Then he started gaining on her, making no pretense of hiding. He started around her.

She already had him figured out. He wanted to get in front of her, make a quick stop on the bridge, then have *her* trapped.

As he started around, she jerked the Camaro over, almost forcing him into the ditch. He backed off, them came at her full speed. The big Mercedes rammed the bumper of her much smaller car.

Barbara floorboarded the Camaro, then hit the blue button below her left knee that turned the nitrous oxide loose. The Camaro stood on its back wheels and flew off down the road.

Then it dawned on her. She should let the Mercedes get in front of her. That way Preecher and Polo Kiwanda could trap it on the bridge. So at the first curve, she pulled over and hid behind a tree.

The Mercedes went flying past her.

Perfect.

She got back on the road and accelerated after him.

Huh oh. In her rearview mirror, she got a glimpse of another car coming down hard on her, about to turn onto the loop-road...and it wasn't the yellow roadster and it wasn't the blue Lamborghini.

She was the one who was trapped! Tumbler had tricked her! She was now trapped between him and his henchmen. And if Tumbler had planned that far in advance, he had also probably planned a roadblock back down the road somewhere to take out Preecher Kinser and Polo Kiwanda.

Grandmother Dare, I've gotten us both killed, she thought. If you aren't already.

The bridge was over the next rise.

She was doomed. The Camaro was fast, but it couldn't leap cars.

Just as she hit the crest of the next rise...

A loud roar like thunder!

A flash of yellow and blue!

Tumbler screeched to a halt on the bridge.

Facing him, bumper to bumper, were Preecher Kinser in her dad's yellow roadster and Polo Kiwanda in his baby-blue Lamborghini.

Barbara jammed her Camaro against the back bumper of Tumbler's Mercedes, blocking his escape. She leaped out and yelled, "Look out, he's got someone on our tail. There's another car on the loop just over the rise."

Polo Kiwanda raced to Barbara, shoved her into the ditch

and stood against the Camaro's bumper, aiming an assault rifle over the horizon.

Preecher Kinser belly-leaped on top of the hood of the Mercedes. He rammed the barrel of his pump shotgun through the windshield, splattering glass everywhere.

Mickey didn't move.

Preecher stretched out longways on the hood, propped himself on his elbow, and started heehawing.

Tumbler sat in the backseat, behind the steering wheel, his hands meekly raised in surrender.

"That other car should have been here by now!" Barbara said. "I was certain it turned onto the loop road!" Then she heard a noise in the distance. The mystery car was flying around the "one way" loop the "wrong way." He was almost to the front door of the cabin.

"Grandmother Dare," she screamed, and went racing across the wildflower meadow. "No, no!" she screamed and kept screaming.

She could see in the distance a big man wearing a white turban, climbing the steps to the porch. He kicked the door open and rushed in.

Barbara came racing past the barn and through the yard, yelling, "No, no."

She leaped to the porch and dashed inside. She heard him in the loft. Instinct told her to flee, but her raising told her to risk it all. She looked for a weapon. Grandmother Dare's homemade sagebrush broom was leaning in the corner.

She grabbed the broom and started up the steps, holding the sharp end like a soldier with a rifle, stalking the upstairs darkness. "Grandmoth—"

She saw his feet first.

The big man met her on the stairs.

Their eyes met.

"Todd?!"

"Sweetheart!"

Her knees buckled as Todd drew her into his arms. He kissed her and kissed her and kissed her until finally the reality

369

that she wasn't dreaming hit her. So, laughing and crying, she kissed him and kissed him and kissed him back.

She wanted to stay in his arms, but couldn't. It wasn't over. So, she moved from his embrace and clutched the broom. "What are you doing here? How did—"

He grabbed her again and held her close.

She melted. "Oh Todd. Oh, Todd." That's all she could say. Then her senses started coming back to her. "Was Grandmother Dare up there?"

"No," Todd said, still holding her.

"I'm afraid she's gone," Barbara said. "The man I think did it is sitting in his car over yonder." She pointed to the bridge where the four cars were parked and where the three men were standing.

"Let's go ask him," Todd said and started leading her toward the bridge. As they trotted across the cornfield toward the meadow of wildflowers, he held her hand, and, with his free hand, gently lifted the brown wig off her head, letting her hair fall free. "We're through with that," he said, tossing the wig at Mr. Scarecrow. "We'll let him wear it."

"Hello, Todd, my boy," said Preecher Kinser, when they arrived at the cars. "In all the excitement, I forgot about you."

After greeting Preecher, Todd turned to Tumbler who was standing belligerently beside his car. Todd rubbed the bandage on his wounded head, and said to Tumbler, "I should have fed you to the shark."

For the first time, Barbara realized the white turban on Todd's head was actually a bandage.

"He won't talk," Preecher said, pointing at Tumbler.

"Where's my grandmother?" Barbara demanded of Tumbler.

Tumbler ignored her, but did not look away. He just tried to stare her down.

"The lady's speaking to you, sir," Todd said with more authority than Barbara had ever heard him speak.

Tumbler spat at him.

Polo Kiwanda, the boxer, spoke up. "In my country, we take heem behind tree. You want to go behind tree, Meester?"

About that time, Old Ned came sauntering through the

370

wildflower meadow. He sidled up next to the fence, getting as close to Barbara as he could. She reached across the fence and patted the nose of the tired old horse.

"Too bad there aren't four of Ned," Todd said, pointing at the horse. "We could do what Roland's uncle did."

"*Roland*!" Barbara yelled.

"You thinking what I'm thinking?" Todd asked.

"There are *four of us.*"

"Giddy up."

"That's it," Barbara said. "He wanted a ceremony. Let's give him a *ceremony*. Preecher you and Polo take Mr. Tumbler to the middle of the meadow...there by the apple tree. He'll talk."

Tumbler shrugged and gave an amused look.

Barbara then turned to Todd. "Sweetheart, there's some rope in the barn, in Ned's stall." She was pushing him toward the barn as she spoke. "Run and get it. Cut it into four pieces, about fifteen feet each. Hurry."

Within minutes, Tumbler was lying spread-eagle, flat of his back in the middle of the meadow beside the barren apple tree, his amused look gone.

Barbara hurried as she spread the four heavy ropes out on the ground. There was not a second to waste...Grandmother Dare might still be alive somewhere.

And that's when she saw it, one lone apple blossom, all dried and withered—a holdover from an earlier harvest—clinging precariously to the tree. Like a promise of future harvests.

She quickly tied the end of one rope to Tumbler's left wrist. She then tied the other end to the back bumper of her father's yellow roadster. Preecher Kinser was already at the wheel.

"What do you think...you're doing?" Tumbler demanded.

"You were going to have a *Kneeling* Ceremony. We're going to have a *Quartering* Ceremony.

Todd stood there gawking at her.

"Do his ankles," she said, already to the second rope.

"All I know are naval knots."

"That'll do," she said, tying the second rope to Tumbler's right wrist. She then attached the other end to the back bumper of the Lamborghini.

"You tell me…what you're doing!" Tumbler shouted.

"She's giving you a lesson in French history," Todd said as he tied Tumbler's left ankle to his Vette.

"Ha," hooted Tumbler.

"Here in the Smoky Mountains, Mr. Tumbler," Barbara said, "you don't mess with our kin. Our people didn't always live in *these* mountains. A long time ago, they came from across the ocean and they brought with them memories and stories of how to treat men like you, men who threaten the family."

"I don't need a lecture from you, missy," Tumbler said in a demeaning tone.

"Such a story came to us from the mountains at Roncesvalles Pass. That's in Spain," she said. "The year was 788. The boy's name was Roland. He was a dreamer. His uncle sent him on a mission of mercy. But a man, pretending to do good for his country, not too different from you and the tobacco cartel, waylaid him in the Pass. Trapped, Roland sent a member of his party for help. He believed help was coming. But it wasn't. Roland was slain there in the mountains at Roncesvalles Pass. The villain's name was Ganelon."

"That's a stupid story. You have no right…to tie me up like this," argued Tumbler.

"*Stupid?*" Barbara said, calmly, all the while going about tying his ankles and wrists. "You don't know how the story ends. You see, Roland's uncle was Charlemagne, supreme ruler of the land. When word came to him that Ganelon had slaughtered Roland, his favorite nephew, Charlemagne said, "Round up the four finest steeds in the land, tie one to each foot and one to each hand…'"

Tumbler started getting the picture. "Turn me loose…You'll be sorry."

"Do you know what Charlemagne said then, Mr. Tumbler?"

Tumbler turned his head away, his jaw on the grass.

"'Giddy up.' That's what he said. So you see, Mr. Tumbler, when you come to the mountains, you had better know who a

372

person's kin is. You see, Buzzard Mackelroy was my father. Grandmother Dare is his mother—"

"Buzzard Mackelroy's dead," Tumbler interrupted.

"But not what he taught me," Barbara said. "Grandmother Dare told the story of Roland to my father, and he told it to me. Now *I've* told it to *you*. The name of the story is *The Song of Roland*. It's a Medieval French epic. In the olden days, they called it a *chanson de geste*, a war song. Here in the Smokies we call it *justice de montagne*, mountain justice. However, I do need to apologize for one thing...."

Last, she tied the fourth rope to his right ankle and the bumper of her Camaro. She jerked on the last knot, securing it. "Instead of horses, we're using horse*power*."

Now, everything was all set for the Quartering Ceremony. Barbara walked to Tumbler's side and stood over him. "One last chance, Mr. Tumbler. Where's my grandmother?"

"You're bluffing," he said. "You wouldn't dare."

"Oh, I'd dare all right. *Dare's* my name." She turned to the other drivers. "Looks like he still doesn't want to talk."

She looked into the afternoon sun. A lone buzzard floated among the fluffy white clouds, as if salivating in anticipation of the dissection and its drippings. She imagined it was her father, taking in the bird's-eye view of the apple tree, the wildflowers, his yellow roadster, her silver-gray Camaro, the baby-blue Lamborghini, and the red Corvette. All four automobiles faced in opposite direction, Tumbler tied to the rear bumper of each.

Tumbler's white Mercedes sat off to the side. It wouldn't be involved in the Ceremony. Old Ned stood at the rear of the luxury automobile, staring blankly at the goings on.

Barbara hurried back to her Camaro, opened the door, climbed in, and called through the window, "Gentlemen, start your engines."

Tumbler started rocking his head from side to side.

"Take up the slack," she yelled.

Each of the four cars eased forward, making the ropes tied to Tumbler's limbs taut as violin strings.

Tumbler shook and kicked and jerked like a snake with its head cut off.

Barbara rammed the Camaro into low gear, raised her left hand out the window, and yelled above the idling vehicles, "Rev your engines to full throttle. When I drop my hand, gun it."

Thunder broke loose in Grandmother Dare's valley of wildflowers. All four vehicles roared to full force and sounded like a dig-out race at Alcoa Speedway. The cars shimmied and shook and rocked from side to side under the awesome power, begging to be unleashed from the monster tied to their tails.

To Barbara, the twin bazookas on her daddy's yellow roadster roared loudest of all, cackling like a ghost from the grave, and spitting blue fire out its exhaust, singeing Tumbler's hair. Tumbler was thumping his buttocks up and down on the grass like a wild man.

Barbara raised her left hand a little higher, ready to thrust it down in full force, all the while watching Tumbler in her rearview mirror. Just before she slung her hand toward the ground, she saw his lips moving. There was no way of hearing his voice over the thunder from the cars. She opened her door and leaned her head out.

"Wait! Wait!" he screamed. "I'll tell. I'll tell."

Barbara straddle-walked *her* rope back to him. "You better not be playing games." Then she saw the evidence of his sincerity. He had wet his pants, and maybe more. "Where is my grandmother?"

"In the trunk. In the trunk of my car."

"The keys?"

"My right pocket."

She yanked his pocket inside out.

"Don't you hurt Mickey!"

A single key and a bloody pocketknife spilled out onto the grass.

At that instant, the dried and withered apple blossom, the only one left in all of Cades Cove, turned loose and drifted out on the wind. Barbara watched it finally settle, ever so gently, beside the blood-stained pocketknife.

She grabbed the key, dashed to the trunk of the Mercedes and popped the lid open. By now the men had gathered around.

374

Grandmother Dare lay bound and gagged and all crumpled up in a pile. She didn't move. Her eyes were closed.

Todd gently lifted her out and laid her on the grass, while Old Ned looked on. Barbara sobbed hysterically as she bent over and rubbed Grandmother Dare's arms and legs, trying to bring life back into her.

Todd gently pulled the duct tape from her mouth and leaned over and listened to her chest. "Heart's still beating. Barely though." Then he yelled to Preecher Kinser, "Call an ambulance!"

"No!" Barbara said. "We're too far away. An ambulance would take too long. Put her in my car. Just set her in the front seat and strap the seatbelt around her. *I'll* take her to the hospital. Go with me, sweetheart." She called him *sweetheart.* He was back.

As Todd raced with Grandmother Dare in his arms to the Camaro, Barbara said to Preecher and Polo, loud enough for Tumbler to hear. "Leave him tied until I get back."

"I told you where she was," Tumbler said. "Kept my part of the deal. Let me go."

Barbara knelt and whispered in his ear, "This is Intermission. If she dies, I'll be back and we'll finish the Ceremony." Then for the first time she noticed he was wearing a purple polka-dot bow tie. Something about the tie offended her to the core, but, right now, she was too lost in saving Grandmother Dare to mentally process the information. She yanked the tie from his neck and stuffed it in the pocket of her jeans and dashed to her car. Todd had Grandmother Dare strapped in in the shotgun side, and his big frame was cramped into the small rear seat.

"I need a drink."

Barbara turned and looked at Todd. "What?"

"I didn't say anything," Todd said, innocently.

"I need a drink," Grandmother Dare said, weakly, and wiping her mouth with her wrinkled, freckled wrist.

"Grandmother!" Barbara screamed. "You're alive!"

"Sure. I'm alive," she said, glancing out the window. "What's Ned doing out here? He knows he's not allowed in the meadow."

Grandmother Dare seemed to be okay, but Todd and Barbara spent the night in the cabin with her just to be sure.

Tumbler was not *okay.* Besides the mess in his pants, he spent the night in jail.

The next day, Saturday, Todd said to Barbara, "Let's go home. I have a surprise for you."

68

After the Senate hearing, Charlie Carrington received a strong reprimand from the Democrats for his involvement with the tobacco cartel. They wanted a full scale censure, but the Republicans, being in the majority, killed that by arguing that Kaufman was blackmailing him. Charlie Carrington may have sponsored some bad legislation, but if sponsoring bad legislation was the criterion for censure, they might all be censured. After all, powerful lobbyists were always using their resources to entice senators to vote this way or that. Besides, Charlie Carrington had already resigned. "What do you want, his blood?" The Democrats fumed, but Charlie Carrington, though wounded, left the Senate with most of his reputation intact.

As for Kaufman, he went to prison. All his assets were seized, and his fraudulently obtained stock holdings in tobacco companies were sold and the money distributed among various cancer fighting causes, especially those fighting nicotine. Kaufman would later die in prison, a babbling imbecile.

As for Tumbler, no one knew how many people he had killed, but he was sentenced to die in Georgia's electric chair for killing one of their own, and it would be Tamika Brown who would strap him in. At his trial, his only defense for killing her was, "She called me stupid."

Aunt Maudie, sitting in the courtroom, leaped up and yelled, "You *are* stupid!"

When they had found Tamika in the trunk of Barbara Dare's car, in her right fist she was gripping a purple polka-dot bow tie.

69

Back home in Asheville, Barbara's *surprise* had not arrived. Todd told her to be patient; it would be there in a few days, and that he'd had to order it at the last minute. That was Friday.

Saturday afternoon, Preecher Kinser called and said he was going to retire the yellow roadster, and that he had promised her dad that before it was raced for the last time, he would invite her to the race. Could she come tonight?

Wild horses couldn't keep her from that event. So, as she had promised her dad that she someday would, that night Barbara went to the Alcoa Speedway to watch the yellow roadster race one last time. Todd went with her. As they walked in, "Daddy Was An Old Time Preacher Man" was blaring from the loudspeaker—Dolly and Porter of course.

Barbara sat in the stands, inhaling the aroma of the race track, listening to the roar of the hot rods, and holding Todd's hand. The head bandage was gone and his hair was a little longer now, but his twinkling eyes were that same old blue. In the purse in her lap were her father's goggle-glasses. She vowed she would never go anywhere without them. She had told Todd everything, and she was beginning to heal, but she didn't know if she would ever be completely well again. Such was her loss. Gene and Sally Chastine sat beside them, and since Todd had announced his candidacy for the Senate, he had hired Gene as bodyguard.

Preecher Kinser did the color analysis over the loudspeaker. "Tonight we have a new driver. Let's hear it for Hot Rod Harry, fresh from his Air Force tour of duty in Thule, Greenland. He's at the wheel of the yellow roadster."

Barbara whispered to Todd, "That was Daddy's car. I'm sure Preecher's doing this just for me."

Todd nodded as if to say, "Probably so."

The yellow roadster roared and spat blue fire as it dug out. Hot Rod Harry took the lead and kept it.

Memories came at Barbara so hard and so fast that she thought she would pass out. This should have been a homecoming. Grandmother Dare had told her of how, as a little girl, her father used to bring Barbara here. How different things might have been. It was as if she was burying his memory. Axe had called, after the fact, and told her about the "no visitors" funeral.

Barbara removed the goggle-glasses from her purse, strapped them on, and tried to watch the race through *his eyes*, as she had promised she would. But the goggles were too thick. So she put them back into the purse and just sat and enjoyed the roar of the hot rods.

The yellow roadster won.

After the race, Todd jumped up. "Wow. I'd like a closer look at that rod. I might even buy it for you." He grabbed Barbara's hand and went bounding down the bleachers, Gene and Sally right behind them.

Now Barbara knew what her surprise was. Todd had bought the roadster! It evidently hadn't dawned on him that the car was already hers. By inheritance. But she wouldn't rob him of the pleasure. It would mean a lot to him, and Preecher Kinser could use the money.

The yellow roadster was pulling into the Winner's Circle by the time they got there. Hot Rod Harry, dressed in a yellow racing suit, and, wearing a yellow crash helmet with tinted mask, climbed out to accept the accolades.

"You're quite a driver," Todd said to him.

"Thank you, sir," he whispered.

Then Todd asked Barbara to open her purse. When she did, he removed the goggle-glasses from the purse and said to her, "You won't be needing these." He turned back to the driver. "Mr. Harry, how would you like to be my personal chauffeur?"

"I'd like that just fine, sir."

"I hope I can afford you. What would you charge?"

"How about a peanut butter pie?" the man said, removing his helmet.

Todd tossed the goggle-glasses to him.

Barbara's knees buckled as if she had seen a ghost. She crumpled to the ground. Todd and the driver pulled her to her feet while Gene and Sally quickly crowded around, forming a privacy circle.

"Try to act composed," Todd said to her. And then he explained. "Congress appreciated what your dad did, so Father arranged to get him into the Witness Protection Program. But first we had to kill him; the warden was in on it. Shake hands with our new chauffeur, Hotrod Harry, just furloughed from a two-year stretch with the Air Force in Greenland."

Barbara stood there heaving. Finally she whispered, "Hello," and reached, weakly, to shake hands with the ghost.

When she did, the man cupped her hand, embracing it, then placed something inside it. "I believe this is yours."

She opened her hand and there lay her Cherokee mud-bead necklace.

That night Barbara Dare-Carrington started her family.

About The Author

Dr. O. J. Bryson—friends and family call him "Jay"—and his two "pound" dogs, Silver and Shadow, live on a mountain overlooking the Tennessee River, in the shadow of the Smoky Mountains. The suspense/thriller A Trace of Smoke is his first published novel. He is published in Writer's Digest, in American Airline's magazines, in the YMCA's magazine Focus, and in Amway's Amagram. Bryson, a university professor/administrator turned businessman, has nonfiction books published in English, French, and Korean, and the Tennessee Humanities Council has featured him at their annual Southern Festival of Books. In high school and college, Bryson raced motorcycles and boxed in the Golden Gloves. As a professor, he toured for the State Department with the USO. He has two sons, Scott and Chris, and one daughter-in-law, Tina. Tina is about to make him a grandfather.

Printed in the United States
1581